IMAGINE MY SURPRISE!

A NOVEL

K.S. HADDOCK

UNBOUNDED CREATIVITY
HERESY PRESS
FEARLESS EXPRESSION

Heresy Press books may be purchased in bulk at special discounts for sales promotion, corporate gifts, fund-raising, or educational purposes. Special editions can also be created to specifications. For details, contact the Special Sales Department, Heresy Press, 307 Fifth Avenue, 4th Floor, New York, NY 10016 or info@skyhorsepublishing.com.

Skyhorse Publishing® is a registered trademark of Skyhorse Publishing, Inc.®, a Delaware corporation.

Visit our website at skyhorsepublishing.com.

HERESY PRESS LLC
P.O. Box 425201
Cambridge, MA 02142
heresy-press.com

10 9 8 7 6 5 4 3 2 1

Library of Congress Cataloging-in-Publication Data is available on file.

Cover design by K.S. Haddock

Print ISBN: 978-1-949846-84-3
Ebook ISBN: 978-1-949846-85-0

Printed in the United States of America

For Claudia, Stella, and Sawnsee.

Editor's Note

The following work is the edited transcription of audio recordings made by seven-year-old Keenan Harris in the early 2030s. The story of Keenan Harris is a celebrated case study in the field of Transmigration Science. Events herein have been corroborated and verified, though the names have been changed to protect the principal actors' privacy.

R. Adams, PhD

AUTHOR'S PREFACE

[TRANSCRIBED FROM RECORDING]

TIMESTAMP=2032-07-06T:13:42:17-13:44:03Z

Is this thing on? Check-one-two. Hi. My name is Keenan. I'm seven-and-a-half years old. Well . . . at least on the *outside.*

If you are listening to this, you found my device! And you opened the package that said, "Please open and listen to my story." You discovered my digital recorder in the crawl space in the back of our attic—the very attic I'm sweating my balls off in right now. I'll hide it after every session because my parents would have me committed if they ever heard this. Not that they'd be all that surprised.

So, I'm about to tell you a long and crazy story. It'll sound like it's made up, but it's not. This shit really happened. You probably won't believe it anyway. You'll think that some grown-up put me up to it as a weird publicity stunt. But that's not what happened.

The reason I'm doing this now is because my memory of everything is slipping. My brain is glitching; I want to say, like a kaleidoscope. And I have to get this all off my chest so I can go live a normal kid's life, the one that's waiting for me.

One more thing—can you do me a favor and give the recording to a publishing company? I know it's not as easy as that, but if you find some cool, open-minded editor, I think they'll publish it. I'm even going to helpfully include formatting notes so you'll know how to lay it out. Remember this: I'm very fond of Garamond.

So, with all that being said, before I forget my story . . . here it goes.

Title the book: *Imagine My Surprise!*, with an exclamation point at the end. Chapter One! By that I mean, just put the number one and a period. And maybe a subtitle, like . . . "So, there I am, dying."

PART 1 - KEENAN

TIMESTAMP=2032-07-06T:13:42:17-14:59:02Z

1. So, There I Am, Dying

Imagine my surprise—I was dying!

I remember the lovely prick of the needle in my arm. It was a clear January night, and I was slouched on my black leather sofa watching the distant, twinkly lights of downtown San Francisco—watching them fade. Franks had come by with a birthday bag of really good heroin, and I fixed on my couch in front of those twinkly lights like I'd done so many times before. And *mmmm*, the Pavlov prick of the needle is exciting in its own right—you almost don't need what follows. Unfortunately, what *did* follow was an overdose. A *murder*-dose. I didn't see it coming.

But that moment—that *rush*. It's like . . . love ascending. Then after you're an addict, it's like a glancing moment of love quickly plummeting into spiritual disappointment. Like an entire relationship in one shot. Exhilaration and heartbreak. One second, you're on top of the world; the next second, bitter, inevitable loss. And then you need more.

So, there I am, dying, and my heart is breaking—literally—under the weight of a heavy overdose of some very fine Afghani white heroin . . . cut with fentanyl. First of all, that anyone would sully such a high-grade narcotic with crap like fentanyl was a crime unto itself. Second, this was my unfortunate introduction to fentanyl. I was unable to move. Not twenty feet away in the kitchen drawer was a lifesaving dose of Narcan.

I remember the feeling of liquid on my chin, dripping down my gray goatee onto my chest, ruining my expensive Brunello Cucinelli button-down. I had vomited: *so* rookie, so preschool.

But if you're on your way out, overdosing on smack is probably not the worst. (I've heard drowning, just before the end, is quite pleasant.) All my anger had vanished, even my anger toward Franks for murdering me. Heroin being heroin, it was hard to give a shit why, hard to care that I was dying at all.

And so I slipped down a rabbit hole, and with me went reality, the world, and the aforementioned beautiful prickly lights of downtown San Francisco. I slid comfortably back into the womb of creation, its arms enfolding, drawing me back into the birth canal of existence, back to the atoms, to Adam, to the beginning, and I didn't care because I was full of careless heroin love. I was either going to wake up in the hospital or not wake up at all, and either seemed a perfect outcome.

Happy birthday to me. I was fifty.

!!!

Imagine my surprise—and my dismay—to find out I didn't exactly die. After a brief period of the most ravishing, rhapsodic blackness, the rabbit hole appeared again and was coming back toward me. I couldn't breathe. I was cramped and wet. I was sure I was regaining consciousness in a giant pool of my own vomit. And the smell! Hard to describe, like fish and feces and gut-stink, and it took my breath away. My lungs seemed filled with fluid. And there was a taste, a taste of bile and something else, something indescribable yet somehow familiar.

Also, I wasn't approaching the rabbit hole—I was being squeezed *out* of it. Slowly. I was losing patience, my careless heroin love vanishing. I thought, *Whatever bad trip this is, I'm going to kill someone, someone like Franks, that halitotic Irish motherfucker.*

To make matters worse, I couldn't move. I was bound in a wet sleeve with no muscles. A kind of goo gummed my eyes; my hearing was a sluiced white noise. It would suck if the heroin had left me too brain damaged to personally kick the shit out of Franks.

The warm fuzzy of the heroin vanished. My senses were a disquieting swirl, like a really bad acid trip. Then—I was suddenly out of the hole and into the daylight. Yay!

Hold it. No—not *daylight*—it was *surgical* light! I'd made it to the hospital! It's just like I said, you either wake up dead or in the hospital.

I was freezing and everything was a blur, both sight and sound. Air filled my lungs, and I screamed like a baby. I was alive!

2. The New Drug

Imagine my surprise when I realized what the fuck was going on.

"Holy Christ!" I shouted. But what came out was more like a squawky rattling shriek. I couldn't control my mouth and tongue, and I had no fucking teeth! I had *no fucking teeth*!

The world was a cold, blurry cacophony. I bawled like a—*yes*—baby. I was uncontrollably angry, having a tantrum. Something was tugging on my stomach. Latex fingers passed me around.

I was insane.

Somehow, I found a moment of focus. I obviously was not a screaming gore-covered nine-pound baby boy. I *was* a boy, right? What was probably happening was that back in the real world I was in my death throes on my leather couch, puke running down my face and ruining my expensive shirt. I was *not* being wiped clean of a thick coating of placental goo and being swaddled in a warm blanket like a full-body tourniquet. I was *not* being weighed and measured; I was *not* being nestled into someone's warm, protective arms.

I was clearly in the throes of a full-blown drug psychosis.

Perhaps it was some new designer drug with a name like *Womb* or

Rebirth, and it made you feel like you'd died and been reborn into a little bitty baby. That *had* to be it.

Suddenly, it was quiet. I'd stopped bawling.

I couldn't see worth a damn. It was like being drunk with Vaseline in your eyes. Except without the drunk. My hearing was all a-jangle. My skin felt bathed in Novocain: vague, fuzzy. Sight, sound, and touch happened in shapes without definition.

And, oh—the smell! Never had my olfactory sense been so acute. Thirty years of smoking had taken its toll on the ol' sniffer. That, and, well, let's face it—the kilos of coke I'd snorted. But now I could smell with canine acuity: Pine-Sol, floral hand cleanser, sweat on a woman's skin, the smell of . . . what? *Aftershave*. Two aftershaves. There was cheap jasmine perfume. Coffee—with cream and sugar. I could smell blood. Blood and urine. A hint of shit. I smelled three types of bad breath, and the minty fresh breath of someone chewing gum. I could even smell the cigarette somebody had smoked. A cigarette! I would've killed for it. *Killed*, I say! I smelled the liquor from somebody's pores after a night's hard drinking. A man's sour drunk-sweat. Probably the sweat of my new father in this increasingly vivid hallucination. And there was a curious sweet smell, directly below me.

I tried prying open my weak eyelids. Why couldn't I do it? As I wedged them open more, images were a white burst of overexposed film. Colorless shapes bobbed before me; I realized the shapes were people looking down at me. I wanted to fend them off but I couldn't lift my tiny flaccid arms, leaden encumbrances without purpose. Minutes ago, before I injected myself with this new designer drug that I'm calling *Womb*, I was a tallish, brawny, white male who could break somebody in half with one well-placed roundhouse. Now I was tiny and helpless, and I was pretty sure I was about to piss and shit myself.

What a fucking nightmare. I *hated* this drug.

I began crying again. I was lifted, passed around. Then I was back in my warm swaddled arm-crook. I liked it there, so I stopped crying. I managed to open my eyes a little more; the blur sharpened. But I was seeing in black and white.

Sound was also blurry, voices distorted. It sounded something like this:

Male-sounding voice 1: *Hhheehehee rhrrhllooookss lllrrike mheheheeee.*

Male-sounding voice 2: *Rheee jdduuuzzz rorrloook rrhrrichhe ywhooooo.*

Female-like voice coming from behind my head: *Djddooodgggedd uhhh bbbhhuulleeeettt. Whheeeeheewww!*

There was a crash of noise that I'm pretty sure was laughter. Everyone sounded drunk.

Female-like voice 1: *Hhhhhggheeeeezzz ppprorrbbbaabbleee zhuuunggrreee.*

Male-sounding voice 1: *Gggccchiiive ghhhiiiim tthhshshhhhuahhh ttiiitt.*

They sounded drunk, but it was *me* who was *hearing* drunk. All those little pieces of the ear? Cochlea, vestibule, the stapes, and the something-or-other along with a host of auditory nerves going to and coming from my baby brain. All that shit wasn't strong yet so I had the ears of a drunk, which was apropos since I had the life of a drunk—albeit a highly functional drunk.

The sardonic female voice coming from under me was my new mom, which made that pervasive sweet smell her breast milk. *My* breast milk. It hit me then that the growing pain in my stomach was hunger. I was famished. But I couldn't turn my head. There were no fucking muscles in my neck. My body was a flopping paroxysm. So instead, I squirmed. My head, like my arms, was a useless leaden appendage. In my brain I was making the words, *Please, someone, I'm so hungry!* But in reality, I was croaking like a dying asthmatic cat.

Somebody said something and there was laughter. Weird echoey laughter. They all knew what I wanted, it seemed. Mom turned me over. That smell was overpowering, sweet. If the idea of love had a smell, this was it: mother's milk. It *was* love. It was everything I ever wanted. It was my new heroin. That's what it was like! I had found my new heroin and it was my mother's own milk. How convenient!

I needed it. I had a brainless zombie desire that controlled my rubbery, boneless body. I groped with my mouth and pried with useless fingers, and for the first time in living memory I suckled a breast for the primary reason breasts exist: sustenance.

When the milk passed through my gums, I heard radio waves. Almost deafening—an aurally synesthetic response to the mother's milk. And it was Beethoven.

All I could hear, shutting out the world (save for this warm nectar slurping past my gums), was the chorus to *Ode an die Freude*.

Ode to Joy.

3. The New K.S.

I was born. Again.

So there I was, at a midwifery center, a wriggling newborn.

A couple days limped by, and I alternately sucked, shat, and pissed with little or no control whatsoever. I cried some—not the wail of a newborn, but the confused weeping of someone dumbfounded by his predicament. At least that's how it sounded in my small head.

Soon enough, through all the cooing and handling and suckling, through all the shitting, pissing, and vomiting, through all the passing around to different relatives and complete strangers—my senses grew stronger. Smell and taste were off the charts. My past life held no memory of such richness. My new vision, not so much; I couldn't get my eyes to focus. I could make out my fingers, stuff right in front of my face, but that was about it. As my baby-hearing became less drunk, I heard a phrase oft repeated: "Introducing Keenan Solomon Harris. Nine pounds, three ounces. Over eighteen inches! Big as a salmon!" This charmer was my new father.

Big as a salmon. He must've said that every day for two weeks.

The invariable response to this was, "Keenan Solomon? Sounds like a black name."

This was the first hint of the culture awaiting me.

Dad, from what I could gather, was a skinny, tall, white blur with red hair. He held me in his arms like I was made of eggshells. I felt impossibly small; I remember what a trip it was. I still believed I would wake up.

Giant, garish faces were thrust at me, making *ga-ga* nonsense words and smelling of perfume, liquor, cigarettes, coffee, and bad breath. These were primarily Dad, Gramma and Pop-pop (Mom's side), and Uncle Joe and Aunt Shelly (Dad's side). Mom didn't have any siblings, and Dad's remaining parent, his father, Edward, was hobbled by dementia back in Boston. I was handed off to and prodded by strangers, doctors, visitors—all manner of human flotsam to whom parents willingly hand over their little babies. I'd been reborn in Hell, a Sartrean character stuck in a room ripe with the stench of provinciality, quotidian aspirations, and junior college degrees, unable to run away, unable to form words, unable to escape at all, straitjacket-swaddled in a baby blanket. Holy shit.

The only person who didn't baby-talk or change her vocal register to me was my new mother. After a day or so, I started to understand a bit of what I was hearing. But sound was rattled and tinny, like a stereo EQ with the treble jacked and the bass missing. A bad cassette recording. One of the first things I noticed was that my new mom—Louisiana, as everyone called her—had something of a Southern drawl, gravelly, and filtered through a California accent. My new dad sounded like he might've originally come from Boston. They called him Drew.

All these things I quickly registered within my short stay at the midwifery.

I had a sort of rolling consciousness that I chalked up to my developing brain. My old self might've been reborn inside this new shell, but it was still at the mercy of human biology.

About that—human biology—of course I realized, even then at the hospital, that I shouldn't have been able to think the thoughts I was thinking. A newborn human brain is like a third the size of an adult's and it should not be capable of complex thought (thank you, psych degree).

Its cerebral cortex is vastly undeveloped at that point. But the mysteries of the brain are numberless, and reincarnation wasn't supposed to be scientifically possible. But here I was. I strained to remember my World Religions class. Reincarnation was what, Buddhist? Hindu? Both? Where was the Internet when I needed it? Hold it, had I even been reborn in the time of the Internet? *Fuck!*

On the first morning of my rebirth, I woke to my mother handing me off to a blur that I identified as Dad, and some other guy whose seriousness suggested he was a doctor. They wheeled me away in a plastic crib into another room. A flurry of faces floated above me in surgical masks. *Curious*, I thought.

Dad said, "It's okay. You won't feel a thing."

Uh-oh. I felt a sharp something down below. I couldn't lift my head to see what the hell the doctor was doing down there. There was this tugging feeling. I suddenly thought, *HOLY SHIT!* And by the time I realized I was being circumcised—it was over. I didn't even have time to cry or protest, and the aftermath was not much more painful than, say, fucking yourself raw. With none of the pleasure of getting there.

Later that day, as I lay in my mom's arms, a man on the TV delivered the top of the news. It was my biggest revelation yet.

"Good evening, on this Monday, January 27, 2025 . . ."

I began to cry.

Lou kissed my head. "What is it, honey?"

Five years had lapsed. I struggled to turn my head toward the television but, as mentioned, my neck could not support my head. Had I heard correctly? Was that right? January 27? I was born yesterday. That meant I died and was reborn on my *old* birthday. Exactly five years earlier, alone in my house on Potrero Hill, I had died, a junkie loser.

My new name was Keenan Solomon Harris. K.S.H. Being reincarnated into my own former initials and on my former birthday—January 26—was proof of a higher . . . *something*. This was a cruel cosmic prank played on a lifelong atheist and denier of all things supernatural. If I had only known in my old life that death wasn't the end, I could've done away with a shitload of existential dread.

Why five years?

I had been reborn on my birthday in the middling Northern California suburb of Campbell—in Santa Clara County, the Silicon Valley. I'd been reincarnated forty miles south of where I'd died.

!!!

On the third day, they drove me home from the "birthing center" in what I could only discern was a Japanese car owned by a chain-smoker. See, my new mom was a smoker, and she could barely wait to be wheeled from the facility before lighting up. As they released her on the steps of the midwifery, she handed me off to Pops and searched for a pack of cigarettes. Actually, the pack of cigarettes was in the form of a bow-wrapped gift from Dad's sister-in-law, Aunt Shelly. Uncle Joe pulled up in the car, a faded red Toyota Corolla. Meanwhile, Mom savagely ripped the gift wrapping from the cigarettes, a pack of Winston Reds. She gazed at them tearfully, long-lost friends. Then she tore into the pack and, with shaky hands, guided a cigarette between her chapped hospital lips. She searched for a lighter in her voluminous purse, cursing. But she found it and lit up, drawing deeply, with pleasure.

Pops carried me away from her toward the idling Toyota.

"Honey," Pops said, "Joe's here. Let's go."

Louisiana gazed at him with slow-burn defiance, plucked the lit cigarette from her lips.

"I haven't had a fucking cigarette in nine fucking months and if I don't smoke this fucking cigarette, I'm going to rip both your and Joe's fucking heads off and shove them up your own motherfucking asses. *Capisce?*"

My dad nodded his head obsequiously and knelt, opening the rear passenger door with one hand while holding me in the other; he slid into the back. They didn't have a baby seat yet so he belted up and held me tight. *Genius.* Pops noticed Uncle Joe was also smoking.

"Um, Joe . . . snub the butt. A newborn child is in the vehicle," Pops said.

"Oh, shit, Drew, sorry." Uncle Joe, a short, taut man with a shock of black hair, quickly flicked the cigarette out his window to the asphalt. Joe had a considerably stronger Boston accent. He looked back and smiled at me, sticking a stubby finger in my face. *Hell, yes! Nicotine!* I could smell it, and I grabbed his giant finger with my little hands and suckled on it greedily. Uncle Joe grinned.

"What's taking Lou so long?" Joe asked, adjusting his head to see his sister-in-law through the car window.

Pops sighed. "Well, I guess the best way to put it is that she's having her first *fucking* cigarette in nine *motherfucking* months. To paraphrase."

Uncle Joe nodded appreciatively. "Ah . . . that's gotta taste good."

I gurgled in agreement.

!!!

Biology erased all misgivings I might've had about breastfeeding. *For a while.* The Milk was hardwired into my brain like a heroin mainline. This evolutionary instinct to attain milk was impossible to override.

And what a delicious, intoxicating drug the milk of Louisiana Harris was!

After she left the birthing center, she started smoking again, and thus my craving for nicotine—which had followed me into this new life—was sated.

She was never going to win Mother of the Year.

Her magic milk likewise satisfied the ghostly pull of my former heroin habit. I mean, at this point, my opiate addiction (likewise nicotine) was only a psychological habit, with me in a body so fresh from the womb. But my urge to get opiated on schedule still existed. Louisiana's milk was a fix, a cigarette, and a nutritious meal all wrapped in one. My milk-sense could smell her enter a room. On top of this, when she had her afternoon vodka martini, I'd get a taste of that, too. She was my walking, talking, foulmouthed corner bar happy hour on two legs.

Stop. I know what you're wondering, you depraved listener of the future: did my time on the tit arouse me sexually? First of all, you're sick for even thinking that. But truly, the growing conflict between breastfeeding and what used to be a sexual act became an unbearable dissonance. It was just too weird. Baby food was the answer to this: a sad methadone.

But as long as we are on the subject of the earthly desires of my previous life, I came from the womb with them fully intact. I had so much time to think, lying around helpless, that every pleasure that I'd previously enjoyed taunted me: the booze, the sex, the drugs, the endless creative projects. Yes, I could someday regain my vices, but for now, how was I going to get a smoke and a glass of bourbon?

Of course, as the years lurched by, chances to experiment presented themselves. The first time a cigarette or highball was left unattended, I quickly had a taste. The effects were catastrophic. At my body size, one cigarette puff made me sick for a day; one sip of Lou's martini and I was hammered . . . and sick for a day. It took death to straighten me out. A new motto: *Reincarnation—Better than AA.*

!!!

Listen—don't think I had forgotten the betrayal of my henchmen. Well, hench*man*—Franks. Like I said, being a completely helpless newborn, I had nothing but time to examine every granule of my previous life.

But my memory of that last day was tricky. The morning of my fiftieth birthday, I woke up alone. Maybe my cat, Joplin, was there, I forget. My head was in the reverse fugue of the recently sober: I'd just emerged from the three-week cycle of kicking heroin. Being sober was just as disorienting as being intoxicated.

The day previous, I'd taken back control of the business, demoting everyone back to their old positions as my minions. They had minded the shop while I went through the intense hell of withdrawal, and they were not overly keen to hand it back. I reassured them I was fine to handle it.

It was a cheap (and calculated) move for Franks to come over that afternoon with a full bag of high-priced works, saying he'd bought it for me as a Christmas present before I decided to kick. He didn't use the stuff himself, and he asked me what I thought he should do with it.

I magnanimously told him I'd get rid of it for him. He knew I couldn't handle it.

That story seems cut and dried, but there was a lot of doubt. Something from that day was missing, and I couldn't tell if it was my drug-scrambled brain playing tricks on me or if indeed there was more mystery to unravel.

In any case, I had a few years of growing up before I could feasibly take revenge. Meanwhile, I had to find a way to survive suburbia. Again.

4. *Logistics of Helplessness*

Ma and Pa Harris took me home to a shitty little three-bedroom house in Campbell. It was an old seventies tract home flanked by poorly groomed oleander bushes and a yellowing crabgrass-choked lawn. They rented it month to month from an unseen landlord who never maintained the property but was quick to make a phone call if the rent was late.

These things were of minor importance to me at the time, as I was squirming, helpless, confused, and pissed off.

While it was near impossible to accept this current version of my reality, I knew if I was going to survive, I had to push my disbelief aside, which was the same as accepting insanity as fact. So, I began to work on a game plan. First order of business was that I needed to become mobile, but as a newborn, I had physiological and instinctual hurdles to contend with. For instance, I was wracked with random body pains—literal *growing* pains, and digestive pains. My sleep patterns were practically narcoleptic. I'd be sitting there, helpless in my auto-rocking super-pram, ruminating over my predicament when I'd suddenly conk out and wake up hours later in my crib. On top of this, I shat a river of sweet-scented poop, I had no control over my tiny ever-spouting penis, and I often vomited. I was a miniature quadriplegic junkie.

Previous to this nightmare, I had no experience with babies. That said, maybe it was all the child psychology classes in college, or just absorbing the world around me, but when it came to the baby-care department, I was *leagues* ahead of my ignorant millennial parents. I mean, had they ever even picked up a parenting book? Did they have a game plan at all?

They were excited to change the first diaper—they googled it immediately when they got home. They actually looked forward to changing me, even as my penis let loose an uncontrollable stream, and I vomited like someone possessed. Cutest fucking thing they'd ever seen. This enthusiasm over my bodily excretions lasted about a week.

After a month or so into this new life as a prisoner inside a rubbery doll, I started to gain control over my bowels, my sleeping patterns, and my crying jags. I was so under control that our pediatrician was concerned that something was wrong; perhaps I was developmentally disabled. I was not behaving as a normal newborn. Regardless, I began to shit and piss on a sort of a schedule (unavoidably in my diaper) and I slept through the night from about eight o'clock to seven o'clock the next morning. There were a lot of naps.

If I was going to move around independently, I needed to build some body strength, had to build my core. Zero musculature in my neck made it feel like my head was attached to a 700-pound weight. Add to this quadriplegia. So I started an exercise regimen. Head lifts, leg lifts. It took me three weeks before I could lift my head. This might sound paltry, but it's way ahead of schedule. In the end, physiological milestones took about a third of the time compared to a normal baby.

It went like this: the *grups* (see original *Star Trek*, episode 8) would lay me out on the filthy, bacteria-laden floor to change or watch me. They spent a lot of time watching me. They'd lay me on the floor and I'd take this time to, well, exercise: twitching up and down, rolling side to side, trying to lift my massive head. I'm not quite sure what it looked like—perhaps like I was having a fit, or autistic repetitions. Nonetheless, in a few weeks I could indeed lift my head. In four weeks, I could turn over. At around six weeks I could sit up, and before ten weeks had passed, I was crawling. I was standing at about three months. The parents were amazed. The aforementioned pediatrician, Dr. Claveria, was also amazed. A little *too* amazed because, unbeknownst to me, she kept a detailed longitudinal developmental chart that would later prove to be problematic.

Learning to talk was a different matter. My mouth was about as useful as if I'd eaten a tablespoon of cocaine and chased it with a quart of whiskey. Not having any fucking teeth didn't help either. And the mushy high-pitched slur that issued from my tiny lips was disturbingly dissonant to what my ears expected to hear: my former adult voice. Very upsetting. But in the end, I was able to form words even sooner than I could crawl. This is when I had a very important talk with myself.

Self, I said. *You can either behave with your full intellect and go the way of all child prodigies: stick out socially, be hovered over by overzealous parents and teachers and puzzled at by ever-probing scientists. Or, little man, you can go incognito—undercover—and gain the upper hand by playing the role of a baby human, albeit a very bright one with advanced physical skills.*

So I chose the latter. I chose to not behave like an adult; I chose not to articulate my thoughts; I chose to fly under the radar.

But still I trained. I relearned how to talk by unplugging the baby monitor in my room and reading Lou's women's magazines aloud on the sly.

The state of babyhood has become that of house arrest. Long gone are the days of the simple audio-only baby monitors. Now it's Wi-Fi-Bluetooth-controlled baby monitors with full video capability, night vision, infrared, pulse detection, sound- and motion-activated transceivers, all packaged in baby-soothing pastel hues and manufactured in blunted baby-safe shapes made of water-resistant rubberized plastic. In every room, every hallway, even the bathroom, every nook and cranny. Spy on the baby twenty-four-seven—let's face it—spy on the *babysitter*, the relative, the stranger, even the errant spouse. It's a sick state of things, and I fear there is no going back.

Being a critical observer of human behavior, you can imagine how disconcerted I was that (after I accepted my predicament) I'd been reincarnated into a working-class millennial disaster. This might've embittered me, but I had to admit that it was little different from the white trash beginnings of my *first* life.

My new dad—Drew—was the sort of nadless dork that I previously had little use for. Luckless and ineffectual. Yet he was painfully optimistic and loving in a way I'll grudgingly describe as unconditional. Guilelessly devoted to his wife. He was a total sucker.

He was thirty when I was born, brown-red hair, tallish at around six foot two, thinnish at about 180 pounds, and smartish, in a B-average engineering-student sort of way. What he lacked in artfulness, he made up for with a tinkerer's ingenuity.

He had a corny streak; he was a punner. He had no concept of the value of money and had the slightly unfocused, abstract ambition of an inventor. And, while I often wanted to kick his milquetoast ass, I had to admit that I found him amusing. His other saving grace was that he was handsome. He almost had to be a loser just so he wasn't so intimidatingly good looking.

Then there was my new mom: Louise Anna Solomon Harris. Total piece of work. She was slim-hipped with medium brown hair and Mediterranean skin; she had a semi-angular runner's shape, but she never exercised—one of the lucky ones. I knew her type—she was the sort of woman I'd dated and broken up with for most of my before-life. She was a real pistol. The opposite of Drew, she was a self-loathing pleasure-seeker who had grown to detest her honest, devoted, *naive* husband over the short span of their marriage. I'm pretty sure that she'd already started to cheat on him before she got knocked up with me. More on that later.

Lou is a great case study, though: headstrong, non-practicing Jew from Baton Rouge who had escaped her overbearing parents. She ran away to San Francisco and met Drew. She was smitten by his good looks, the ease with which he made her laugh, his ability to make her cum, and the talent to piss off her conservative parents. Louisiana, as she grew to be called, had very few scruples. Though she never finished college, she was often smarter than those around her. She was a real ball-buster, and while I could tell early on that she hated her predicament (i.e., not being able to divorce Drew because they now had a baby), she really did love *me*—her bizarre little boy. In fact, I think if she'd had your run-of-the-mill baby boy, she would've abandoned the family altogether. But parenthood made her rethink things, possibly for the first time in her life.

But that self-examination was a few years away. For now, she was still a bitch on wheels.

5. *Learning to Walk*

At five months I took my first steps.

I waited until the grups thought I was napping, then escaped from my crib, dropping onto the stained shag carpet. This was the second time I had made it out of the crib, both times a cinematic escape from baby prison. My arm strength—particularly my hands—developed faster than any other part of my body, so climbing became relatively easy. I slowly pulled myself up over the bars, pushing up with my tiny legs, and thumped down, crumpling to the floor.

The TV droned loud in another room—I was safe.

I struggled to my feet, using the leg of the crib for support. Baby sweat is a weird thing. It smells like mother's milk. I'd been strengthening my chubby little legs every day by holding onto the crib and doing squats. Yes, a tiny red-haired baby doing squats. My balance was pretty good, but these fucking baby legs were almost useless. I was motivated by one thing—no, not escape, not freedom, not even the ability to get a snack on my own schedule. I was motivated by the need to shit—perchance to piss—in private. I was determined to walk so as to spare myself the insufferable indignity of shitting and pissing myself inside a diaper on a daily basis. Being breast-fed was humiliation enough. Hell, having no teeth was humiliating, if not somewhat emasculating. There is nothing more emasculating than infancy.

As I prepared myself, I took stock of my surroundings. My bedroom was a mélange of whimsical babyisms, hand-me-down cast-offs, and silly impulse buys. It was a garish upside-down Norman Rockwell brought to you by your local big box and neighborhood Goodwill. The color scheme seemed to be survival of the tackiest: avocado-green desk lamp on a fire-engine-red metal desk (with rounded corners); a piercingly cyan-colored vinyl chair most often used by Drew while reading Shel Silverstein poems to me before bed; a pastel yellow flat screen beaming cute duckling and kitten pictures accompanied by a soothing female voice cooing infantile Orwellian bon mots on a loop: "the house cat says meow," "the mailman says hello," and, oddly, "the farmer works all day," among others. Even now, I sometimes nightmarishly dream the creepy prerecorded voice: "The farmer works all day." Over time, I managed to turn off the audio in the system settings, but not before they were etched indelibly into my tender cortex.

Back to the action. I had escaped, and I stood precariously next to the crib, dressed in a little blue T-shirt and diapers, not quite two feet tall. The knees were kind of wobbly and my spatial sense was kind of skewed. I think my muscle memory was still trying to adjust from six feet tall to just under two feet. I stood with my arm outstretched to the crib leg. I let go and made my first hands-free step. Then another. It was like that first time on skates: you can stand, but you're waiting for the fall. And fall I did. Then I crawled to the dresser and pulled myself back to my feet. Finally, I made my first drunk-like series of steps all the way across the room—

"Oh, my God! Keenan!" Drew blurted. The surprise knocked me down. I glared up at him. *Motherfucker! I had it!*

He rushed forward to help, but I stopped him with a hand, a rather age-inappropriate gesture. I struggled to get up on my own.

"Honey!" Drew shouted. "Come in here! Keenan climbed out of his crib and is walking around."

I somehow got the legs standing, and I pushed the rest of me up from the ground with my palms. Baby bodies are held together by rubber bands. But there I was, standing. From the other room, I could hear Lou's approach.

"Drew . . . he's five months old. It's impossi—" She rounded the corner just as I righted myself. I swayed a little, steadied, and slowly . . . staggered . . . about . . . and came to a wobbly stop, looking up at them. I threw up my hands, giving them a *Ta da!*

Their mouths dropped as they looked at each other, then back at me. It was the *Ta da!* They fell to the ground in front of me, belly laughing. It was infectious. I staggered over to them in a mad giggle and fell between Lou and Drew. It was my first real laugh as Keenan Solomon Harris.

And I thought, *Maybe I* can *work with these guys.*

!!!

My mission, however, was not fully accomplished, and a couple days later, I again escaped my crib. My primary reason for my crash course in walking, after all, was to use the toilet on my own and regain a sense of dignity. Why this was so important at the time escapes me now, but at least it got me off my diapered ass.

Lou was in the kitchen on the phone. Drew was at work; he drove bodies for a funeral home. Encouraged by my recent success, I again scrambled over the side of the crib and made it to the bedroom door, slightly ajar. The world from this low angle was disorienting. Being miniature is like being stuck in a German expressionist film. I peeked through the door crack across the great expanse of dirty burnt-orange shag carpet that lined the hallway. Lou and Drew had little time for aesthetic thinking. Imagine if Courtney Love married Homer Simpson and all they had to decorate with was the Salvation Army. It wasn't just my room—the entire house was a study in secondhand furniture, doodads from their adolescence, rock posters, and sad, yellowing houseplants. Oh, sure, here and there lurked a new appliance or a piece of accidentally tasteful flotsam, but the house and all its contents could do worse than total destruction from a sudden flash fire.

Anyhow, back to my toilet training.

By now I *really* had to piss and dump, so I did a little reconnaissance, peering down the ugly hall. The ugly bathroom was ten feet away. I stopped to listen for Lou; I could hear her in the ugly kitchen, still talking on the phone. I crept into the ugly bathroom and closed the ugly door behind me.

Aaaaaahhhhh!!

That sound was me gasping in alarm as I saw myself in the scratched floor mirror affixed to the back of the bathroom door. It was very unsettling to look through Kurt's eyes and see Keenan's tiny form. Gathering my composure, I looked more closely. *Hmmm.* I was a type. There're a lot of types: ugly babies, pretty babies, long-faced babies, squoosh-faced babies, bald babies, hairy babies, unfortunately shaped babies, vacant-eyed babies, alert babies.

I was the pale, redheaded, big-blue-eyes type. There was nothing very special about me, and I was a little on the small side. I had Drew's pale Irish skin, with maybe just a hint of my mother's olive in the creases. My blue eyes looked way too big for my face and maybe a little too far apart. But I think I lucked out, looks-wise, which wouldn't be hard with parents like mine. My lips were much poutier than the former thin lips of yester-life. The problem was that the set of my head, the look on my face, and the expression of my brow were all absolutely out of place. I wasn't convincing. I resembled a possessed child.

Had to stay on task.

I looked around at the ugly bathroom. It was sunburn pink. I'd only previously experienced this bathroom when Drew bathed me in the shower. *With* him. To save time. That said, it was better than the kitchen sink, which is where Lou usually bathed me.

The one thing I hadn't figured into my plan was how to actually squat on the toilet without falling in. I was very tiny, the bowl very big. Slipping out of my diaper, I reached up and put down the center seat with a clatter. I held my breath, listening for Lou in the kitchen; she bantered into the phone. I exhaled. Though my legs were already a little tired, I was determined to go through with it.

Flipping the hot pink garbage can upside down, I used it as a stepping stool. I climbed up on the wastebasket, using the toilet tank for balance; I took a breather, then pulled myself up onto the center seat rim. Suddenly, I was on the bowl! Even with the center seat down, the gap was easily wide enough for me to fall all the way through into the water. There was no way I was big enough to sit on the seat normally, so instead I stood up on it with a foot on either side, legs spread. I looked down past my small hairless baby's penis to the water below. The bowl looked clean enough, but I was ever skeptical of Lou's cleaning practices. I guided my piss stream—for the first time in this new body—into the bowl.

Freedom! Well, freedom, stage one. Next: pooping.

I listened for Lou: nothing.

Peeing accomplished, I carefully steadied myself over the porcelain chasm and tore free some toilet paper. I was going to have to squat a bit to clear my legs, which were starting to shake. Easing down, I tried to force some out, to no avail. I was nervous. I squatted a little lower and tried again. This time it squirted out in a semisolid light brown jet from my tiny ass and went straight in. I sighed a little bit and straightened.

And then my left leg gave way.

My left hand, filled with toilet paper, frantically grabbed for the counter but came up with nothing, and—*whoosh!* I slipped, hitting the back of my head on the seat as I fell right into a bowl of my own fresh excrement.

Plop! Splash!

I fell at such an angle that my head was in the bowl and my right leg was sticking out. I was trapped! I reached my tiny arms down to keep my head above the waterline—rather, the piss-shit line. My hands kept slipping and I couldn't entirely keep my head out of the goop, just my face, so I started to scream. And scream. Where was Lou! *Fuck!* Was I going to *re-die*? What an embarrassing second ending! "Motherfucker!" I shouted.

The door suddenly burst open, and the yellow bathroom light flicked on.

"Keenan! Oh, God! What the fuck?!" my lovely mother blurted. She was quick, and she grabbed my right foot with one hand and gingerly lifted the rest of me out of the bowl, dipping the top of my head in the poop water for good measure. "Oh, God! How . . . ?" The scene was too much for her to compute as she dangled me shit-dripping and wriggling over the bowl as to not fling poop soup all over her tacky pink bathroom. "Keenan? How did you get in here and . . . *fuck*!" Realizing I was safe, I finally shut up. She was too confused to be angry.

She held me aloft by one leg and my only thought was, *So, this is how Jack felt with that giant.*

Lou sighed and made something like a chuckle, then gingerly cradled my poopy head and slid open the shower door with her elbow, setting me down gently on the tub bottom. Turning on the faucet, a puddle of cold water gathered under me and I let out a surprised shriek.

"Oh, God, Keenan!" Lou's hand shot in and turned on the shower. Warm water rushed over me as I squirmed in the tub basin, washing the fecal detritus from my tiny head and body. Then she joined me in the shower, stripped of her clothes, and she lifted me up under the jets, washing me at arm's length like a filthy puppy.

Then, the chaos was gone. It was just us and the sound of the shower. Water cascaded across my face and body. Still held at arm's length, she turned me around. "You okay, honey?" Our eyes met, and Louisiana again began to chuckle. I smiled. We laughed a little while relief washed over us, and she hugged me to her body. She squirted soap into her hand. "How the hell did you do this, Keenan?" she asked herself. "What is it about you, baby?"

And with warm water cascading over both of us, she started to sing. I think it was a Fleetwood Mac song.

6. *At About Seven Months*

At about seven months, I discovered Lou was having an affair!

When you're twenty-seven inches tall and supposed to be a helpless, clueless baby, adults tend to break rules around you. Like you're invisible. They act like they're alone, like they're with the dog. All adults do this.

Check this shit out.

So, I'm hanging out around the house in my pull-ups, which at this point were really a prop. By now, the grups were used to this—me cruising around the house in just my pull-ups. They were relieved, in a puzzled way, that I didn't run around burning myself on the stove, stabbing myself with sharp objects, or drinking toxic cleaning products. Instead of accidentally hurting myself or breaking things, I focused on finding a place where I could page through one of our stolen doctor's-office magazines to catch up on what was going on in the world. Also, Drew was old school and liked to get the Sunday *Chronicle*. I'd take a section and hide under my crib, perusing the news in half-light.

There I was, one weekday afternoon, lying under the crib, naked but for my prop diaper, reading the news ("President Rescinds Political Promises") when I heard Louisiana greet somebody at the door. Normally,

I wouldn't've paid much bother but there was something about the timbre of her voice—surprise and affection—that made me realize that it wasn't Dad or anybody I had yet met in the short time stuck in this tiny body. I rolled out from under the crib, stood up, and crept toward the paint-chipped doorjamb, peeking around.

There was dear Mum, lip-locked to some big brute, a stranger in a cop uniform, handsome in a young Gary Busey sort of way. Lou was drawn into this officer's body, swept into it rapturously; imagine a reed bending to the will of a skiff's bow. She issued a sigh, and when both heads turned toward me, they froze. They saw a tiny child dumbstruck in the hallway.

I remember thinking, *You traitorous bitch!* They stood looking at me, I at them. My face must've been the picture of contempt . . . or was it, dare I say, good old-fashioned Freudian jealousy? And what does jealousy look like on the lineless face of an infant? Probably like a tantrum brewing. Either way, I was shocked. I mean, the scenario was all very obvious to the fifty-year-old in me: my so-called mother had clearly been having an affair with this P-I-G before I was even born. It was clear that they hadn't seen each other in forever, and after all this time, they finally found a moment to reconnect. So, he came over. Their lust was real, palpable, and right in front of me. Surprise registered on his face, guilt on hers. She straightened.

"Keenan, honey!" She glanced at Dude, then back at me, then back at him. "Wade, this is Keenan."

He was a little perplexed. "Um . . . he's already walking?"

"Yeah, couple months now," she said, as though this was the most normal thing in the world. "Keenan, this is my friend, Wade."

Wade. I glared up at him as only an infant can glare. He stepped forward, slowly falling into a crouch. I didn't budge, gazing at him stonily. He continued toward me, and I could tell he was going to pick me up.

I saw it in my head: I would go up to this home wrecker and fake with a right hook; he would react, then I would push-kick his unprepared right leg with my right leg, snapping his knee. As he came down in excruciating pain and confusion, I would grip his head with my finger-crossed hands, slamming his surprised face into my left knee, bouncing his head up as my right elbow came down on his temple. He would collapse like a sack of apples, and I would shoot a rueful glare upon my adulterous mother.

Unfortunately, I found myself, inconveniently, a mere twenty-seven inches tall.

Wade swept me up with a genuinely good-natured swing and happily waggled his giant face in mine saying, "Hey, li'l buddy! I'm Wade!"

He handed me off to Lou and she held me between them. I was inert in her arms—not stiff, not wiggly, just there. I had actually started liking Lou for a little bit, and I don't mean just because I loved breathing her cigarettes and sneaking sips off her drinks. She seemed like a fun-if-not-hard-edged woman stuck in a boring marriage. But this was different somehow. While I could understand the obvious mismatch between her and Drew, I *liked* Drew. And, while he was a chump, he was my biological dad and yada yada . . . so what was going through my little skull was, *How could you do this to him, you slut?!* I thought all of this in a split second before Lou said, "Say Hi to Wade, Keen." I could sense the shame and fear in her voice.

I made a dismissive grunt and looked back at Wade. He waggled again and said, "C'mon, li'l—"

And I grabbed his big nose, shoved my tiny thumb into his nostril, and wrenched it upward as hard as I could with my undeveloped arm. He yelped and sprang back, grabbing his nose.

"Jesus!" he said, his eyes watering, looking disbelieving at Lou and me.

Fuck, yeah!

I giggled in the most annoying little baby's voice I could muster.

Lou was aghast. She stepped forward and Wade put a hand up. She swung me around.

"Keenan! No! Why did you do that?!" She looked at Wade, looked back at me. I made what I think was my first shrug.

Because he's a fucking cop and I can finally get away with it.

Wade took it, though, and composed himself. I mean, what was he going to do?

"Hey, it's alright, Lou. He's just a baby," he said, looking out the front window. "Look, I gotta go—"

Lou was crestfallen. "Wade, I haven't seen you in eight months! I can put Keenan down for a nap."

He looked at her, then at me. I smiled.

"I don't think so."

"Wade!"

"Hey, I didn't have time for that anyway. I just wanted to see you. Let's do it . . ."

He actually looked at me skeptically . . . then whispered like I was deaf, or didn't understand English. "*Saturday.*"

Lou was beside herself. "But . . ."

Wade leaned over my head, kissed her lingeringly, then stepped back. "Bye." He looked at me and gave me a tiny wave. "Bye, Keenan. Sorry to cramp your style, li'l buddy!" The ripped screen door slammed behind him. He was gone and Lou hissed out a breath.

"You're an evil little devil, Keenan. I don't know what's got into you."

Then, just to fuck her up, I gently grabbed her face with my tiny hands and rubbed my downy head against her cheek. Then, I formed my first words to her.

"Mommy. Wuvooo."

Yeah, I said it as gooey as possible, and it was highly manipulative, but it probably saved me some sort of punishment.

But for Louisiana, everything stopped. Her heart may have literally ceased beating. My sin was instantly erased. Tears formed in her eyes. She looked at me in awe.

"Keenan?" she asked breathlessly.

"Mommy, wuvooooo," I repeated, relentless.

She staggered with me to the couch and collapsed onto it.

She held me up with (I have to admit) a heartbreakingly beautiful, loving awe etched on her face. It made me feel like an asshole. But it also made me half forgive her, too. She hugged me, weeping and kissing my face and head.

"I love you, too, Keenan. I love you, too. I'm sorry I'm sorry I love you I'm sorry oh Keenan you *talked*, oh my God, oh Keenan . . ."

Maybe I cried a little, too. So what?

!!!

Saturday.

Lou reeked of perfume. I couldn't really see her because I was tucked up under her arm. I *could* see that she'd put on a pair of red pumps. She was up to something. Cigarette smoke wafted from her free hand. She hefted me down the hall.

"Drew!" she called impatiently. A muffled response from the other room. "Drew!"

Finally, she reached Drew's study and set me unceremoniously on his lap between him and his computer. On his screen was a stock trading site; on his desk next to this was a half-empty beer mug; wafting nearby in an ashtray was a joint.

I got a look at Louisiana. She was in a denim skirt and a tight red T-shirt that read MeThree. She was mascaraed, bronzed, rouged, lipsticked, and linered. No bra. What class! Her dark mass of hair was tied back with a scrunchy. "I'm going out for a while. Watch the Monkey."

Drew had been shaken from deep thought—well, deep thought for Drew—and he was just then registering our presence. "What? I thought I had the day to myself!"

"Change of plans."

"Um . . . I . . . where are you off to?" He stood up and set me on the chair.

"I'm going to meet Roxanne. She's a little down," Lou told him. I looked at her, and she glanced down. She was lying. She rubbed my wispy head. I jerked away from her.

You're meeting that fucking cop, aren't you? I was jealous . . . maybe betrayed. Whatever my feelings, why did I care?

"Rox is *always* a little down," Drew said. He gestured at the screen. "I'm working on Dottie's portfolio. I think I'm getting the hang of it." He paused. "Can't you meet Roxanne later?"

"*Portfolio.* It's not Dottie's anymore. And no, I can't meet Rox later. I watch Monkey all week. You can watch him for a couple hours." She headed for the door.

Really? That redneck piece of shit Deputy Wade? You trollop!

Drew put on his best pouty face, but Lou would have none of it.

"Drew. Roxie just got dumped. I'll be back after a few drinks."

Floozy!

She looked at me as though she might've read my thoughts. "You wanna hang with Daddy, don't you, Monkey?"

I stared at her stonily.

"Alright," Drew said, "but you gotta give me some time tonight, and . . . bring back some dinner." He put me on the chair and followed her out of the room and down the hall.

I looked up at the computer screen. *Shit, Pops has freakin' stock! Somebody must've died.*

Alone in the room, I saw the smoldering joint. I reached out with my tiny eight-month-old hand and snagged it. I took as big a drag as my little lungs would take and held it in. I quickly replaced the joint in the ashtray and sat back in the chair, exhaling with a cough. I giggled.

I awoke ninety minutes later in my crib. I sat bolt upright.

Jesus! What the hell happened? I felt dizzy. I stood up and peeked over the bars at the door. It was an easy climb down, now thoroughly mastered. *Oh, shit! That's right—Drew's joint. Note to self: I weigh only twenty pounds. Do not smoke sticky green indica until you at least hit sixty pounds, you lunkhead.*

I hopped the crib rail and stomped down the hall, finding Drew in front of his computer, fretting over a stock portfolio he couldn't understand. I said, "Dad?"

I was still easing them into the idea that I could talk. I kept it to one- or two-word communications.

He turned around, clearly buzzed. Drew loved beer. He had jugs of home brew fermenting in the garage. He was soused and stoned on the very marijuana that'd laid me out.

"Keenie!" he exclaimed, red-eyed and bushy tailed. "It's about time you escaped from the pen." He hefted me up. "Let's try to make sense of this stock business one more time." He sat down, me on his lap. "This, my little son, is like reading Aramaic. Totally unintelligible."

I looked at it. It was totally intelligible. It showed 31 shares of Apple and 140 shares of Cal Solar. That was it. That's what he'd spent hours fussing over. I looked up at him and gestured at the display. "Apple."

He looked at me in amazement. "What?" He looked at the screen. "Apple? Apple Computers? Ah, jeez, Keenan, don't tell me you can already read."

I pointed at the Apple logo.

"Oh . . ." he said, then gave me a sidelong glance.

Jesus, Drew, just keep the fucking Apple, sell the Cal Solar . . . they were tanking before I was dead . . . or born . . . whatever.

He talked at my downy head. "You know, I'm just going to sell the

Apple. Solar has gotta be big, right? I mean it's the twenties for chrissake. Solar good, Apple bad. Like Microsoft used to be, but more pretentious."

You louse! Who gave you a computer driver's license? Somebody help him.

He snagged the roach out of the ashtray to relight it. "Daddy's going to take one more drag and then you and I are going to check the beer." Then under his breath. "Where the hell is Louise?"

I looked at him apologetically.

On screen, he clicked the box next to his Apple stock, then hovered over the SELL button. I watched his finger tremble over the mouse. Sweat beaded his forehead. Then a beeping sound went off in the kitchen. He perked up. "Ah! That's our taquitos, my li'l buddy." He got up, setting me in the chair. Looking down at me, he pulled on the joint. "Back in a sec. Don't fall asleep on me this time, Monkey."

He left. I had little time. I stood on the chair and grabbed the mouse, massive in my hands. I unclicked the Apple stock and clicked over to his Cal Solar, selling immediately. A window came up asking me if I wanted to transfer funds toward another stock. I looked at the screen and saw a link that said "STOCKS TO WATCH". I clicked it and it gave a top ten up-and-comers. I scrolled down quickly, hearing my father burn his fingers on the plate in the other room with a gasp. I focused on a stock: Integral Wave Devices. I'd just read about it: a wave-motion electricity generator company out of San Francisco that had just got picked up by Pacific Gas & Electric. I transferred all the money from Cal Solar to IWD and pressed the mouse button. It was done. I heard my father approaching from the kitchen, so I stretched my tiny hands to press CONTROL-ALT-DELETE on the keyboard. No menu came up—the computer just froze.

I sat back down and pretended to play with my belly button.

Drew came in and almost dropped the taquitos. He saw the crashed screen.

"Ah, hell! Jesus on a popsicle stick, Keen!"

He tapped the keyboard fruitlessly. "Goddamn it!" He looked at me, then at the computer. "Keenan, did you touch the keyboard? Shit!" He paced around the messy little office, grabbed a taquito and chomped on it. He looked at me, angry, then at the rebellious computer.

"Keenan, screw it. Let's check the beer. I'll take care of this later. It's not worth it. Never trade stocks while you're high, Keenan." Laughing, Drew wedged me into the crook of his arm, and we both giggled our way to the garage to check on his beer.

!!!

Later, Drew and I, molded comfortably into the recliner, watched the current American political disaster as portrayed by what they used to call cable news. That's when Louisiana returned from what I gathered was an afternoon rendezvous with Deputy Dawg. Drew was quite inebriated and not a little bit disheveled (being on his sixth home-brewed brown ale and his second spliff) when Lou walked in. We looked up in tandem as she suddenly hovered over us.

"Look at my two little boys," she said, billowing out a plume of smoke from a freshly lit cigarette. There was a curious edge to her voice. On her upper arm I detected what might have been a sex bruise.

With barely a glance, Drew replied, "Hi, baby. Did you have fun? How's Roxie?"

I watched Lou's face. She suddenly remembered her lie. "Ohhh, Roxie'll be fine. Just needed an ear." She exhaled another billow. Secondhand smoke was a secondhand thought in the Harris household. "I'm going to take a shower and change," she said.

She disappeared.

Drew and I continued to watch the news. I realized that Drew had gone quiet. I looked up at him and followed his gaze through the hallway and into the master bedroom. Lou was visible through the door frame, stripping down. Lust in my father's eyes.

Oh, God.

This was horrifying for a couple reasons: first, there was the image of my parents screwing; second, I was 90 percent sure my mother had just fucked another man. I forced my gaze back to the TV and heard the shower turn on in the bathroom. Drew suddenly lifted me out of his lap.

"Hey, little buddy. Why don't you sit here and watch the funny news guy while Daddy goes and helps Mommy in the shower." I looked up at him as he placed me in his warmed-up seat.

Jesus, I thought. *Sloppy seconds or not, at least he's getting laid.*

He disappeared into the bedroom. The door closed with a click, and I heard a distant squeal from their bathroom. I climbed down from the recliner and trod toward Drew's office. I closed the door until it just touched the jamb, and climbed the office chair, restarting Drew's computer.

I had been waiting for this moment; I estimated I had maybe twenty minutes. Bringing up the browser, I typed "Franklin Franklin O'Donnell"—*Franks*, my traitorous lieutenant. I found several addresses for Frank F. McDonnell, his business DBA, and an appraiser's license. If I had more time and a credit card, I could find out his phone number and social security number. Gotta love the Internet.

I heard the shower cut off.

Next, I typed in "Steven Hightower," also known as Poindexter, part of our crew, but really, he was Franks's man. Pugnacious little Poins, too smart to be working for Franks, but apparently not smart enough to stay out of prison. Looked like he was popped on an old warrant for second-degree armed robbery. Nice. California State Prison, Sacramento.

There was the sound of bedsprings down the hall.

Then I searched for "Bartholomew Montgomery." Oh, Bart. He was my favorite. Used to work for me as my number one in the drug business. He'd cut his criminal teeth on fencing stolen property and second-story work before working for me. Unfortunately, when I last saw him, he was on his way to a three-year stretch in Folsom. I'll get to that later. I found no current information on him.

I looked up Dolly Velasquez: my fabulously wanton and marginally scrupulous sweetheart. I discovered she had her own counseling practice now. Good for her. That would make it easy to find her.

Then I remembered the newcomer to the gang, August Williams, a young white techie dude who seemed an unlikely drug dealer—which of course was a feature, not a bug. He had a built-in techie clientele with loads of money to burn.

The growing orgasmic crescendo issuing from the bedroom told me I had better wrap it up.

The first search on August Williams yielded a brief article about my very own death: three short paragraphs in the *San Francisco Chronicle* archives.

Alleged Drug Dealer Charged in Fentanyl Death

San Francisco—An alleged drug dealer in San Francisco has been charged with murder after prosecutors say he sold fentanyl to a man who was found deceased from an overdose.

August Williams, 24, who reported the death, was set for arraignment Thursday afternoon in connection with the death of 50-year-old Kurt Houston, according to the San Francisco County City Attorney's Office.

Houston was found dead at his Potrero Hill residence on January 26 by San Francisco fire paramedics. In a subsequent search of Williams's vehicle, police investigators found prepackaged narcotics. Investigators later discovered text messages in Williams's phone indicating multiple narcotics transactions . . .

I thought: *What?!—but August didn't kill me!*

This was all wrong. August must've found me dead and told Franks, who had assumed my role as drug boss, then sacrificed August. What a fucker.

In some distant part of the house, I heard a harmony of ecstatic wails.

A second article read:

> **Fentanyl Dealer Sentenced to Two Years in Overdose Death**
>
> San Francisco—August Williams was sentenced in federal court today to 24 months in prison for distributing fentanyl that caused the death of one person, announced Drug Enforcement Administration (DEA) Special Agent in Charge Spencer Frendlon. The sentence was handed down by United States District Judge Kris Shteil.
>
> "The death and destruction caused by fentanyl knows no boundaries. From coast to coast this poison is devastating families," stated Special Agent Frendlon. "Holding accountable those, like Williams, who ruin lives with their criminal actions, is our priority."
>
> Williams, 25, of Redwood City, California, pleaded guilty on June 20, to two counts of distributing fentanyl. In his plea agreement, Williams admitted that in January, he sold heroin combined with fentanyl . . .

The sex noises ceased down the hall.

I quickly powered down the computer, climbed from the chair, and used all my might to shove it back toward the desk. As I passed the master bedroom, I heard low murmurs and smelled a cigarette. I closed my bedroom door behind me and climbed up and into my crib.

Staring at the ceiling, I puzzled darkly over the new information.

My guess was this: August was sent to check on me to find out why I hadn't answered my phone, or he needed to re-up his drug supply. He found me dead and called 911. The kid was pretty green. Franks and Poins would've *never* called for help at all, or at least not from the scene. Then, I'm sure Franks and Poins hired an attorney for August, and when that attorney found out that the city attorney and the DEA were not going to budge, Franks leaned on August to take a deal and do the time. You know, to ensure his own health.

Fucking Franks.

But now I knew how to find Franks and Dolly when the time came. I'd long considered that they'd had a fling behind my back before I died. Was Dolly also in on my death? Did she help frame August? And what was my angle anyway? What was I going to do about it? Surprise them as a five-year-old? Get them arrested somehow? Find a way to have them killed? What kind of person was I now? I had to make a plan.

7. About Nine Months In

About nine months in, I started to go a little stir crazy. I was itchy for unrestrained experience. None of this chaperoned baby bullshit anymore. If you're cognizant of the outside world, babyhood is like prison: constantly watched, fed, and forced to live by someone else's schedule. I reasoned that freedom was not going to happen unless I freed myself . . . *in the middle of the night.* I went from being daunted by my tiny earthly form to being excited about new earthly possibilities. This took the form of my top secret "nightwalks."

There was a lot of intelligence gathering. I studied my parents' sleeping habits. From two in the morning until dawn, they kept an unchanging sleep schedule. But just before sleep, one of them—usually Lou—would get up, check on me, empty her bladder, and return to bed; shortly after, Drew would get up and do pretty much the same thing. Then they'd sleep undisturbed without deviation. When I became confident of their schedule, I decided that it was time to rediscover the outside world—even if that outside world consisted of a one-block radius of our marginally employed neighbors.

I figured that like any cat burglar, I should dress in black. A midget in commando drag. Sadly, the darkest clothes I owned were a black toddler-size AC/DC T-shirt (courtesy Uncle Joe), dark blue pajama bottoms, a dark blue Disney cap, and tiny dark green sneakers. I dressed as a sneak thief by way of a concert parking lot.

On the big night, Mom checked in on me at one o'clock in the morning, and about forty-five minutes later my sleepy-eyed dad lumbered in to peek at me. After his ghostly face disappeared, I waited about five minutes and climbed out of bed. While the grups didn't get up until seven, I had to be inside well before sunrise, lest someone think there was a monkey loose in the neighborhood.

In the four months since I'd learned to walk, I'd grown very sure of my new body. I was a big lug in my past life, but the unlikely combination of musical theater and kickboxing had made me a big, *agile* lug. Keenan Harris was pretty sure-footed, his dexterity had improved, and he ran amok all over the house climbing anything taller than, well, me. That's why the grups called me "Monkey."

Now, dressed in that aforementioned tiny commando costume, I peeked down the dark hallway echoing with snores from Mom and Dad. I trod lightly past their bedroom and made my way to the back door, eyes adjusting to the darkness. I held my breath as I stretched up and unlocked the door, turned the knob, and slowly opened it.

The intoxicating smell of Indian summer breathed sweetly in my face. A dog barked in the distance. I stepped out and eased the door almost closed but not all the way. I didn't have a key.

Imagine my surprise to find myself unfettered in the outside world after nine months of captivity . . . in a body the size of a capuchin. *Unreal!* My lungs filled with night air scented with jasmine.

Now what do I do?

I kept close to the bushes and made my way toward the side gate. The fence was about six feet tall—from my height, it looked sixty. I swung up onto the gray iron water meter, then onto the top of the plastic garbage can, unlatching the gate. The squawk of the hinge seemed deafening. It surprised me and I pressed myself into the shadows to listen. Nothing. Carefully climbing down, I exited the yard, leaving the gate open.

Relying on slightly open doors and gates was getting me edgy, but being out of doors was worth it. It was so odd being under the night sky. Exhilarated but vulnerable, the size of a terrier but lacking teeth, lacking speed. All I had was the protection of the shadows.

I rolled under the hedge on the side lawn, then lay prone. I inched forward toward the street, and the leafy hedge perfectly concealed me from the hard yellow sodium light beaming down from the streetlamp high above. The neighborhood was quiet except for the odd car passing by every so often, piloted by a tired waitress, a drunk teenager. I'm not sure how much time went by as I lay there, taking in the alien night.

Under a car across the street, glowing eyes fixed upon me. The cat finally got curious enough to cross toward me. Halfway across it stopped to lick a paw, studying me. It was a big orange-striped tabby. It trotted straight up to me and meowed. I reached forward and it rubbed its nose against my small hand. I pulled my hand back, sinking deeper under the hedge. We sat in silent conference for some minutes. As it purred, I thought about my next move.

Footsteps! Suddenly, the cat was snatched up!

"Tristan!" the woman said. She breathed heavily. All I could see were yellow running shoes and the cuffs of matching sweats. This woman, of whom I could see little, was on a three o'clock in the morning jog.

"What's up, kittiwittikins?" Yellow Sneakers said. "What are you doing all the way out here?" She set the cat down again, patted it on the head, said, "Hurry home!" and jogged on. The cat named Tristan looked over at me, meowed, turned and trotted away.

When they were out of sight, I poked out my head, looked around, then scuttled across the neighbor's lawn to the next house, two doors down from us.

Avoiding the light, I skirted the yellowing rose bushes and made it to the far side of the neighbor's yard. I was a small escaped simian, a Curious George, hiding twixt battered garbage can and metal gate.

Young voices issued from the side yard.

I carefully pushed through the neighbor's unlatched gate; voices came from an open window adjacent to a junk-strewn side yard. Perfectly still, I listened. There was a boozy syrup in their young voices, perhaps pot. I should've left right then, but my curiosity got the better of me and I took a look around. Under the window there was a convenient stack of threadbare tires, and I climbed them until my eyes were level with the bottom of the open window. My tiny nine-month-old head, Disney-capped, peeked through the rickety blinds.

My nose picked up sandalwood incense masking the funk of pot, sex, unwashed clothes, spilled beer, and perhaps a hidden pizza box.

Amid the gothy punk rock decor, it took me a second to figure out that I was looking at the bedroom of a teenage girl. Concert posters hung on the wall next to draped screen-printed banners of rock stars I'd never heard of—Mitori and Whitechapel? There was a mishmash of stuffed animals, softcore S-M accoutrements, and marijuana paraphernalia. Against the wall, on top of a dorm-room mini-fridge, was an altar of sorts to grunge prophet Mark Lanegan. A legion of spent, half-melted candles (only one lit) pooled at the foot of a picture collage of Lanegan doing his howling, scowling, rockstar best.

I thought: *What the fuck?! Mark Lanegan is dead?*

This severely bummed me out, but I didn't have time for that.

At the edge of the bed, on top of the purple leopard-print comforter, a shaggy-haired guy with brown-olive skin gurgled a hit from a tall red plastic bong covered with stickers. His ears were bedazzled with steel, his naked torso glistened with sweat. The guy's accent was so very San Jose: "Yeah, man, so Rico is all up in the shit with Chanelle 'n' shit. Like white on, you know, whatever." *Suuuuuck, guuuuurgle.* He held the smoke in, red faced.

His companion was a skinny, pale, pixie-haired white girl of seventeen-going-on-thirty, pacing back and forth, wearing nothing but a thin skull-emblazoned tank top. Smeared lipstick, smeared mascara, smeared expression. She was nursing a bloody nose with a wadded-up paper towel. She also glistened with sweat. Her voice was a husky staccato.

"Rico don't know shit from nothing. Chanelle still got her cherry and she ain't givin' it up to no banger from South Hoser, David." She pronounced his name "*Dah-veed.*"

Oddly, I sensed that this was their version of pillow talk but I couldn't tell if they were pre- or postcoital. Finally, he put down the bong and swept her mid-pace onto his lap and into his sinewy brown tattooed arms.

"David!"

"How's your nose, baby?"

"That shit's messed up, man." She kissed him. "It's okay." She planted another one on him and they tongue-wrestled for a sec. Then his eyes drifted over to the window and—*he saw me!*

Fuck! I thought.

"What the fuck was that?! *Fuck!*" David shouted.

I was already gone. I launched myself off the stack of tires, landed squarely on my feet, and headed for the gate. I heard a thump from inside the house—the girl ejected from his lap. Once through the gate, my little feet propelled me as fast they could across the neighbor's lawn back toward our house.

In the silence of the night, I could clearly hear him at the window, frantically telling her, "I swear to God there was a little gnome or some shit at the window. I *swear to God*!"

"David! You saw a *what*? You're high!"

"A gnome! Fuck me! I'm going out front."

"Come on—you're all loaded 'n' shit. There ain't no . . . *thing* . . . out my window . . . you'll wake my mom!"

I heard him scramble through the house. I was across the lawn and through the rose bushes and under our hedge again. I froze. I heard David careen through the backyard, clamor and curse through the side yard, and then burst out of the gate, coming to a stop in their driveway.

The young man came all the way out onto the sidewalk, shirtless, his bare, tattooed chest puffed out. He flashed a pistol about. Gangbanger-in-training, high as a kite, looking for a gnome. Priceless.

Across the street I saw Tristan-the-Cat's eyes glow at me from under the car.

The girl hissed from the porch: "Get in here right now, you freak! Someone will call the cops!"

After a few glances up and down the block, David cursed—"Fucking fuck"—and went back inside. When I was sure the neighborhood was once more at peace, I crawled from under the hedge, closed the gate, slipped through my back door, and locked it. I stopped and listened to the house and the parents' gentle, rhythmic snores. Satisfied I was in the clear, I snuck back to my room, changed out of my commando night-walk gear, and snuggled very contentedly in my crib.

It was almost four in the morning.

8. *Here There Be Monsters*

At a year old, my nightwalks expanded, ever enlightening. I got to know not only the neighborhood, but the neighbors, all by the stealth of night. By this time, I had pieced together an entire black cat burglar outfit—sweater, pants, and a little black cap. I nicked a small watch from inside the back of Lou's dresser drawer. I kept it in my pocket. I'd sneak out at two in the morning and sneak back in by dawn, finding all the quickest and darkest routes through hedge, bramble, fence, and yard. I learned the yards with dogs, the houses with cats, the inhabitants who burned the post-midnight oil. Down the block was a vacant early-2000s tract home into which a teenage couple trespassed and utilized for romantic purposes most nights. Of course, there was also that teenage couple two doors down. I'd sometimes watch them take drugs and screw, but that soon grew boring. The adult couple a few doors up from them was far more interesting with their bondage equipment and role reversals. There was also the woman, a mother of two, who snuck inside her next-door neighbor's house. Lesbian tryst, I believe. Also, there were many professional drunks on our street. At least four or five of the dads or moms or both simultaneously stumbled home each night. They'd lurch down their front walks, fall inside their doors, and knock things crashing to the floor before the door was shut. Loud fights followed. One of the neighbors was some kind of a drug dealer, but I could never quite tell what kind. I mean, obviously it was either speed or coke. Cars stopped by for quick ins-and-outs all night long. It was a neighborhood of working-class reprobates—and a democratic mix of all races.

The travels on the particular night I'm about to recount were a little different. My plan was to make it all the way to the 7-Eleven, four long blocks away. I'd been as far as two blocks from home, and that in itself was quite a way, hopping shadow to shadow on tiny legs.

Drew took his nightly piss and checked on me at 2:06 a.m., right on time. Under the covers, I was already dressed, and I bounded out of bed five minutes later.

The night was brisk, the moon partly obscured by clouds, and the noisy sodium streetlamps cast their yellow glow on the street. I carried no flashlight; my young eyes were better than any eyes I had in yester-life.

I made my way to the end of our court by my usual route, stopping at the neighborhood gazebo, a structure buttressed by a forest of yellowing grass. At *my* height it was a forest. This little section of lawn was the longest stretch of my route that lacked real cover. There was a five-second sprint during which I was completely exposed. The shrub-enshrouded fence on the other side of this gazebo was the demarcation line between our shoddy subdivision and the next slightly more posh neighborhood.

Remember the pair of wayward teenagers I mentioned? This was where they resided, and tonight I came upon them as they sat on an iron bench that faced the grassy breezeway.

"Did you hear that?" I heard the girl whisper.

I froze.

"What?" a guy's voice answered in a hushed and annoyed tone. "C'mon. I gotta get back."

I disappeared into the ivy that blanketed the entire fence line.

"I heard, like . . . *little footsteps*."

"Probably a raccoon—they're everywhere around here," he replied. I heard the muffled slurp of making out. "Let me do something about this bra strap."

"Please don't lose it. That was hard to explain." A moment later, she let out a quiet moan.

He chuckled, then said, "Your mom counts your bras? Does she number them?"

"Mmm . . . you'd be surprised. Now hurry up."

I crept slowly away toward the hole in the fence that led to the street behind our court. Tristan, the neighbor's orange tabby, blinked at me in the darkness, directly in my path. I scuttled past him and he leaned into me with a purr. Like always.

"Hey, Triss," I whispered, rubbing his ear. "I'm in a hurry." I scurried past.

I was now in a slightly newer, more affluent subdivision. Ours was run down; this one was probably built within the last decade. The houses were bigger, more thoughtfully planned; the cars were more expensive, the lawns mowed. And, thank God, it was landscaped with plenty of tall shrubbery and flower beds. At my height, most of these yards were little jungles, jungles filled with lost balls, empty beer bottles, baby rattles, gardening tools, sprinklers, crackling snails, odd vegetables; cats and raccoons patrolled there, rats and opossum lurked there, with impunity; dogs barked frantically from behind scratched wooden fences; people stumbled drunk through this jungle, people slept coma-like in this jungle, slept until morning, wafting with the stink of vice.

And this pre-cognizant baby with an insatiable urge for escape called these jungles his wilderness home.

On that night, I traveled through yards I didn't know very well, and I reached the furthest perimeter of my previous nightwalks. I stopped to study what lay in front of me. A dead-end street and a row of houses lay inconveniently between me and my goal: the convenience store. This was the great unknown. That said, while this journey seemed epic to a thirty-inch-tall baby, by age seven it would be a five-minute walk.

Beware! Here there be monsters.

Crossing the street wasn't difficult, but I needed to find clear passage beyond this barrier of houses. It took me a couple tries to find a climbable stretch of fence. My shoes squished as I crept through shrubbery and across stretches of lawn.

I was almost to the 7-Eleven; a little over a half hour had elapsed.

A gated community was my final challenge. I slipped easily through the gap between barred gate and stucco wall. Rolling lawns, gurgling fountains, and three swimming pools. As I skulked past the fountains and pools, I heard the occasional quack or frog-splash. The frogs and insects at this time of night affected something of a low roar.

Finally, I reached the last boundary. The convenience store was just over a tall cinder block wall that kept the commoners out of the gated community. I could see the top of the 7-Eleven sign. I scanned the line of the wall until I found a tall, bushy olive tree that had a branch just within reach of a good running bounce off the wall. This I did, and once I was on the branch, I monkeyed my way up to just above the top of the wall, nestling myself comfortably into a sturdy dark crook. For perspective, just know that first branch was four feet off the ground and the wall was maybe seven feet high on the condo side, and had a nine-foot drop on the 7-Eleven side.

But I had done it! This was my nightwalk's goal! I just wanted a ringside glimpse of social interaction that wasn't my parents, the neighbors, or the fucking playground. I was close enough to hear snippets of conversation and remain wholly undetected. My perch overlooked both the side parking lot and the back area of the 7-Eleven, where they kept the dumpster and crushed boxes. I checked my ladies' watch: it was 2:50 a.m.

A 7-Eleven (and its parking lot) is a social microcosm of America, analogous to the fractured intersection of community and commerce, warped by our sick obsession for convenience: raw need delivered by a financially leveraged workforce, prepackaged and served up like smack to junkies.

You will never find a more wretched hive of commerce and villainy.

I breathed it in: three cars in the cracked asphalt lot, bright fluorescents, young adults smoking, laughing, sipping brown-bagged forties chased with Big Gulps. All I really wanted was a visual piece of the action. Twelve months trapped in this baby-flesh cage was killing me and I was desperate for any stimuli that wasn't the stultified life I'd been born into.

At least I could glimpse the local depravity, and that was definitely enough.

Safe in my shadows, not ten yards distant, I was rewarded with my first sighting: parking lot tweakers. Some things never change—jeans, flannels, long hair, and California drawls, with a tinge of San Jose homeboy. They rounded the corner of the store next to the dumpster and busted out a pipe.

"This Lonnie's shit?"

"My cousin's."

"I thought he don't cook no more."

"Guy's gotta make rent."

"Sweet. This is like Walter White shit."

Click of the lighter. Big draw. A cough. Pass the pipe. Click. Draw.

A bottle rattled loudly from over near the dumpster.

"Shit!"

They watched a beer bottle roll toward them across the uneven asphalt.

A beat, then one of the guys said, "Stoli, that you?"

A groan and slither issued from the other side of the dumpster area.

In the dim light of this dark side of the building, a large ragged-headed form scuffled forward. The silhouette of a shambling homeless man.

"Who's asking? That Shep?" grumbled the dark form.

Both young men laughed at this.

"Shit, man," said one of the guys, who I assumed was Shep. He wore a baseball cap.

"Got something for an old veteran?"

The shambling man stepped into the light where I could kind of see him. He had a beard and pale skin. Shep gave this Stoli fellow the pipe. The other guy said, "Remember me, dude?"

Stoli turned to the other fellow. From what I could see in the dim cross-light, the kid had a long scraggly red goatee and a shaved head. Stoli said, "Bam Bam."

Shep and Bam Bam let out a laugh.

"Fuck, dude," Bam Bam said. "Good one, man."

"I may be crazy but I ain't stupid." Stoli took a small hit off the pipe and coughed, handing it back to them. "Aw . . . that's not what I thought it was." He crept back toward his shadow. "But whatever. You know where to find me."

"Right on," Shep said.

Stoli disappeared into the garbage area as Shep and Bam Bam giggled.

"That dude's a trip."

A beat.

"Well, man, I gotta get."

"I hear ya."

The two men disappeared, and not long after, a silver late-model Camaro shot out of the lot.

I waited a little longer to see if I could absorb any more real world. Chilly night. Damp air. Dog barking far away. Electronic bell of the 7-Eleven door bing bonging.

Finally, I peeked at the watch: 3:20. Time to go.

My heart almost stopped when I heard a voice from the dumpster area: "I know you're there."

It was the bum, Stoli. Frozen, I said nothing.

"It's okay. What are you anyway? Raccoon? Possum? *Elf?*"

Another long silence. I was dumbfounded, terror stricken. I began to edge down from my perch, toward my escape route.

He continued, not quite a yell, "I know you're there. I can hear you. Feel you. Are you one of the *Watchers*?"

He was clearly funny in the head.

"It's cool. I'm a friend. Just wanted to say hi. No biggie. Just wanted you to know, when you come around again, it's all good. I'm not afraid. I'm ready to go. I'm tired of this place."

I was somewhere between panicked and exhilarated.

"I can smell you. Strange smell. Sweet." He mumbled something to himself as he waited for a response, which I did not offer. "What's your name?"

I took a breath, nervous. Was I really going to do this?

"Kurt," I said. I was not going to lie to this man—I didn't have to.

Stoli stood up with a start: a rangy wild-haired silhouette against the yellow streetlight. He said, "Goddamn! I thought I was crazy!"

"Well, you *are* talking to a voice in the fence."

"Ha *ha*!" He took a couple of steps toward me, out of the shadow.

"Don't come any closer or I'll vanish," I warned. Like I was going to outrun an adult. But he didn't know what I was.

He backed up into his niche. "Alright, alright. Don't get excited. It's just not every day you get to talk to an elf."

"What makes you think I'm an elf?"

"Shit, I dunno. You have a tiny little voice. Like a child's. But you speak like a grown-up." Pause, exhale of smoke. "And you're small. I can tell by your movements, by the way the tree shakes."

"You're telling me you can smell me and hear my movements. Quite a talent."

"Yeah, well, I spent a lot of time hiding myself." Slurp of beer. "Sniper."

Oh, great. He was a cliché, a homeless veteran. "Which theater?" I prodded.

"Curious choice of terms . . . *Afghanistan*," said Stoli. "What's your story?"

"You wouldn't believe it if I told you."

"You know I would . . . *Kurt.*"

Fuck! Hearing my name jarred me, spoken to me for the first time since I died. He mused, "That ain't no elf name. Curiouser and curiouser."

"I'm not an elf. I'm not sure what I am or how I got here."

"You some sort of ghost?"

"In a way. But ghosts don't have bodies, so not really."

"Fair enough."

He popped another beer.

"Why are you a bum?" I asked.

"Ha! A *bum.* No one uses that word anymore. No, I got a home—I just don't like it there much."

A beat. "PTSD?"

"Ain't you cheeky. Yeah . . . something like that."

The cherry glow of his cigarette danced in the dark. An ember flurried to the ground.

He continued. "You see a lot of dead people. Body parts in the dirt. You never really know if they deserve it. I reckon now they didn't. Deserve it. I lived in a cave for a year. I started to enjoy it."

"I bet it had running water."

"You're right. And great sunrises. And a delicious supply of animals who wanted my cave. When the army found me, I was fat."

"You were Zarathustra."

A hitched breath.

"What did you say?" he asked suspiciously.

"I—" *Ah . . . he knew who that was.* "You heard me."

He took a moment. "When you're on a mission you pack light.

Technical gear, med-pack, MREs. I also brought a small e-reader with sixteen books on it. One of them was *Thus Spoke Zarathustra*."

"It's hard to dog-ear an ebook."

"Who the fuck *are* you?"

I looked at my watch. Ten minutes.

"I'm not your guardian angel, if that's what you're hoping."

"You have the voice of a child. I'm going crazy."

"Much to our surprise, you are not. Let me put it this way: I was once someone else, and I came back. I don't know why. It blows the hell out of my rationalistic notions."

I heard the pop of a fresh beer, saw the flash of a lighter.

He asked, "You're a reincarnation? Are you like a talking badger or something?"

I laughed. "Shut the hell up." I said evenly, "I'm not a talking badger. There are no such things as elves. I'm not an alien. You are not hallucinating. I used to be Kurt Sebastian Houston, failed writer, petty drug lord, a real dickhead. Murdered at age fifty by his henchman, six years ago. Ish."

There. I said it. To the crazy 7-Eleven bum. But I knew he would believe me. He had nothing else to believe in.

"Nothing you say matches up with the way reincarnation is supposed to work."

"*Supposed to work?*"

"In *The Tibetan Book of the Dead*. It was on my e-reader."

"Holy shit! Of all the 7-Eleven bums, I get a scholar."

"Wow, you *are* a real dickhead."

"I'm working on it." I paused. "Look, you say I broke the reincarnation rules? I'm right *here*—a talking toddler!" I shook the tree branches.

"You're supposed to spend forty-nine days in limbo, not six years."

"Well, the *Book of the Dead* got it wrong." I added, "And I was in your so-called limbo for five years. It's been a year."

"It also says that if you made it back as a human you weren't such a bad guy in the previous life."

I pondered this. "Well, maybe I *wasn't* such a bad guy."

There was a very long silence.

"I gotta go," he said. But he didn't move.

For some reason, this ticked me off. "Don't be such a pussy." This coming from the child voice through the fence. But I was desperate. I said, "I just spilled my guts for the first time. You are the first one to hear my story. You're not having a psychotic episode. You are behind a convenience store and you're talking to a reincarnated human. Why was it easier when I was an elf? Or alien? Don't leave me. This is fucking real and you better fucking believe it. Cuz I know now that I need *you.*"

I heard him get up, start to gather his things.

"Where are you going?"

"I drank too much."

"You've had four beers."

"I need my medication."

"Oh, please."

"You sound like you're . . . like three years old!"

"I'm much younger and much older."

Stoli stood out of the shadow, looking toward my black slice of the fence, frozen.

"This isn't real."

"It *is* real. You're not having a flashback. *Amor fati*, my friend. This moment is *supposed* to happen. This is what we were waiting for. We're each other's ticket to finding ourselves again. It's all very clear. Believe me, the old Kurt would never talk crunchy granola bullshit about destiny . . . but then he died and was reborn. Listen: I'm going to help you, and you are going to help me fulfill my mission."

I'd never stated it so plainly before: *I was on a mission!* The details were becoming more defined that very moment, and I was sure that

Stoli, a very rattled homeless guy, was part of this infernal puzzle. I had known for a while I was going to need outside, grown-up help if I wanted to face down Franks.

Stoli turned around like he was about to go, but remained still, *stuck*. "This isn't happening," he said.

"Look, I gotta go, too. It's almost dawn. I'll be back, and next time don't be all freaking out on me. We have work to do. I'm not some hallucination; I'm a being from a past life who needs your help. Because you're an adult and crazy enough to believe me." I paused. "I might not be back for a month or more. Anyhow, if you have the cojones to show up every night waiting for me, it'll be worth your while. Both monetarily and spiritually. Can we agree on that?"

Stoli was completely mortified. I'd gone from being a mysterious elf figure into an apparition who had just made him what probably sounded like a Faustian offer.

The parking lot was empty. He started to walk away again, saying, "I hope to hell you don't actually exist."

I called after him, "Probably like two weeks!"

He didn't reply, and I watched him disappear into the night.

The whole exchange made me tired. The watch said four in the morning. I eased myself down from the branches of the olive tree . . . which was probably really the size of a tall bush. As I slunk through my now familiar shadows, my shrubs and gardens and gates that kept this elf safe from harm, I tried to absorb what had just taken place. I had revealed myself for the first time.

After months of secrecy, I'd come out. It'd been a long time since I'd felt such relief. I sprinted through the gated community and past the pools and over the back fence that led to my neighborhood.

I'd exposed my true identity to a crazy man, and it suddenly dawned on me that I'd been sent back to fix everything, to make amends for the bridges I'd burned and the resulting casualties.

As I skulked home through the back door, dawn crawled up the chilled autumn sky, and I quietly nestled in my bed, finally understanding that this wasn't a purgatory that I had to wait out. It was a story that I had to finish.

9. At Sixteen Months

One day Drew broke the news to Lou that he'd lost his job at the funeral home. There was a colorful fight. A table lamp was dashed against the wall. Afterward, Drew moped around, surfed job sites, vaped pot. His resume was a mess of disparate jobs, most of which he'd gotten fired or laid off from. He just wasn't very employable.

Fortunately, the Malkmuses down the street (I would later befriend their son, Ralphy) had a friend whose family owned a music store in the Willow Glen neighborhood of San Jose. They needed a bookkeeper, and Lou had an associate degree in accounting. Thus, the Harris family paradigm soon became reversed: Drew got up early and fixed us breakfast; Drew did the laundry; Drew took me for walks (something Lou *never* did).

Then, our piece-of-junk car broke down, which meant Lou had to get up early and take the light rail all the way into Willow Glen. Morning was the enemy of Louisiana Harris. I was already awake in my room when I heard them get into it.

"Goddamn it, Drew! I can't do this alone—I'm going to be late."

He grumbled and said in a gravelly voice, "Why are you up so early?"

"The car's busted, remember? I have to take the fucking train. Take the fucking car in!"

"Oh, yeah. Shit."

"Get the hell up and fix us some breakfast, I have to get ready."

He groaned. "I have to control the alcohol content on my beer."

"It's not the alcohol content you have to control."

I stood at my door wearing a fluffy red Star Wars robe. Drew stumbled into the hallway in his boxers. "Hey, Monkey . . . up and at 'em already, I see. Breakfast in twenty."

"Okay," I replied.

As I walked past my parents' room, I heard Lou's hushed voice. "Hey, are you on duty?" Pause. "Oh, good. Can you do me a favor and pick me up at the train station? The car's broke. I need a ride to work—I am *not* taking the fucking train." Pause. "I'll make it worth your while . . . ."

Oh, my God! You cheating tramp!

I was silent during breakfast, seated in my silly cartoon-covered vinyl booster seat, shooting dark glances at Lou. She said, "Keenan, you look like you need to go to the toilet."

At the door, she checked her lipstick in the coat-hook mirror, telling Drew, "If you happen to get the car fixed, please come pick me up. I can't stand the fucking train. It's filled with creeps."

"Yes, dear," he said without a hint of irony.

"If not, I'll be home late for dinner. Just leave it and I can microwave it when I get here." She managed to give him a little peck on the cheek before exiting. "Thanks," she said as the door slammed.

Drew looked at me and sighed.

"She's not a morning person is she, Keenan?"

"No," I replied.

He smiled. "That said, I've got a little surprise for you later."

At about eleven in the morning, there was a knock on the door. I looked up from the magazine I was reading, and Drew bolted up from the couch. A broad grin stretched across his stubbly face. He exchanged words with the deliveryman outside, then he shot back through the house to the garage; I heard the grind of the garage door opening. Out the front door, I saw a plain white box truck backing into our driveway.

Oh, dear lord, what have you done, Drew?

I watched the men efficiently unload the boxes into the garage, slam down the truck door, and leave. As the garage door screeched closed, I looked at Drew in disbelief. In the brightly lit, cluttered garage, Drew gleefully sliced open two large boxes stenciled with THIS END UP. When he was done, we were looking at two expensive-looking stainless steel barrels with conical bottoms: Drew's new brewing equipment.

"These, my dear Keenan, are two fourteen-and-a-half gallon conical fermenters. Stainless steel, no welds. The next step on my way to becoming a master brewer."

"How?" I asked. I labored to keep verbal responses very short.

"I got this random dividend check from a company called Integral Wave Devices."

"Mom?"

He looked at me askance.

"I got a great deal on them. Now I can do away with all those stupid plastic buckets and giant bottles."

He picked me up, smiled, and planted a kiss on my cheek.

"What do you think?"

"Hide it."

His smile faltered, and he puffed out his cheeks, exhaling. "You're probably right." He put me down, but gave me a sort of double take, realizing we'd just had something like a conversation. He said, "Now go inside, I have a garage to rearrange."

At the door I looked back at him and thought, *Not so bad, you crazy bastard.*

10. The Long Good Nightwalk

It'd been a long time since I had a nightwalk. I'd put it off, and I felt bad because I told Stoli I'd be back in a couple weeks. It'd been five months. But I started to realize how risky these adventures were. They were exciting and fun at first, and I got away with them. The getting-caught part wasn't my fear, but getting attacked by a raccoon or coyote or pervert was a real possibility, against which I had little defense. Still, I got itchy for busting out, so I got up in the middle of the night and skulked through our neighborhood to the 7-Eleven. I even brought a sippy cup.

I'd barely scrambled up my olive tree before he addressed me.

"Finally! The phantom elf child returns!"

I hadn't even settled in yet. I was about to reply when I heard, "Who are you talking to, man?"

Stoli was smoking a joint with the long-haired graveyard shift manager, Stan. Their breath plumed in the frigid night. They looked in my direction.

"Nothin'," Stoli said, passing the spliff to Stan.

"You're such a trip, dude," Stan said, pinching the joint out with his fingers. "I'm going to head back inside and front the shelves. You have enough beer?"

"Yeah, I'm good."

"Cool."

Once Stan was gone, Stoli did a quick look around. The parking lot was empty and the faint crunch of heavy metal issued from within the store. It was chilly and misty on this mid-January night; a low fog crept up from the creek. Stoli stepped forward.

"Kurt!" he whispered loudly. "That you?" He walked toward the fence. It made me a little nervous, but I was well tucked into my shadowy tree and there was still a seven-foot cinder block wall between us.

I said, "Yeah, it's me. I'm back."

He walked up to the fence, then abruptly turned his back to it, I guess to appear as though he was just standing in the lot, beer in hand, smoking a cigarette.

"I believe you are real now," he stage-whispered.

A beat. "That's good. I need you to believe that."

"Look—"

"Stoli, stop stage-whispering."

He paused. "What?"

"Whispering loud is still loud. You can talk normal. Everybody thinks you're crazy anyway."

He thought about this. "Fair enough. This is good because . . . would a hallucination be so reasonable?"

Oh, Jesus. Still have to be careful.

He said, "I missed you, little buddy. I've come to a place where I don't care if you are a hallucination."

"I'm not a fucking hallucination." He still didn't believe it.

"Agh . . . your little voice makes cursing sound so wrong."

"Goddamn it, I don't have a lot of time."

"You turned my world around and I want to talk to you about it."

A white minivan pulled into the lot and a security guard stepped out and waved at Stoli, who half-heartedly waved back. Almost into the store, the guard, an aging, overfed white guy, changed his mind and waddled toward us.

"I'll handle this," Stoli said, starting off. He met the guy halfway. "How ya doin', Mike?"

"Pretty good, Stoli. Cold. Gotta juice up on the caffeinateds," the man said.

"Good. Good."

"You seem in a cheerful mood."

Mumble. "GA check today."

"How was the hospital?"

Stoli coughed again. "Don't want to talk about it."

Moment of leaden silence.

"Okay then. Well . . . take it easy, Stole."

The man walked off to the store.

Stoli returned and said nothing. He knew I heard what was said.

"Yeah, so what? I got admitted for a little bit, so what?"

"Hey, man," I said. "Three hots and a cot with a therapist thrown in. It's paradise." Then I got it. "Tell me you didn't check yourself in because you thought you were crazy—because you met a 7-Eleven elf."

"I feel better now."

He turned around, facing me, the fence, the black tree branch dark, searching. Then he turned right back around and sipped his beer, chuckling. "Whatever you are, you sound like you know your way through the system. But that could be my head talking."

"Ah—you want proof." I thought about it. "I could tell you stuff you don't know."

"Like what?"

"I don't know . . . stupid minutiae." I paused. *What stupid minutiae?* "Are you a musician?"

"I'm tone deaf."

"Well, how about . . . the main chord progression for 'Mother' by Pink Floyd is G-D7-C."

"Yeah, I couldn't know that."

"Oh, this is odd—did you know the famous gunfighter Bat Masterson died sitting at a desk as a New York City sports reporter?"

He thought about this. "Alright. Pretty good." He paused. "You're kind of a hard-ass. I bet you were a real dick back in the day."

"The dickiest."

"Karma's a bitch, huh?"

"Cute."

Another moment plodded by.

Finally, I said, "So I have a plan. A *master* plan. You could say it's our mission."

"Wow. Okay. Uh . . . *our mission?*"

"Look, Stoli."

"John."

"*John?* John, then. Look, John, I was born on January 26, 1970, as Kurt Sebastian Houston. I was reincarnated on January 26, 2025, as Keenan Solomon Harris. Tell me that's not a fucked-up coincidence."

"Shit."

"Yeah. You're the only person I've ever told."

"Also, it would make you a little older than me."

I had a great view of the back of his raggedy brown and gray head. There was a pop of another beer. The seriousness of my voice was diminished by the . . . well, its diminutive nature, but I continued.

"Listen up, John. I didn't believe in *anything*—certainly not a fucking afterlife—but I was proven wrong. It made me realize there is no coincidence. I died and was reborn fully conscious with my same initials, on the same day of my previous birth. Meeting you is part of this whole thing—we *gotta* do this. I need your help . . . and I think you need mine."

"Keenan Solomon Harris. Kurt Sebastian Houston. This is really actually happening, isn't it?"

"Yeah, this is actually happening. Don't worry, it drives me crazy, too." We watched an Uber in the shape of a Toyota Camry drop off a couple of drunk girls who giggled their way inside the store. Finally, I said, "Everything has meaning now. Nihilism was so much easier."

"I hate this. I thought everything would be over after I died."

"We are going to solve my murder."

"Your *murder*?"

"I was murdered. That's how I got here." I paused a second to have a drink from my sippy cup. "*Obviously*, I was reincarnated to solve my murder, and I found you so you could help."

"Whoa there, little fella. How are we going to bring someone to justice with this cockamamie story? How do you know it was murder?"

"I know. There had been something of a coup d'état just before the guy killed me."

"Hold it—were you the president of a third world country or something?"

"Ha! No, but I had something of a, um, criminal operation going and my lieutenant offed me. He gave me a hotshot."

"Hotshot? Like . . . *drugs*?"

"A lethal overdose of heroin and fentanyl."

"Ah, shit, man."

He crooked his head to peer over the fence into the blackness, trying to see me, to behold this mad person, the crazy elf, who now proposed some ridiculous pact with a former junkie.

"For a second you were sounding a little Buddhist with all the connections and whatnot, but revenge ain't no karma trip, it's the opposite of that. Maybe dying on junk was just your destiny and now you're in some sort of purgatory."

"Well, that's dark." *Shit.* "Also, you can't mix karma and purgatory, totally different religions."

"You don't believe in religion."

"Dammit, look—if being murdered was my destiny, then being reincarnated was, too." Stoli turned his back to me again and lit another cigarette. I continued, "The guy who did this was an evil, fucked-up person and he deserves payback. I'm too little to do it on my own."

Stoli grumbled incoherently, then said, "If I didn't think I was crazy before, making a pact with a reincarnated junkie elf is pretty convincing."

That's when I hit him with it.

"There's *money*."

He turned around, peering into my darkness.

"*Money*?"

"You can verify that everything I say is true when you dig up the ninety-two thousand dollars buried in my old backyard in San Francisco."

"Oh, Jesus. I'm supposed to go to San Francisco, break into somebody's backyard, and dig up buried treasure?"

"Ninety-two thousand dollars, Stoli."

"Call me John. How do you know it's still there?"

"It's well hidden, and not in a place likely to be dug up randomly. I was the only one who knew about it."

"And where exactly is this?"

"1836 Twentieth Street on Potrero Hill. It's buried under a bench under a tree at the top of the property."

More grumbling. "This is so crazy." I watched the back of his head sink and shake. "I gotta think about this." He turned around and rattled the fence. "But . . . I gotta see you."

I considered this. What did I really have to lose?

"Okay."

The moment of truth. I climbed up to the next branch, then edged out along it until my tiny baby face was illuminated by the yellow glow of the security light above the dumpster. We both froze as Stoli—*John*—saw me. From this angle he was huge.

"Oh, my God," he whispered. He sank to his knees, sobbing.

"I told you."

He reached a hand out toward me, shaking. He was too far for us to touch. I sank back and lowered myself out of the light.

"I gotta go. Remember everything I said. 1836 Twentieth Street. It's in the backyard on the hill under the bench. It's under my parents' ashes. I'll meet you back here in two weeks, if I can, and we can start to hatch a plan. If for some reason I don't show up, don't forget about me."

"Oh, my God," he repeated.

"This *is* really happening, Stoli."

With that, I lowered myself from the tree and scurried away, disappearing into the shadows. It was done. I was counting on a clinically insane dumpster bum to rescue me.

I raced back home, slinking through ivy, lawns, and gardens, trying to figure out my next move. But as I cut through the neighbor's hedges, I was met with a shocking surprise: two patrol cars, their cherries flashing, parked out in front of my house.

Holy shit! Fuck me! The jig is up! Damn! What do I do? I suddenly realized this moment was inevitable. How long could my absences really go unnoticed?

I crossed the neighbor's lawn and decided to just walk through the front door. How much trouble could I get in? I'm just an innocent little baby, right? As I trod up the front walk, I could see two officers, male and female, talking to my grief-stricken parents in the living room. I stepped inside and Lou saw me immediately.

"Keenan!" she screamed, shoving past the surprised cops. She ran to me and fell to her knees, whisking me up into her arms, crying. "Oh, Keenan! Where have you been?!" She hugged me tight, her face a wet smear. One of the cops mumbled into the radio attached to her chest.

"I just went for a walk" was my lame excuse. This statement seemed to perplex the officers, but it angered my mother.

"You stupid, stupid child!" Lou said, inspecting me for damage.

"Told you," Drew said. He was grim and weary, sleepy in his scruffy plaid robe.

One officer clucked his tongue as the other filled out a form. "Folks, we'll still have to file an incident report."

Lou brought me into the light where she could have a better look at me. Tears spilled down her face as she planted kisses all over my head.

Lou was right—I *was* stupid. Because this little mistake cost me my freedom and my plan. I was soon under lockdown, under kiddie house arrest for the next two years.

PART 2 - KURT

TIMESTAMP=2032-07-10T:10:21:40-12:00:12Z

11. The Month of Darkness

I've put this off long enough. Let's talk about Kurt Houston.

Yes, Kurt Sebastian Houston was the old me, and instead of going into my whole backstory, I'd like to cut to the beginning of the end, to the series of events that led me to throwing in the towel: The Month of Darkness. That's how I referred to it back then; that's how I refer to it now. This happened in the early twenty-teens. First my mom, then my dad, then one of my best friends. They died in the same thirty days. This was preamble to my fall from both human and artistic grace. It's emo bullshit, but it's true. I broke.

My mother, Bunny, who suffered from Alzheimer's disease, had what I like to think was a glimpse of clarity one morning. She hid herself in the sterile white communal shower at her board-and-care, equipped with a paring knife stolen from the kitchen; she closed the pebbled Plexiglass shower doors, turned on the water, and opened up her wrists, leaving behind a note: "Please take care of kitty."

This was the first thing that fucked me up.

Mom left my sister, Rae, and me nothing, and I had to borrow money from a friend for her cremation. The mourners were few: a handful of our über-Christian relatives and some of my friends who knew Mom before she got sick. She was legendary with my friends. The most affordable memorial facility we could find was in San Francisco's gay Mecca, the Castro district. Mom would've loved it. The über-Christians clutched their pearls.

Brad, my father, was invited to her memorial. He had retired to a small town near Yosemite called Groveland. He stopped for a couple of scotches before driving the three hours to his ex-wife's memorial. He never showed up and we thought a forest fire near Groveland had cut him off.

About four days after Mom's memorial, we got a call from the Tuolumne County sheriff with some strange news. They thought they had the remains of my father, found at the bottom of a ravine in the burned-out hull of his Subaru. They also had a theory that it was my father's car wreck at the bottom of this deep ravine that started the fire that destroyed thirteen thousand acres of Sierra foothills and almost burned down the historic town of Groveland.

Yes, so my mother's death led to my father's death, as well as four people caught in the fire, as well as the destruction of thousands of acres of flora and fauna. All from a suicide with a paring knife.

While my mom had been destitute, my dad had somehow squirreled away about seventy thousand bucks—Rae and I split it right away. This would become seed money for my upcoming fall from grace.

I spent the rest of that week licking my psychic wounds, drinking heavily, letting people booze and drug me up. Even worse, at that time I had also (stupidly) set my hopes on a script I'd managed to get into the hands of an up-and-coming director. It felt like I was on the verge of a writing success after more than a decade of disappointments. I kept expecting Hollywood to call me personally and tell me how brilliant my work was. I'd been through the LA screenwriter grind house before, a place where you send things out, they get looked at by an assistant, you get promises, then nothing ever happens . . . *ever*. Unsurprisingly, all communication with my latest Hollywood contact went dark. Another dream was over; a realization that, combined with the grief of my parents' deaths, fueled even more debauchery.

A couple days later, sitting in the little garden in front of my in-law apartment in Glen Park, halfway through a bottle of whiskey, my good friend Chris Feist called, seeking to distract me from my recent losses. He and I had gone through prep school, college, girls, and apartments together, and we had an easy but very close friendship, maintained with nights of pool and cocktails and the occasional late-night consultations on matters about which only we could trust each other. He'd been at my mother's funeral; he helped me clean out my father's trailer.

And thus, with me having just buried what was left of my dad, Chris was ready to again console me with a ritual night of drinking and crying. I took his call from the garden. He was getting off work at a job in the Dogpatch.

"Need anything?" he asked.

"You're my savior. Please, um, some cigarettes . . . maybe pick up some beer or whatever," I said.

"How're you holding up?"

He seldom asked questions like this, and the words hung there curiously.

"Ah, you know. It comes and goes. I guess I'm maintaining, though . . . I've been pickled for the last week."

"I see. So . . . cigarettes and beer, Export As and Pabst?"

"You got my number."

"I know."

I ended the call and finished the half pint of whiskey. I smoked my last Export. An hour went by, which was strange because he was literally ten minutes away, fifteen with the purchase.

I waited.

Finally, I called him on his cell but somebody else answered.

"This is Officer Morley . . . who is this?"

I sucked in a breath. Everything went into slow motion.

No. Fuck. No. No. No.

"Um . . . I think I have the wrong number. I'm calling for Chris Feist."

There was a pause and an exhale on the other end.

"You have the right number. How are you related to Mr. Feist?"

"I'm a close friend. He was on his way to my house. Is everything alright?" *Was he busted or something? This was very far-fetched.*

I heard the officer say something to another officer that sounded like "I have a friend of Feist on the phone." A muffled reply. Back to me, he said, "Um, there's been an incident. Mr. Feist isn't available . . . we need to get in touch with his partner or relative . . . do you know who I might call?"

Fuck. "What happened? I'm a *very close* friend . . . since high school . . . you can tell me." *Please don't tell me, please don't tell me.*

"Feist—Mr. Feist . . ." Officer Morley was equivocating. "There was a liquor store robbery. We need to contact a wife or a relative. Do you have a name that might be on this phone?"

Time got even slower. He was . . . what—*dead*? This was much different than Mom or Dad. This was *me*. This was like *me* being killed. This was me being killed and presented to myself by Officer Morley. "Andrea is his sister."

"Thank you, sir. Please call the San Francisco PD or the family or . . . for more information. That's all I'm allowed to tell you. I'm sorry." His voice was nervous as he abruptly hung up.

And I blacked out.

My eyes fluttered open to find my good Irish landlord, Mary, cradling me, dabbing up blood from a goose egg coming up on my forehead. I'd fainted in the garden. My cat Joplin watched from the wood railing above us.

This is what happened:

At a San Francisco liquor store one Thursday evening in September, two armed and masked men entered and pulled guns on the large Palestinian cashier. The Palestinian, having seen worse, pulled a small 9mm pistol from under the counter and aimed it at the robbers. The gun never quite reached its trajectory before one of the robbers shot the large Palestinian man in the stomach. This caused the rotund cashier to pull the trigger of his pistol several times in an erratic arc. The first bullet took out some Snickers and a bottle of Chianti. The second bullet passed through the ear of one Jorge Barca, who later gave a brief description of the gunmen as masked, pale skinned and "white" sounding. The third bullet entered the chest of Christopher Sigmar Friedrich Feist. It pierced his left atrium and lodged in his spinal column. The cashier fell to the floor, pulling with him a shelf of pint-sized liquor bottles with a crash, and the two gunmen, unprepared for such violence, fled immediately amid a cacophony of breaking glass, screams, and curses.

Mr. Barca was stunned, but managed to dial 911 on his cell phone and crouched over the quickly fading Mr. Feist. It was only at this point that Barca noticed that he couldn't hear out of one of his ears, that he himself had been shot. His phone was covered in blood, yet he felt no pain. Barca handed the phone to a bystander who had entered the liquor store to help.

"Take the phone! It's calling 911. I'm shot in the ear," Barca shouted. He looked at the dying man before him; the man's face showed no pain, only confusion. Barca tore open Chris's shirt to see the damage, and he saw that it was bad indeed. He'd never seen a bullet wound before and he watched as the blood pulsed out with every waning beat of the man's heart. Chris looked sleepily at Barca, who thought the man looked serene in his dying. Chris was trying to tell him something. Barca leaned in with his good ear. "Tell Kurt I'll be late," he said. And the man died.

Barca wept a little for the man. He was a little puzzled—he knew a Kurt. He sure as shit hoped this wasn't Kurt's buddy.

Yes, Barca was my coworker. We were digital photo retouchers at a studio in the Dogpatch, near Potrero Hill. Jorge lived across the street from this liquor store, a neighborhood bodega I had frequented almost every workday for many years. I also knew the lumbering and quite affable Palestinian cashier who'd been shot (and not killed). Chris Feist and Jorge Barca had probably even met over the years and, in the hazy consciousness of his dying breaths, Chris somehow remembered this, deliriously asking Jorge to pass on a message to me.

!!!

So, you can imagine my surprise that Chris Feist was dead.

If I hadn't already become unhinged by my parents' deaths, Chris's demise surely was my, *ahem*, coffin nail. Not only was it unfathomable that he could die, but the fact that he was in that liquor store because he was buying me beer and smokes was catastrophic. To top that off, on his deathbed, he gave a message to Jorge that I would actually receive—an *apology*. For being late. Why couldn't he have said, "Tell Mom I love her"?

Days passed. At least this time I didn't have to identify someone's body, I just had to show up at the funeral a week later. So, one Sunday morning, I was dragged to San Jose by Rae. I had hardly slept in days—not because of drugs or alcohol. Indeed, with this real nightmare nestled in my noggin, I had no desire for anything, including food or leaving my apartment. I just couldn't wrap my mind around it, or run away from it.

Rae held my hand as we walked into the funeral chapel. I remember four things distinctly.

First, I remember the way people looked at me as I was led by my sister, led like an old man, down the aisle. My face rubbery, red, and sunken, my life force shattered; I was like what people mean when they say "he was a shell of a man." But there was something else. I suppose it could've been my own guilt working me, but I could swear that behind the glances of Chris's mom, dad, and sister were slivers of blame. Their glances said, *Oh, Kurt, you must feel awful, seeing as he was on his way to comfort you about your recent losses, and he stopped off to get your cigarettes. You must feel terrible that he sacrificed his life trying to placate your emotional neediness.* This is what their eyes said.

Second thing that stuck with me was the seedy burgundy carpet of the chapel. It was stained and threadbare. It was the carpet of a bus depot damaged by heavy foot traffic. It made the chapel feel, well, pedestrian . . . *used* . . . like a Greyhound station.

Third, the stunned hush. The quietness and the muffled murmurs. This wasn't the funeral of the patriarch, or the jovial uncle or crazy aunt, or the dying relative who "took his approaching death with the same dignity as he lived his life." This was the blackest of funerals, enshrouded by the shocking and untimely death of someone deeply loved and more deeply lost. It wasn't silence, it was the communal inability to breathe, to catch a breath.

The sudden death of a friend is a sucker punch.

Fourth, Rae led me through the viewing line, the mourning queue. She coaxed me into viewing position, and there was Chris. There lay the truths to every question I'd ever asked. There lay the existential resolution I'd been waiting for my entire life: the cold, made-up flesh of a dear friend, one of the best people I knew, Chris Feist.

This was confirmation that life was meaningless.

A while later, people said things from the stage. Somehow, I was one of them. A paraphrase of my eulogy:

"Chris and I went to Bellarmine College Preparatory for Boys. When I met him, he had a Flock of Seagulls haircut. I was a rocker; he was a new wave lame-o. In reality, he was way cooler than me. I'm sure he thought the opposite. We really weren't close until we landed at UC Irvine together. He introduced me to art history. The thing is, him and me, we were very different types, but we were connected by our mutual discontent: *This so-called adulthood is a rip-off? This is not what was promised. Society lied to us.* When my parents recently died, Chris was there to help me cope. And one day, on the way to my house, he stopped at a store to get me cigarettes, and he got shot dead."

I paused so long that people began to whisper.

Finally, I said, "I can't come back from that. Thank you for your time."

I stumbled down the steps, and the audience gasped. But somehow, I kept my feet. I wiped the tears from my eyes, looked at Rae, looked at the congregation, then walked outside and down the street, found a cab, drove to the airport, bought a ticket for New Jersey, and got on the plane.

12. AWOL

Imagine my surprise when, after the Month of Darkness, I found myself in New Jersey.

Hillsdale, New Jersey, was where my remaining best friend, Dennis, lived. We'd both gone to high school with Chris. Back in the day, when I wasn't living with Chris, I was probably living with Dennis. In San Francisco. Chris and I might've been more emotionally aligned, but Dennis was my brother, my drinking buddy, my longtime writing partner. Then Dennis, the bastard, wised up, found a great wife, and moved to Jersey. I was left behind, not quite forty at the time, a wayward bachelor, still partying like the rock star I was never destined to be.

So, when I suddenly showed up at his house in Hillsdale, New Jersey, at nine o'clock at night on the Sunday of Chris's funeral with a bag of groceries and no warning, Dennis showed only mild surprise.

"Surprise!" I said.

"Yeah, get in here." *Why wasn't he surprised?*

I stumbled into his house, eyes red, smile full of fakery. Then I saw the kids on the floor in front of the TV.

"Hi, Netta, Randy!" They turned their heads.

"Hi, Uncle Kurt," they said together in monotone out of the sides of their mouths, returning their attention to the movie.

Damn. I forgot about the kids. I forgot all about families and Sunday nights.

They all clearly knew I was coming. Someone, probably my sister, gave them a heads-up, though no one could've possibly have known exactly where I was going when I so abruptly left the funeral. Rae probably called all over the country in the six hours I was in the air, warning out-of-state friends and family that a half-crazed Kurt might show up at their door.

I must've been standing in the foyer for too long, listlessly pondering this train of thought, grocery bag still in hand, when Dennis nudged me gently along. "C'mon, Kurt. Let's go in the kitchen." His voice was somewhere between compassionate and annoyed . . . and *weary.* He was close to Chris, too, and he couldn't make it out to the funeral because of work. Then, on top of this stress, Kurt shows up to his house in full mental breakdown.

I made myself at home in their kitchen, talking brightly, inanely, making Dennis and me both drinks, tossing ice cubes into a couple highball glasses and splashing into them the bourbon I had brought. I can't remember the conversation. Dennis took it all in, solemnly letting me have my psychotic episode unhindered. His short dark hair was peppered with gray, and he sported a close-cropped beard.

"Kurt," he said, evenly. I stopped. "You keep calling me Chris."

I gazed at him, lost. *What had I even been talking about?*

"Sit down," he instructed.

He nodded toward the dining room. That's when I noticed his wife, Helen, had been sitting in the dining room the entire time, listening to my meaningless babble, a stemmed glass of red wine set before her. The dim yellow light made her skin glow.

She looked at me much like Dennis had, but perhaps with more concern. "I'm sorry, Kurt. About Chris. And your mom and dad." I sat down, cradling the bourbon bottle. I averted my eyes to my glass and rattled the cubes.

"Oh, well. Anyway, man, it's good to be in Hillsdale. Right at the end of summer. Feels just like San Francisco. Doncha think?"

Helen grabbed my hand across the table and said, "No one says 'it's good to be in Hillsdale.'"

"Kurt—" Dennis started, taking a seat next to me.

"You look great, man," I said, trying to obstruct serious conversation, trying to fill every pause. I took a large gulp of bourbon. "The kids are *so* fucking big! And it looks like you spruced the place up a bit."

"Kurt—*stop*." Dennis pressed his knees against mine and leaned in. I couldn't look at him. He was trying to connect, and I was trying to disconnect, to completely unplug from reality. And I couldn't get drunk enough. I drained my glass and refilled it from the bottle, now half empty. I could smell my own boozy reek, enabled by six hours of unfettered drinking on the airplane.

"Let me tell you," I continued, "a last-minute flight to Newark is fucking *expensive*. Not that it matters now that I inherited some *pretty nice* insurance money." Dennis's mouth opened wordlessly.

A cell phone ringing inside Dennis's pocket broke the tension. We locked gazes, his eyes filled with knowing. He finally took the phone out. "This is Dennis." Pause. I sipped my drink. He looked at me and spoke without dropping his stare. "Yeah, he's here. I'll have him call you in a while. He's okay." Pause. "*Ish*." I could hear a distressed voice at the other end. "Okay. Talk soon." He ended the call and said, "That was your sister. You should call her when you're ready."

I looked at Helen. "Do you like the *Ninth Symphony*? You know, Beethoven?"

Her face was pained. "Sure."

"He wrote that shit at the bottom. The *bottom*. *Ode to* fucking *Joy*, and he wrote it when he had lost *everything*." I drained my glass again. "The agency representing me in LA dropped my script," I blurted. "Fuckers." I refilled. "It felt like my last chance." Pause. "Fuckers." Sip. "But hell, eleventh time's the charm, right?"

I hummed *Ode to Joy*.

A tear slid down Helen's cheek.

"Kurt," Dennis said, seriously. I hummed louder. He stood. I stood. "Kurt, stop." I sang the notes louder, in his face, crazy tears now sliding on my cheeks.

"*La la la la, la la la la, la la la la, la—la-la!*"

"Kurt!" he shouted. I sang louder. "Kurt, STOP!" I was now shouting the melody.

Dennis gave me a good hard stinging *slap!* across my face. I collapsed back onto my chair.

A shocked silence hung in the air. Helen abruptly left, and I heard her voice in the other room, talking to the kids. The sting lingered on my cheek.

"Kurt, you gotta pull yourself together," Dennis pleaded, pulling up his chair again. "You're stronger than this. Chris is *dead*. Your mom and dad are *dead*. I know this is harsh, but self-pity and booze will not bring them back. It won't make the pain go away. It'll make it worse."

I sobbed. He handed me a paper napkin from a pile on the table and put a hand on my shoulder.

"I'm sorry, man." He pulled my forehead to his. "I loved Chris, too. And your mom. I didn't really know your dad."

"Neither did I." We both made something like a laugh.

He let go of me, tried to meet my eyes. "You can stay here as long as you want, but you can't run away from this. New Jersey is just a change of scenery. A piss-poor one at that. Chris and Bunny and Brad are dead and you're alive. You can stay here as long as you need but you aren't going to bury this shit with booze . . . or drugs." This was a rare version of Dennis: love and rancor, determination and fraternity, duty and fear. I loved him more than ever at that moment.

I had a death grip on my whiskey glass. I put it down and watched the blood flow back into my knuckles. A tear puddle had formed on the oaken dining table. I hugged Dennis tight and the sobs poured from both of us. Helen came back to the room and joined us. We all three wept.

!!!

In New Jersey—well, Hillsdale, to be more exact—I figured out that I was done with being a digital artist. I was also done pursuing the futile exercises of writing, acting, and playing music. It had gotten me nothing but heartbroken and poor, and now I was in my mid-forties without any safety net whatsoever. With the various insurance policies and inheritance that I'd suddenly come into, I found myself sitting on about forty thousand dollars. I needed a change. I'd been living on hope, and that was clearly fucking gone.

I let my beard grow, as well as my usually shorn hair. I put on ten pounds from Helen's home cooking. I looked like a different person.

I spent my days wandering aimlessly around Hillsdale and northern New Jersey. I rarely made it into Manhattan. I often drank with the locals and even started to look like them, but opening my mouth was the dead giveaway that I was from California. You don't know you have an accent until you go somewhere else. Dennis and Helen had day jobs, but at night and on weekends they would seek to distract me from myself. I might've served as a useful distraction for them as well. I was their third wheel as they made the social rounds that suburban parents are obliged to make, and I was a sure curiosity to their friends. I didn't think of writing or acting or playing music. I didn't even listen to music or read. I fled the one Broadway musical I attended at intermission.

Then it happened. One day late in November, the trees almost bare of leaves, I sat alone at a bus stop in Paramus. I'm not sure where I was going or if, indeed, I was going anywhere. An advertisement inside the bus stop shelter said: BECOME A REVERSE MORTGAGE BROKER AND MAKE $$$! TAKE ADVANTAGE OF NEW MORTGAGE LAWS! DAILY SEMINAR JUST $299!!

I looked closer at the details. The seminar was one block away, and it was going to start in twenty minutes. I shrugged and started walking. At the door, I paid $299 and started the second to last phase of my life: Reverse Mortgage Broker.

I was handed a plastic badge on a lanyard, a photocopied seminar binder, and a ballpoint pen with a house and dollar sign on it. The meeting room was really more of a small theater, with a digital projector displaying the same stylized house with a money sign woven into it. The lights dimmed and a handsome bespectacled Asian man in his fifties appeared on stage.

His voice was clear and smooth. "Welcome to ZLO Finance's Introduction to Reverse Mortgage Law. I'm Edward Lau. I'm a certified accountant, mortgage broker, and appraiser. I'm also your benefactor, because after today, you'll not only be happy you paid less than three hundred bucks to change your future, you'll be on your way to being a millionaire in less than two years!"

I left the seminar elated. Helen and Dennis were puzzled by my new attitude, and even more puzzled that someone like me was doing a creepy 180 with his life path. I left Hillsdale on the first of December. Within two months, I was a certified California reverse mortgage broker, selling short-term solutions to unsuspecting old people and the desperately bankrupt.

I sold my soul to the devil. Imagine my surprise.

13. Evolution of Kurt

Turns out Ed Lau from ZLO Finance was formerly a senator's aide who helped write some very loose reverse mortgage legislation. Those classes in Hillsdale were the first classes taught about the new regulations of reverse mortgage broking, and I got a jump on a large chunk of the Bay Area business. It turned out to be mostly about pushing papers between desperate homeowners, the banks who held the mortgages, and the federal government. I got a cut from every transaction.

These mortgages were usually taken out by elderly couples with liquidity problems. These couples were homeowners over the age of sixty-two with considerable equity in their property, and this equity was paid back to them in the form of a mortgage loan. They were basically selling their equity (and property) back to the bank so they could have some money before they died. To them, it felt like they won some sort of lottery. It was and is a fear-based predatory practice that leaves nothing behind for the family when Grampy dies. I didn't give a shit. I had lost all pretense of earning money in any moral fashion. I even started advertising on AM radio, recording the spots on the same home recording studio setup with which I used to record my own music. The recording equipment finally paid for itself.

At a year or so into the reverse mortgage biz, I had a little storefront, a shop off Twenty-Second Street and Third, and two brokers working full time. Surging property values had rescued many elderly San Franciscan homeowners from liquidity death, and many of those folks wanted to live in their homes but burn the money on their way to the grave. I was delighted to help them with that. My two employees were just the sociopaths for a job like this. They took relish in leveraging and manipulating people, banks, and the government by any means necessary: emotionally, financially, fearfully, even intellectually, although intelligence was rarely required.

One of my sociopaths, Bart Montgomery, was thirty-seven and a former petty criminal who'd gone straight(ish) after a stint in the pokey. He had some college, and at some point, before I met him, he acquired a real estate license and profited on the occasional sale.

I taught Bart how to be a reverse mortgage broker and paid for his licensing. He was as tenacious as a pit bull and had a predilection for vice that made me look like a freaking altar boy. We became fast friends. He was whip thin with mocha-colored skin, had a too-slick style that suggested criminality, and possessed the ability to be candy-cane nice one moment and junkyard-dog mean the next.

My other employee's story is less interesting. Her name was Clara Horowitz, and she was an online date gone awry. We didn't hit it off romantically, and I quickly found out that she was pathologically overbearing and had a talent for both bookkeeping and deception, ideal for her new line of work. While finishing her broker certification, she managed the office.

This leads me to the day I met Dolly.

I was sitting in the back office listening to AM talk radio, waiting to hear my self-produced Seven Hills Brokerage ad. It was about two in the afternoon, and I sipped a beer at my desk while lazily signing a stack of reverse mortgage applications. Birds twittered through the big open window behind me.

My office was more a prop than anything else. It was a study in peacefulness and safety: greens and beiges, with a few scenic San Francisco and California prints, comfortable chairs, a comfortable moss-colored leather couch, plenty of houseplants, good lighting coming in from the communal backyard. There was a well-stocked liquor cabinet and beer and wine in the mini-fridge.

There was also a steady supply of coke and pot in my desk. My employees loved me.

I yelled through my open door, “Bart, did you close the Berger thing yet? That jackass downtown keeps calling me.”

“Bart’s on the phone,” Clara yelled back.

“Did he close it yet?”

She poked her head into my doorway. “I think he’s talking to her now.”

Bart said, “Look, if you don’t think your house is worth saving, that is another option.”

“Bingo,” I said. Clara’s head disappeared.

Bart’s voice was wistful. “Mrs. Berger—*Janet*—you’ve poured your life into that garden of yours. Don’t sell. Stay in your home. Use your home to pay *you* back. You deserve it.”

Bart was a good closer. I sat back down and looked at some online porn for a while until I heard my latest Seven Hills radio ad come on. I shouted to the office, “The ad is on the radio!” I turned it up.

The radio spot opened with a sinister synth chord.

I wrote the music and performed the voice-over myself, and the irony didn’t escape me that years of recording my bullshit songs had finally paid off in this very cynical way. These little radio spots grew my business by a hundred percent. The voice-over went like this: “Times are tough. A lot of us got thrown some real curveballs in the last few years. You didn’t build a life just to turn around and *not* enjoy it.” Then the music changed into a fun, folksy acoustic guitar. “Hi, I’m Kurt Houston, president of Seven Hills Brokerage. At Seven Hills, we specialize not only in government-funded bailout refinancing, but also reverse mortgages for senior homeowners over sixty-two facing the challenges of the current economic climate. Enjoy the golden years in style. Call (415) 555-0916 or log onto www.sevenhillsbrokers.com for more information. Take back the good life. You deserve it."

"Whoo-hoo!" Bart hollered. He and Clara came and loitered in my doorway. Bart held up a white whipping cream dispenser in his hand. There was no cream in this dispenser, just nitrous oxide. He hissed its contents into his lungs. These were my trusted employees.

My smile faltered. "What have I told you about huffing at work?"

Bart shrugged.

"Very effective radio spot, Kurt," Clara complimented. "Really kicks 'em in the nuts, then hands them a bag of ice." Clara took the bottle of nitrous oxide from Bart and inhaled. Bart let out a peal of deep, nitrous-augmented laughter behind her.

"Yeah, it does kind of grab and twist, doesn't it," I agreed.

I was about to huff some nitrous myself when the metal bell on the front door jangled, signaling that we had a customer.

"Oh, shit. Somebody get that and close my door." I emptied the rest of the canister and set it on the window sill behind my desk. I popped a breath mint. Soon, there was a light knock on the door.

"Yeah?"

Clara poked her head through. "There's a lady and her nurse here who want to take out a reverse mortgage." Then she whispered, emphatically, "St. Francis Wood."

My head swam from the nitrous. "I'm . . . can't Bart take care of it?"

"*St. Francis Wood*, Kurt," she repeated. Clara peeked back into the office, then back at me. "I think you'll want to handle this yourself, boss." She grinned and winked.

I was intrigued. "Really?" I straightened my bowling shirt and tested my breath.

"The ol' lady's name is Mrs. Lazarus."

I popped another mint.

"Well, send the nice Mrs. Lazarus in."

Clara opened the door for Mrs. Lazarus. Pushing in on a fancy walker, the ol' dame wore a slightly rumpled vintage Chanel dress topped with a matching sun-damaged hat. At her side was a pretty young nurse pushing an oxygen tank. A *very* pretty young nurse.

"Greetings, Mrs. Lazarus. Have a seat. How can I help you?"

She stopped in her walker tracks. "How do you know my name?"

"My assistant told me—"

"Are you the fella on the radio I heard yesterday?"

"Maybe, yes. Kurt Houston, Seven Hills Brokers. Have a seat." The nurse, who had longish dark brown hair, wheeled the oxygen up next to Mrs. Lazarus and helped her into one of the seats in front of my desk. The nurse was dressed, well, *nurse*-like, fetishistically so. She even had the white hat thing on her head. This was Dolly. She told me later that the old broad had instructed her: "Dress like a nurse! I don't want anyone thinking you're my friend."

I beckoned to the nurse to sit as well. "Please, have a seat, Miss . . ."

"I'm Dolly. That's okay. I'll stand." She stood behind Mrs. Lazarus as though she were ready to restart her heart if it suddenly failed. Dolly smelled faintly of amber. I resumed my seat behind the desk.

"*Houston*? Like the city?" blurted Mrs. Lazarus.

"What?" I watched Clara close the door, shutting us in. "Oh, my name. You can say it like Houston, Texas. I prefer *How-stun*, but your choice. Right. Now, Mrs. Lazarus, what can Seven Hills do for you?"

"I read about this reverse mortgage thing and then I heard your awful ad on the radio," she said.

"Ah, yes, my *awful* ad," I agreed. I took a good look at Mrs. Lazarus. Her wrinkled skin looked hard as porcelain; her hair thinner than mine. She was a haughty eighty-year-old West Coast blue blood—Getty style, or Hearst. But cash poor.

Her dry, papery voice spoke in rapid fire. "I brought all my records. The dump is on Maywood Drive. Thirty-seven hundred square feet. Last appraised at three-point-five. Worth more now, I expect. I've got about eighty percent equity in it, but Harold didn't leave me any cash."

"Uh . . . um," was all I could say. The nurse, Dolly, was trying to get my attention. I saw her nod toward the whipping cream canister I'd forgotten to clear from the windowsill. *Shit!* I casually stood up and meandered to it as if to look contemplatively out the window. I said, "So, I always ask my clients to consider a few things before going through the reverse mortgage process."

"Oh, don't worry about that crap," Mrs. Lazarus spat. "I'm not a fucking idiot." She clutched an accordion file atop her knees. "Dolly and I here are going to take a trip, then I'm going to blow out of San Francisco forever. Place is filled with homos! Screw Max."

I casually backed into the nitrous bottle, knocking it outside the window into the geraniums; I sat my ass on the sill. "*Max*?" I asked, looking at her.

"Her *son*," Dolly said. Her voice was silk with an ever-so-slight Mission District accent. Think of Salma Hayek, but relatable.

"*Max* . . . oh, Max is your son."

"He's not my son! Not anymore!"

"Anne," Dolly soothed, "it's okay. Mr. Houston is here to help us."

Mrs. Lazarus leaned toward me. "I think he became a *gay*. And an artist! I'm cutting him off. And me—I'm going to . . ." She considered, eyes tilted. ". . . to *whereabouts unknown*!" She laughed a crisp, vindictive laugh and heaved the heavy accordion file onto my desk with a thud. "You figure it out, Texas. Where's the toilet?"

"Right outside the door there," I replied. I felt elation tinged with fear.

Dolly helped her matron stand up, positioning the walker.

I grabbed the accordion file. "It's on the left. If you need any help, ask Clara. I'll just look over your records."

As Dolly helped Mrs. Lazarus toward the bathroom, she cast a glance back at me and gave me a lingering once-over, following it with a half grin that I would soon know and love. She said, "Thanks for your help, Mr. *Houston*."

14. *Tastes Like Success*

After I got Mrs. Lazarus a hefty reverse mortgage, the lovely Nurse Dolly Velasquez and I started our affair. Fast forward seven months: Dolly moved into my flat in the Dogpatch. My existence had taken on the surreal quality of a cross between a raunchy porn and *The Grifters*. All done with a certain cocaine-and-alcohol-fueled panache.

It didn't stop me from doing business.

Imagine my surprise finding myself the owner of a beautiful Potrero Hill Victorian with a magnificent, sweeping northern-exposure view of downtown San Francisco. This was spring of 2014 or '15, I think. Time is getting fuzzy for me.

I had had my eye on this large, restored Victorian on Twentieth Street, not far from my office. I knew all about the ins and outs of the property because I'd negotiated a reverse mortgage about a year earlier with an eye on the declining health of the octogenarian owner. The day the owner died, I called the bank and arranged a walk-through with an acquaintance of Bart's—an acquaintance who would soon become my right hand. His name was Franklin Franklin O'Donnell. You know him by now as Franks. By this point in his American criminal career, he had his grubby paws in about ten different scams. One of his big moneymakers was knock-off black market sports apparel, mostly San Francisco Giants. He was a rabid Giants fanatic, which is odd for a guy from Dublin, Ireland. Another lucrative sideline was fake property appraisals. He had a legit license, but there was nothing legit about his appraisals, which were always paid for by assholes like me. He was slick, if not a little careless and loud. The Dublin lilt added a certain charm. All this would've been funny if I didn't know that he'd cut your heart out and sell it back to you for a profit.

Bart, Dolly, and I, dressed in our most expensive business attire, pulled up in a rented black Mercedes and parked right in front of the Victorian. Bart even got out of the car to open the rear passenger doors for us. I emerged from the back seat, gray Italian suit crisp, sunglasses hiding my dry, red eyes. I spied the property reps, Sandy and Jeff, nervously watching us from the big bay picture window. The bank wanted to turn over the property so bad, they were salivating for an offer.

We approached the door.

"Alright—everybody in character," I whispered. "Dolly, you love the place; Bart, you wander around tsk-tsking everything; and I'll stand around magnanimous, but checking my watch. Got it?"

"Roger that," Bart replied.

"The usual," Dolly added.

"What's what's-his-name's ETA?"

"His name is *Franks*," Bart replied, then added, "I dunno . . . maybe ten minutes."

"Who's got the blow?" Dolly asked.

"Bart does. Now straighten—"

The door flew open. It was Jeff.

Jeff blurted, "Kurt! Dolly! Um—"

"Bart."

"Bart!" Jeff repeated.

Bart sniffed arrogantly, then whisked past Jeff inspecting the place with pursed lips. Dolly gave Jeff's hand a courtesy shake and once inside said, "Oh, my God! It's gorgeous, Kurt! I *love* the hardwood floors!"

Jeff and I shook hands in the foyer. I asked, "Where's your . . . *partner*—Sandy?"

"Upstairs. She'll be down in a sec."

Jeff closed the door behind me. He was about fifty, white Euro-mutt, sandy-gray receding hairline. Thin. His partner was a little older, fixed by quite a bit of plastic surgery.

The house had been gutted and restored: fresh plaster, new floors, new electrical and plumbing. Sadly, they had staged it like a Williams-Sonoma catalog. Gauche. But I kept my grin, nodding in fake approval.

"Can I get you a drink?" he asked accommodatingly.

Fuck yes! "No . . . I don't drink except for weekends," I lied. "Gotta keep sharp."

"I meant water or a soda."

"Oh." *Really? People drink water and soda?* "Um, no, that's fine. What did it last appraise for?"

Then Dolly screamed from somewhere in the house, "Oh, my God! A *bidet!*"

I chuckled and elbowed Jeff. "We could sure use that sometimes. Heh heh." I walked past his blank expression. "When did you do the remodel?"

Bart shouted from somewhere, "Hey, Jeff! This balcony railing looks short. Is it regulation?"

He looked at me, then shouted back, "Well, it should be." Then to me, "They remodeled when the market came back."

"Oh, good. New pipes?"

"Copper."

"What did it last appraise at? I forget." I hadn't forgotten at all: $1,554,500.

He faltered just long enough. "One-point-seven."

"Right."

I walked into the kitchen, where Bart had crawled under the sink to check things out. I asked, "Bart, what are you doing under there?"

He didn't budge, kept puttering. "Well, it's relatively new. But it is Chinese."

That's when Sandy emerged from the dining room, done up as ravishingly as possible in a low-cut blouse, flowery knee-length skirt, fake tits presented, smelling pretty.

"Kurt!" She darted toward me for a hug. I smiled, and she embraced me in a warm—too warm—embrace. These folks were desperate. "You look great!"

"Um . . . thanks?"

That's when she noticed Bart, in his shirtsleeves, backing out from under the sink. He looked at all of us, shaking his head. "Yeah, Chinese."

The electronic doorbell bonged. We all looked at each other.

"That must be the appraiser," I said.

"Hellooo?" said a broguey accent from the foyer.

"I got it," I said.

I went to the foyer and beheld Franklin Franklin O'Donnell for the first time, head poking in the door. He had a blond flop of hair swept above a semi-handsome face; his cheap yellow tweed suit was draped over a tall skinny body. He smiled at me, hand extended.

"You must be Himself. Kurt."

I took his hand and smiled. "*Himself.* Nice. Listen." I led him into the Williams-Sonoma living room and said with a hushed voice, "So, these guys are desperate to flip. This is the lowdown: 1894 Victorian, two-year-old remodel. Property last appraised at one-point-five-fifty-four five; he just lied at a one-point-seven, houses on either side are selling for under one-point-four. I had it appraised high originally so the bank is desperate to unload it. Bart just made the 'Chinese' plumbing gag. I want it for under one-four. Got it?"

He looked at me with a wide, impressed grin. "Done, Chief." That's when I noticed his odd-smelling breath. He turned and walked toward the kitchen, shouting, "Nice! Niiiiice!" I followed, hiding my smile. Franks was shaking hands. Dolly burst in from the hall.

"Oh, Kurt! The bedroom has a Jacuzzi tub!" she proclaimed in a suggestive singsong voice. She acted surprised when she found everyone gathered in the kitchen. She saw Franks. "Oh, hi! I'm Dolly!"

A beat. Then everybody laughed. Franks rushed up to her.

"Ah, darlin'! Yes, the place is excellently accommodated." He actually took her hand . . . was he going to kiss it? She pulled it back. Jeff and Sandy gazed at Franks skeptically. I intervened.

"This is Franks—"

Bart interrupted. "*Mister* Franks . . . can you please follow me to the basement, where we can check out the foundation?" Franks saluted Bart.

"Yes, Bart! The foundation! Excellent idea."

"Jeff, Sandy," I offered, "Would you like to join us in the basement?"

Sandy deferred to Jeff. "Oh, you boys go on and do that technical stuff."

Dolly took her arm. "Let's go look at your gorgeous garden, Sandy."

The boys were left alone in the kitchen.

I gestured to Jeff. "Well then, Jeff. Where's the cellar?"

15. Sniffs Opportunity

So, I got the house on Potrero Hill. After my people had done their dubious assessments, I got it for about a hundred thousand under the reverse mortgage appraisal I had ginned up originally, what with the "bad pipes" and "old foundation."

I decorated the place tastefully minimalist, with simple antiques and artfully distressed furniture here and there, a touch of fifties modern—but not to clash. A thoroughly functional *Iron Chef*-class kitchen, roofed outdoor hot tub, reclaimed redwood deck, and a contemporary garden with native flora, a tiny patch of lawn, and a small herb garden. From the high point in the backyard, you could see over the fence to the top of the buildings of downtown. You could even see the white-hot beacon on top of the Transamerica Pyramid.

Dolly moved in with me. It's hard to describe our relationship. I wasn't capable at this point of real love, not anymore, not after the accumulated hurts and setbacks of an entire adulthood of loving and losing. I had so little functional heart left that the working chambers remaining were relegated to my sister and the thin instinct to stay alive. Well, and there was one dark chamber that held a private altar of regret, death, and unrequited fulfillment.

But Dolly was a piece of work in the most stereotypical "Kurt's girlfriend" fashion. Horny, hedonistic, sassy, smart, and morally corrupt, all wrapped up in a witty, ironic package. We had a lot of fun, and we skirted serious issues with a healthy amount of liquor, drugs, and conscious avoidance.

In that sense, we were happy.

Around this time, the US Congress started passing legislation that curbed the very predatory mortgage practices that had made me well-to-do, and business began to fall off. Damnable liberal nanny-state, damnable checks and balances! Why was I ever a Democrat?!

Then something weird happened.

I was at my office in the Dogpatch one day when an old man in a gray suit graced my office doorway. I was unusually sober at the office that afternoon, reviewing a highly leveraged appraisal that Franks had sent me. The man in the gray suit tapped lightly on the door frame.

"Kurt Houston?" he inquired.

I looked him up and down. Maybe seventy, longish hair for an old white lawyer; I detected an edginess right away.

"You're not trying to serve papers to a *Kurt Houston*, are you?"

He chuckled. "Heh heh. No. You're not in any trouble. But this is a grave matter. Can I close the door?"

I looked at him: serious but congenial. Past him, I saw Bart and Clara leaning from their desks trying to see what the man was up to. I waved him in. "Sure. Close the door. Take a seat."

He quietly shut the door and sat on one of the chairs in front of my desk, briefcase on his knees. He said soberly, "My name is Laurence Potts. I'm the attorney for the late Hobson Sward."

I did a mental double take. "Late? *Late* Hob Sward?"

He adjusted himself in his seat. "Hob passed last week."

This caught me totally off guard. Hob was an old friend. He was also my coke dealer, my longtime connection. I'd wondered why he hadn't answered my calls lately. This was all a shock.

"Hob is dead?"

"Yes."

"*Hob is dead*?"

Mr. Potts shifted uncomfortably. "I'm sorry, Mr. Houston."

I looked at him—*through* him. This Laurence Potts. Twenty years of lurid memories shot through my head all at once. I managed, "How?"

"He found out he had brain cancer and killed himself the same day. Pistol."

Talk about a long moment. We looked at each other and he let me take it in. I was floored. Gobsmacked.

Potts sighed. "I was a good friend of Hob's, too. I, well, saved his ass for about four decades . . . if you know what I mean."

"I know what you mean."

It's hard to ever know how deep a friendship runs with your drug connection, but I considered Hob and myself pretty close. We had been seeing each other on a regular basis for twenty coke-filled years. He was a great dealer because he was consistent, had a set schedule. Most impressively, he was a prolific artist—he was a master etcher and painter. Had a hundred life-size nudes of women hanging on racks in his flat. His abode was a madman's lab of vintage furnishings and outdated gadgets, like your crazy uncle's garage. He was a collector of quality junk, and he'd lent me props for just about every show I'd ever put up, back when I cared about such things.

But why was this guy really here?

"Killed himself, huh? Is it okay if I smoke?"

"Be my guest," he replied. Potts was freaking cool. Like if Jeff Bridges was your lawyer.

I exhaled a plume toward the open window. "Suicide. Sounds like Hob. Always the realist."

"Indeed. That's what everyone says when they get the news."

"So . . . why are you here? Laurence, is it?"

"Call me Larry, Kurt." He clicked open his case and brought out some papers. "Hob left you some money . . . and something else."

He held up a small key.

Whoa. "What?! Really?" I was actually taken aback. I took the key. "Safe deposit box?"

"Ninety-two thousand in cash," he said with a shrug. "And something else." He was clocking all my reactions.

I coughed. And coughed. "Fuck! I knew it . . . there was no way that guy could spend what he was making."

"The money was only a small part of what Hob had squirreled away."

"Okay, so . . . money. What's the *something else*?"

"A Glock nine-millimeter—the very Glock that took his life. Took a while to get it back from SFPD, but I know people. Also . . ." Laurence paused. "And he left you his business. If you want it."

Silence. Moments thudded by. I didn't know how to process this.

"His *business*?"

"Well, while he was the last person to display affection to anyone, he was apparently quite fond of you, thought you were smart. He still has product to get rid of and clientele that needs service. Whether you want the business or not, he left you the product. But he left instructions that should you want to continue in his stead, his connection would be ready for you, and his clients will be assured you are safe to call. You probably know some of them."

"Probably." I ruminated, looking at Larry, then down at my hands, then back at Larry. "Well, fuck me in the ass with a crowbar. How much product did he leave?"

"Ten—well, now, *nine*—ounces." Cheshire grin, then he added, "There's a half pound of grass. And of course, his . . . well, what you might call his Rolodex."

We gazed at each other. I rolled my office chair over to the wooden cabinet next to the desk, opened the door and found the bottle of bourbon. I set two glasses before us. He slid his glass over slowly and tasted it, took a sip.

Larry said, "Also, as I understand it, the profit margin in reverse mortgage brokering is about to fall drastically."

I nodded my head. "It's true. I can't believe I used to be a Democrat."

"Maybe this is a chance to supplement your income."

I smirked. "What was Hob taking in, if you don't mind me asking?"

He didn't blink. "He wasn't just a gram here and there sort of guy. He was actually moving sizable weight to very connected people on a regular basis."

"He always seemed kinda small-time."

"He was small enough to stay under the radar, big enough to be happy, and to keep his nieces and nephews on the other coast happy. Cleared fifty a month, give or take."

"Well, well, well."

"Yeah, not too bad for a guy who barely left his house." Larry put the papers on my desk. "There are a lot of movie stars and politicians in the Bay Area."

"So . . . I don't mean to sound skeptical, but I'm not sure signing papers for this sort of thing is exactly . . . *prudent*."

He downed the bourbon, reached over, and poured himself some more. "You're signing for the safe deposit box. The money is all legit . . . after some considerable effort."

I slid the papers my direction and gave them a look. It was kind of like a receipt. A receipt for a couple decades of friendship.

Hob was gone. Shit.

It would've been awkward to say something like, *I'll have my lawyer go over this friendship payoff from my drug dealer and get back to you.* As a professional reader of people, I knew this guy was solid, solid like Hob was solid. The language was simple. I found a ballpoint and signed it in blue, sliding it back to this Larry character. Looking at him more closely, I realized I'd bumped into him at Hob's place during a pickup.

Laurence Potts looked at the papers, then stuffed them in his briefcase, closing it with a snap. Reaching into his suit pocket, he produced an envelope and put it on the desk, setting the safe deposit key on top of it. "That's the safe deposit box paperwork, bank card, and key."

"Alright."

He poured himself another quick one and downed it. "I miss Hob, Kurt. I wish the fucker hadn't made me his executor."

I let a moment thunk by. "I have to think about all this shit."

Larry turned to leave. "Don't wait too long making a decision about the business. Before the end of the week, if you please. And, depending on what you decide, maybe I'll be seeing you around."

"We'll see." As he left, I said, "Can you close the door behind you?"

The door clicked shut. There I was in my little office, with my future facing me in the form of a little key and a white envelope. And in a metal box somewhere was ninety-two big ones in cash, a felonious package of drugs, a Glock 9mm, and a notebook full of numbers that could bring down the California government.

There was a timid knock on my door.

"I'm not here!" I shouted. I lit a cigarette and looked out the window at the tiny garden. I could hear Bart hammering a client on the phone in the other room.

Fucksake. Death kept altering my trajectory. And just when I started to worry about keeping my employees employed, an answer came. A dark, dark answer.

An iridescent green hummingbird lit upon the window sill.

Sometimes when people, like a Hemingway or a Hunter Thompson, blow their brains out, you feel sad—but also a little impressed. Hob died as he lived: on purpose.

Playing the role of Drug Dealer was my final project, and I did it largely in the spirit of wrong-headed loyalty to the idea of Hobson Sward.

!!!

The day after Larry paid me a visit, I went down to the bank to check out the safe deposit box. I was presented with a metal box, bigger than you see in the movies, inside of which was an old-fashioned leather briefcase. The bank clerk left me alone with it in a secured room. I opened the case, quickly looked through it, and decided it would be more prudent to do this elsewhere.

Alone at home on Potrero Hill, I fixed myself a whiskey, lit a smoke, and sat down with the briefcase set before me on the big dining room table. I was nonplussed to say the least. I breathed in the battered leather, a kind of deep, woody, oily smell. Clicking open the latch, I slowly opened the case. Inside were two rectangular plain-wrapped packages, a triangular chamois cloth bundle, and a stuffed manila envelope. I went for the chamois cloth, immediately guessing that it was his gun—the suicide weapon. I unwrapped it and held the pistol, ejecting the clip. Empty. Also in the cloth were a loaded clip and a box of 9mm rounds.

I spoke to the gun: "So you're the culprit." It was a fine specimen. I had gooseflesh. I put the pistol down and grabbed one of the brown paper packages. I hefted it before tearing the paper away: four stacks of hundred-dollar bills. I'd never seen so much physical cash at one time. It made my dirty greedy heart go pitter-pat. I toasted the stacks of money. "Fuckin' aye."

The other paper-wrapped package was half the size and considerably lighter. This of course turned out to be my dealer starter kit. It was a pint-sized chunk of pearly white cocaine, double wrapped in a ziplock bag. I opened and smelled it. Yep, that would be it. I broke off a crumb, crushed it on the table with a credit card, and whiffed it with a bill.

Holy Jesus, it was good!

Lastly, I picked up the manila envelope and unclasped it. Out slid a very worn pocket-sized black address book, tabbed with colorful Post-its and tattered scraps of paper. I cracked it open; it was filled busily with the names, addresses, and numbers of clients, a book from a different age, when people wrote things down. Many of the names were familiar. It was a dangerous book to even own. Names and numbers were crossed out, as though he'd updated the book for decades or more. Inside, there was a single sheet folded in half with KURT written on it. I flipped it open and spread it on the coffee table. His fluid hand bore me this note:

Kurt—

Seems stories of my demise—

Fuck me. I had to stop. It was *that* note. It was hard to take, so I set the paper aside, poured myself another bourbon on the rocks, and smoked a cig on the porch. I looked out at the City and my eyes searched for the place down the hill, eight blocks distant, where Hob wrote this note that I was about to read, before he shot himself in the head.

I flashed to years ago, sitting in his cluttered flat, surrounded by life-sized nudes dangling on racks, talking about Egon Schiele. I thought life was crazy back then, but I truly didn't know what crazy is.

In any case, I went back inside, braced myself, and started again.

Kurt—

Seems stories of my demise finally haven't been exaggerated, eh? Sorry to leave you in the lurch like this, but you know me—no Mr. Sentimental. Hope the money helps out, and the rest of my stash. Do what you want with it. Also, enclosed is my little black book. This is more for reference—and leverage—than anything. If you decide you want to take over the family store, then call Larry and the clients will come to you. Larry will supply you with the name and number of my source. If you decide not to take on the business, just give the book to Larry and I'll see you on the other side.

Right.

I'm not sure if Larry will be able to get my gun back. If he did, I want you to have it because I think you are one of the few people who will understand my choices—and me—after I'm gone.

So it goes—

Hobson

I wiped a tear and folded the letter, putting it back in the address book.

On the table before me was a picture-perfect narcotics bust: a gun, money, coke, and an address book with the names and numbers of politicians, rock stars, doctors, lawyers, and yes, beggar-men and thieves.

I gazed at the money. *What to do . . .*

I decided not to touch the money for the time being, wrapping it back up and sealing it tightly with masking tape. I went into the garage, dug into the mess, and found an empty plastic detergent canister with a lid. Upstairs, I double wrapped the money in a garbage bag and sealed it with duct tape. Then I did it again. I put this inside the plastic detergent canister. Next, I took the gun in the chamois cloth upstairs to my gun cabinet. I fished out a can of gun oil. I saturated the cloth with the oil and wrapped the now-loaded Glock inside it, putting this bundle inside a waterproof red vinyl pistol case. I also threw in a fifty-round box of 9mm hollow points. Zipping this up, I took it downstairs and wrapped it in another plastic bag and wrapped that with more duct tape. I placed this atop the money in the squat plastic detergent container. There was a little room left.

I was quite cognizant that I was packing this treasure for the future, and in that future, I might need this money in a very desperate situation. I was thinking in noir film logic, and gangsters always hid the loot with a gun, just in case. I was betting that the future me, in such a dire circumstance, might need a drink, so I found a pewter flask (a best-man's gift with KURT engraved on it), filled it with eighteen-year-old scotch, and put this in a plastic bag.

I pictured myself, ten years hence with the mob or police on my tail, limping into the backyard, wounded in my leg or shoulder. I dig up the cash and unwrap the gun just in time to blow away the bad guys. Uncapping the flask, Future Me toasts the Mafia corpses I just made, and I take a gulp to kill the pain in my bleeding leg, saying, "Sorry, boys, just had to dig up an old friend." And I flick my cigarette at their bodies. Music swells. Credits roll.

As ridiculous as this was, I continued putting together the package, placing the flask on top and stuffing crumpled newspapers to pad in the extra space. Sealing the plastic canister with its airtight lid, I duct taped the lid closed, then the entire package; then I wrapped this in a garbage bag and taped it tight. I toted this out to the backyard and took a look around for a likely place that might not be disturbed even by future tenants. The backyard was terraced, with a deck attached to the house and a small lawn and indigenous bushes. Next to this was the hot tub, and some switchbacks led up the hillside to a wooden bench under a big willow tree, from which you could see downtown San Francisco and the Bay. The bench had a little brass plaque affixed to it: In Loving Memory of Athel Dillon "Brad" Houston and Faith Ann "Bunny" Kreiner. Dad and Mom, divorced in life, together in death.

Their ashes were mixed in a stone box buried under the bench. California golden poppies blanketed the hillside.

So, shovel in one hand and my criminal time capsule in the other, I trudged up the hill.

When I got there, I said, "Hey, Mom and Dad . . . want some company? Meet Hob. Sort of."

I moved the bench aside and dug down. It didn't take long to hit the green marble box that held their ashes. This green marble box itself had been shrink-wrapped in thick clear environmentally resistant plastic. I set Mom and Dad on the bench. "Take a breather, you guys." I had to dig a considerably bigger hole for Hob's container. About a half hour later I had a four-foot-deep hole, two feet in diameter. With little fanfare, I placed Hob's money-gun-scotch time capsule in the hole and covered it with a layer of dirt, packing it with my feet. On top of this, I placed Mom and Pop.

"Rest in peace, all y'all. Hey, Mom and Dad—if you think about it, I finally paid you back all that money I borrowed . . . with interest. Don't spend it all in one place."

I finished reburying them, stamping the dirt as hard as I could, sloughing the extra in the bushes near the fence. I scattered some leaves and sticks and humus over the spot and replaced the bench. I sat on it and lit a cigarette.

I had a good cry, and when I wiped my face, the tears were muddy.

"Oh, well."

I pulled Laurence Potts's card from my wallet, read the number, and made the fateful call.

Thus began the life of a drug dealer.

PART 3 - KEENAN

TIMESTAMP=2032-07-14T:15:43:10-17:32:28Z

16. Daycare is a Halfway House

Imagine my surprise when I found myself under house arrest.

If you recall, our young hero was caught nightwalking, much to the chagrin of the parents and the police. And thus, a burglar alarm (the cost of which I was ever reminded) was installed. Rather a reverse-burglar alarm, on all the windows and doors, designed to keep me inside at night. The keypad code for which I could never crack.

Imagine yet another surprise when I got relegated to daycare. You see, after many months of unemployment, Drew finally got a job—selling commercial pest control—and Lou kept her bookkeeping job, but cut her hours in half. So . . . *daycare*.

This did not make me happy, and it did not make Lou or Drew happy, seeing as daycare was another expense they could scarcely afford. But there we were, Lou and I, pulling up in front of the brightly painted green and blue single-family home that doubled as a daycare facility: Happy Feet Daycare. Strapped helplessly in the car seat, I gazed glumly at the high white picket fence, the red plastic top of a slide peeking out above it. The car smelled of perfume and cigarettes. Lou opened the door and knelt to unbuckle and extract me.

"Mom!" I whined.

"Keenan, I know you hate this, but after your last stunt, if we don't appear to be a normal, sane family, Lydia from Child Protective Services is going to whisk you away, and then where will you be?"

Couldn't've put it better.

"And if you get foster parents, they will want to send you to genius school and poke and prod you and mess you up. Is that what you want?"

"No." While Lou left a lot to be desired as a mother, she sure understood me. I mean, she didn't know for sure about my intellect, but she intuited that I wanted to be left alone. And she felt lucky not to have to chase after a toddler all day.

"Believe me, I'd rather just leave you at home in front of the TV, but even I'm not sure anymore if you won't get into trouble. You're too damn smart."

She lifted me out onto the bright morning sidewalk. She had dressed me in little jeans, little sneakers, and a little blue plaid button-down. The car door slammed. She knelt down again, looking me in the eye as she fussed with my wispy ginger-blond hair. The high-pitched cacophony of twenty children of various ages drifted through the fence, which I now saw was constructed of molded white plastic.

"Keenan, I know this isn't your scene." She looked pretty in her knee-length business skirt, sun glinting red through her dark hair. "*Your scene.* Hell, I don't know what your scene is, but I know it's not with kids your own age. Frankly, you sometimes remind me of your grandfather. Anyway, don't freak out the teacher or caretaker or whatever they call the people who watch over the kids."

I looked skeptically through the fence. Kids running. "Okay."

"And don't organize any coup d'états against the management—this is the only place we can afford."

I grinned a little. "Okay."

"Ready?"

I nodded. She stood and grabbed my up-stretched hand.

Fifteen minutes later I found myself seated on a tiny red plastic chair at a little kelly-green table in the corner of a large playroom, all a-bustle with kids aged two to five, a kaleidoscope of races, and an even mix of girls to boys.

The director and owner of Happy Feet, Dorothy, was a pudgy, middle-aged white lady with thinning brown-gray hair and a no-nonsense demeanor. She was capable and a little tough. Dorothy was assisted by a young lady who I assumed was either her daughter or niece: late teens, very cute, name of Tabitha. What I could deduce from Tabitha's chipped black fingernail polish, nose piercing, and deep goth-red lipstick was that, under her accommodating façade, she was bored, bitter, and didn't much care for Dorothy. Tabitha would rather be smoking pot and drinking beer with her friends in Santa Cruz instead of chasing little monsters like me. I immediately liked her.

There I was at the little table with a box of Crayolas and a few sheets of newspaper-grade art paper. I argued in my head which level of kid-mode I should affect to integrate into the mix. The black crayon in my hand was poised over the paper. A miniature showcase of human sociology seethed around me and left me pondering. What was clear right away, as my eyes darted everywhere, was that the little girls directed most of the playtime activities—except for those outlier boys with blocks, dump trucks, LEGOs, or trains. Trains were very popular. But most of the boys were sucked into playtime as directed by the girls.

A boy a little older than me with straight black hair whooshed past, snagging the crayon from my hand without a thought. This did not distress me. Tabitha was busy on the floor reading Dr. Seuss to several very interested children. Dorothy patiently and expertly changed a diaper on a table across the room. A little blond girl pounded relentlessly on a plastic toy piano in the middle of the floor, performing a dissonant and somewhat psychotic aria for her playmates, who ignored her.

One—*indeed*—flew over the cuckoo's nest.

Is it any wonder that when your life, as such, springs from this kind of insanity, many of us so readily return to the loony bin? Some kind of gravity was in play.

"Hi, I'm Lulu. You wanna play Barbershop?"

I jumped at the sound of her voice. A girl with golden curls in a stained pink flowered dress stood over me. Lulu was probably four and she had little bee-stung lips and liquid pale blue eyes.

"Barbershop?"

"Yeah, come here with me."

She took my hand (which was still frozen in place, empty of its black crayon) and led me to three plastic milk crates that she'd arranged into a sort of counter. Behind the counter was another boy, dark—Southeast Asian, I think—who stood there as confused as I was.

"Rakesh, you sell him the books."

Whew! I feared scissors might be involved. Rakesh pulled a thin hardcover children's book from behind the counter and set it before me.

"That'll be five dollars," Lulu demanded.

Oh, shit. These people were insane.

"I thought this was a barbershop."

Lulu got a little surly. "It is! Five dollars! Pay up!"

Er . . . use my improv skills! Yes, and . . .

I reached for my nonexistent wallet. "I left my wallet at home. I'll pay you six dollars tomorrow. Okay?"

She looked at me skeptically. "Okay, you can pay me tomorrow."

She handed me the book along with a scrap of paper from her pocket.

"Here's your receipt. Six dollars!" She took the book back and put it behind the counter. "What's your name?"

"Keenan."

"Keenan, you can be the casher now. Rakesh, you can go on your lunch break."

Rakesh stood there. "Rakesh, go!" she insisted. I watched him trot off to get bossed around by some other girl.

"Keenan, you are the casher now. Stand behind the counter and I'll find us another customer."

"Cash*ier*."

Lulu tilted her head. "What?"

"It's not casher, it's cash*ier*. I'm the cash*ier*."

"Whatever. Get to work."

Sur-fucking-real. I came around the milk crate counter as Lulu went in search of another customer. Behind the counter were the aforementioned children's books and a mangled plastic Barbie doll head. Quite an inventory. Lulu dragged over a little black girl, hair in rubber bands, thumb in her mouth, orange top and brown pants.

"We are open for business!" Lulu shouted at her.

I looked at the little girl, she at me. I realized I was expected to do something.

"Thanks for coming by our little . . . *barber*shop. A shipment of new products just came in. I think you'll be happy with the depth of our inventory."

Taking her thumb from her mouth, the little girl said, "I'm Trisha."

I paused. "I'm Keenan. Glad to meet you. Can I interest you in some fine literature from the latest authors." I placed the three battered yet colorfully bound children's books on the counter. "Short-listed for the Pulitzer." Trisha put her thumb back in her mouth.

Lulu grew impatient. "Buy something!"

"I see you're skeptical," I continued with Trisha. "I've been holding onto this next item for just the right customer. I think *you* are that special customer." I placed the ruined Barbie doll head on the crate. "For you—only *one thousand* dollars."

"Okay," Trisha replied.

I caught Lulu's eye, and said, "Can I just put this on Ms. Trisha's tab, Ms. Lulu?"

"Yes." Lulu was supercool with credit. She dug another scrap of paper out of her pocket and handed it ceremoniously to Trisha. "This is your receipt. Please come again." Trisha, sensing her part in this craziness was over, grabbed the doll's head and disappeared. Lulu was pleased with me, seeing as I played along and said things that sounded like what shopkeepers say.

"Good work. You can go on break." I was dismissed. She shouted, "Rakesh!"

About an hour later it was story time. This meant we could nap while the daycare assistant, Tabitha, read us a story about a hungry worm.

I sat cross-legged in the first row on my appointed spongy yoga mat.

"In the light of the moon a little egg lay on a leaf," she read. I watched her face as she formed the words. It was like watching a statue speak. She was completely still, her skin porcelain but for sunburnt ears. Her expression was placid as she spoke, but her eyebrows danced, and her eyes glanced up to see who was still awake, who was paying attention. Catching my eye, she read on. "One Sunday morning the warm sun came up and—*pop!*—out of the egg came a tiny and very hungry caterpillar." Her carpenter pants seemed new and pressed; her red Converse All Star high-tops were speckled with blue paint. She wore a simple black T-shirt under a black-checked flannel. This girl had clearly smoked a lot of weed in her short time. "He started to look for food. On Monday he ate through one apple. But he was still hungry."

The timbre of her voice was a sonorous alto. Somehow this Tabitha infused her monotone with cadence; there was a storyteller in there despite her deadpan delivery. My eyes began to droop, my head nodded. I struggled to stay awake.

"On Tuesday he ate through two pears, but he was still hungry."

I awoke to a slowish modern cover of a Schoolhouse Rock song and rubbed the sleep from my eyes. The clock high on the wall read eleven thirty. Only one more hour to kill.

After all the kids had been gently awakened (oh, the tears of newly awakened youngsters), Dorothy, with her maternal equanimity, announced to the room, "Boys and girls, please get your juice and fruit from Tabby in the back, and feel free to have open play inside, or out in the yard. Lulu, can you help Ms. Tabitha?"

I glanced over at Lulu, who perked up all smiley with such a privileged responsibility. "Yes, Ms. Dorothy! Thank you." And she rushed to the back of the room where a straight-faced Tabitha set a box of juice bags and another of assorted fruit on a folding table.

Ah . . . I remembered this. I guess it's not really déjà vu when you really have gone through it before: story time, nap time, playtime, and snacks. The memory of it now, sitting here in my attic recording this, is that I had—have—a bird's-eye view of the socio-behavioral microcosms that inform us all: the interactions between children, dominance and submission, the power hierarchy, the need for order, the raw fear and confusion . . . and the wonder.

I stood in line, tripping on those very notions, tripping on the Schoolhouse Rock songs, and for a second, I even forgot myself and I felt like one of them, a child, stepping one step at a time toward the juice and fruit, in front of me a redheaded kid who smelled of cut grass, in front of him a shy Asian girl looking back at me with giant wonder-filled brown eyes.

Then the kid with the straight black hair and red sweater, who'd swiped my crayon earlier, cut in front of me without even a glance. I found this amusing.

"Hey, buddy, what's with the attitude?"

He ignored me. He smelled like burnt rubber.

"You know, that's very rude to take a guy's crayon when he's about to sketch a masterpiece." Still nothing. "Also, the red sweater is an atrocious fashion choice. Who dresses you?" Again, nothing. I wasn't upset or anything; I was just in an experimental mode of communicating to other kids, seeing as this was perhaps the third time I'd ever been in a large-scale kid situation. I quickly learned that as long as no adult was within earshot, I could speak freely. It was interesting. Finally, I said, "Hey, dude in the red shirt—no cutting!"

The boy turned around. He was about six inches taller than me and had emotionless almond eyes. I wasn't about to give in. "Look—you can't just cut in front of me. Get to the back of the line."

He looked me up and down. "I'm Vincent," he said, then walked to the back of the line.

This is how kids around this age identify themselves. It was a greeting: I'm Lulu, I'm Rakesh, I'm Vincent. This was often followed by their age: I'm three, I'm four. It was the preschool equivalent of name-rank-and-serial number.

At the table, I was presented a choice of juices and fruits by Tabitha and Lulu. "Hey, Keenan," Tabitha greeted, "You want apple or orange juice?"

"You got anything else?"

She looked at me, amused. Oh, that's right . . . *no coherent sentences.* Maybe just pointing or repeating a word, apple, orange? I was pretty bad at this.

"Apple, please." I realized I was flirting with her. Sheesh.

And she gave me a reward—she tousled my hair and handed me a cold, sweaty juice bag with attached straw. "You're funny, Keenan. What kind of fruit?"

I looked over at Lulu, Tabitha's so-called assistant.

"Lulu loves to play Barbershop," I said. Lulu stared vacantly, not really understanding what her job was. "Lulu?"

"Barbershop?" Tabitha asked.

I wanted to say, *Lulu here thinks that barbershop means any store situation.* But I'd already gone too far, so instead I said, "Nothing. Grapes, please, Lulu."

Lulu continued to gaze uncomprehendingly. "Lulu, give Keenan some grapes." Tabitha actually handed Lulu the grapes and Lulu slowly relayed them to me; then Lulu leaned over and gave me a quick impetuous kiss. I jumped back.

Whoa!

"Hey!" I shouted.

Tabitha laughed a deep laugh, knowing all too well what was going on. My face must've been deep red. Tabitha put a hand on Lulu's shoulder and said empathetically, "Lulu, we don't kiss other people unless they give us permission." The children behind me tittered, and Lulu, formerly my bossy barbershop overlord, shyly buried her face in Tabitha's bejeaned thighs.

I stood there, lost for a second, juice packet in one hand and table grapes in the other. I scurried out to the play yard, beelining for a little wooden bench in the corner behind the blue and green hard-plastic merry-go-round. *Whew!* Day one was turning out to be both interesting and harrowing: a harbinger of much drama to come, preschool-style.

Stabbing my straw into the juice bag, I drank quickly of the appley goodness. Looking around, I saw that the yard was a long rectangle bordered by the tall white plastic picket fence. On the far end from me were little tables littered with crayons and coloring books (childhood *is* all crayons and coloring books) and a sandbox with buckets and shovels; adjacent to that was a hard-foam play area strewn with plastic and rubber balls; next to this was the obligatory multicolored plastic play tower constructed of puzzle-like panels that formed tunnels and parapets, equipped with a monkey bar and rope swing. A slide slanted down from the top of the tower and child after child slid laughing to the rubber-padded bottom, only to gain their feet and race around for another frolic. Kids scrambled monkey-like everywhere. Next to me the small merry-go-round twirled, the centrifugal force tossing gleeful tykes everywhere. That's when Vincent and his cronies showed up.

Vincent and his kid gang.

Vincent had a crew cut of bristly black hair and was the biggest three-and-a-half-year-old you ever saw. A bully in the making, he was flanked by a hapless crew of post-toddlers who clearly didn't know they were part of a gang.

Vincent approached me, sized me up and said, "I'm Vincent," he repeated. He paused. "I'm almost four." Talk about throwing down the gauntlet!

I calmly put down my juice bag and grapes and stood. The two kids on either side of him really didn't know why they were there. I think they thought candy was involved.

I looked them up and down. "So, *Vincent* . . . who are your buddies?"

They looked at me blankly. I kept forgetting I had to speak in child-speak. "I'm Keenan. I'm almost three. Who . . . are . . . you guys?" I pointed at them simultaneously.

The one on the left said automatically, "I'm Julian!" But before the one on the right could pipe in, Vincent stopped him, all the while staring at me. "I'm three . . . and a *half!*" he announced threateningly.

If this was prison, say, this would be my opportunity to shank the alpha dog so I wouldn't later get ass-raped in the shower. But it wasn't prison. *Per se.*

"Jesus fucking *Christ*," I cursed, but then checked myself. Not because I shouldn't swear, but because swearing wasn't on their radar yet. It was meaningless. Instead, I said, "Excuse me. Did you say three . . . *and a half?!*" Vincent nodded. "That is so freaking cool."

"I'm Walter," said the other kid, finally.

Rescue arrived in the form of a pink flowered dress and gold curls. Lulu appeared, fearless and oblivious. She gave a cursory glance at Vincent's preschool mafia and said, "Good*bye*!"

Vincent gave me a "this isn't over" look and shuffled away with his grateful henchmen. Lulu asked, "How was the grapes?" Oddly, she said this with a scowl.

"*Were* the grapes . . . I *loved* 'em."

Then she stole a kiss from me again and ran away at full sprint.

"Ugh!" I said, in spite of myself, once again feeling the heat in my face.

The impressive weirdness of the day made me realize being out of doors and socializing with miniature lunatics was way more fun than reading old magazines and surfing the web at home. This was a George Orwell allegory come to life: politics and absurdity. Hell, Lou and Drew had become an overwrought Greek tragedy compared to this living metaphor of society as portrayed by preschool. *Lord of the Mud Pies.*

A bell rang and the kids immediately headed for the door. Dorothy appeared in the school yard. "That's it, my precious children. Time to go home!" The kids had disappeared, except for me, near the merry-go-round. Dorothy said, "C'mon, Keenan. Your mom's here."

She led me to where the kids were queuing up. "You have a good day, Keenan?"

"The best," I replied.

Outside on the sidewalk, Lou, looking a little tired, opened the rear car door and helped me in.

"Was it a disaster?" she asked, seriously.

I climbed into the kiddy seat and buckled myself. "It wasn't so bad."

Amused, she kissed my forehead. "Good, cuz you're gonna be spending a bit of time here."

Dorothy and Tabitha waved as we sped away.

!!!

Lou dropped me off at Happy Feet every morning, picked me up at twelve thirty. Because we had only that one piece-of-shit car, Drew and Lou had to negotiate who got it and on which days. Drew had use of a company pest control car, but he couldn't take it home.

Lou devised a disheartening work-around.

We sat at our kitchen dining table, me on my booster chair, spooning Kraft mac 'n' cheese into my mouth. Delicious at any age.

"You know that sheriff's deputy, Wade? I bumped into him the other day and we got to talking. He offered to help us out for a while," Lou said.

"Help out?" Drew asked. He scrunched his face as he sipped his beer. "Ooh, jumped the gun on this one."

Lou affected a nonchalance into her voice. "Well, he lives pretty close by and the preschool is near the sheriff's department. He said he could help pick up and drop off if he was available or didn't have a call; he said that he'd be glad to help a neighbor."

Wow. Some fucking nerve.

Drew looked surprised, too, but for different reasons.

"Hell, that's like a police escort!"

"And he'd drop me off at the light rail to work."

"Well shit, that's fantastic. Invite him over for dinner . . . and beer."

There was a cruel self-satisfaction under my mother's placid veneer. "Nice. I'll call him and let him know." She glanced at me and caught my eyes burning into her.

"Something wrong, Keenan?"

I put my tiny spoon down. "Not hungry."

Drew, the fucking moronic cuckold, chimed in. "Well, eat your broccoli and you can go watch TV or read *Scientific American* or whatever you're into these days." He smiled at himself. Sometimes I couldn't blame Lou for having an affair.

!!!

The day arrived in which Deputy Wade had taxi duty.

I stood at the front door of our little house, peeking through the screen at Wade's civilian Ford SUV. He sat in the driver's seat, looking over at me peering through the front door. Lou gathered her things as Drew put on his coat.

"He's outside waiting," Drew told her.

"Good. I'm almost ready."

Drew came up behind me. "You get a police escort today, Keenan. Only the finest for our little monkey. Whaddya think?"

"Great."

"Hey, honey, I'm gone," Drew said.

"Have a good day!" She almost sounded convincing.

Drew kissed the top of my head, opened the screen door, and shuffled down the walk. On his way to our car, he stopped and chatted to Wade, all sunglasses, through his SUV window. I watched them in disgust until Lou, with her coat and purse, beckoned me.

"Ready, Keenan?"

Without glancing up at her, I pushed through the screen door, heading toward Wade's SUV. I was surprised there wasn't a gun rack in it.

"Wake up on the wrong side of the bed, Keenie?" Lou called after me as she locked the door behind us.

I said nothing. My little legs marched on toward the SUV, engine idling, Limp Bizkit thumping from the speakers. When I got to the SUV, I couldn't reach the door handle. I angrily jumped up and down trying to open it. Suddenly, the door flew open as Lou took hold of me.

"What has gotten into you?"

Still, I said nothing. She went around to the front passenger side, sliding in and sitting me squarely into her lap, securing a seat belt over me, over both of us.

Wade glanced at her, me. Limp Bizkit still blared. He turned it down. "Don't you want to get the kid's seat?"

"Drew just left with it."

"It's illegal."

She looked at him coquettishly. "So, bust me, big guy."

I stared ahead at my tiny sneakered feet.

Wade made a growl that I assumed was supposed to be sexy. He scrutinized Lou and said, "You look like you might be *coming down with something*."

She replied in a whisper, as though that would either keep me from hearing or understanding: "I already called work."

"Right on."

Gunning the engine, he sped off toward the daycare center.

!!!

On the way back home that day, sure enough, Lou and Wade glowed with a postcoital sheen, grins and all. I had a clear view of the side of Wade's chiseled face.

Oh, how I loathed his presence.

I resolved to hit the Internet immediately and look up everything about Wade Johnson: sheriff's department, public records, wives, exes, siblings, parents, phone numbers, address, social security number. Everything in his past must be on the Internet: transgressions, reprimands, suspensions. I had only to plumb this material and present it to him so that he might see the error of his ways. On my side was the fact that he would no doubt question his sanity when I, a tyke of almost three years, accused and threatened him using a vocabulary above his own education level. My goal was to freak him out into compliance. Certainly, an adult-speaking infant threatening to notify his superiors that their employee was fornicating with someone else's wife on the department's time would make him stop. Right? I devised a plan.

A couple days later, Wade was back on the scene delivering me to preschool, no doubt turning around and heading back to our house where

Lou would shag him, or vice versa. So I consulted Lulu as we shared our favorite plastic bench in the play yard, kicking it with juice and grapes.

"Oh, Lulu . . . I love these special moments with you. You know, when you and I can push the curtain aside and really get down to brass tacks."

Lulu looked around. "There is no curtains, silly!"

"You're a very observant little girl, Ms. Lulu, but your command of the language leaves something to be desired. There *are* no curtains, Lulu. *Are*. *Curtains* is plural." I paused. "I know what you're thinking, that I used *is* with *curtains* just now, thus contradicting my assertion. These are a few of the intricacies of the English language, Lulu. Hopefully you'll come to love them as much as I."

She promptly took half of my grapes. Then gave me one back.

"Thanks. Look, Lulu, remember our little powwow a couple days back? Well, I'm going to attempt to unsaddle that fiendish deputy on the way home today. But I need a ruse, a diversion. I was thinking of going for the spoiled kid gambit, demanding ice cream or . . . or what? What do kids like us need and need *now*?"

"Cookies!"

I shook my head, sipping the juice.

"That isn't going to fly. We have cookies aplenty at home." I snapped my little fingers. "A-ha! I'm grumpy! I'm so so, *so* grumpy, Lulu, because I have a *tooth*ache and need some clove oil or some shit to numb the pain."

"Look at my teeth," Lulu demanded, flashing a crazy smile. Her teeth were little white pearls dotting her pink gums.

"Lovely. Are your parents British perchance? But seriously, this ruse may well work . . ." I paused. "Unless they take me to a freakin' dentist." I stood up and caught sight of Tabitha. "Yes, Lulu, I feel a bad toothache coming on, and I think I better alert Ms. Tabby of this unfortunate development. Excuse me."

!!!

At twelve thirty, when Lou came in to get me, Tabitha, bless her goth-rock heart, was at my side. I held my left cheek and put on my best look of distress. Lou's face, still aglow from her recent rogering, fell at the sight of me. She knelt down and felt my forehead, looking up at Tabitha.

"Everything alright?"

"Keenan has a toothache or something," Tabitha explained. "I looked, but I couldn't see anything out of the ordinary. Might be under the tooth, a cavity or something."

"Cavity? Sheesh, his teeth just came in. Let's see, Keenan."

I opened my mouth.

"Where? In the back?" I nodded as she stuck her index finger in my mouth and touched a back molar. I winced and made a plaintive moan. "Sorry, honey." She stood up. "Great."

"I put a little clove oil on it," Tabitha explained. "It seemed to help for a second."

I reeked of clove oil.

"Yeah, I used clove oil when he was teething. But I think we're out."

Both the ladies sighed and Lou took my hand.

"Let's go, Monkey. We'll pick some up on the way home."

Success!

"Okay," I replied miserably.

She led me to the SUV and strapped me into a baby seat in the back. I hadn't planned on them suddenly getting a baby seat. Wade saw the look of consternation on both of our faces.

"What seems to be the trouble, big guy?" Wade asked.

"He's got a toothache. We're going to have to stop at the drugstore on the way home."

"No problem." He glanced back at me as he put the car in gear. "Be brave, big guy."

Shut the fuck up, you brainless chunk of testosterone.

I was nervous, though. I had my spiel down, indeed had rehearsed it alone in my room this morning before the house had risen. Wade was such a dimwit, however, that it was hard to predict his reaction. Would he properly question his sanity? Would he threaten violence upon me? Would he just ignore me altogether? Would he try to come clean to Lou and tell her that her weird three-year-old son had threatened to expose their infidelities in a freakishly articulate manner?

My little heart palpitated.

Wade swung into a Walgreens parking lot and found a space. Lou got her purse and opened the door. "I'll just be a couple minutes."

"S'all good, darlin'. Keenan and I will hold the fort. Won't we, Keenan?"

He smiled at me and I nodded.

Mom took off. I dropped the act and unbuckled my kiddy seat belt. Wade watched me in the rearview. "Gettin' comfortable, big guy."

"Actually, Wade, we need to talk."

He chuckled. "Awesome. Sometimes you're so . . . like . . . whatcha-macallit?"

"Articulate?" I leaned in between the front seats. "Look, you fucking moron, we don't have a lot of time because I want to get this out before Lou gets back."

Wade's brain was having trouble registering these words coming from a three-year-old. This was expected.

"Wh-what? What did you just say, Keenan?"

"Oh, God. I'll . . . talk . . . slower. Look, jackass, I know you're having an affair with my mother. I've known for a long time."

"What the fff . . ."

"Fuck? What the *fuck*?"

His face had lost its color and he twisted around in his seat to be sure it was me who was talking, not some prank.

"I'll tell you what the fuck, *Wade*. I'm going to make this quick because my mom is going to come back soon. By the way, I have no fucking toothache. That was a ruse. So, look: you must stop seeing my mother *immediately*."

"What the hell?" He unbuckled his seat belt so he could look behind the seat, like there might've been a recording.

"Calm down and pay attention." I continued. "You will make up an excuse to leave Lou, or you will simply *never call her again*. If you *don't* do this, I'll not only tell my dad that you are fucking his wife, I'll email the sheriff's department and tell them you've been having an affair with Louisiana Harris . . . and that you've been molesting her son."

"You can't . . . this is impossible . . . *email*?" I think he was going into shock.

"Look, idiot. You'll keep quiet about this because people won't believe that a kid my age could say shit like this. The fact is, the true story is, if you must know, is that I've been reincarnated and I'm stuck in this body. I used to be a writer. Or drug dealer. Take your pick." I chuckled. "That's the second time I've ever admitted that." I looked at him; he was walleyed. "You probably think you're going crazy. But let's get this clear: if you don't stop seeing my mother immediately, I will send the email that says you had an affair on duty and molested a young boy. I know the molestation thing is a cheap shot, but I have to make sure you're paying attention. If anything happens to me—like if I suddenly have an unfortunate *accident*—the email will still be sent. So, you better hope I stay alive . . . on all accounts."

"This isn't happening." Panic cracked Wade's voice. "Who put you up to this?"

"This is no joke. This *is* happening." I paused. "Look, I see Lou coming out of the store. You will say nothing of this; you will drive us home; and you'll never ever come back. Got it?"

He said nothing and sat back in his seat, rebuckling his belt. His breathing had quickened.

"Nod your head if you understand."

He gave an almost imperceptible nod just as Lou got back in the car.

"I got some clove oil and some knock-off Orajel just in case," Lou said, looking back at me as she buckled herself in. "How're you doing, sweetheart?"

"I'm great, Mom."

"I mean, how's your tooth?"

"It doesn't hurt anymore."

Her brow furrowed. "Really? Well . . . good, I guess. Well, we have stuff in case it comes back." She glanced at Wade, who looked positively ill.

"Hey, honey. You okay? You look like you've seen a ghost or something."

Wade nodded, looking straight ahead. "I'm not . . . well," he said, and started the car.

Lou put a concerned hand on his leg. He flinched, glancing back in the rearview nervously.

"Don't." He put the car in gear.

And that was indeed the last we saw of Deputy Wade.

So, that last part where I told him if something happened to me an email would be sent? This wasn't true, but I was prepared to firebomb his career if he crossed me. He was one of the few—the lucky few—to whom I have revealed my reincarnation. They always say the same thing: "This isn't happening." With all our lip service about seeking the afterlife, when actually presented with a glimpse of it, no one believes.

If you say you talk *to* God every day, you're pious. Say you talk *with* God every day—then you're crazy.

17. *Kids These Days*

The effect of losing her lover was heavy on Louisiana Solomon Harris. The explanation Mama Lou gave to Papa Drew about Wade's sudden unavailability was pretty convincing: "He was reprimanded for taxiing civilians in a patrol car." For weeks, she was taciturn, lachrymose. I felt a little sorry for the broad—just a *little*. I'd come to appreciate—even *love*—my milquetoast father, who may have been hapless, but possessed qualities that I strongly admired—curiosity, humor, and vision. And by vision, I mean believing that if you try at things, those things sometimes work out.

Anyhow, in his new pest control job, Drew had built a little bit of confidence, and it showed. This self-confidence bled over into his brewing life, and he entered a few cases of his home brew into a local brewing competition. A strong brown he called Brownout Ale and a breezy lager dubbed the Lou Lager. Both had placed in the contest. Cash and prizes were at stake. My father was giddy; my mother perplexed; both of them pleased.

It was the night of the awards ceremony in the spring of my fourth year that these honors were bestowed upon my father. I now had a sort of entry level computer tablet, and I was reading it on the living room floor.

Lou, looking fabulous in a little black dress and black heels, puffed on a cigarette outside the front doorway, sipping her martini. She had cut back on her smoking while also taking said habit outside onto the porch.

Drew appeared in the hallway in his one threadbare suit, fussing with a striped burgundy tie. He asked, "Honey? Can you . . .?"

Lou and I gazed at this nervous, forlorn man, handsome even in that ratty suit.

"Hell, Drew—what makes you think *I* can do it?" Lou replied. "You'd have better luck with Keenan."

"I *meant* Keenan." A beat. He winked at me. "Kidding. Come on."

She closed in and took each end of the tie, experimenting, remembering the knot, figuring it out and pulling it taut. Then Lou kissed Drew on the lips. Not a peck, but a real kiss, a kiss of . . . what? *Love?* Yeah, a wife's loving kiss. Drew hesitated and smiled.

"Thank you, honey," he said. Drew snaked an arm around her and returned his own lingering kiss. They got lost in that moment and my little four-year-old heart jumped for them. This was something new! Then they looked over at me and caught my slack-jawed expression. I averted my gaze back to the tablet, and they laughed.

"We better get going," Lou said.

"Where's Tabitha?"

My head jerked back up. *Tabitha?!*

The doorbell donged.

My little crush for Tabitha had grown over the ensuing months since I'd been at Happy Feet Daycare. It was difficult to maintain my four-year-oldness all that time. And yet, there was Tabitha at our front door, all of twenty, dressed conspicuously normal: no death metal T-shirts, no goth eyeliner, no black lipstick. The door closed behind her; she sloughed her denim coat and dropped an overloaded book bag to the floor.

Drew put on his suit jacket, Lou, a red suede coat. Lou said, "We should be back before midnight."

"I'd ask you if there is anything I should know," Tabitha said, "but it's just Keenan. He'll probably bury his head in his tablet. He's had dinner?"

"Yeah," Drew said.

"He's been going to bed late," Lou added. "It's best not to fight it."

Oh, yes, I'd trained them well.

Tabitha walked over to me and rubbed my wispy hair, which was losing its towhead strawberry, turning brown. "I can tell who wears the pants in this family."

"Be nice to Tabitha, Keenan," Lou said on her way out.

In the last year since I'd been going to daycare, I'd let Tabitha discover that I could communicate like an adult. I didn't tell her about Kurt, and I gave her the impression that I was selective about who I shared my abilities with.

Tabitha stood in the doorway as the car pulled out of the driveway; she waved goodbye and closed the door. As soon as the parents had left, she quickly sat down next to me and declared, "Now, Keenan, I know you're not a normal four-year-old—shit, I don't know *what* you are—but since you know what's going on around you, I won't beat around the bush."

This was interesting. After a moment, I replied, "Yes?"

She grinned. "Is it cool if I invite some friends over? I mean, can I invite them without you spilling to your parents?"

This wasn't surprising. I mean it's right out of the cool babysitter playbook. I considered the possibility of some real excitement around the Harris household. Young adults on drugs! Drunk boys and girls! Petty dramas!

"Don't worry," I told her, "Just don't let it devolve into pandemonium. And don't let anybody get into my dad's beer or there'll be hell to pay."

Tabitha wore a stunned expression. "'Devolve . . . into . . . pandemonium,'" she repeated, then hugged me. "Oh, my God, you little freak! You're so awesome!"

And so, she began texting her friends.

!!!

Not long after, said friends came over. They were quite something. They referred to themselves as G-Punks, which was short for goth-punk, and their style was indeed a marriage of the two, with new variations thrown in. Sterno, Jasper, Gigi, and Philip; Mohawk, Drag-Queen, Lip-Piercing, and Pretty Boy, respectively. They reminded me of my theater geek friends of yester-life.

I nestled myself into the corner of the couch as the five of them got stewed on alcohol and cannabis. These youngsters (it's the only way I could view them) took over the living room, passing around a vodka bottle, chasing it with cranberry juice. Within an hour, the living room was strewn with jolly supine forms and clouded with the strong scent of marijuana and fruit-scented vape.

They seemed amused by me, but a little nervous, so I left them to their vices, literally, and headed to my room. After waiting a few minutes, I sneaked into the hall, darting into my parents' bedroom. I listened from behind the door.

Philip said, "That kid is . . ."

"*Weird.*" Sterno interjected.

"Stern!" Tabitha chastised.

"I was gonna say he is like the little sister in *Dune*," Philip added.

There was a silence. Gigi laughed.

"Oh, Philip! Reading books is *so* cute!"

Then: "Sean just texted," Jasper blurted.

Sean?

"Where the hell is he?"

"He's on Camden. He'll be here in a sec."

An excited titter swept through the room.

Then from Tabitha, calling searchingly: "Keenan, you okay? Another one of our friends is coming over."

I scrambled from my hiding place and scurried down the hall.

"Keenan?"

When Tabitha poked her head inside my door, she found me stretched on the rug.

"Oh," she said.

"Yes?" I replied nonchalantly.

"Another friend is coming over."

"Alright."

"You okay in here?"

"Fine."

"Alright."

She disappeared. The clock over the doorway read nine forty-five. They probably had a couple hours, give or take, before Lou and Drew returned.

A short while later, the doorbell rang, and this Sean fellow was greeted with enthusiasm. I was reasonably sure I knew the source of this enthusiasm—*he was the drugs*. The buzzing vibe in the room wasn't just the large amount of pot the kids had smoked and vodka they'd drunk, it was the promise of drugs (powdered, no doubt) anticipated from this Sean fellow.

"Hello, my pretties." Sean greeted them devilishly in a gravelly baritone.

I had to see this guy for myself. Rising from the floor, I crossed down the hall and peeked into the living room. Sean wasn't what I expected at all. He was maybe thirty, with a thick chest and ponytail down the middle of his back. He wore a black fedora and a dark gray leather blazer. Sheesh, I knew this uniform.

But that wasn't all. I *knew him.*

I was astonished and must've stood walleyed in the doorway because Sean was suddenly looking at me, clearly wondering what the fuck a toddler was doing in their midst. Tabitha saw me.

"Keenan? You okay?" Tabitha asked.

"Hi," I managed.

"This is Sean."

Sean smiled, took two steps toward me, and knelt down. "Hello, little man. How's it going?"

Little man.

"Alright, I guess," was all I could muster, tarrying in the hallway. Sean chuckled and looked at the others, who tittered knowingly.

"Careful, Sean," Jasper warned. "He's an alien."

"Jasp!" Tabitha said.

"Are you from another planet, Keenan?" Sean inquired good-naturedly.

"I am from earth."

This got the predictable laugh, but I saw Philip nod at Tabitha, who crossed toward me.

"Hey, Keenan . . . can you entertain yourself in the kitchen or your room for a little while. We have to talk *adult* things with Sean."

I rolled my eyes. "*Adult* things. Sure. I'll be in my *room*."

"Thanks, Keen. We won't be long."

Sidelined from the party, I lay on my bedroom floor, studying the Manet and the Lichtenstein on the wall, and thought of Sean. Sean was, *is,* Franks's younger American cousin. On the growing list of cosmic accidents in my new life, I had to add my henchman's cousin coming to my very abode. I wasn't sure what it meant, but it reminded me that I'd gotten sidetracked from my mission of righting the wrongs of my previous life. It reminded me of the nightwalks and that guy Stoli. Stoli hadn't seemed like an accident either, but the plan I'd hatched had collapsed due to my own carelessness. Anyhow, maybe I could still find out something about Sean's cousin Franks, whose exact location was not easily found by a simple web search. Franks had a lot of former addresses. On top of that, after Franks got his citizenship, he immediately went off the grid and seldom, if ever, filed taxes. I wasn't entirely sure "Franklin Franklin O'Donnell" itself wasn't an alias.

Shutting off the light in my room, I slowly turned the doorknob and peeked out. Coast was clear. Creeping down the hall, I again darted into my parents' room, wedging myself behind the door.

Bauhaus thrummed in the living room. I heard the telltale sniffing of drugs, the idle chatter, the clink of glasses, the smell of cigarettes and pot. My parents would not be pleased with the stench.

I think it was Philip who asked, "How much time do we have?"

Tabitha: "Not long. Probably be getting a text anytime, unfortunately."

Big snorting sound, then Sterno: "This is Uncle Franks's?"

"Always."

Bingo. Franks was still in the area. Jesus Christ. I wondered if there was an Aunt Dolly.

"It's kinda stepped-on."

Sounds like Franks to me.

"Fuck you," Sean said casually.

"Where are we going to bounce after this?" Jasper asked.

Silence.

"C'mon you guys," Tabitha said. "I gotta straighten this place up a bit. Someone open a door. It smells like a dispensary in here." I heard the squeak of the front door, and I went back to my room.

A short time later, she tapped on my door. "They're gone, Keenan, and your parents are on their way home. Wanna come back out and hang until they get here?"

"Sure."

So we sat in front of the tube, Tabitha trying to suck down as much diet soda as possible to cut the effects of the booze, pot, and blow.

"It smells pretty bad in here," I told her.

She got up and resprayed the living room with an oppressively scented air freshener, waving her arms in the air near the door as though the miscellaneous aromas of vice might all magically flow outside.

"I told your parents I had a few friends over," she explained.

"Don't expect a tip."

"Do you think they'll get mad?"

"It depends." Then I had an idea. "I'll vouch for you if you tell me something."

She looked at me. "Name it."

"What's Sean's last name?"

Tabitha gave me a look. "Um . . . O'Donnell, I think. Why would you want to know that?"

"Just curious."

"Keenan, you're not thinking of saying something, are you?"

"I would never cause trouble for my favorite babysitter. Seriously, I was just curious."

"You're something else, Keenan."

When Lou and Drew arrived home around eleven thirty, they were plenty lit themselves, both holding trophies and ribbons and certificates, falling inside the door, giggling, greeting us. Then they stopped, smelling the night's activities.

"Whoa," Drew said.

Lou tilted her head at Tabitha. "Just a few friends over, huh? Smells like a burnt skunk."

"Well . . . we may have smoked a joint . . ."

Drew tried to head off his wife's wrath. "Lou, no biggie."

Lou thought she was being smart when she turned to me. "Keenan, what went on here tonight?"

I resisted the urge to glance at Tabitha, holding Lou's gaze. "Her friends came by. They were nice. Then they left."

Lou narrowed her eyes at me, then at Tabitha; then she sighed. "Okay. Whatever. Anyway, Drew won three prizes! He was like a beer superstar!"

This was a surprising achievement for my ne'er-do-well dad. I stood up on the couch and bounced. "Way to go, Dad!"

Drew, who was still holding his trophies—two bronzed beer steins overflowing with stylized hops and barley—set them down on the table with a clatter. He grabbed me.

"I did it, Monkey! They liked my beer!" He planted a sloppy beer-smelling kiss.

"That's great, Mr. Harris!" Tabitha said.

Lou whipped out her wallet and handed Tabitha four twenties. "Thanks, Tabby."

"You're welcome, Mrs. Harris." Tabitha turned and tousled my hair. "G'bye, you little punk. Be good."

I winked at her. "*You* be good."

18. *Happy Return*

A few days after Tabitha's party, after being visited by Sean, the Ghost of Junkie Past, I searched online for Sean O'Donnell on my crappy tablet. My fever for revenge against his cousin Franks had been rekindled. I had no idea how I would enact revenge short of growing up and getting a driver's license, and I didn't have that kind of patience.

In any case, I distracted myself by researching my target, but my kiddie tablet just wasn't cutting it. Even with all the parental filters turned off, the weak operating system and infantile browser just weren't up to tasks a normal computer would accomplish instantly. On top of that, its native word processor only showed characters in big cartoonish fonts, maddening. We would have to fix this somehow. Sneaking onto my dad's computer just was not an option anymore.

My mom tapped on my door and stepped in.

"Hi, Keen. Dinner in an hour."

"Alright. What's the menu?"

"No child asks that question."

"How would you know?"

"Your Dad's beer brats, sauerkraut, potatoes, and corn."

"Whoa . . . what's the occasion?"

"We are having a guest over for dinner. This man we met at the brewing awards wants to talk to Drew about opening a brewpub—" Lou hesitated.

"I know what a brewpub is, Mom."

"Of course, you do. My four-year-old." She shook her head. "Anyway, it's pretty exciting."

"Great."

"Whatcha doin'?" she asked me.

"Nothing." I paused. "Mom, can I get a new tablet?"

She snorted. "Right after I get a new computer. And a new phone. And a microwave that is faster than the toaster oven."

"Forget about it."

"I'll call you when dinner's ready."

When supper was announced, I trotted out to the dining room to the heady aroma of Drew's porter-soaked bratwurst and artisanal sauerkraut. *Ah, Drew, putting the bräu in low-brow*. I climbed up on my booster seat as Lou brought in the steaming brats. Drew and his guest came in from the garage-brewery. By now, the garage was used solely for the purpose of making beer. There was always a batch being mashed, sparged, boiled, cooled, or fermented. You get used to the smell. Not only was Drew producing cases of beer, he'd been paid to keg his brews for friends' parties. I believe if Drew hadn't won awards at the competition, Lou would've blown a gasket by this time. He'd really gone beer crazy.

Drew carried a pitcher in each hand as he led our visitor to the table.

"Ah, look. It's my little monkey. Keenan, this is Mr. Galvin."

"Hi, Mr. Galvin."

The man, maybe fifty, a little red-faced, trimmed gray and brown hair, glanced at Drew, then back at me with a twinkle in his eye. He said, "Hi, Keenan. You can call me John. No need to be so formal." He held out his hand and I shook it. He held it for a little longer than necessary and winked at me.

Creepy.

When he took his seat at the table, he examined his plate and asked, "So what have we here?"

Drew poured beer, replying, "Porter-soaked bratwurst, my favorite sauerkraut, au gratin potatoes, and local-grown sweet corn from up the street."

"A feast!" said John.

Lou joined us with the potatoes and corn. "Very posh. And most of the food groups," she said, sitting down. "Dig in."

John Galvin had the cracked cheeks of someone who'd spent a lot of time in the sun, like a fisherman or farmer: rosy Irish cheeks beset with lively hazel eyes. His grayish hair was neatly trimmed, almost military, and he sported a close-cut salt-and-pepper beard. He was dressed for business in a light blue button-down and gray tie. A matching suit jacket hung on the back of his chair. There was a gold service ring on his finger. He caught me looking at it.

"You know what this is, Keenan? That's an Army Ranger ring," he said instructively. "Seventy-Fifth Regiment. I was in the army. You know, like the army men you play with." He piled a dollop of kraut on his brats. Annoyed, I glanced at Lou, then at Drew. Our guest caught the look. "Did I say something wrong?" he asked, grin faltering.

Drew chuckled. "No."

"Well . . . Keenan is, uh . . ." Lou was weighing her words. ". . . *smart* for his age. He knows stuff." She shrugged. "Hell, he can probably tell you the history of the Rangers."

Galvin was amazed. "What? No . . . *really*?"

"He's funny that way."

Drew nodded, shook his head, shrugged. "Ask him a question."

"How old is he? How old are you?" Galvin asked.

"Four."

"Four?"

"And four months."

"Well, well." Then he asked, "Do you know anything about the Army Rangers, Keenan?"

I shrugged. "I know they used to fight Indians."

Galvin whistled, impressed.

"*Native Americans*, Keenan," Drew corrected.

"They were like scouts." I wanted to Wikipedia his ass, but it was too soon. "Now they are commandos or something."

Galvin laughed heartily. "My goodness! Sorry I talked down to you, son! I didn't know you were so . . . *advanced.*" Then he said out of the side of his mouth to Drew, "Is he like some sort of kid genius?"

"Um . . . I guess you could say that." Drew looked at me pointedly. "But he's still a kid."

It was about this time that I smelled something fishy about this John Galvin character. He seemed a little . . . *disingenuous*? Maybe that's not it. Too *earnest*? I watched him as he forked many sausages into his face. The grown-ups continued to make small talk until Galvin set his fork down and pushed back from the table. "Well, you folks make a very savory meal! And this beer—what can I say, that's why I'm here." He drained his glass and smacked his lips. Drew emptied the rest of the pitcher into their glasses. "And with that, maybe we should talk a little about this brewpub idea I'm dreaming up in San Francisco."

Ah! So *that* was it! He had been ingratiating himself to Drew. Lou rose, collecting the dishes, suppressing a hopeful smile. Drew stood as well, empty pitcher in hand.

"I have just the new ale for the occasion. Maybe we should take it to the other room. Keenan, you can go"—Drew hesitated with some embarrassment—"play, or read—or whatever you do—if you want." Thus, Lou and Drew disappeared, leaving Galvin behind in the kitchen with me. Feeling awkward, I climbed down from my booster chair.

Galvin was suddenly at my side, whispering excitedly "Keenan! It's me!"

It didn't register at first, but the tone of his voice made me stop.

"It's *me—Stoli!*" he whispered.

Lou rushed back in to do the dishes. "You guys making friends?" She was not ten feet from us. "John, don't get Keenan started. He'll talk your ear off."

"That's alright," he told her, ushering me just outside the kitchen. He knelt down and continued, voice low. "It's Stoli! The dude from behind the 7-Eleven! I found your buried cash! I made good."

What. The. Fuck.

"Holy shit," I exhaled.

"I came back for you!"

My throat was knotted closed. My eyes darted over John Galvin anew. He was markedly different, but . . . *it was him*. Who else could it be?

The nightwalks. Stoli. Buried cash. The abandoned plan.

I jumped at Lou's voice. "Is he pestering you, John?" She stood in the kitchen doorway, hands working a dish towel.

Stoli didn't miss a beat. "Just asking Keenan if he knew where he was going to college."

Lou laughed. "Funny . . . I've never even thought to ask."

"Ask what?" Drew returned with a large foamy pitcher of brown ale.

Stoli held my gaze, smiling. "Where Keenan's going to college."

"Ha!" Drew set down the beer and winked at me. "Well, all I gotta say is that he better get a scholarship or something. We'll be lucky to afford *community* college."

Lou shook her head. "One thing at a time. Let's at least let him reach puberty."

"That'll be a joyride." Drew nodded toward the other room. "Shall we retire to the living room?"

Stoli rose. "Excellent idea."

I watched them leave and realized Lou had stopped to look at me. "Well?"

"What?"

"You are standing there. Are you expecting dessert or something?" she asked.

I was a perplexed statue in the doorway. "I don't know."

"You can join us, if you want."

"Okay."

She said in a half whisper, "I think John is going to offer your dad a job."

"Making beer?" I whispered back.

"I guess. Maybe we can reclaim the garage."

"I wouldn't count on it."

I had to hand it to Stoli—he'd really thought this out. In the living room, he spun quite a yarn, a personal history, partially fabricated, about how he came into a little money, turned that little money into a lot of money, and decided to pursue his dream of opening a brewpub. He described this found money as an inheritance, sinking it into a friend's personal fitness invention—a series of webbing straps that, when combined with a particular workout regimen, made it possible to stay in shape in a confined area—a patent that was purchased for millions of dollars by the US Army. That was about a year previous. Since then, he'd diversified, made even more money, and was ready to settle down with a business that would engage him and make him happy into his retirement: a brewpub. He had grown up in a restaurant family, but knew nothing about brewing. Along came the Silicon Valley Brewing Competition. When he tasted Drew's microbrews and heard the passion in Drew's brief acceptance speech, John "Stoli" Galvin knew he had his future brewmeister.

The real story was different. The part about investing in his friend's company, then reinvesting and making a mint is true. But what happened on the way to the money, and on the way to Drew and me, was different:

When Stoli met an invisible elf by the name of Keenan Solomon Harris on the other side of the fence from his 7-Eleven garbage area hangout, he thought he'd seriously lost it, that he'd had a breakdown. *But it seemed so real.* Either way, he was in some bad shape. So, he went to his caseworker and told her he wanted to clean up, to get his head straight and swim out of the debilitating undertow of his PTSD and substance abuse. Thus, he began his final foray into rehab. He told no one about the reincarnated man-child he had met through the fence behind a Campbell convenience store. He looked up Kurt Sebastian Houston and found out that the troubled writer-musician had died of a drug overdose some years earlier. Still, this did not convince him that he wasn't looney toons. After thirty cleansing days, he borrowed a car and went up to San Francisco to verify or discredit the address given to him by said dead-writer-elf-phantom hallucination.

Discovering that the address—1836 Twentieth Street—actually existed almost sent him back to rehab. Stoli parked the car inconspicuously behind a contractor's truck about fifty yards down the street from my old Victorian. There was a shiny black Land Rover in the cobbled brick driveway. Stoli waited. And waited.

About ninety minutes later, a robust-looking middle-aged blond lady in a pale green business suit came out of the house, got into the Range Rover, and drove away. That lady was my sister, Rae . . . well, Kurt Houston's sister. After a few minutes, Stoli (who, I have to keep reminding myself, was clean-shaven, sober, and dressed business casual) got out of the car, crossed the street, walked up to 1836, and rang the doorbell. Nobody stirred within. He knocked persistently. Nothing. And no dogs. This was good. He looked around, went to the side of the house, and without hesitation jumped the fence.

He told me the yard wasn't kept up very well, but he could see that it had once been very nice. He saw the hot tub, the deck, the overgrown wooden steps leading up the hill to the bench and the willow tree. He hopped these steps two at a time until he stood at the top. There was nobody in the neighbor's yard and he had a view down Twentieth Street, the direction my sister had driven away. He studied the windows at the back of the house. He saw movement and froze. A fluffy white Himalayan cat sunned itself in the window. He thought it might be watching him.

Joplin, still breathing well into her teens. *Oh, Joplin.*

Stoli read the brass plate on the back of the weathered bench: In Loving Memory of Athel Dillon "Brad" Houston and Faith Ann "Bunny" Kreiner. He grunted in acknowledgment and hefted the weathered bench aside. He took a hand spade out of his pocket and, yanking handfuls of grass from of the soil, he quickly dug down about two feet before he hit a green marble box wrapped in tattered plastic. He was about to crack the seal when he stopped, weighed it with his hands, and glanced at the brass plate on the bench.

"Oh . . . Athel and Faith. Pardon. Not what I'm here for."

He set the box aside and sank the hand spade down another foot or so before it hit the top of a plastic detergent canister wrapped in garbage bags and duct tape. It took him a few minutes to unbury it. Pulling out his pocketknife, Stoli quickly cut through the disintegrating plastic and tape and ripped off the top of the canister. He was in a sort of frenzy now, sweating, filthy. He dumped the contents of the plastic tub out: a taped plastic brick, something triangular wrapped in a white garbage bag and a silver flask with Kurt engraved on it. He went straight for what could only be the money. He cut open the brick and held stacks of hundreds in his shaking hands. *Unbelievable.* He looked around. Nobody—no neighbors—paid Stoli any mind, just Joplin, at eye level in the second-story bedroom window of the house. He tossed the money back into the bucket, then ripped open the white plastic bag, which held the red vinyl gun case. He unzipped the case far enough to see a gun handle, then threw it in the tub, followed by the flask.

He stopped and took a breath.

It was all real.

A reincarnated criminal stuck in the body of a child had told him where to find buried treasure. He found the treasure. *Hold it—reincarnation is real? The universe isn't really a nihilistic void without meaning?* Even as he was bulldozing the dirt back into the hole with his arms, he felt the urge to vomit—so he let himself do so and covered it over. He replaced my parents' rectangular green marble urn into the hole and buried it, and dragged back the old weathered bench. He felt time was running out. With the plastic tub under his arm, he scrambled madly down the hill, skidding, slipping, and almost falling on the crumbling wooden steps.

When he got to the side yard gate he was panting. Muddy rivulets of sweat and tears ran down his red face. His button-down was in ruins, the knees of his khakis soiled, his head abuzz with the swarm of questions that now had answers. Deep from somewhere, he found the presence of mind to shut the panic off, like an actor about to go on stage subduing his butterflies. He took a breath. Anybody could be on the other side of the fence. The big blond lady could suddenly pull into the driveway; a neighbor could be out in their yard; the police could be pulling up. The best exit was to walk quietly through the gate and make a relaxed beeline to the car like nothing was amiss. So, wiping his eyes with his sleeve, he nestled the plastic detergent container of money under his arm, unlatched the gate and . . . strode through.

No car in the driveway, no one approaching. He walked calmly with the bucket, put it in the trunk, got in the car, and drove away.

This was two years before that fateful dinner at my parents' house, and it changed his life. He was now afraid of nothing except perhaps the infinite possibility of existence. The PTSD was gone and he hadn't been on medication for a month. Within a year, he'd be able to drink alcohol again without the urge to guzzle until his consciousness was erased. Loud noises didn't juice his adrenaline. He could sit at a restaurant without his back against the wall. He was, in a sense, born again—via the *fact* of a hereafter, not the faith of a false heaven. All these things he later told me.

But let's go back to that night in our living room.

That night when Stoli/John met the Harrises in Campbell, he convinced Drew and Lou about the viability of his business plan. By the time he left, Drew had agreed to meet Stoli/John up in San Francisco that next Saturday to check out the commercial space he'd just put a deposit on.

"Hell, bring the whole family and we'll make a day of it up in the City," he said, eyeing me. "Would you like to see San Francisco, Keenan?"

I was nearly breathless at the thought. "Yessir!"

My mom chuckled at my enthusiasm. "Look who wants to see the big city."

I let Drew lift me into his arms as Lou opened the door for Stoli, who was in the process of putting on his jacket. Stoli pulled a business card from the inside pocket. "So, I'll email you the address and you guys can meet me up there . . . say . . . noon?"

Drew and Lou paused. A feeling of *is this really happening*? made them both dumbstruck. Stoli stood in the doorway, understanding.

He said, "Look, I know all this is weird and happening so fast. I mean, you don't know who the hell I am, not really. If you haven't, look me up on the Internet. But what I do know is—" He nodded at Drew. "—is *talent* when I see it. The microbrew business is cutthroat in the Bay Area and someone is going to snap you up, Drew, if I don't. So I'm just asking you all to consider my ideas, and meet me at this space I'm renting. Worst that could happen is you get a free lunch and Keenan can see the big city."

Drew pursed his lips and looked at Lou. "I'm in. How about you?"

"Why not?" Lou agreed.

"Can I have your card, too, Uncle John?" I asked in my sweetest kid voice.

Lou looked at me. "Uncle John?"

"It's okay," he said. "Here."

I grabbed Stoli's card.

"For his Rolodex," Lou said.

"Ha! Rolodex," Drew said. "Keenan will never know a world with Rolodexes."

"Uncle John," Stoli repeated. He tousled my hair and winked at me. "Yep. Never again." He shook Drew's hand and gave Lou a slight hug. "Well, until Saturday. I'll send you the address. Look over the business plan. We can sort out any details then. Drew, I'd really like to work with you. I think we can build a great brewery."

"I feel good about it. I hope I'm up to the task."

"You'll be fine." He gazed at all of us. "Bye now."

"Bye," the parents said.

They closed the door behind him, and we all looked at each other excitedly. They embraced, sandwiching me between them.

Drew was elated. "Can you believe it?"

Lou was pleased but wary. "It sounds almost too good to be true. I hope he's not a crackpot."

"He does seem a little wacky, but I like him. I looked him up online and his story checks out. What do you think, Keen?"

"He's okay," I replied. His business card safely in my hand, I felt rescued.

19. Old Haunts

"This is it, Keenan," Drew said. "San Francisco. The big, scary city."

Imagine my surprise when I found myself back in San Francisco. I lowered the window and let in that air—crisp air, fog burning off, complex tapestry of sounds and smells, cars, exhaust, ocean, street food, Chinese bakery. We were where the Mission meets the SoMa, and I had a prescient feeling about where we were headed as we cruised down Harrison toward Eleventh Street.

"It's not scary," I said.

There was a lump in my throat. Somewhere within San Francisco's seven-by-seven-mile expanse could be found my sister, Rae; could be found Franks, still a drug dealer, I assumed. Somewhere on the San Francisco streets and in the neighborhoods around me were elements of my old life, theaters I had performed in, bars I'd drunk in, buildings I'd worked in; women I'd made love to, musicians I'd jammed with, friends I'd laughed with; hearts broken, messes left behind, promises laid to waste.

I felt sorry for Kurt Houston. What a chump.

Lou turned around in her seat, tilted her head at me. "If it's not so scary, why do you have that look on your face."

I shrugged. *Big boys don't cry.*

Drew parked the car at a meter, and I unclipped the belt and knelt on the seat, head swiveling. Across the street, Stoli stood in front of what used to be the Twenty Tank Brewery. *I knew it!* It was an old haunt of mine. Because . . . this was how the fate thing worked. This was how destiny rolled out.

I'd spent a good portion of the 1990s in this exact neighborhood, sauced and stumbling from the Twenty Tank Brewery to Paradise Lounge to Slim's to the DNA. Streets crowded with grunge-era twenty-somethings, adorned in supercool thrift clothes, hipster leather, vintage boots, piercings and tats galore. Soon after that, the hipsters switched to zoot suits and the swing music revival. Finally, the soulless real estate grab of the dotcom boom gutted this neighborhood—not unlike my own soulless real estate avarice following the great recession.

After worrying over the parking meter for way too long, Drew led us across Eleventh Street, Lou's hand in his, my hand in Lou's. Stoli, all smiles and dressed casually in jeans and a blue short-sleeved button-down, met us in front of the boarded-up windows and chained doors. He had bags of Chinese takeout in his arms.

"Greetings!" Stoli hailed us, setting the takeout on the sidewalk. He shook hands with the grups and put his paw on my head, giving me a wink. "Welcome to the big city, Keenan. What do you think?"

"It smells." Laughter at my deadpan.

He turned and made a dramatic gesture at the face of the old building.

"I present to you the future home of Eleventh Street Brewery."

"Impressive, John," Lou said. "What was here before?"

"Well, it was built in the 1930s. It was a machine shop for a long time, then, oddly enough, it *was* a brewpub in the '90s." He fished through a ring of keys and unlocked the padlock. He accordioned the creaky gates apart, exposing plywood-paneled doors defaced with graffiti scrawls and the tattered paper and rusty-staple detritus of band advertisements and lost dogs.

"Eleventh Street Brewery," Drew repeated. "Great name! Any of the old equipment left?"

Stoli turned another key in a dead bolt and pulled the handle, explaining, "There's no actual brewing equipment as far as I can tell, but it still has industrial water, power, and ventilation. The electrical is wired for heavy machinery and there are two silo-looking-things on the roof—you'll have to tell me." He ushered us inside.

The place was cleared of all that had been the old brewery. Now it was all dusty cement floors with industrial carpets rolled up against the wall and a large pile of scrap wood and disassembled cubicle walls. Beer cans and food wrappers eddied in the corners. The kitchen counter and long wooden bar were no more. But the high windows and skylights let in a comforting diffused light, and the stairs to the second level mezzanine were still intact.

In the center of the room, Stoli had set up a card table and four folding chairs. He put the takeout on the table and three gift-wrapped boxes.

Lou whistled. "Eleventh Street Brewery."

Drew's face worked as he designed the brewpub in his mind. "This is fantastic, John."

"Thanks. The possibilities are endless." Stoli took a chair at the table and started to unpack food containers from the bags. "Hope Chinese is okay."

"That's perfect," Drew said.

I tugged on Lou's hand. "I'm going to go look around."

"Alright. Don't step on a nail or something."

I was off, up the stairs like a shot. I stopped at the top. *How many times had I climbed these stairs?*

A little while later, as we finished our meal, Stoli presented us with the wrapped boxes. The first two, for Lou and Drew, were new phones.

"John . . ." Drew protested.

"Stop. This is business. In fact, these are company phones. Of course, you can use them however you like, but I'm going to need to be in touch with you, and you are going to need to be in touch with each other," Stoli explained. "The corporation I've set up around the brewpub is covering the tab for the phone bill."

Inside my gift box was a new tablet.

Lou gestured toward my gift. "But . . . *really?*"

"He's going to have to have something to do around here . . . unless you can afford a babysitter."

She sighed. "What do you say, Keenan?"

"Thanks, Uncle John!"

It was a high-end tablet with its own cellular provider and Wi-Fi.

John said, "As an actual uncle, I long ago learned that when bringing gifts for one, bring gifts for all. It cuts down on the tears," he added with a wink. In fact, the whole gift-giving exercise was really a ploy to get some technology to me so he and I could communicate directly.

"John, I don't know what to say," Drew said, sitting back in his folding chair.

"Say you'll help me open up a brewpub. I can hardly do it myself . . . and I already signed a five-year lease."

Drew shrugged at Lou. She said impatiently, "For chrissake, Drew." She smiled at Stoli. "Of course he'll take the job, John."

"I'll take the job, John," Drew repeated. "When do we start?"

"That's the spirit!" Stoli patted my head. "What do you think, Keenan? Feel like visiting San Francisco once in a while?"

I was already absorbed in my tablet. I looked up and said, "I like your plan. Thanks, Uncle John."

!!!

I had to hand it to Stoli. He'd really outdone himself.

When the Harrises got home from that trip to San Francisco, I retired to my bedroom while Lou and Drew celebrated with a cheap bottle of champagne. The new tablet was a stroke of genius because it set me up with not only a real web browser, instant messaging, and email—it was hooked up to a credit card. It was all outlined in an email waiting for me:

Greetings, Elf!

Hope all of this isn't too much of a shock. I feel so indebted to you that it has been hard to contain myself. Sorry it took me so long to find you—it's really not as easy as you would think. All I had was your name, so I had to hire a private detective. Anyhow, it took some brainstorming to think up my brewpub angle, but one of the things the private eye uncovered was all the brewing equipment your father had acquired on his credit card statements. Then the brew contest happened and everything fell into place. That said, I fully plan to open up a brewpub so that I have something to do in my retirement. I like your parents very much. And Lou! What a looker, huh, kid? Sorry if that's weird.

So now we have email. Remember, video chat. My number is in the contacts. Also, plug the credit card information into the payment app of your choice. The card is attached to one of my accounts so the limit is very high. Don't go too crazy! I realized you might be fettered in your search without access to money. Hope it helps.

Now, I'm not so hot on revenge, but it's not every day a guy has the chance to bring his own murderer to justice, so I'll do what I can for you. If you give me his name and any information you have on him, I'll sic my PI on him, get his whereabouts, and we can devise a plan from there. What do you have in mind?

I guess that's all for now. My final question is this: are you going to keep your previous identity secret forever?

Yours, Stoli

!!!

I had this strange feeling. It took me a while to pinpoint it: *Camaraderie.*

I finally had a connection with someone in this new life to whom I could tell all. Someone who wouldn't lose his mind (already lost) or cart me off to a lab for tests. I reread his message several times. There wasn't a shred of doubt. He was committed—in all the ways you could possibly mean by that word.

I hit Reply and began to compose my first email to stolisoldier69:

Dear Stoli,

The man we're looking for is named Franklin Franklin O'Donnell. Also find information on Dolores "Dolly" Velasquez, Bartholomew Montgomery, Steven "Poindexter" Hightower, and August Williams . . .

PART 4 - KURT

TIMESTAMP=2032-07-17T:09:16:53-10:48:11Z

20. Franks

One of Franks's early side jobs was as a part-time taxi driver. This was highly convenient for everyone involved: me, him, our crew, our clients. I was about a year into my final career when Franks began to express a growing streak of individualism.

By now I was well settled in the Potrero Hill house. While the initial appraisal was crooked, the mortgage itself was probably the only fully legal one I'd ever brokered (short term, fixed).

Seven Hills Brokerage was no more. By that, I mean the office. As the drug business increased, disseminating illegal product out of what was essentially a storefront was a bust waiting to happen. It was difficult to fully vet the foot traffic and run the cover business at the same time. A mix of legitimate brokerage customers and profligate pleasure seekers would show up at the office at the same time, at an office rife with vice, loud music, pot smoke, an ever-hissing nitrous tank, liquor, and Internet porn. Not that some of the legit customers wouldn't turn to the dark side once on the premises, but it was getting too risky, so I closed the doors of my firm and took the drug business incognito.

Dolly soon became my so-called girlfriend. She didn't really like the term, and I didn't really like the feeling that she was always doing something behind the scenes. She had become something like my gangster moll, and like all gangster molls, she politicked within her position of power. On this particular evening, Dolly and I had been on a marathon screw, taking breaks only to drink more whiskey and snort more coke. Then Franks came over, all fired up.

I had my personal hours and professional hours. My professional hours were eleven in the morning to two o'clock in the afternoon and five o'clock in the afternoon to eleven o'clock at night. No exceptions. I wasn't the sort of dealer you could call up at three o'clock in the morning and beg for an audience. If you did that, you were out. As far as Franks and the gang went, they had leeway, but you had better have an excuse. And they always did. This schedule was something I got from Hobson—he stayed clear of major police entanglements with this protocol for his entire career, so I figured it was a good practice.

On this particular evening, Franks showed up at midnight, obviously hopped up and ready to lay out what he considered yet another grand business opportunity. Outraged that I'd been disturbed, I wrapped a tattered couch throw around my waist and answered the door, still glistening from the sweat of sport-fucking my so-called girlfriend. I wrenched the door open with surly impatience and glowered at him. He wore a black leather blazer and had aviator glasses tucked back on his head over that greasy mop. His forehead was beaded with sweat but it was sixty degrees and breezy.

"Goddamn it, Franks. What?" I growled when I swung open the door, half-blocking the view into the foyer. Dolly was just around the corner on the couch (the same couch where I died), freshly laid and smoking a cigarette. I looked him up and down and rolled my eyes. "Oh, Jesus."

"Hey, man," he said. "Can I speak with you a second 'bout somethin', Kurt." He tried to look past me; I blocked him with my body.

I glowered some more. "It's fucking midnight and you already re-upped." I narrowed my eyes at him. "Don't tell me you already sold out."

Franks paused for a second. His brogue was a bit choked by all the gear he was on. "Actually, I'm nearly through with it, yeah. I have these frat guys who hit me up every week. It gave me an idea. Can I come in?"

I looked over my shoulder at Dolly lying wantonly on the couch, legs still glistening. Her silky brown-black hair fell about her breasts. My cat, Joplin, who perversely enjoyed watching us have sex, huddled next to the gas fireplace, eyes half lidded. "Hey, Doll, cover up. Franks is here."

She scowled and hissed, "What? What the hell? It's like after twelve." I sighed and shrugged at her. "Goddamn it." She snorted the line on the mirror, swept up all the accouterments, and disappeared into the other room.

I looked back at Franks. "Alright, jackass. Five minutes." I led him into the living room. The couch leather was still dewy with sex. I picked up the cigarette I'd left in the ashtray and quickly tossed Dolly's panties behind the couch. The door closed behind Franks.

"Where's Dolly?" He detected the aftermath of something in the room.

"Dolly? What makes you think it was Dolly?" A musky smell permeated. Breakbeat issued from the stereo; I turned the volume down with my phone. Franks sat down casually next to me and shook out a cigarette. He also plopped a wad of bills on the coffee table. I looked at it. Not bad.

"Check this out, man. I usually don't make that much until about three in the morning." He paused for effect, billowing Camel smoke. "The dorm gauntlet is really kicking."

Joplin crept up to Franks and put a scratchy-but-friendly paw on his pant leg. *Traitor.* Franks, who was acquainted with Jops, pulled on her ears and smiled. "Ah, Joplin, ya fuckin' minx, ya."

"Franks!" I barked, bringing him back to the conversation. "What the fuck is the *dorm gauntlet*?"

"That's what I wanted to talk about. I think we have an opportunity."

What he didn't know was that I was about to tear him a new asshole, but I thought it'd be prudent to listen to him on the off chance that a marginally intelligent idea might issue from his mealy lips. I said magnanimously, "Continue."

"See, I been working this college gauntlet: Hastings Law School, USF, Academy of Art, and SF State. They fucking love our product and have been spreading the news. Every week it's been growing." He stood up importantly, crossed toward the fireplace, and turned to look at me to see if I was excited. I feigned interest. He was in full salesman mode. "For the last month, the buys have been growing. I dealt just two ounces three weeks ago and by tonight, this weekend, I sold over four ounces in just the last two days. But see, these're all momma's boys 'n' girls getting checks from their folks so their money runs out for a wee time . . . *until they get their next check*." He was getting worked up, even though he was mostly acting, and he stopped dramatically to crush his cigarette and light another. He threw his jacket on the floor and again waited for me to react. This was his idea of oration.

"Continue."

"So, see, look, they're going to be out of money next week, as I see it, and they will want more—hell, they said so." He sat down next to me. "The taxi business is going great, man. Sweet cover, like. The key is, Uber drivers are controlled by the mainframe, cab drivers are freebooters on the hunt. They call me, flag me, I come by. I figure if we up the ante and spot 'em credit sometimes, we'll really dig them in. And I drive it to 'em like a fucking service, man."

"Did you just say 'freebooters'?"

"It's an expression! A fucking taxi service with credit, and we can expand a little and deliver to more than just the frat boys and sorority girls. They already do it with pot. We can expand and make some real fuckin' dough, man. Maybe get in with another driver. I know a DJ who works for Yellow who'd be in for a little extra business."

"So let me get this straight: you're dealing en masse to a bunch of college students and you're delivering on call for all your clients. So, are you using Paypal or Square or something?"

Franks was wide-eyed. "That's a *great* fucking idea, man! Maybe we should make an app! I mean, like a secure one, you know." He put his dirty sneakers on my glass coffee table.

I put on a smile, stood up, and grabbed the wad of drug money from the table, weighing it in my hand, nodding in appreciation. Then I threw it at him, hard, in the face. He recoiled with a yelp. Joplin darted off out of the room. Franks looked small on the couch.

I said, "Here . . . you might need this to post bail."

"What?"

"What the *fuck* are you thinking, you idiot? Don't you know that college students are the biggest possible risk you can take in this business?"

"What?" He was blindsided.

My words were articulated with controlled anger. "College students are stupid as fuck. And reckless. And undependable. They're always scared, and they'll drop dime on you without a second thought."

"Kurt—"

I stepped forward and kicked his feet from my coffee table.

"Don't fucking 'Kurt' me, Franks. And keep your fucking feet off my fucking table. You're riding around in your cab giving out your phone number to anyone with a cell phone, a C-note, and a straw. Do you *want* to get busted? Do you want *me* to get busted?!"

"No, I—"

"The first customers that get popped in this business are college students, and they'll rat on anyone so their parents won't find out—so their *school* won't find out. And now your cell number has probably been texted to a hundred phones with the slogan, 'Call City Cab for Killer Coke.' And what happens at dispatch when your fare miles don't match up to how much money you're handing in? You think you're the first Mick asshole driving a cab to think that dealing curbside is a *grand* idea?!" By now my voice had risen forty decibels. Dolly suddenly appeared in a green silk kimono.

She said, "What did you do now, Frankie?"

Franks looked up and turned red. "Shut it, Dulce."

Dulce?!

I rushed him and kicked his legs. "No, *you* shut it, Franks," I hissed. "Now, take your fucking cash roll and finish the rest of your shift and get a new burner phone tomorrow. *Tomorrow*, you dumb dirty-cuff fucking tinker. Cool it on your fucking coeds and stick to our regular clients, you know, the rich ones who aren't beholden to anybody and give us most of our money."

Dolly wheezed out a sigh. "Shit." She turned on her heels and left the room.

There was a long silence. Franks stood up somberly. "Sorry, Kurt, I thought it *was* a *grand* idea."

"Leave the thinking to me, Franks, and just run product. I don't want to be talking to any lawyers or bail bondsmen anytime soon. *Shit.*" I couldn't look at him anymore.

He made toward the door, then stopped. "Kurt . . . hate to ask, but I still need to re-up."

I sat down and lit a cigarette. "Goddammit."

21. Broke Badly

Looking back, I have to admit that my twisted health consciousness did indeed stave off the damage my party warrior habits were inflicting upon my body. I liked sweating out the toxins, but in the end, I was really only concerned with looking good.

Yes, it may seem a little contradictory, perhaps antithetical, for a drug-addicted alcoholic to pursue a health regimen, but even when my brain wasn't twisted by the effects of my daily—hell, *hourly*—habits, I still exercised on a semireligious basis, rain or shine, hungover or not. The impulse to work out was a vanity instilled by my (first) mother. That was the truth of it, and I'm sure I'm hardly alone on this: working out was for looking good, not health. As far as I was concerned, any positive health effects were coincidental—*gravy*—an unintended consequence to be disregarded as soon as another binge was due.

One chilly spring afternoon workout, Franks paid me a visit. Bart held the focus mitts as I drilled. I was also drinking beer and high on coke, sweat gushing from every pore. Bart, while no boxer himself, had learned by now how to hold the mitts and call out the hits, shouting "One-two-five! One-one-two! One-four-kick!" and I'd smack them out in rapid-fire succession. A plastic BOB punching bag, a freestanding rubber mannequin with a water-filled base, sat in the corner, always ready to take a kick to the face. I'd returned to kickboxing to channel a daily growing anger that had crept into my life. I realize now that the anger coincided with my daily use of cocaine. Funny, that.

Franks showed himself in through the side door. "Hey, tough guy," he said, careful to strip the irony from his voice.

I turned and nodded, gasping for breath. "To what do I owe this great honor, Franks?"

"Three, four, five, six," Bart called.

I smacked them out.

"Need to talk to you about a predicament."

"One, two, left and right kick."

"How unusual for you."

Smack, smack, smack, smack.

"Can you give me a sec?"

"Left, right knees and elbows."

I smacked them out, then stopped, reaching for my beer and the towel.

"Franks, I'm in the middle of a workout."

"Well, I—"

"I have an idea—why don't *you* hold the mitts?"

God, I was a prick. Bart took off the mitts and helped Franks put them on.

"I've never—"

Bart was helpful, even as he withheld his grin. "Just call out the hits: one and two are straight punches, three and four are hooks, five and six are uppercuts. Left kick, right kick, et cetera. Hold your arms taut, like this, and turn to meet the hooks and uppercuts." Bart showed him and I turned to Franks. My chemical heart pounded out of my chest.

"Okay . . . one, two, three—"

I didn't let him finish because this exercise was now about

intimidation. I rattled off three rapid-fire punches as hard as I could. Alarmed and flustered, Franks's mitted hands flew akimbo and he took a few steps back. "Shit, man!"

"Jesus. Be ready. Now what's your problem today, my Irish friend?"

"Well, you know that guy—"

"Call out the hits."

"What? Oh, um, three, four, five."

I smacked them out a little slower so Franks could get the hang of it.

"Which guy?"

"The young guy up near Parnassus. You met him once."

"Yeah, Clint or Clay or Cunt or some shit."

"That's the guy. *Clay*."

"Call 'em out.

"One, two . . . five, six?"

I rattled them off, putting a little extra effort into the last uppercut. Franks reeled back; he'd had it.

"Goddamnit, Kurt! Let's just fucking talk and stop this shit. This is serious."

I backed off without smiling, pulling off my gloves and throwing them on the mat. "Jesus, Franks. Hold on." I mopped up more sweat with the towel and went over to the fridge to fetch us all a beer. Bart smoked on the other side of the garage, texting into his phone. "Bart." I tossed him a beer.

I handed Franks a beer and sat down with a smoke. "Alright. So, what's the trouble?"

Franks sighed. "Finally. Shit. Okay. So, I fronted Clay a few ounces and he's dodging me now."

I thought about this. "Not really my problem."

"I knew you were going to say that. But you see, he's been pretty fucking cheeky about the whole thing and he threatened to turn us in if I put any more pressure on him."

"Threatened *us*? You mean he mentioned my *name*?"

"Yeah. He said if I don't back off and give him some more time, he'd drop dime on me, you—the whole deal."

I shot a dark glance at Bart.

"Motherfucker," I muttered.

I stood up, stepped over to Bob the punching dummy and gave him three quick roundhouses to the head. Franks sipped his beer calmly.

"How much does he owe you?" I asked.

"About five grand."

"Hmm. Well, can't have our street levels thinking they have leverage on us. Especially white-bread twentysomething trust funders with a misguided sense of entitlement."

"We should pay him a courtesy call," Bart said.

"Parnassus, huh?" I asked.

"Mm hm. Willard Street," Franks said. His face held both fear and relief.

"Does he live alone or with roommates?"

"He's on his own."

"Good. Okay. Franks, have your guy Poins stake him out to see when he leaves. We'll be waiting for him when he returns."

"What do you have in mind?"

"Put the fear of death into him—hopefully without any actual violence." I thought of something. "What kind of car does he drive?" Bart laughed.

Franks thought about this a second. "I think he drives a Saab. New."

"Shit, that should more than cover our inconvenience."

Bart and I watched Franks, who did nothing.

"Well, what the fuck are you waiting for?"

Franks was surprised. "What? Right *now*?"

"Yeah, *right now*. I intend to talk to him personally. It's not going to take care of itself. Let's shake this motherfucker down and be done with it. Don't you want your money?"

"Um . . . alright . . ." It was all happening too fast.

!!!

Clay Thornton was a twenty-nine-year-old trust funder slowly making his way through nursing school at UCSF, as well as his trust fund. One of Franks's first customers, he had upgraded to low-level dealer, no doubt so he could get his own supply for free, become popular, and pocket a little extra cash. I remember meeting him at a party I'd thrown the previous summer. He had seemed nice enough back then, but spoke too familiarly, a little too arrogant, thinking he was somehow *in* with the big boys.

Franks gave us a call the next day as Clay was seen leaving his apartment building with a book bag, probably going to study, to class, or to make a deal. Bart drove us over to Clay's in his souped-up Subaru WRX.

Bart was valuable for a variety of reasons, the best of which (besides his loyalty) was his second-story ability. He could break into just about any building, through door or window. Parking down the street, we met Franks at a Muni stop across from an Art Deco-style building. His man Poindexter was with him, dressed in a navy-blue hoodie, making him look a bit out of place in this gentrified neck of the woods.

"Hey, Poins, you might want to lose the hoodie. Wrong neighborhood."

Poindexter looked at Franks, who nodded at him. Down came the hood. Franks's outfit wasn't much better: a bright orange oversized Giants jersey. Franks saw me eyeing his shirt.

"What?"

I tilted my head and said, "Nothing. What apartment is he in?"

"301."

"Is there an elevator?"

"Yeah."

I turned to Bart. "Take the stairs. Text me when you're inside." He quickly crossed the street.

"Bart will have us inside in a jiff."

I lit a cigarette, hoping a bus didn't come and mistake us for riders. Poindexter and I clearly didn't like each other. If Franks felt the need for a henchman, the henchman should at least make the effort to make me comfortable. Poins didn't like me because Franks painted me as a petty tyrant. By this time, Franks was more right than wrong.

"Is your real name Poindexter?"

This might have been the first time I'd addressed him personally, and he glanced at Franks, then at me. "No," he replied.

"How'd you get it?"

"Because I'm smart," he said without any hint of irony. I had underestimated him, read him wrong. Poins had a cover of sorts. He continued, "You called me Poins."

"Yeah," I answered.

"Henry IV."

Holy fuck. That *was* smart, and he'd been waiting to show me. All this time.

"Not bad."

"The question is, man," he continued, "are you Prince Hal or Falstaff?"

Franks cut in, "What the fuck are youse all on about?"

I said to Poins, "Well, clearly, Franks here is no Prince Hal."

Poindexter was smart enough to drop the conversation, shrugging dismissively.

That made me wonder why he had partnered with Franks. But that was simple, too. Franks was an opportunity maker; he was an opener . . . even if his closing abilities were wanting. My phone vibrated.

Bart texted: "I'm in. Take stairs. Knock three times. There's a dog. But it's okay."

Franks and Poindexter looked at me expectantly.

I grumbled, "There's a fucking *dog*, Franks?"

"What? Up there? I didn't know, man."

"You could fill a book with what you don't know. We're taking the stairs."

We crossed the street and entered through the building's front door, left propped open with a rolled-up newspaper. Franks and Poindexter flanked me at apartment 301, and I knocked softly three times. There was a muffled yap of a dog on the other side of the door. Franks winced as Bart quickly let us inside.

An excited Chihuahua bounced up and down, panting happily. I knelt down to pet him while making shushing sounds.

Bart said, "Coast is clear."

Cradling the dog, I reminded them, "You know what to do."

The boys scrambled to their respective duties. I handed the happy dog to Franks. "Here you go, dumbass."

!!!

Clay was whistling when he got home. That stopped when he flicked on the light and was confronted by Franks, Bart, and myself, relaxing in the living room of his Art Deco one-bedroom. Franks petted the docile Chihuahua, who licked the Irishman's face.

"Hi, Clay," Franks greeted him.

Alarmed, Clay backed up into the hallway, only to be met by Poindexter, who menaced Clay back into the living room.

Not quite catching the gravity of his situation, Clay said loudly, "What kind of *Pulp Fiction* bullshit is th—"

As instructed, Poindexter executed a double ear-slap on Clay, stunning him. A full six inches shorter than Clay, Poindexter quickly grappled him into a sleeper hold, rendering the poor kid temporarily unconscious as he slumped to the floor.

Clay's little dog licked his master into consciousness a minute later. Nine Inch Nails blared from Clay's stereo, and we all availed ourselves of his well-stocked liquor cabinet. We'd draped him across the Ikea couch, and when he finally came to, he found me sitting in a folding chair across from him, drinking his booze. Poindexter was cozied up next to him, Bart blocked the hallway, and Franks smoked in the kitchen while eating a sandwich. Clay pushed the dog off, and it bounded off the couch and darted toward Franks, who caught him in his free arm.

Clay went from groggy to panic in one second.

"Hey, wait . . . wait—"

"Shhhh," I soothed. "All is not lost, Clay. You just happened to piss us off. I bet your throat is dry. Want some water?"

He accepted the cup of water from me and sipped it. I took it back. About to begin his arguments, his explanations, his et ceteras, I cut him off.

"Thirty-year-old single malt, Clay. *Classy.*" I paused. "Before you start with your . . . *rebuttals*, let me flesh out your predicament for you." I sipped the scotch. "Now . . . we found your stash of blow . . . and your pot and your ecstasy. We also found your big ol' Smith and Wesson. Nice fucking gun. You were gone a long time, so we also copied your personal contacts from your computer. Obviously, we found your liquor." The boys raised to that. "On top of that, we got your social security number and your bank account number. Next time, don't keep your password on a Post-it on your computer screen. *Jesus.*"

He said nothing, unable to believe what was happening to him. Appropriately, Trent Reznor filled the room with his screeching rhythmic angst.

"Clay?"

"I have your three grand," he said, staring at the ground.

I nodded, slowly turning my gaze to Franks.

"*Three* grand?"

Franks didn't miss a beat as he stuffed half the sandwich into his mouth. "Interest."

I maintained a cinematic placidity. "Well, that's a good start, Clay. But even if it was *two* grand, you shouldn't make threats to people like us. It makes us grumpy." My boys all nodded at this. Poindexter smiled and put a friendly arm menacingly around Clay's shoulder.

Clay didn't say anything, so I helped him out.

"Where's the money, Clay?"

"In my backpack."

"Bart?"

Bart retrieved the backpack where it had fallen on the floor and rifled through it.

"It's in the inner pocket," Clay told him.

Bart pulled out a wad of twenties and counted it.

"Now that wasn't so bad, was it, Clay? Why didn't you just tell Franks to give you a couple more days?"

"I did!"

"No, you fucking didn't, you fucking fuck ya!" Franks suddenly burst.

"I told you to wait!" Clay whined.

"Ah," I broke in. "*You* don't tell *us* anything. Now why did you threaten us?"

"I was kidding."

And that's when I turned. That's when I turned a corner that I *still* wonder about. I leaned over in the chair I was sitting on and punched Clay in the face. It was so fast, it stunned everyone, including me. It was a jab, no big deal, but it split his lip. Clay honked this whiny, moany "Owwwww!"

I shot up. "You fucking bitch." I went to the kitchen for paper towels.

I passed Franks, who was also stunned, half-eaten sandwich frozen in his hand. Bart nodded appreciatively from the foyer. Poins, who sat next to Clay on the couch barely reacted at all, stone-faced.

I threw the paper towels at Clay. "Please shut up." I paced the room, lighting another cigarette, pouring myself more scotch. I retook the chair across from Clay. Tears slicked his face, and the paper towel was soaking red.

"This is what we're going to do. We got some of our money back. We're going to take your gun. Sorry about that, but it seems stupid to leave you with it. We're also going to take half your ecstasy. Haven't done it in a while—love the stuff. I was going to take your Saab, but I only drive American. We'll leave you with the rest of your stash so you can stay afloat. What's your dog's name?"

Confusion on Clay's face, then, "Gypsy."

"You can keep Gypsy. Shitty watchdog."

I downed the rest of the scotch, signaling the boys with a head gesture toward the front door. Franks finished the rest of his sandwich and he and Poins joined Bart in the foyer, leaving me standing over Clay, crumpled like a wounded bird on the couch.

I continued, "Now, I don't really have any hard feelings anymore. So if you want to keep on with us, you can talk to Franks about it. If you want to quit, no harm, no foul. But just don't get any weird ideas. We all know where you live, who you hang out with, and what your dog looks like. Are we clear?"

He nodded.

"Yeah?"

"Yeah."

"Gentlemen?"

Poindexter opened the door with care and waited outside in the hall. Franks let go of the dog, who made a beeline to Clay, who sat there trembling, staring at his knees. Bart followed the others with a jacket full of dope and a soft nylon case with Clay's .357 magnum.

I backed out toward the hallway and said, "Breathe easy, Clay. You survived. You just gotta be a little more respectful of your elders." He glanced up at me, then quickly returned to staring at his knees. Gypsy licked the salty tears on his face.

I closed the door and pointed down the hall. "We'll take the elevator, like civilized people."

"Think that's the last we'll hear from him?" Bart asked.

"I don't know. What do you think, Franks?"

"I wouldn't be surprised if he gives me a call. He likes Charlie too much to just go cold turkey, even if we did just put the fear of God into him."

When the elevator doors closed, I hit the STOP button and got all up in Franks's face.

"Look, dumbass," I hissed. Poindexter, alarmed, took a step toward me, Bart took a step toward him. It was all very tense inside that little elevator. I turned to Poins, towering over him.

"Back off, Poins. This is a supervisory meeting, and you'll quickly find out I'm not some pussy old white guy." I turned to Bart and said, "Relax." I returned my attention to Franks, who was handling the tension better than the other two. He just wanted me to finish my reprimand so he could go get a beer—like a teenager letting a parental scolding wash over him. I grabbed his jacket and backed him up against the elevator wall.

"Look, Franks, I can only guess why you didn't handle that yourself, but neither scenario is very cool. Either you were testing me or you're a real pussy. Well, you got your test, and now you look like a real fucking pussy." I restarted the elevator. "You knew I wouldn't come over here for anything less than five grand. Nice play. Now fuck off."

I let him go just as the doors parted. An Asian woman in surgical scrubs waited outside the door, surprised to find four sketchy-looking men emerging from within.

"Excuse me, ma'am." I pushed past her, my gang following closely.

I realize now I didn't visit Clay to protect my business, but rather to look tough in front of my minions, who needed reminding who was boss. What was worse than actually playing the heavy with Clay was believing I really *was* a kingpin, greedy to retain my power.

22. *Kurt Gets a Taste*

It was the kickboxing. It was the age. It was the peculiar state of health I maintained, with the whiskey, coke, and Cobb salads. In my increasingly delusional headspace, all this seemed to balance out, damage and repair, damnation and repentance.

Something had to give, and it happened to be a disc in my vertebrae.

I was temporarily confined to my place on Potrero Hill during the summer of my discontent. Outside on the veranda, I'd made a sort of desk on a tray table in front of my sickbed, a vintage chaise longue. I surrounded myself with pills, raw vegetables, a Bloody Mary, a wheatgrass shake, cigarettes, a poached egg, a 9mm pistol, cocaine, a laptop, and a *Men's Health* magazine. Dolly, in nothing but a loose silky robe, perfect breasts poking skyward, sat across my thighs, rocking back and forth to LCD Soundsystem, kneading my flaccid penis as she offered me a drag off her joint. I waved her off. I was on the phone with Bart.

"Yeah, well thanks for the sympathy, Bart. And by the way . . . *I blame you.*"

I lit a cigarette and sipped my wheatgrass, chasing it with the Bloody Mary.

"Yeah," I explained to him, "you weren't paying attention with the mitts and I overextended. Huh? Well, that's exactly what I'm saying: that's what you always do, and it finally ended up with me throwing my back out. *Dick.*"

Speaking of dick. You'd think with someone as hot as Dolly, she'd at least get a halfie out of me. She fondled my lifeless appendage, simultaneously exhaling pot smoke, then snorting blow off her fingernail. She was talented.

"I'm laid up on the veranda," I continued to Bart. "Dolly's doing her nurse thing. But even the Percocet isn't cutting it. I'm dying here." I eyed the powder on the mirror. "Also, I'm bored as fuck. All you guys are running around making me money and I'm stranded here and can't move." The poached egg was cold, so I threw down a vitamin supplement, chasing it with the wheatgrass shake. "How bad? Well, I can't walk. I can't even get a hard-on. What? Fuck you, it's the meds. Anyhow, I'm waiting for a call from Franks. He says he's got something better than Percocet . . . I don't know, but I'm a little afraid. I told him to surprise me. He's been pretty good lately. Makes me suspicious. Hold on."

Dolly was making progress. Halfie achieved. She looked up at me, busy at her work. I nodded a smiling affirmation at her, lit another cigarette.

"Yeah, ever since the college kid incident, our Irish brother has faithfully toed the party line. I'm sure he's up to something." I glanced at Dolly. She seemed to also be up to something, too, but at the present moment, it was hard to care. "I know you got my back, buddy boy. How's biz with you?" Pause. "Great. Burning Man is one of our biggest paydays. Are you coming by later? Cool. You know where I'll be." I ended the call and sat back.

The phone trilled again, breaking my concentration. Franks.

I let it ring, and finally said to Dolly, "Sorry, baby. Gotta get this."

Dolly looked at me and shrugged. "Your loss," she said, unstraddling me and disappearing upstairs. I answered the call.

"Franks. Great timing."

He had a way of starting most conversations in mid-thought, a conversation he had been having in his head without you.

"That's what I'm talking about, man."

"What?"

"Fuckin' prescriptions. It's just how they keep you down, man. If they satisfied you, you wouldn't need so many of them. If they totally killed your pain, you wouldn't need more. I have news for you, my friend: they've already conquered pain."

"Yeah, it's called death."

He laughed. "Funny man, Kurt."

"I think I know where you're going with this, Franks, and I don't think it's a good idea."

Pause on the other end of the line. "Kurt. Do me a favor and try to stand up."

"Franks."

"Give it a shot, and let me know how you're doing."

"You're a real fucker, you know that?"

"Go ahead, man, I'm waiting."

"Hold on." I put down the phone and started the process of standing up.

I sat up on my elbows and a tinge of pain shot into my fingers. There was some weird nerve damage going on there. With a groan, I sat upright. I could hear Franks make a comment, his tiny voice disparaging inside the phone. Ignoring him, I braced myself on the carved wooden frame of the chaise and slowly eased myself up. My jaw was clenched, my hands clawlike on the chaise. Suddenly I was standing and it wasn't really that bad. I let out the breath I'd been holding.

It was when I smugly reached for the phone to tell Franks "no problem" that a bolt of lightning shot through my asshole and into my head, neck, and arms. I screamed and fell backward onto the chaise longue.

When I was done panting, when my vision returned, when I saw Dolly standing over me, naked but for panties, I realized I could hear Franks shouting at me through the phone that still lay on the tray table.

Dolly was all a-panic. "Jesus Christ, Kurt! What the fuck? Are you okay?"

"Fine," I said through clenched teeth. "Can you please hand me my phone."

She saw the phone lying face up with Franks's face on the screen. Scooping it up, she angrily growled into the phone, "Franks, what the hell are you doing to Kurt?!"

"Give me the phone, Dolly," I said.

She handed me the phone, and I said into it: "You win, asshole. Send in the clowns. I'll be right here."

"Excellent. I'll be there in half an hour. I'll have my cousin Sean with me."

"Wonderful."

Ending the call, I let the phone fall to the floor. Dolly shook her head at me.

"Whiskey," I said.

"I have a bad feeling about this, Kurt."

"Me, too," I agreed, repeating, "Whiskey."

!!!

Sean O'Donnell, twenty-three years: a handsome, ginger-haired buck. He leaned back on my kitchen counter as his cousin, Franks, buttered me up for the inevitable. Sean wore what we called the Uniform: chukka boots, black T-shirt, jeans, leather coat: the zero position of cool. You can never lose with that combination, no matter what race, class, or social stratification. Boots, jeans, T-shirt, leather jacket. It was true at the birth of cool and it's true now.

So there leaned Sean O'Donnell, Franks's cousin and heroin connection. Sean looked on, expressionless, as Franks stood over me, selling me to the Life.

It all makes so much sense to me now. The entire arc. This moment of my vulnerability was the break Franks was looking for—the power grab. I didn't know what I was getting into, but Franks certainly did—like he'd always had this inevitability over me.

Another truth hit me: I was just a tourist in the criminal life. These sociopaths way outclassed me in their lack of moral center, and they did it with ease. Technically, yes, of course I was a criminal—*and then some*—but at the heart of it, I was just a sad, misguided play-actor trying to kill himself via the seductive pull of criminality and danger. I was a criminal tourist who got by on talk, fantasy, perversion, and a death wish. To the likes of Franks, I was just a mark; I was part of a long and difficult grift. Sure, I had a plan and follow-through; I had money and heart. Sure, I was big and I was a bully, but . . . *I was a fake*. Franks knew it . . . or at least sensed it. He had made me the target of a long grift, and heroin was the last step to getting me out of the way.

But back to the action.

Cousin Sean leaned back, sipping a Negro Modelo, and Dolly, now clad in tight jeans and a Kiss T-shirt, sat across the room on a barstool, all happy-go-lucky, idly swirling a margarita on the rocks. It was a summer afternoon, I was in pain, and Franks fussed over me, about to fix everything.

"Kurt! Fuck, man," Franks said. "You look all sorts of fucked up." He leaned over and kissed the top of my bald, stubbly head, almost brotherly. His greasy blond hair fell over his face. A black and orange Giants T-shirt hung threadbare on his skinny frame.

"Where's Bart?" I finally managed, jaw tight. Radiohead's *Kid A* played on the speakers. For some reason, focusing on the gun lying on the tray table next to me distracted me from the pain.

"He's on a run for me," Franks said. He cleared his throat. "Don't you mind about him, Kurt, I have just the thing for you."

I nodded toward Sean. "You must be Sean?"

"Yes, my American cousin, Sean."

"Hey, Kurt," Sean said. "Sorry you're all messed up, man."

They all looked at me like I was mentally handicapped, which in a way I was: feebleminded with pain.

Franks knelt down in front of the chaise. "So, this is the deal. All we could get was some . . . *shit.* Some H. Some heroin, brother. You don't have to do it. Or you can. But I can tell you this: it'll definitely make the pain go away. You can snort it or smoke it or shoot it. What do you want to do?"

Sean gazed at me with what looked like legitimate concern. Dolly, smoke curling around her head, glanced at each of us, then just shrugged at me.

I heard myself say, "Let's shoot it. It'll be faster."

Franks and Sean went immediately into motion. Sean cooked it up in a spoon. Dolly left her stool and closed in to watch, fascinated. Franks did his best to assuage me, rubbing my arm. He actually caressed my forehead.

Mind you, this was early on a summer afternoon. Birds chirped manically outside, and the white noise of Interstate 80 was like breaking waves in the distance. It might've been a kind of urban bucolic, if it weren't for the back pain and the druggies.

Joplin padded in nonchalantly, glancing at everyone, twitching her fluffy tail, recognizing most of them; she jumped up onto the end of the chaise. Like Dolly, the cat calmly watched with interest as Franks helped Sean tie me off. She watched this man plunge the syringe into my arm. I watched her watch him doing this horrible thing to me. And that was it.

So fucking beautiful. It was. The pain was gone instantly. Or rather, I didn't care instantly. I didn't care about anything. But different than that:

we think that caring is a part of love, but it's not. Heroin is the feeling of love without all the caring. It's perfect love. Love without consequences.

Weirder than all of that, it seemed to fix my back.

23. Market Share

Imagine my surprise when I found myself heading up my first gang meeting.

You would think a "gang meeting" would've happened by now. Before this meeting of the drug minds, the strategy of making things up as I went along gave me the moral cover to pretend that I just happened into this business, that being a drug dealer was an accident—or better yet—a phase I was going through.

I've spent a lot of time examining each moment of my first life—all that I can remember, anyway—dissecting the motivations of all those involved, parsing the backstory of each player's circumstance, focusing on my own regrettable final years. I've had a lot of time to think about it, especially in those first nightmarish months of my infant immobility: a plague of regret and confusion, toothless and trapped, no musculature, no bowel control, each day trying to convince myself that nothing was real, that I was in a coma-dream, or indeed in Hell. Hell seemed a more realistic scenario than being reincarnated as a newborn in Campbell, California.

Looking back, my regrets are few. All that happens is necessary to the moment. *Amor fati* and all that. Right? I see my criminal life as sad, sordid, and cinematic, like a sort of Tarantino film produced by inept film students: enjoyable in a way, but embarrassing.

So, on a certain Wednesday afternoon in March, I called an all-hands meeting at the house on Potrero Hill. As I said before, heroin had relaxed the muscles in my back enough to let the tissue actually heal. I had no pain, even when I was sober. Why I never saw a doctor after I hurt my back still eludes me. Oddly enough, heroin also helped me cut back on the cocaine. Blow was now relegated to a pick-me-up or social drug—clear the head or break the ice with houseguests. Looking back, I think there was a collective sigh of relief when my drug of choice became heroin. I wasn't such an asshole anymore—wasn't tense, and the paranoia and quick temper all but disappeared.

Oh, heroin. H. Horse, junk, chiva, smack. Our favorite was simply *H*. The nicknames were endless—Henry, Jones, Kabayo, Helen—*hero.* We made fun of anybody who had a clever name for it. After the first month of being on H, I found my sea legs and learned to become functional. Like all druggies.

The first gang meeting was called for three in the afternoon—first thing in the morning to the likes of us.

My chafed penis strained against my shorts as I dragged myself around the dining room in a fluffy white terry bathrobe. It's not exactly true what they say about hard-ons and heroin. It's a sensual drug, and while it may take some work to get an erection, once you get it, it lasts forever. Sex becomes less about orgasm (orgasm has nothing on a heroin high) and more about connection and enjoying the high together, close up. Nobody ever climaxes, but marathon sex is a fantastic way to exist between fixes. The heroin rekindled my and Dolly's sex life—at first, anyway.

I digress.

So, Dolly was upstairs recovering from the long tumble, and I was downstairs making a very unfocused attempt at taking our gang meeting seriously, padding lingeringly from room to room, returning to the dining room to arrange and rearrange things on the big antique oak table. *Exile on Main Street* played in the kitchen.

Chairs in place. Plastic bottles of water. Electronic drug scale. Drug testing kit. Box of dope, box of cash. Crystal decanter of expensive bourbon. Glasses. Ice bucket. Napkins. What else, what else? Foggy mind was forgetting something. This looked like a job for cocaine.

I heard the sound of the shower upstairs.

What was this scene missing? A pistol tucked in the planter near the sliding glass door. Why? Because I was a drug dealer. What else? The brain started to ramp up after the inhalation of a giant rail of coke. Snacks? Where were my manners? Where was my sense of hospitality? Chips! Salsa! Maybe some of those little frozen quiches! Pop 'em in the oven!

Then I went upstairs to jump in the shower with Dolly.

When I was all cleaned up, I threw on some clothes and let Franks, Poindexter, and Sean into the house. Bart joined us shortly thereafter.

I said, "We're in the dining room, gentlemen."

I was now barefoot in slacks and a white linen button-down. I put on Clapton. Clapton was the perfect music in that it filled up the space but you didn't really need to listen to it. The curtains were drawn but light streamed through the thin white fabric cracks onto the neatly set table. Seated around it were Dolly, Bart, Franks, Poindexter, and Sean. I made sure everybody had a drink. A tray of warm mini-quiches and a bowl of tortilla chips sat next to a bowl of salsa. Standing at the head of the table, I topped off my bourbon as Dolly passed around a mirror.

"I love the light in here," I said, smiling. I stood. "A toast!"

Glasses raised.

"What are we toasting?" Bart asked.

"We are expanding our enterprise."

"Oh, shit," he replied.

"Only a matter of time," Dolly said.

Poindexter raised his tattooed hand. "What's that noise?"

I cocked my head. "Clapton?—Oh, the staticky sound?"

"Yeah, I guess."

"White noise generator. Throws off the listening devices."

Franks snorted. "Who's listening?"

"Exactly."

Dolly rolled her eyes. "Kurt read it somewhere."

"Better safe than sorry, I guess," Bart said.

"Anyway, now that I'm back in commission—thanks to the miracle of heroin—I feel reenergized about business matters."

"It's about fuckin' time, man," Franks said, raising his glass. "Sláinte!"

Everybody chorused, "Sláinte!"

I gestured to Sean.

"And we're welcoming a few new folks to our crew."

Bart looked at me askance, then sideways at Sean. He boldly said, "Alright . . . um, I guess I'm on a need-to-know basis now?"

"Sorry I didn't forward you the business plan."

"Whatever." Bart clucked his tongue. "I mean I get Sean, but . . . who else?"

"Well . . . there's Dolly."

"I thought she was part of the crew already."

"Not officially, no. After much soul-searching—"

Dolly snorted.

"Quiet." I continued, "I've decided to make Dolly my proxy. She gets the combo to the safe and will be my voice if I'm, uh . . ."

"Nodding off," Bart cut in.

"That's very indelicate."

Franks chuckled in spite of himself and it pissed me off.

"What the fuck are *you* laughing at, McFuckface?" He continued to laugh until I too cracked a grin. This was the *new* me. The *heroin* me.

Whereas before I might've blustered into a general dressing down of my crew, now I merely joined in the laughter. "Fair enough," I said.

Bart wasn't smiling. "So . . . what? Who else? Don't tell me—PD?"

Poindexter gave him a small salute.

Franks slapped Bart on the back. "You have a problem with that, Bart-o?"

"Franks," I warned.

"It's alright, Kurt," Bart said. "No offense, PD, but . . . well, you haven't really worked for *us* this whole time—you've worked for *Franks*."

I watched Sean. He was taking this all in with a certain amount of salt, a fair measure of humor. He was definitely sizing things up. Impressive for his age. While I recognize Sean as partially to blame for my downfall, I always thought he was pretty bright and that he held onto a code of ethics. He wore a kind of Mona Lisa smile as he leaned back in his chair, sipping a beer.

"That's exactly why he's being let into the crew," I said. "Better have him working with all of us than having his talents hogged by Franks."

"Talents?" Bart said skeptically.

"Well, I don't want to get ahead of ourselves, but he knows who we need to deal with in the—er—*neighborhoods* of the City."

"And I fuckin' don't?"

Poindexter cleared his throat. "Chill, homes. You got Norteños *and* Sureños covered?"

"Whatever. You got Hunters Point Boys and Sunnydale Mob?"

"In my back pocket, man. And Big Block and Page Street."

"*Big Block*," Bart scoffed, reaching for a quiche and popping it into his mouth. Dolly smoked a cigarette and idly played with the cocaine on the mirror.

"More importantly, Poins has got Potrero Hill Gang and Hill Girlz," I added.

"Why does that shit even matter? We got clientele in spades."

"Because we're adding to our product line." I nodded to Sean. "Sean?"

Without a word, Sean stood, brought up a silver aluminum briefcase, rolled the combination lock, and cracked it open on the table. He pulled out a FedEx box.

"When it positively absolutely has to be there on time," Dolly cracked. She passed the mirror around again. I was starting to feel the slight nag of needing another fix.

"Just camouflage," Sean said, pulling out a yellowish plastic-wrapped brick of heroin and plopping it on the table.

There was a sucking in of air, an appreciative whistle, and Bart saying, "Holy shit."

All to the steady hiss of the white noise machine and the slow hand of Clapton.

I stood and walked around the table picking up the kilo, weighing it in my hand.

"Thanks, Sean." I stood behind him with the brick. "One kilo of ninety-nine percent pure Afghani heroin. An eighty-thousand-dollar investment that should triple itself."

Poindexter and Franks high-fived. Dolly looked on greedily, salivating. And Bart was . . . *blank*. He was unimpressed, silent. I continued to walk around the table.

"Which leads us to Mr. Poindexter. We have our coke niche, but we don't have a heroin niche, and if we suddenly show up with all this thunder and no introduction, we will fall victim to the wrath of the various operations around town."

"Can I see?" Bart asked. I tossed it to him. He smelled the plastic. There was swirly Arabic-looking writing printed on it. "So . . . if you don't mind me asking . . . where do you get it from, Sean? You seem a little . . . well . . . *young*."

Sean looked at Franks and Franks nodded. "Let's just say I'll be covering the Richmond District."

"Ah. So . . . Afghanistan by way of . . . what? *Ireland*?" Bart paused, thinking, then said, "Do you mean the fucking IRA?"

Franks scoffed. "Doncha know the Troubles are over, Bart."

"But—"

"Moving on," I prompted. Bart poured himself some more booze and lit a cigarette. I said, "I detect a little resistance, Bart."

"Well . . . what if I don't want to peddle junk? I don't know shit about it. I tried it once, like ten years ago. I know maybe three people who fix and I wouldn't sell to one of 'em." He put the brick on the table.

There was a silence. All eyes were on me, then Bart, then back on me. This was unexpected. I hadn't figured a naysayer into my plan, especially Bart.

Strangely, it was Poindexter who broke the silence. "Hey, man, it's easy. It's just like selling anything else. In fact, it's easier than selling yayo. Once you got customers, it sells itself."

"That may be true, but I don't think so. I'll stick with blow. I know it. I'm solid. You guys can peddle the H."

Franks was getting a bit hot. He said, "Man, I don't do the shit either. It's called what—*diversifying*, right? If it gets slow with the blow, you got the other."

"Blow is never slow for me."

"Jesus, Bart. You're always a buzzkill."

"Well, motherfucker, I'm a buzzkill with two strikes, alright? Blow is within my comfort zone."

"Your loss, *team player*," Franks said acidly.

I had to laugh, and did. "Alright, you guys. Calm down. If Bart doesn't want in on this part of the business, it's more for you all, right?"

"I don't even have an opinion," Sean said. "I mean, who cares? 'S all good, Bart."

Poindexter shrugged but Franks was still miffed. "Yeah, well, it means we may have to find somebody to cover Bart's territory."

"What territory? I don't have a territory, I have clients. I know who they are. Dude, like Kurt said—more for you. Enjoy."

By now the coke, the tension, and the huge bag of H was taunting me. "Well, good. We're all settled then," I said, "I'm pretty itchy to check this shit out." I reached over and picked up the kilo and handed it to Dolly. "Hey, honey, let's weigh out ounces to those . . . *who are participating* . . . then relax with a nice little fix." Bart looked sullen. "Bart, we'll talk about it later, but your concerns are noted."

"Okay," Dolly said. She turned the brick over in her hand. "How do I, uh . . . *open* this thing?"

"Knife."

Bart, always slick, produced a switchblade and, clicking it open, presented it to me handle-end first. I carefully cut a slit into the end of the brick and slowly wedged it open until powdery white heroin sifted down onto a large plate. Dolly scooted the scale toward her and turned it on with a beep, donning a surgical mask and pulling gloves on with a snap.

I downed the last of my whiskey and said, "This concludes the business portion of our meeting. Everybody, make yourselves at home."

24. *Erase Mode*

By the spring of the year before my death, my sister Rae had just about written me off. She was very acquainted with her wayward brother using and abusing drugs and alcohol—she dabbled herself—but even she had her limits. Who could blame her? I wasn't the same brother she'd known. Not only was I emotionally disconnected, but the ravages of my habits and trade had left their mark.

In the meantime, things had been looking up for her. Rae'd found a job in the human resources department of a cosmetics company, and she had a new apartment and an actual boyfriend. Because I felt guilty about our sad situation, I had a momentary lapse of family and decided to do something for her.

On her birthday, April 4, I dropped by her place in Alameda to bribe some sort of love out of her by showing up with a fifty-inch flat-screen TV.

"Happy—happy birthday, sister!" I shouted, massive TV box leaning outside her door.

I don't think she saw the box right away, because a big smile cut across her face. "Oh, thanks, bro!" Then, this massive box registered in her brain. She looked at me, at the box, back at me, grin faltering. She clocked this glaring tokenism—she tweren't no dummy. "Really?" she said.

"Let me bring it inside."

"Leave it for now, my place is a mess. Let's go to the bar."

"Say no more."

As we descended the steps to the sidewalk, we both looked at the giant box obstructing her door. She huffed out, "Oh, my God."

The tiki bar was a dark dive with carved Polynesian masks and plastic palm fronds. We settled on sharing a flaming scorpion bowl and picked through a pile of coconut prawns.

"What's this boyfriend's name again?"

"Michael."

"Michael," I repeated, measuring how such a name tasted in my mouth. I lazily scratched my shoulder. It was nice in the tiki bar because it was dark as a cave, and only the light peeking under the entrance hinted at daytime. Perfect.

She polished off the last prawn and said, "You seem pretty *itchy*, Kurt. What's up?"

This caught me off guard. Her tone was sort of bemused? Fishing?

"What do you mean?" I asked.

"Kurt, you look like hell. I've never seen you this . . . *thin*. You're antsy but you haven't got up once for your usual coke fix in the bathroom. What's the new drug?"

This was a very cynical accusation. I could see anger behind her suspicion. I didn't have the will for excuses and deflection anymore. "Well, it seems you have it figured out."

Rae's face fell. She couldn't believe it. The use of this particular drug was further than either of us had ever considered—*way back when.* We had an unspoken agreement that certain drugs were off limits: heroin and PCP. No one in our considerable group of druggie-artist friends had ever gone that deep (as far as we knew). Oh, sure, we'd done *all* the other drugs: pot, coke, meth, mushrooms, acid, peyote, mescaline, MDMA, Oxy, 2C-B, Vicodin, amyl nitrite, nitrous oxide, ketamine—we'd even smoked opium. Yet *smack?* That was taboo.

"Heroin?" she hissed incredulously. The word hung in the air. She grabbed my wrist and quickly slid the sleeve up my arm, revealing a trail of scabby bruise marks in the crook of my arm. She gasped, letting go of me.

I pulled my arm back and rolled down my sleeve.

A beat. A *heavy* motherfucking beat. Her glance was filled with . . . *verdict.*

"Whatever," I said. "Now you know. Happy?"

She slowly shook her head at me and gathered her purse. Her eyes were wet. She managed awkwardly, "I'm not happy."

I said: "What? So *what*? It's not like you think. It's not a big deal like they want you to believe." It was the argument out of an after-school TV special.

Rae couldn't look at me. She stood and threw a couple twenties onto the table next to the scorpion bowl. Leaning over, she kissed me on my stubbly forehead. "Get some help, Kurt. I'm done."

"Rae . . ."

Halfway to the exit she called back, "Don't call." There was a crack in her voice. That was the last thing she ever said to me: *Don't call.*

I remember looking around the mostly empty bar. The bartender wore a vacant expression as he wiped down a table across the room. A pale brown-haired lady looked up from her book at me and blinked. I drained the rest of the scorpion bowl and left. I had business to attend to.

She sent the TV back.

!!!

Around the time I last saw Rae, our drug profits had doubled.

I'd given Dolly the keys to the kingdom, going as far as making her the go-between with our heroin supplier. While she occasionally used opiates, she had a clean record, and was the safest bet among us. Also, I'd skipped past the young Sean O'Donnell by now and bought straight from *his* source, a guy who ran his business out of Pedro Point in Pacifica.

I should've known that something was up with Dolly when I had to make the bimonthly restocking run myself. This was unusual, but I was itchy and mindful of the dwindling supply, so I ignored this hiccup in the process.

My connection called himself Jim, and from what I could tell, he'd attended one too many Burning Mans. (*Men?*) He was older than me, but way better put together, and rumored to have formerly been a professional surfer.

He greeted me at the door with a squint.

"Kurt?" he said. "I mean—hi, *Kurt*! Come on in."

He spoke with a heavy California surfer drawl. "Lock the door behind you, por favor."

He had barely recognized this skinny version of me.

The thump of trance turned down low drifted through the sunlit beach house. The place was a study in poorly thought-out nautical themes and peeling rattan. A half-clad couple sat on the couch watching a superhero movie amid a cloud of pot smoke. Another pretty, semi-dressed young lady trimmed a pile of pungent green bud at a table clearly suited for just that purpose.

Gesturing, he said, "That's Amanda—"

"Hi!" she said in a bright London accent.

"—that's Billy and Billie. I think they're living here now."

"You think?" I said with a chuckle.

"You know how it is around here."

After we made our deal, a transaction paid for via phone apps, I asked, "Mind if I fix?"

Jim said, "Sure. Don't bother breaking into yours, though; I'll sort you out. Then you can kick back with the Billies for a while. Glad you're not gonna eat and run."

Hours passed. The Billies, as Jim called them, were from Olympia, Washington, transplants who were currently tearing through an inheritance. As I was preparing to leave, I dumped out a pile of coke to perk us all up. As we were sharing this, Jim said, "Good of you to give Dolly some time."

I looked at him. "What do you mean?"

"You know, for the move and shit."

Uh-oh, I thought. But I didn't break character. "Yeah, well, I do what I can."

In a panic on the way back to the City, I called Dolly. She actually picked up. I tried to sound nonchalant.

"Hello?" she answered.

"Hi, honey . . . what're you up to?"

She paused. "Where are you?" She was fishing for context.

"I'm on the way back from Jim's."

Another pause. "We need to talk."

"That's great! I'd love to talk," I overemphasized. "See you when I get home?"

"If you know already, why are you doing this?"

Heroin and cocaine contrived to make a venomous cocktail in my bloodstream. "Know *what*, dearest?"

"Kurt."

"Know that you had it on easy street with free drugs and a nearly bottomless allowance?"

"Kurt."

"Normal people have a talk before shit like this goes down."

"Kurt, we've *had* talks. And you're always too high to remember."

"Why, Dolly? Why now?"

"Because you're not present anymore. You're not here. I have to share you with your other girlfriend—heroin."

"What the fuck are you talking about? So using a shit-ton of blow is fine, but using H is off limits?"

"Heroin makes you a bore, Kurt. And I'm tired of trying to get your attention."

"Fuck you." Then I stammered, "So you're leaving the company?"

"The *company*? That's rich." I could hear her exhale a cigarette. "Yes, Kurt, you're going to have to go back to running things and not lying around in a stupor all day."

"It's not *all* day."

"I got a place out on Taraval near the beach. I got a new job."

"You'll never make it at these rent prices."

"And you don't have to worry. I'll forget everything about your business. I know you'd probably have me disappeared."

This last bit from her was melodramatic . . . but at that point quite possibly true.

"If Franks has anything to do with this, I'll kneecap him."

"Goddamn it with you and Franks. I'll have you know that Franks advised me against it. He actually said we should try to work it out. But fuck it—I'm steering clear of all y'all. We had our time, Kurt. It was fun for a while."

"You'll be back." My eyes welled up.

Ominously, she said, "I hope you make it."

"Dolly."

"I'm hanging up, Kurt. I cleared out everything that was mine. I left you the bed and the Schiele print."

"Dolly . . . what if I went to rehab?"

"It's too late, Kurt." I could hear her voice start to hitch. "Good luck."

"Dolly."

The call ended.

I screamed "FUUUUUCK! FUUUUUUUUUUUUUUCK!!" in the car all the way to Potrero Hill.

PART 5 - KEENAN

TIMESTAMP=2032-07-18T:13:07:39-15:01:37Z

25. *Talking Out of School*

After the nightwalk incident, Santa Clara County social services had assigned me a social worker named Lydia. Meeting with us (me), she thought it best that I be clinically assessed, both psychologically and intellectually. That was almost three years ago, and kindergarten was approaching. So Lydia was again activated to visit and ask us all a question: was Keenan a savant or a psychopath? More tests were required, they said. Voluntary, they implied. Loaded with consequences, we knew. This was what I'd been trying to avoid. But in a rare moment of wisdom, we Harrises all decided I would take the tests, with the caveat that Santa Clara County would accept the results and stop micromanaging the Harris child.

A month later Lydia paid us another visit. She was warm and gracious, greeting us like old friends. She sloughed off her coat and extracted her work tablet, ready for business. She had more silver in her hair than before, but time hadn't been unkind to her. Also, she handled us like we were a special case, giving me the feeling that long conversations about us had taken place within the therapeutic bureaucracy of county health. And she was direct.

"Keenan, can you come here?"

Oh, shit. Here it comes.

I looked at her, at Lou and Drew. They said nothing. I got up and went to Lydia; she took my hand. She looked me in the eye. It was a little weird.

She said, "Keenan, because you're so together, I thought I'd give you the choice of leaving the room or sticking around as I talk to your folks about some heavy stuff. Do you understand? What do you want to do?"

I was done with the pretense. "I'll stick around."

Lydia chuckled through a half grin. "That's what I thought."

My parents, of course, paid attention to none of these subtleties but instead were breathless for some sort of verdict—shit handed down by the *Man*—Santa Clara County.

"We've been in contact with a Dr. Claveria, Keenan's former pediatrician," Lydia said to us.

Lou and Drew nodded with interest while I concealed my panic.

"Claveria thinks Keenan is a prodigy. County thinks Keenan has autism spectrum disorder—what we used to call Asperger's." She looked at me, gauging my reaction. I couldn't hide my consternation.

"Keenan. You know what that is?"

I nodded. I just couldn't figure out a good old-fashioned lying response. Nothing about this seemed surprising to Lou and Drew. I literally couldn't surprise them anymore.

She said, "Keenan, I don't think you have autism."

And I said, "I'm *not* autistic."

"Your test scores look like an adult sat in for you."

"Hey!" Lou and Drew protested.

"Hold on! They *know* an adult did not sit in for Keenan, it's just that in addition to the hundred percent score on the multiple-choice questions, the written responses were grammatically complex."

I shrugged. The parents didn't react at all.

Lydia continued, "You see, in my opinion, clinicians and educators are too tired and unimaginative to really look into the reasons a young boy is preternaturally smart and aware. It's easier to slap a label on them. In this case, I think it works in your favor, and I feel we should officially designate you as a child with autism."

Lou and Drew hitched their breaths, but I was already there.

"I get it," I replied.

This was unsurprising to Lydia, who believed in this alternate universe in which a five-year-old had an adult mind. "This will open up a lot of advantages to you, Keenan. A lot of leeway. A lot of lenience." She gave me a pointed look, and I nodded okay.

"Some more interesting news is that we want to skip grades for Keenan; we just have to decide the proper amount."

Lou and Drew could only look at me. By this time, Lydia had all but forgotten about them.

Drew said, "But how does that work? Do autistic kids skip grades?"

"Children with autism who are intellectually advanced often skip grades," she said. "Look, my governing philosophy is to construct a path through which Keenan—*and you all*—will be most successful."

I cleared my throat. "Let's skip kindergarten and take it from there," I said. They were skeptical. "Look," I continued, "If I advance too far, I'm going to get picked on. I'm pre-K size. They'll stomp me. Let me skip further ahead in a couple years. I can wait." They still weren't convinced. "How about this: first grade, local public elementary with an afternoon program that lets me hang in the library and use the Internet."

"That is reasonable," Lydia said. "With me in your corner, you'll never take another psych test unless you want to. Is *that* okay?"

"Sold," I said.

On the way out, Lydia reassured my folks, "Don't worry, I'll submit my report, write up an IEP, and send you guys the details."

She was about to exit the screen door when she hesitated, holding it open. "Keenan. Come over here a sec."

The parents stood back as Lydia drew me near. She smelled faintly like a perfume counter. She said into my ear: "This might surprise you, but I've run across a couple more like you, Keenan. Well, maybe not exactly like you, but seemed like grown-ups stuck in kid bodies."

This was reassuring. I shrugged, whispering, "Okay."

She sighed, and that sigh told me that those kids had had mixed success. "Just thought you should know." She stood. "Bye, Harrises. Talk soon."

Lydia turned and stepped off the porch. But before reaching the sidewalk, she turned her head and called back: "You be careful, Keenan."

26. *First Grade*

Imagine my surprise when I found myself in first grade! Again! My first time was Del Roble Elementary School in San Jose. Ms. Otani. Very nice, as I recall. Big black bun on her head, always smiling. This time around it was a lady named Gina, at a place called Village Elementary, a few blocks down from our house. I don't remember Gina's last name because it's been a couple years and kids don't use their teacher's last name to identify them in school anymore. No more Ms. Otani, or Mr. Friesen, or what have you. It's passé. Now it's Gina or Ron. The role of teachers has been equalized. It's first-name basis now.

First day of school and Louisiana and I walked down the block, the late August sun already breaking down what remained of the morning cool. I wore a version of what I'd worn for the last forty years or so: jeans, T-shirt, and black Chuck Taylor high-tops. The T-shirt had a baby Yoda on it giving a peace sign. In my little backpack there was lunch, a water bottle, a pad of paper, pens, *The Crying of Lot 49*, and a cheap flip phone that I talked the parents into buying me. A flip phone was all I could get because (a), *You're too young for a smartphone!*, and (b), *We don't have that kind of money! Are you crazy?*

Lou wore white jean shorts, red sandals, and a salmon-striped boatneck tee. And yellow cat-eye sunglasses. Always on parade.

Across the street from the school, we had the talk.

"Keenan."

"Yeah, yeah."

"Don't frighten the children."

"Mom."

"Actually, the children will be fine. Don't frighten the grown-ups. Keep your mouth shut unless you're called on, but for chrissake don't raise your hand."

"Don't raise my hand? What am I even *here* for?"

"That's a good question. And the answer to that is so that I can start setting up the books for John and you don't get in my way by telling me how I should set up the books for John."

"So, I'm going to school so you can get me out of your hair?"

She knelt to my level and dropped her sunglasses. "Keenan, most parents embrace the notion that school is just daycare with learning. Otherwise, we'd get nothing done."

"Great."

She put a hand on my shoulder. "Look, I just want us to appear normal, Keen. Now let's go meet this Gina lady."

"School is a parental conspiracy."

As we crossed the street to the school she casually pleaded, "Please don't make Gina insane, Keenan."

!!!

Gina's first grade classroom door said GINA'S 1ST GRADE! in tilted block letters, alternately purple, red, blue, yellow, green, repeating. It was Room 8. Louisiana knocked sharply three times, a little too hard. I looked up at her.

"Sorry," she mumbled.

We heard approaching footfalls and the door swung open.

"Hello?" The woman who answered the door was a pale figure, towering, with a freckled face.

"Hi," Lou said, "I'm Louise and this is Keenan." I elicited a half shrug and half smile.

"Oh! Hi, Louise and Keenan! I'm Gina. Welcome to school! Come on in—we've still got a few minutes before first bell. Sorry I couldn't meet with you sooner."

Louise?

We sat down at a low crafts table, all three of us in kid chairs, which looked comical for my mother, but somehow natural for Gina. The room was a kaleidoscope of colorful die-cut cardboard numbers, letters, animal pictures, place names, and planets all hanging by strings from the ceiling, stapled to the wall, or taped to the window. Gone were the days of the chalkboard; it was now all whiteboards and dry-erase markers.

Gina glanced into a manila folder. "Lydia said that Keenan has special needs and has been approved for an extra library period and extended learning for language with Mr. Luber at the contained learning center."

An alarm went off in my head. "What do you mean by—" Sensing my concern, Lou cut me off and finished my sentence, patting my leg.

"When you say 'extended learning for language' at a 'contained learning center,' what do you mean, exactly?"

Gina cocked her head, strategizing on just how to choose her words. "Well . . . the *contained learning center* for language is the portable classroom where Spenser—Mr. Luber—teaches English and writing to children with special needs. Each period, he teaches a different group. The ASD group is the last of the day." Gina's eyes flitted up to the wall clock behind us. She said in a slightly more confidential voice, catching my eye, "Sometimes language needs for children on the autistic spectrum require tutoring outside the classroom so as not to distract the other kids."

"I see." I could hear the breath tight in Lou's throat. I knew it wasn't so much that she was getting upset; it was that she was concerned about how I was taking it.

Gina continued casually, as though she was explaining the behavior of a captive breed of, say, chimpanzee. "Kids with autism can usually handle math, and they can memorize a list of planet names, but language and communication can sometimes be elusive. Some spectrum kids are very verbal, just not in a very linear way. Do you like planets, Keenan?" Eyes flicked across the wall clock.

"Yes, Gina," I said in my puny five-year-old voice. "Planets are lovely."

"Keenan."

"It's okay, Mom." Gina's gaze bounced between me and Lou. I decided to go big, to give Gina the full monty, as it were. I said, "You see, Gina, my mom was asking about the—what'd you call it? The *contained* learning center?—she was asking about it because I think she has misgivings about its capacity to educate so-called spectrum kids (your term) in a direction not *less* advanced than grade level but *more* advanced."

There was a painfully leaden pause. I rarely or never unleashed my full adult articulation to an actual adult, except to Stoli. But the arrogant and careless way Gina had referred to children with autism had made me, only nominally a child with autism, angry, and thus arrogant and careless in suit.

"Wow," Gina managed.

And that's when the bell rang. This provided a convenient segue for Gina. "Well, I figured you were somehow gifted, Keenan, skipping kindergarten. I didn't mean to talk down to you. I apologize. I'll talk to Spenser and make sure he's ready for a kid like you." She winked at me, and I'm not entirely sure "kid like you" was meant in a friendly way, seeing as I had just dressed her down.

"Okay," I said.

"Thanks for coming in, Louise. We'll make Keenan feel right at home."

"Great."

The second bell rang. "Let's go outside and meet the class, Keenan," she said, standing and crossing to the door ahead of us.

As we stood to follow, I needled my mom, hissing, "*Louise*?"

She donned her sunglasses. "What can I say—sometimes I'm a Louise."

!!!

The working relationship between my folks and Stoli (John, to them, of course) had grown very solid. Trust was implicit and explicit in both directions. The advantage to this was that he had become "my favorite uncle" who would pick me up from school every now and then when visiting from San Francisco, giving my mom a break as she worked on the brewery financials. He'd pick me up and we'd go for ice cream on our way home.

One day in October he picked me up from school and I unloaded on our way to the ice cream shop.

"So, this thing with Spenser has taken a curious turn," I said to him as he piloted us away from the school in his SUV. Spenser was the special education teacher in the Contained Learning Center.

"Ah, yes. Spenser with an *S*. Do tell," Stoli replied.

"Yes. Spenser with an *S*."

I checked out Stoli; he was looking slick and shiny in new jeans and a green sweater over a collared pale-yellow shirt. He asked, "Is Spenser-with-an-*S* still mistreating your, um, *classmates*?"

"Well, not when I'm in the room. Not after that first week. But today I come in and he's already working with Patrick with some flash cards."

"Patrick is the red-haired kid who has some sign language? Sweet kid, likes to hug?"

"That's the guy," I continued. "Patrick hugs once, only once, and will not play with you unless it's drawing, and you have your side and he has his side. In the back of the portable, Alexandra is setting up rows of LEGOs by color, headphones on. That's her jam until she has her time with Spenser."

"I feel you should respect your teachers more," Stoli said. He turned the SUV into the strip mall parking lot in front of the ice cream shop.

"Right. So, after a few minutes, Spenser takes me aside and says, 'Keenan, why are you even *here*?' And I'm like, 'What?' And he says, 'Why are you here? I'm pretty sure you aren't on the spectrum at all.'"

"Whoa," Stoli said as he parked the car.

"Right? This was a little surprising, but I managed a 'Why would you say that? I was tested.' He says, 'C'mon, Keenan. I mean, the only thing spectrum-y about you is that you're kind of like a savant, and you like to be alone, but really, I could put your brain in an adult's body and you'd be just like my Uncle Harry. The district just parked you here, didn't they?'"

"Holy shit!" Stoli exclaimed. "So, he knows you are perfectly cognizant?"

"I don't think he's sure, he just feels he has nothing to lose. Which is stupid. Anyway, all I could say was, 'Well, you figured it out, Spenser. I'm part of a conspiracy orchestrated by the school district and a team of Stanford psychologists to hide me in a portable classroom in Campbell, California.'"

Stoli chuckled. "That's actually partially true."

I nodded at the shop. "Shall we get our ice cream?"

I got vanilla chocolate chip in a cup. Stoli is a strawberry ice cream fan. Only one I've ever met. We sat at a lone table outside where no one was within earshot.

"So, Spenser-with-an-*S* has your number—what did you say?" Stoli asked.

"I said to him, 'Look, Spenser, I may sound older than I am, but I'm still five and don't get along with other kids. That's a lot for a first grade teacher.' And Spenser said, 'Got *that* right.'"

"When did all this happen?"

My ice cream had melted because I'd been too busy talking. I drank it out of the cup and chewed the chocolate chips. "Right before you picked me up."

"Oh, *man*." Stoli looked at his watch. "We should go. I got some info for you."

"Awesome. Thanks for the ice cream."

As we headed toward my house, Stoli got quiet and handed me a flash drive and explained, "It's a flash drive and you just—"

"Yeah," I stopped him. "I know what to do."

"Of course."

After my lively tale about the special ed teacher, it seemed I'd used up all the good humor and we were stuck with an odd silence. "What is it, John?" Calling him by his actual name always meant I was serious. He looked pained.

"Well, I called up that investigator pal of mine. He helped me dig up information on the names you gave me and he, well . . ."

"Yes?"

"He found a lot. A lot, a lot. These are some bad dudes that you were hanging out with."

"Yes, they were, Stoli."

"And, well . . ."

I knew where this was going—I'd been expecting it. "Spill it."

"You don't come out looking so hot yourself."

"No shit."

"You were a drug dealer and a junkie."

"I told you I was."

"You said you 'ran a tight little outfit' but got into your own supply."

"Same thing."

"Please, Keenan."

"Look, I dealt drugs for five years and I was a heroin junkie for that last year." I paused, weighing the inevitable. I was going to have to tell him everything but it couldn't be right now—it'd take too long. "I made a wrong turn at some point." I weighed my words. "Much like you, I had a reaction to a highly stressful period in my life, but instead of becoming lost on the streets, I became morally lost and wound up in a dark world of bullshit. It's a little embarrassing."

"This guy who killed you—he *worked* for you? Don't get me wrong, I'm grateful, but I have to ask myself, what did I get myself into? Was that money you gave me drug money that someone is going to miss? Or *has* been missing?" Stoli was getting that panicky tone in his voice that I'd grown to recognize.

"Hey . . . slow down. It's not like that. That money you dug up was inherited from a friend. Yes, he was a drug dealer, but it was cash legally inherited by Kurt Houston, via legal probate. I didn't know what to do with it, so I buried it in a hole. Even by that time, I was a little confused."

"What about these guys—Frank O'Donnell? Bart Montgomery, Dolores Velasquez, Steve Hightower—"

"*Poins*," I said. "You memorized their names?"

"*Poins*—and August Williams. I've read a lot of police reports. Those are on the flash drive." He paused. "You were never caught, though. No police record. You had a couple DUIs."

"Your man is thorough."

"Yes, he is." He had calmed down. "This Dolores person, though."

"*Dolly*," I corrected. "No one called her Dolores. What about her?"

"She ended up doing a little time after you died. Possession. That's how we found out about your checkered past."

I was getting uncomfortable. I hadn't counted on anybody investigating *me*. "How did your guy get his information?"

"My *guy* interviewed Dolly while gathering material for a where-are-they-now article about washed-up Gen X writers."

"Oh, God. That was really his cover?"

"I told you he's good."

Stoli pulled over about a block from my house and turned off the engine. He looked down at me. It's illegal for a kid my size to be strapped into the front seat in California. I stared back up at him. I was a former drug dealer in the body of a five-year-old and he was a former Special Forces sniper in the body of a businessman.

He said, "Look, I don't care about all the illegal shit: drug taking and dealing and criminal behavior. I spent over a decade on the streets, all over the Bay Area, drugging and drinking and whoring and stealing and lying and being generally psychotic, and I turned over a new leaf and got my shit together. All because of *you*. Your death *cured me* . . . what about you? Did it cure you of . . . *anything*?"

"I'd like to think moral corruption."

"Yeah? Are you sure? There are two big questions we need to ponder, Keenan. Before I ask them of you, I want you to know that I am still all in, one hundred percent. We are going to find this son of a bitch and, well, serve justice, I guess. I'm in. I'm not backing out because of the heaping shit of gray area I just discovered about your past."

"That's a relief," I said. My little brain was mush at that point. I'd been hiding from this conversation with Stoli for a long time, I just hadn't known it.

He continued, "Question one: did . . . did you *do* something . . . *bad*? Did you . . . um, did you deserve to die?"

I looked down at my tiny hands. *What a reality check!* I hadn't been called to the mat by anyone in my entire five-year life. It was about time. Stoli was truly my friend. I knew it for sure at that moment. He was literally the only real friend I had, which was funny and sad.

I said, "I did plenty of bad stuff. Illegal stuff. I was mean to people. Only once resorted to violence." I looked at Stoli when I said, "I've never killed someone or had someone killed." It was his turn to look away. I continued with resolve: "No. I didn't deserve to be *murdered*. Dying is a different thing. If I deserved to die, it was for more philosophical reasons, like how useless things shouldn't exist, that sort of thing. But no, I honestly believe that I didn't deserve to be murdered."

He studied my eyes.

"Good." He paused and breathed a relieved breath. He reached over and used his thumb to wipe a tear from the edge of my eye. He continued, "Okay—more confusingly, by all accounts, you were overdosed by a guy named August Williams. He went to prison."

I shook my head. "Naw. That was a setup. Franks gave me a zipper of works with bad dope inside. As a *birthday* present. Total asshole move, as I'd *just* gotten clean. I've read the reports on August, and from what I can sort out, he found me dead at my house, got caught with his supply, and did the time . . . probably to cover everyone's ass. And probably to save himself from an early death."

"Funny you should say that."

"What do you mean?"

"Cuz he was murdered in prison. Shivved about six months in."

Fuck me. I crushed my eyes closed.

"Goddamn them. He was just a green little punk. He was a rookie. Fucking Franks. Fucking Poins."

"Oh, *man*. You think they had him done in lockup?"

"Yeah. Poins has people inside. August was a loose end."

"So, that gives me a little context for my next question: what are we going to do when we catch up with these guys? Shoot 'em? Get them arrested? Tell them that the Ghost of Junkie Past has come to get his due? You're going to be the dog that catches the car—*then* what?"

"I . . ." I was bereft is what I was. I'd had ideas, of course, but they all seemed stupid now. "I haven't worked it out."

"That's actually good. It's okay. We'll work that out together. That's actually really good news." Stoli made a long wheezing hooting noise that seemed to say, *Oh, we are in for some weird adventures ahead.*

He rebuckled up and started the car. "Now let's get home. You'll find a shit ton of interesting stuff on that drive. Make sure you have some privacy."

"You got it," I assured him. We seemed to have reached a critical inflection point. And prevailed.

Eyes on the road, he said, "You have some ice cream on your chin."

27. Whole New Ball Game

After Stoli had asked that critical question, that obscenely obvious question that I'd somehow buried all this time, I struggled to find the right answer. What were we going to do to Franks? The notion of violent revenge had long been my impetus. But when you chased down the series of events necessary to achieve that outcome, the feasibility of it diminished. I'd have to be willing to die and/or have someone die in my stead, in this case Stoli. He was more than equipped to be an assassin, and would indeed probably pull the trigger for me, but I wouldn't risk him, nor myself, nor my family, in the name of some twisted past-life honor killing. Years of living a reexamined life had cured me of such base revenge . . . but it didn't mean I wasn't out for justice.

After I'd eliminated the idea of killing Franks, I considered what might be the next best thing—sending that Irish jackass to prison for my murder. This was also a tall motherfucking order.

The flash drive had a lot of answers.

According to the coroner's report, my demise was ruled accidental death by combined heroin, fentanyl, and alcohol toxicity. Fentanyl, just as expected. Though I'd never been near the stuff, no one was going to believe a five-year-old reincarnation of a drug-dealing junkie.

I learned that the gang, as it existed at my death, had moved on. According to the files on the flash drive, Bart Montgomery had been released from prison at thirty-six months exactly and had spent two years on parole before moving to Atlanta. Dolly had done fourteen days in county for possession not long after my death and went on to start a harm-reduction therapy practice in San Francisco. Poins had been picked up on an old warrant related to an armed robbery cold case and did a couple years at Solano. He currently resided in the Excelsior District of San Francisco.

And that young, average-looking white kid, August Williams? So seemingly well-adjusted? He fell in with the wrong crowd and met an untimely end. It was hard not to blame myself for that.

But my focus was on the Irishman.

Somehow that asshole had dodged a number of bullets. Franks, who in the past had seemed anything but lucky, had done no time and did not go bust. In fact, according to city tax records, he had bought a foreclosed house on Bernal Hill a few years after my death. He also applied for a fictitious business name under GameDaze Merchandise, no doubt a crooked storefront for one of his ill-begotten money-making schemes. GameDaze shared a lease on a private suite at the Giants ballpark, not an inexpensive endeavor. Finally, Franks's image was all over social media, and while he was mostly careful, Steven "Poindexter" Hightower was often by his side.

Where did all this leave my prospects for justice? It meant the justice to befall Franks was to be *my* justice—a personal comeuppance. There *had* to be a showdown.

After I absorbed the copious information provided by Stoli's detective, Stoli and I decided to put some old-fashioned shoe leather toward our goal. Before we could feasibly do this, however, we would have to establish a certain amount of freedom, and that meant my folks had to be comfortable with Stoli and me pal-ing around for long periods of time. I would become a brewery brat, an honorary child mascot of what would indeed become one of a growing number of family-friendly San Francisco brewpubs. Daycare is expensive.

!!!

I spent every weekend up at Eleventh Street Brewery. Drew's first job was supervising the installation of all the tanks, fixtures, lines, and systems needed to keep the place supplied with a rotating variety of beers. Stoli's job, besides being the manager and financier, was building out the pub itself with a comfy, classic atmosphere and a simple but well-appointed kitchen and bar. The kitchen itself would be run by a guy Stoli and Drew had found at a food truck park. His name was Hiroto Salinas, and he brought both his trendy customers and his curious brand of Mexican-Japanese fusion street cuisine to our kitchen. Hiro was cool but high-strung—or maybe he just felt out of his element going from food truck to full kitchen. Lou became, at least for the time being, the keeper of the books, accounts payable, et cetera, for the brewery.

Between sitting on the second floor surfing the Internet with my tablet and hanging in Stoli's office, I'd sometimes help contractors fetch tools, and they were amazed that I knew which ones to fetch. These long weekends at the pub helped bring clarity to my goal, and finally one day, about three weeks from the pub opening, while Stoli and I tested Hiro's Japanese street taco experiments in the manager's office, I laid it on him.

"I think we do it at the ballpark," I told Stoli, as I shuttled loose cabbage and seaweed salad from the taco to my mouth. "This taco is pretty amazing. If you can call it a taco."

"He calls it a Tokyo Taco," Stoli said. "A little on-the-nose, if you ask me, but it's a winner." He wiped his mouth and went back to the subject. "The Giants ballpark? Public space, security check, private suite . . . not bad. But we can't just knock on the door and invite ourselves in."

"I say we take a field trip. GameDaze has interest in Suite 903. Overlooking third base. Let's get seats near that suite and scope it out. Believe me, if Franks shows up, we'll know it. He's like a beacon of crazy. Can't miss him."

"Let me get this straight: you expect to *just bump into him*? Now that's crazy."

"Well, my plan requires him to invite us to his suite."

"I think you've been in the beer."

"Beer doesn't agree with me anymore."

"I thought GameDaze has a website? They rent the suite."

"That site—GameDaze.com—has nothing to do with Franks. It's a shop out of Phoenix. Franks doesn't have a site."

"I'll have you know, I'm not much of a baseball fan. What do we tell your folks?"

"We tell them I suddenly have an interest in baseball."

"That sounds far-fetched."

"They are too tired to question my motives. Have you seen them?"

"I tried to give them the day off."

"Also, you are going to have to wear this." I handed him my pad.

Stoli looked at the images quizzically. "Wrong sport," he said. On the screen was the St. Patrick's Athletic Football Club site. Football, aka *soccer.*

"Naw. It's Franks's other love affair. It's his hometown soccer team. He used to wear their jersey all the time. If you are within eyesight wearing those colors, he will be all over you."

"This is your plan: we are going to hang outside his suite wearing a soccer jersey and he is going to befriend us."

"It's almost as far-fetched as a guy being reincarnated to chase down his own murderers."

!!!

We spent two baseball games standing around the bar outside Suite 903 . . . and we had nothing. Oh, people came and went from Suite 903, but not our wayward Irishman. No sign of Poins.

I wasn't a big baseball fan either. But back in the day I enjoyed going to games every now and then, when somebody had a free ticket. That said, navigating a baseball stadium when you are less than four feet high isn't fun. You can't see anything and you can get trampled at any second. While I didn't like holding Stoli's hand like a five-year-old, it was necessary in this situation. Our routine was to find our seats, then dawdle at the food stand near suite 903. That was it. Frankly, with all the foot traffic, it was a shitty place for a stakeout. A lot of hot dogs were had, nachos eaten, sodas drunk, beers imbibed. Baseball games are long.

I guess from a certain standpoint, we were adorable as grandad and grandkid—me in a little Giants cap and a kid's cream-colored replica home jersey, and Grandad in a camo Giants cap and a bright red St. Patrick's FC soccer shirt. Cute or not, we grew weary of this unlikely method of finding Franks. Worse than that, it was midseason with an endless number of home games in front of us. We were running out of patience.

Back in the manager's office of the Eleventh Street Brewery, Stoli complained, "I feel like we'd have more luck standing outside his house on Bernal than this cockamamie method. I mean, we have his address."

"That's way too suspicious. Criminals are highly paranoid."

"I was kidding, but we can't loiter around the ballpark forever."

"Look," I said, trying to sound convincing. "The Diamondbacks are playing a series this weekend. Franks hated the Diamondbacks. Let's give it another shot."

Stoli looked at me sideways, narrowing his eyes. "Hold it—you aren't actually beginning to *like* baseball, are you?"

I hesitated. "The Giants are on a streak. They could go all the way this year."

"Oh, God."

So we went back that weekend. Saturday afternoon, we again struck out, as it were, but I pushed Stoli for one more day, since the Giants had won, and the Diamondbacks were in for two more.

It was the end of June, and the fog had finally burned off to give us a rare sunny San Francisco day at the ballpark. At the third inning break, Stoli and I were waiting in a long line for the men's room that stretched into the pedestrian walkway. That's when I saw Poins talking to a roaming churro vendor in the bleacher hallway around the corner from Franks's suite. Poindexter looked just like himself, just a little heavier, and he'd let his hair grow out, now salt and pepper. Age had given him that spread-out look, like it does.

"Stoli!" I hissed.

I looked up at him, he down at me. I was about to tell him about Poins when we heard a loud Irish brogue issue forth: "I can't believe it, man!"

We both turned and looked toward the voice; a tall, thin blond man approached us, a plastic cup of beer sloshing in his hand.

"How do you have a Saints shirt?" he continued, amazed. "Tell me you're not from Dublin." Franks came toward us with a smile, his hands held out in the sort of open genuflection he used to affect in the old days. He had on a Giants tracksuit, but under the jacket was his red St. Patrick's jersey. His blond hair was thinning, but his body hadn't caught up to his middle age. His teeth had been straightened; hopefully so had his chronic halitosis.

I have to admit, I was a bit frozen. But Stoli did not miss a beat. We'd practiced this bit of introductory patter.

Stoli looked down at his red shirt and tugged on it. "Oh, this? No, I got it at a game in Ireland while I was on vacation. My cousin is Irish." I could see Stoli giving Franks the once-over; Stoli's brain was finally able to process this fabled criminal in real life.

But I internally winced. The “my cousin is Irish” line could open up a whole can of worms, since everybody in Ireland is somebody else’s cousin.

Franks shoved his hand forward for a shake, ever the charmer. Stoli took it firmly. Franks said, “Ah, good man. Who were they playing?”

“Ah . . . what’s it? The Rovers?”

“Ah, dammit! I knew it!” Franks was intoxicated. By his voice and body posture I could tell he was in the buzzed-but-not-quite-all-the-way-drunk phase of his trajectory. He looked down at me. “Hey, little man. Aren’t you a cute little guy.”

It was all happening so fast, all I could do was raise my little hand and say, “Hi.”

Franks took a gulp of his drink and opened his Giants warm-up jacket to reveal his St. Pat’s jersey. “I’m a fan, too.”

“I saw that—very cool.”

“So, the Rovers, huh? Who won?”

Stoli sighed. “Rovers, one-nil.”

Franks shook his head. “That sounds about right. Fuckers.” He looked over his shoulder at Poins. Turning to leave, he said, “Well, cheers, man!”

Stoli said, “Sláinte!”

This dash of Gaelic made Franks turn mid-stride, and still moving, he grinned, answering back, “Sláinte!” He raised his beer a little, but continued on toward Poins, some fifteen yards away.

Stoli hadn’t been ready for such a quick end to the exchange. We both stood there stunned.

“Keenan, what should we do?” he asked. The bathroom line had barely moved.

I scrambled to think. “I don’t know.” Surely, we couldn’t just come to more games hoping to run into him again. I watched Franks: he said a few words to Poins, then to the churro vendor. Poins handed something to the vendor. Of course! They were still dealing—right here in the ballpark. Franks glanced over at us; his line of sight followed the queue to the restroom. He said something to Poins and headed back toward us. I tugged on Stoli's leg.

"He's coming back."

Franks said as he neared, "Hey, that's quite a line to the loo you got there."

Stoli replied, "Yep. Keenan here really has to go."

Franks looked down at me. "You doing the pee-pee dance, there, Junior?" I shrugged, nodding innocently.

Franks offered, "Look, we got our own suite over here with its own bathroom. You're welcome to use it, if you like. Fourth inning is starting."

Stoli stammered, "Um, well . . ." I couldn't tell if this was an act anymore.

Franks shot out his hand again. "My name is Frank. It'd be my pleasure to let a fellow Saints fan and his boy use our lavatory."

"Um . . . Hi, Frank, I'm John, I . . ."

I whined at Stoli, "Uncle John, I gotta pee!"

He looked down at me, then at Franks. "Well, Frank, we'd be delighted to use your bathroom."

"Good man, John!" He slammed the rest of his beer and carelessly let the cup fall to the ground. "Follow me."

As Franks led us toward his suite, he signaled Poins to join us. At the door he said, "Fellas, this is my good buddy Poindexter." Poins acknowledged us with a nod. "PD, these fine gentlemen need to use the bathroom, and John here is a Saints fan." This last bit of information seemed all Poins needed to know as to why Franks was inviting total strangers into their suite. Franks waved his hand in front of John's shirt, then to his. "Look at that!" Then Franks said to us, "We sell VIP seats, so there's a few guys in here with us. Don't mind them."

And with that, Franklin Franklin O'Donnell ushered us inside.

!!!

I remember trying not to freak out as Stoli locked the bathroom door behind us. I did indeed have to empty my bladder. The bathroom was nice: classic photos of famous Giants moments hung on the wall and a gleaming basin was crowded with soaps, towels, and personal care items. After I did my business, I took a couple deep breaths while looking into the mirror; my face came up just inside the bottom of the frame. There was a jagged psychological dissonance between me as a five-year-old sharing the same physical space with my former henchmen. I felt close to the edge of my sanity.

"What's the plan?" Stoli whispered.

I centered myself. "Let's just see where it takes us. Knowing how Franks is after a few drinks, odds are you're about to become quote-unquote *good friends*. They'll invite us to stay, buy a round of drinks, and probably suss out your money situation to see if they can use you somehow. My cue to leave will be me getting tired after a few innings."

Stoli took this in. "Okay. We can do this."

"We don't have a choice. Get in character."

As we emerged from the bathroom, Stoli said, "Whew! Thanks for that." All the people in the room turned to us. Four drunk guys—techie dudes, quite apparently—sat at window seats with cocktails and an armada of snack plates in various states of consumption. Behind them was a cocktail table at which Poins sat, paying no mind to us. Franks, however, was ready.

"Where are you off to?" he asked courteously.

"We have a couple seats just around the corner."

"Why don't you stay? We have plenty of room."

"Oh, well, I wouldn't want to—"

"I'll get the first round of drinks." He knelt down to my face. "Hey, little man, you want some fries? How about a soda?"

Turns out Franks's bad breath wasn't gone. But I ignored it and gazed up at Stoli. "Can I, Uncle John?"

Stoli sighed. "I guess we're staying."

"Great! What can I get you, John?"

"How about a pale ale and a shot of Jameson?"

"Perfect."

Not long after, we were sitting at the window next to the four techies, who were garrulous and sloppy and sniffly. I had the notion they got the *executive* package from GameDaze, replete with an endless supply of cocaine. John had drinks and chicken wings and I had a cola and a plate of fries.

Franks broke the ice: "So, John, tell me about yourself. You've got Irish heritage, I take it."

Stoli was very ready. "On my dad's side. German on the other."

The Giants were behind the Diamondbacks, three-one. The game seemed of little concern to Franks, but the techie boys delivered a growing litany of obscenities.

"Boys!" Franks shouted at them, gesturing to me. "Language! We have a child in our midst."

Someone managed a "Sorry."

Franks turned his attention back to us. "Where was I? Oh, so you have a cousin in Dublin. What's his name, maybe I know him?"

Dammit.

"Damien Galvin. Lives in Dublin . . . in Inchi-something?"

"Ah, *Inchicore*," Franks corrected. Stoli had clearly been studying up, but this kind of improvising only made me more nervous. "Galvin . . ." Franks searched his mind and took a sip of beer. Poins had left the suite on some errand. "I know like three Galvins, actually. Not sure about a Damien . . . Anyhow, that's grand. So, are you from here in the City, or just visiting for the game?"

Franks was fishing.

"I live in town," Stoli replied. "Keenan here is actually a friend's son. I take him to baseball games sometimes."

"Keenan is a great Irish name! You like baseball, do you, Keenan?"

"Yes," I said.

I kept mostly quiet, but absorbed absolutely everything. The end of the fifth inning arrived. The Giants had scored but were still behind.

"What about you, Frank?" Stoli asked. "Do you do this sort of thing for a living? Renting out ballpark suites?"

Franks thought about his answer a little too long, then said, "Oh, this is just a little side hustle—a way to pay for my baseball addiction." I had the feeling he was choosing from a selection of prepared remarks, contingent on how he was reading his mark. "Let's just say I *facilitate*. I make things happen. I'm semiretired."

"Ah, must be nice. Cheers!" Stoli was working it well. "Let me get the next round."

Just as the drinks arrived, Poins returned. He and Franks shared a meaningful look: a transaction had been made. I knew all the looks. Initially, the excitement of this far-fetched plan coming to fruition had canceled out the revulsion I felt toward these characters. This excitement had worn off, and I wanted to seal the deal and get away from them as fast as possible.

"So, John—you said something about a brewpub?" Franks asked.

"Yeah. I'm pretty excited. The Eleventh Street Brewery."

"Hold on—the new place opening up on Eleventh and Folsom?"

"Yessir! Opens next Thursday."

"That's fantastic! What do you do there?"

"It's mine! I own it."

"Fucksake! That's great!"

This bit of news piqued Poins's interest, and he finally chimed in. "That's dope, bro. Can we come down?"

Franks looked annoyed at Poins. "PD. It's not—"

"Of course you can come!" Stoli cut in. "For one thing, it's open to the public. But you'd be my guests. Why don't you fellas come by and let me repay you for your hospitality?"

I rested my head, eyes heavy, against Stoli's arm. Stoli looked down at me.

"Uh-oh." His hand brushed my hair. "Must be close to the seventh inning. Happens every time."

I opened my eyes and Poins was looking straight at me. Odd and unsettling. I glanced away.

"Little guy looks ruined," Franks said.

"Yeah. Look, fellas. I think I have to get Keenan here back home."

"Oh, well . . . okay." Franks seemed genuinely disappointed.

Stoli made a show of rousing me and preparing to leave; I complied docilely.

"Look, guys, come to the event on Thursday. We open at three. There'll be a DJ. You'll love the food, Poindexter."

"Right on," Poins replied. He continued to clock me. It was weird.

Franks, quite loaded by this point, came in to give Stoli a hug. "Great meeting you, John." He pressed a card into Stoli's hand. "Here's my card. I may be of assistance somehow. Let's talk."

Stoli took the card, held it up. "GameDaze. Franklin O'Donnell, president."

"That's me."

Stoli took my hand. "You ready to go, Keen?"

"Yes, Uncle John."

"Say thank you to Frank and Poindexter."

"Thank you, Frank and Poin—"

I almost said Poins.

"Poindexter," Stoli finished.

Franks laughed.

"Poindexter," I repeated.

They showed us to the door, and we were gone.

Making our way out of the stadium, the urge to gush on what had just transpired was overwhelming. But these particular words coming out of a five-year-old were too strong for public consumption. Stoli saw my frustration.

"You can vent back in my office." Stoli called us a ride. "That Franks is a great actor. Puts on a good show. But you can't bullshit a former Golden Gloves champion of bullshitting." I looked at him. "That would be *me*. He was completely full of shit. We'll definitely have to watch our backs."

As we climbed into our ride, I blurted out, "He's the lyingest crooked piece of shit on the fucking planet."

Stoli rolled his eyes, and I looked over and saw the gray-haired driver's eyes on me and Stoli. She asked, "Are you John?"

28. *Stoli's Dream*

Stoli often talked about creating a brewpub that "gave you that feeling." His vision involved making the pub a destination in which every visit felt like a homecoming, a paradise filled with beer and food served by friends who'd been eagerly awaiting you. A cozy Irish pub feeling without the shamrocks. He installed a fireplace with a stone hearth in the bar area; it was a little prefab, but you could sit on it. The tables were sturdy enough to dance on.

Children of five aren't usually given the latitude that I was at the brewery, but children of five weren't *like* me, a fact recognized by the entire staff. My presence was accepted wholesale and everyone watched out for me, and me them.

When three o'clock arrived on opening day, Lou and I sat on the stairs facing the door, I with a Little Monkey Root Beer (brewed with me in mind), she with her Lou Lager. The crew lined up behind John, standing at attention, a loose, grinning phalanx of maroon and cobalt T-shirted staff. John unlocked the double doors and greeted the not-small crowd waiting outside.

"Hellooo! Welcome to the Eleventh Street Brewery! We've been waiting for you! Come on in!" There was a cheer. "You're the first ones, so sit anywhere. The upstairs is closed until dinner time. Welcome!" About thirty people or so filed in, most heading straight to the bar.

There was a good chance Franks might not show up that day, out of laziness or forgetfulness or disinterest, in which case the plan was to call up GameDaze and rent a seat in his suite. Easy enough, but the idea of Franks coming to *us* felt more organic, from the long con point of view. We were performing our own little grift, and if we gained his confidence, he would be prostrate when I revealed my true identity. Grifters, like vampires, prefer to be invited inside before they do their dirty work. In any case, this was our plan, daft or not, and Stoli and I had discussed all these contingencies before the big day.

By six o'clock, the lower dining room was full, and they opened the mezzanine. If management had any concerns about a successful opening, they were now allayed, and the already good mood turned great. I wandered from post to post as day turned to night. I even played cohost at the door with Drew, the brewer and his son.

Thus, we waited for the Irishman. I stationed myself on a stool behind the bar, tucked back in my spot against the wall. Everyone understood the risk (and illegality) of a minor in this environ; everyone shrugged it off. Around eight o'clock, Stoli, all handshakes and smiles, cut behind the bartenders to check in with me.

"I guess we go to Plan B," he said quietly as he dried a pint glass.

"It was never a good plan to begin with," I admitted. *It was my plan.* "Don't give up—it's early."

But in due time, I spotted Franks and Poins. Squinting, Franks waved at me and I back at him. They got beers and made their way over.

"Hey, little man! Keenan! Remember me? From the baseball game?" Franks had on what he supposed was appropriate dress for this occasion: his best satin soccer jersey under a tweedy dark gray sport coat. At least he'd combed his hair. Poins had traded his hoodie for the leather blazer, which reminded me immediately of Bart. Fucking Bart.

I got into character, chirping, "I remember, Uncle Frank!"

"Where's your Uncle John?" he shouted over the music. I looked around.

"He's shaking hands and stuff!" I shouted back.

Connor the bartender was suddenly at my side, looking Franks and Poins up and down.

"Hey, guys," Connor asked, "can I help you?"

"Yeah, boss, we're here to see John—*by invitation*—we're his baseball buddies."

Poins stared blankly at Connor.

"Ah. Well, let me get him."

"Cheers," Franks said. He gulped from his glass and asked me, "What do you think of the beer?"

I said, "I don't know. I'm too young for beer."

"I was kidding, kiddo." He turned to Poins. "PD, loosen up. Say hi to the boyo."

"Hi," he said.

Uncomfortably long beat.

"Well," Franks continued, "I can tell you this beer is pretty good—brewpubs usually don't make lagers. It's all that hoppy flowery shite." He saw that Poins had drained his glass already. "But Poindexter here loves the hoppy flowery shite, don't you, PD?"

"This shit's good," Poins said.

I was saved from this small talk by Stoli's sudden appearance next to me. I could tell he was half in the bag already.

"Frank! Poindexter! You made it!"

"John! Your place is killing it! And the beer is great!"

"Thanks. Keenan, have you been entertaining our guests?" Stoli asked.

"Yes, Uncle John. Frank and Poins like the beer."

Poins. This came out of my mouth before I could stop it. I said *Poins.*

Franks and Stoli didn't seem to notice, but Poins sure did. That got his attention *real* quick. Nobody had called Poindexter "Poins" except Kurt Houston. And Kurt Houston was dead.

"Let me give you a refill and I'll show you guys around. What're you having?"

"I'll have the lager again, and PD has the Dennis Hoppy."

Thing is, I'd seen Poins get rattled. He always looked for what he thought were signs of danger. His paranoia had served him well, but it could make him jumpy. And I just used the nickname a dead man had given him, and he bore holes in me with his fierce glassy eyes.

John handed them fresh pints and said, "Alright, let's have a tour. C'mon, Keenan!"

Not wanting to get crushed or left behind, I made a rare request: "Uncle John, can you carry me?" John looked at me.

"Um, *sure*, Keenan. Up!" And there I was, going for a free ride with the giants. John started his tour: "So this is the bar, as you could see. I thought the fireplace would make it homey."

"That's a good touch, John," Franks said.

Poins stared at me.

John continued, "You should try the food. Our chef used to run these really popular Japanese fusion food trucks. Sushi tacos. Sounds weird but they are very good."

We came up to the main service nexus, where kitchen, bar, and cash registers met near the back. My mom sat nearby on a stool, phone surfing with a glass of red wine. She looked up at John and his entourage. "Well, well!" she said.

"Louisiana, this is Frank and Poindexter. The friends we made at the Giants game with that fancy suite. Lou is our bookkeeper. Also, Keenan's mother."

"Thanks for coming," Lou said.

Franks was predictable and crossed to meet her. "Happy to meet you. The bookkeeper is the right one to know." This weird non sequitur made Lou wince.

"You're right about that, Frank."

Stoli said, "Lou's husband is the *brewmeister*. He's the magic behind the beer."

Frank hesitated. "Ah, the genius. I'd like to meet *that* guy!"

Stoli set me down. "Keenan, you're getting a little heavy. I'm dropping you off with Lou for a sec as we go find Drew."

This was disappointing, but I said, "Okay."

They disappeared, and I climbed up on a stool next to Lou.

"The Irish guy is a little creepy," she commented.

"That's a word for it," I replied. She tilted her head at me and turned back to her phone.

About ten minutes went by and Stoli hadn't returned. I had a hunch, so I told Lou, "I'll be back in a sec."

"Okay. Be good."

I cut down the hall and stood at the closed manager's office door. Muffled laughing came from within. *Those bastards.* I tried the door. It was unlocked, so I boldly strode in.

"Whoa!" cried Drew, his hand on a nearly empty bottle of Paddy. *Everybody*—Stoli, Franks, and Poins—turned to see me suddenly in their midst. They had clearly taken a time-out from the opening night mayhem to have a nip of the good stuff. Each held a glass of Irish whiskey.

"Oh, Keenan!" Stoli said. "Sorry, buddy. We found your dad and now we are drinking a toast to his health."

"You gave me a fright, little man," said Franks.

Poins stared at me.

"Actually, this is good timing," Drew said, draining his shot glass. "I'll go steer the ship, John. You entertain these fine men. Keenan, come with me. This is grown-up stuff in here."

I shot a look at Stoli. "Grown-up stuff, huh?" This brought a laugh from Franks and Drew, but not the other two.

"I'll be back out in no time, Keenan," Stoli said.

"Come on, you," Drew said, ushering me out the door. "Lock this," he told Stoli.

The door closed behind us, and as we headed down the hallway, I heard the clack of the lock. Soon we were back with Lou.

"Look who I found, nosing around," Drew said, giving Lou a quick kiss.

Lou looked at us knowingly. "Did he catch you drinking with the boys?"

Drew said, "Keen, why don't I get you some fries. Hang out with Connor, stay out from underfoot, please."

By ten o'clock, the word on the street must've got around because the already busy brewery was suddenly very packed, loud, and fueled with boozy energy. Connor and his bartenders were a whirlwind behind the counter. I impatiently watched it all from my barstool perch against the wall.

There had been a time, within those very walls, at the previous brewery whose ghost still haunted that address, when a certain Kurt Houston had quaffed and laughed and philosophized and strutted, when he'd been a fixture there. He'd been one of those impetuous, earnest, young, drunk twentysomethings that I observed that opening night, watched them flirt and puff themselves up, trade embellished stories, cast about for a dream. What a time Kurt had had before things turned to darkness, before he gave up.

Connor busted me out of this reverie. "Keenan! Helloooo! Hey!"

"Oh, hi—what?"

"Hey, can you do me a favor?"

"Sure."

"Can you run this envelope to John's office? I need to make a drop but it's too freaking busy."

The manila banker's envelope was fat in his hand. "You got it."

"Thanks, Keenster!" He pointed an invisible gun at me and pulled the trigger.

I raced down the narrow aisle behind the bar, cash envelope in hand, dodging the waitstaff.

Stoli's office door was papered with employee compliance posters. I stopped and thought about what I was doing: walking into a room that held a couple hardened criminals with an envelope full of cash. But them seeing the cash was part of our grift, right?

I pounded on the door; nobody answered. My little fists just couldn't cut through the clatter and shouting. I took off my shoe and really let the door have it. There was a muffled shout on the other side, and the door came open.

"What?!" Stoli shouted, irritated. He looked down and there I was. He was now fully in said bag. Soused. Seeing me reminded him that he wasn't merely at the opening night party of his brewery; he was, in fact, on a secret mission. I was just in time. Past him, I saw Franks hide the coke while Poins half-blocked the view.

"Oh—hey! Keenan!" Stoli said over his shoulder, "It's just Keenan."

I yelled, "Connor gave me this for you!" My eyes said, *let me in, you drunk fucker!*

He grabbed the envelope and ushered me inside, closing the door. The little office smelled of whiskey and sweat. Franks turned, blocking from view whatever was behind him atop the filing cabinet.

"Hey! Little man! Enjoying the party?"

"Yes, Uncle Frank," I said.

He looked at the other guys. "He calls me Uncle Frank now."

"So, what's it, Keenan?" Stoli asked. I couldn't tell if he was acting.

"Connor told me to tell you that we had to make a drop, whatever that means," I said importantly.

Stoli looked at the manila brick of cash, and understanding dawned on his face. He said, "Oh! Hey, Poindexter, I need to get by you."

Poins moved aside. Behind him was a heavy-duty drop safe bolted to the floor, a keypad and readout on its face. Stoli hefted the cash and said, "Looks like it's gonna be a good night!" He then quickly flipped open the hopper and dropped the bundle inside, letting the drawer close with a clang.

I asked with pointed innocence, "What are you guys doing in here, Uncle John?"

"Well, we're just, er . . ."

They'd switched to bourbon, half-mast bottle on the desk.

"We're just talking about business stuff, little man," Franks cut in, helpfully. Poins stared at me stone-faced, eyes darting to Franks.

"That's right, Keenan," Stoli said, "We'll come and join the party in a second. Go tell Connor you made the drop."

Quietly furious, I said, "You have something on your nose, Uncle John."

John brushed his nose self-consciously and opened the door for me. "I'll be out in a few minutes." And with that, he ushered me out and closed the door. I heard it lock.

!!!

The next day back at home, while the parents slept it off, I squirreled myself away in my backyard fort and called Stoli on my tablet.

Stoli was eating lunch at his apartment.

"Ho-ho! I was wondering when you would call," he said, mouth smacking with a sandwich.

"Oh, my God, you bastard. Tell me everything!"

"Well, you can probably deduce most of it."

"Jesus Christ, how did the fucking cocaine get introduced?! Bad boy, Uncle John!"

"Well, you know how it is—and I guess you really do, from what you've told me. We got good and lubricated and Franks just up and asked if I cared for a line of coke. So I went with it. I was having a hard time differentiating between being myself and being undercover."

I said, "I could tell you were in some sort of way. You were heated. Did you remember to talk about renting his suite and all that?"

"Yeah, he jumped on it easy. Why wouldn't he? Paying customer. At the next Diamondbacks game."

"Holy shit! When's the game?" I asked.

"Like three weeks."

"Plenty of time to talk myself into it."

Stoli was suddenly serious. "I'm unclear on what we are going to do."

"I'm starting to put something together," I said. "A little performance."

"Oh, dear. Well, lay in on me next time you come up."

The ballpark luxury suite was perfect for the showdown. It was a public space, it had a lockable entrance, ballpark security made it near impossible for people to bring guns and knives, and we could alert security if things somehow got out of hand. The likelihood of violence was high.

This will all make more sense to you soon. I anticipate your surprise.

PART 6 - KURT

TIMESTAMP=2032-07-24T:21:00:39-22:56:13Z

29. *If It's Not One Thing*

It takes a lot of discipline to be a successful heroin dealer. Especially when you get high on your own supply. I know this sounds antithetical—being disciplined while succumbing to your addiction—but it's possible. For a while. With that much product around, the compulsion to fall into the loving grace of H all day long is overwhelming. But you can still be functional. So you might wake up with a good strong fix to get you through the morning, then snort little bumps all day to keep the itchies at bay, finishing with one last good heroin nightcap before bedtime.

I was in the muddle of one of these sleepy nightcaps when my phone vibrated on the nightstand. I forced myself awake. The bed next to me was painfully empty without Dolly. I quickly thought the caller might be Franks, but I remembered he was out of town. The phone continued to vibrate. I didn't recognize the phone number, but it was local. I had a funny feeling so I answered.

"This is Kurt."

"Kurt, Bart here. Got some trouble."

Shit.

I could hear the telltale cacophony of jail noise behind him. "Damn, I know that sound," I acknowledged. "I have a guy. I'll call him."

"It's worse than that, man." Bart paused. "It was, um, the *start* of my workweek."

"Say no more." *Literally, say no more.*

"Start of his workweek" meant that he was caught with a sizable amount of blow—he'd taken three ounces—though I imagine he didn't have it all with him; it was probably separated out into half grams, grams, and eight balls, ready for a night of selling to clubbers, yuppies, students, businessmen, and assorted druggies. The kicker was that he had a prior intent-to-sell conviction, so he was in double trouble. There was also an old burglary rap. But I had a legal machine ready and waiting—a certain Larry Potts, Hobson's lawyer, now mine; he was well equipped to handle a popped dealer.

"You down at 850 Bryant?"

"Yeah. Thanks, Kurt. But . . . one more thing."

"What's that?"

"They were waiting for me."

Pause. "What are you saying exactly?"

"I was covering for an out of town someone."

Goddamnit. "Alright. Let's not jump to conclusions. I'll have you out by dawn."

"Thanks, Kurt."

"Keep the bangers at bay."

I hung up. My clouded mind struggled to parse the information. I reached into a drawer, found a bag of coke, scattered some on the flesh between thumb and forefinger, and snorted deeply. Way better than coffee. The mind began to clear.

Did Franks set Bart up? This was huge in a couple different ways. But whether or not Franks had anything to do with Bart's arrest, Bart was facing heavy time because of his priors. A couple ounces with intent to sell is a hard rap no matter how you finagle it. The question now facing me was who did I call first: Franks or Larry Potts? Franks was no doubt going to deny everything. I probably needed more than Bart's estimable instincts before I accused Franks. So I called Larry, who was still awake; he was surprised to hear from me, but he assured me that it would be handled. He'd arrange the bail.

After I hung up, I sat there still wondering if I should call Franks. Clouding my thought process was the need to fix. *Think, think.* Finally, I dialed Franks and got his voicemail.

"Franks. Kurt. Bart's at 850. Bad scene. I know you're out of town, but you probably want to come back so you can follow through with the *plan*. Call me as soon as you get this."

Time went by. I texted Franks. Nothing. I was at wit's end. Texted again. My paranoia and fear got the better of me and I made a crucial mistake: I called Dolly. It was two thirty in the morning. I still hadn't got out of bed. Surprisingly, she picked up.

I said, "I can't believe you actually answered the phone."

Her voice was cranky and filled with sleep. "Oh, Jesus, Kurt. I only picked up because something would have to be *very* wrong before you would fucking call me, *especially* at this hour. What happened?"

"I'm looking for Franks."

I could feel the seething in her pause. "How the *fuck* should I know? *Really*, Kurt?!"

"Bart got popped. He's downtown."

Longer hesitation. "Shit. What for?"

"For the worst."

I could hear the cogs turning in her head. She knew the drill.

"Are you going to do a sweep?"

"Yes."

"How is Bart?"

"Bart is solid. He knows what I'm capable of."

"I was asking if he was okay, Kurt." She paused. "Everybody knows what you're capable of."

But I replied, "Do they?"

I couldn't tell if she was mocking me, because even *I* didn't even know what I was capable of. I may have acted like a crime boss at times, but it was pretend. Or was it?

She asked, "What are you going to do?"

God, I need a fix. I lit a cigarette.

"I called Larry. He's doing what he can." I exhaled a plume into the dark of the room. "I need to fucking find Franks so he can batten down the hatches. I'm sorry I called you. Just me and my bullshit."

Dolly didn't disagree with me. I could tell she wanted to go back to sleep, but she asked disingenuously, "Is there anything I can do?"

"Naw. Not your concern anymore. Go back to bed. Sorry to bother you."

"Okay. Hope it works out, Kurt." Dolly hung up.

The *plan* wasn't some sort of genius escape or anything. It was just getting rid of the criminal evidence without actually sacrificing it. I moved fast. I got out of bed and put some sweatpants on, heading for my primary stash box for some encouragement. I was still drowsy from my fix three hours earlier.

After a pick-me-up and pouring myself a big drink, I took mental inventory of my task: one unregistered 9mm, a half kilo of heroin, a full key of blow, a half pound of grass, about eighty hits of MDMA, a quarter pound of mushrooms, two sheets of acid, a large bottle of Mexican valium, and a small ziplock of DMT. It was a real Hunter S. Thompson weekend party list, but it was the truth. The heroin and coke were business inventory, the rest was social scaffolding. Anyhow, *all* of it was a bust. So, drink in hand, fresh coke buzz in my head, and a large duffle under my arm, I got to work.

I put on shoes and a shirt, got my keys, shouldered this weighty bag of sin and stepped out of the house. It was everything I could do to keep paranoia from paralyzing me. I stood on the street under near-dawn glow with a giant bag of contraband right after my lead henchman was arrested. In my head, video cameras were surely rolling. But it was too late for second thoughts, so I simply walked to the Prius, stowed the shit in the hatch, and silently drove away.

At the storage facility, the security guard let me in with nary a glance, and I went to my unit and slid the door up with a grinding clank. Everything had gone smoothly, but I still couldn't shake the idea that I was under surveillance. In the storage unit, most of what filled it were the remaining boxes of my deceased parents' belongings. As I threw the bag of contraband among their stuff, I felt my depravity in full view of my parents' ghosts. And while I certainly didn't believe in ghosts then, I'm not so sure now.

30. *Bart, Adieu*

Things get real when the law's involved.

My only scrape personally with the law was two DUIs thirty years apart. A far cry from the sort of trouble I could've gotten into, with all the shady characters with whom I'd kept company; the drug deals in ratty apartments, street corners, coffee shops, and bars; with all the air travel while holding contraband in secret places. That's not even counting the *real* crime I'd got up to in that last five years: brokering fraudulent loans using doctored assessments, lying on federal forms, buying and transporting Schedule 1 and 2 drugs around California in bulk, roughing up a guy, committing all sorts of conspiracy-related crimes. Getting away with such things for a good long time has its own kind of seductive power; it is its own kind of drug, lulling you into a sense of invulnerability, a criminal privilege. And thus, you get caught.

Bart getting popped was a shot across my bow. My reaction wasn't to stop, of course, it was to remove myself from the process and arrange for myself to do little more than manage the money and shoot heroin—itself a foolhardy combination.

A few hours after I had stashed all the contraband, after Bart's arraignment, we all met in Larry's law office on Bryant. Bart and I sat on a brown leather couch, across the mahogany coffee table from Larry, in a blue leather high-backed armchair. We were arranged marriage-counselor style, with Bart and me as the unhappy couple.

Larry quickly poured us all a little bourbon, neat, and said, "This is to equalize us before Bart spins his tale of woe. Bottoms up." We drank. Then our host poured us all cups of coffee. "Everybody comfortable?"

"Yep," I said.

"Sure," said Bart. He was doing his best to take all this in stride.

"Good. Let me get my notebook." Larry sat down with a legal pad. I was impressed that he was going to take this story down longhand, but he was in his seventies. "Okay, Bart—I want you to tell me everything, starting with why the hell you were doing an errand for this Frankie Irish guy to begin with. Include all details, don't rush it—any detail might prove important. Especially the interaction with the supposed customer and then the arresting officer, and the *phone incident*—"

"Phone incident?" I interjected.

"You'll like this, Kurt," Larry said.

So Bart spun his tale of how he ran this errand for Franks—who was away at Giants spring training in Arizona. When Bart got to the meetup (a sidewalk café on Russian Hill) to do the deal with a customer named Jericho, it turned out to be a full-on San Francisco Police Department narco sting operation, except they were expecting "The Irishman," a storied drug dealer who was moving a lot of product around town.

Bart said, "Jericho must've been wearing a wire, because right when we made the deal, he said a code phrase, 'I always love your stuff'; I heard a metal chair scrape backward, and a chick stood up from the next table and I could tell that she was totally a cop. Hard face, boy haircut, eyes clocking her crew and everybody. Then my phone randomly buzzed, and I looked down at it—it was my next customer—and I knew what I had to do. I just let it fall to the ground. It worked great, like I'd practiced or something, because right when it hit the ground, I looked back up at the cop and crunched my boot super hard into the phone, totally fucking it all up, and I don't know why but I smiled at the cop-lady who shouted 'Motherfucker! Stop him!' because they wanted my phone, of course, so they can get everything off it. And I fucked them out of it. At least for the time being."

I looked at the bruise on the left side of Bart's face. "Oh, shit," I said.

"Yeah, so right when I did that, the lady cop and three other guys grab me, and two cop cars with their rollers blazing come up and give the sidewalk audience that loud squeaky cop horn blast. It's like a whole fucking cop show and I'm the fucking star. And that bitch cop lunges for my phone on the ground and picks it up and it sort of crumbles in her hand and I can't help but laugh and she gives me a big ol' fucking smack to the side of my head." Bart touched his cheek.

"Epic move with the phone," I said.

"Yeah, well, my face didn't think so. So anyway, the lady cop actually apologizes and says, 'sorry about that, I got excited,' and she throws me a handkerchief, like that's going to help me, and she says, 'I guess you're not The Irishman.' And I say, 'I don't know what you're talking about.' And she says, 'sit down and put your hands on the table, please.' She sits down next to me and says, 'I'm Lieutenant Jacey Sloan. I'll be your arresting officer this evening.' I think she thought she was funny. 'You may not be Irish, but you'll do.'"

They got the dope in his Subaru, all baggied up, but Bart didn't let them railroad him into saying anything. Larry tried to be as gentle as he could as he laid out the bad news that Bart's prior intent to distribute could mean ten years.

Larry let out a grim sigh and told Bart, "If I had my guess, because the cop hit you, I can get it down to five years and with any luck you'll be out in thirty months. Also, there'll be a $10,000 fine."

Heavy, heavy silence in the room.

"Fuck," Bart cursed grimly.

Larry continued, "If we plead guilty tomorrow morning with a deal, we can get the sentencing hearing pushed a couple weeks, then we can get a couple weeks on top of that before you start your sentence."

Then Bart did something I hadn't expected: he cried. Into his hands. And this brought it all back into focus that we were humans, and we make horrible decisions and Bart was about to really be locked up and have his upside-down life turned upside down in another direction.

I scooted over right next to him and put my arm around him and he put his arm around me, and Bart literally sobbed in my arms, this sketchy dealer dude, petty criminal. I knew him by this time as my friend, confidante, my number one; he was funny and smart and he knew a shitload of stuff unrelated to the life. For instance, he could tell you what every tree or plant was that you saw. Like a naturalist. He was well-read. He did three years at San Francisco State University. But this dangerous and exciting life caught up with him, and his only recourse was a good cry in his buddy's arms.

More proof of my brokenness was that I didn't cry with him. Crying had pretty much left me after the Month of Darkness.

I grabbed a napkin from the table and gave it to him. He straightened up, wiped his tears, and blew his nose. "Sorry, guys."

"Dude, you wouldn't be human if you didn't cry."

Bart said, "We gotta contact Franks and tell him to lie low."

I stood up, feeling the rising anger. "That fucking Irishman is going to do more than lie fucking low."

"No, no, Kurt. I been thinking about this," Bart said, pouring himself another shot of bourbon. "At first, I was pissed, of course. But the way it all went together, I don't think Franks could've known. I mean, what would he gain by sending me in there to make a deal only to risk exposing our whole operation?"

Larry cut in. "Look, Kurt will handle Franks, Bart. Let's focus on what we can do for you. First order is getting you to bed. I'm going to have my secretary get you a ride."

"Thanks."

Larry got up and opened the office door. "Jody, can you call Bart here a car? Fella needs some shut-eye." To Bart he said, "What's your address? Kurt and I will figure out all the rest. I need you rested for tomorrow. I'll pick you up myself at seven."

Bart stood. "So that's it? For now, I mean?"

"Yep."

Bart and I went back to the bro-shoulder-hug. "I'll call you later, Bart. Don't worry about Larry's bill."

"Thanks, man."

And so, Bart left.

That's when Franklin Franklin O'Donnell, *The Irishman*, finally called back. Taking it right there at Larry's office, five minutes after Bart's departure, I faked calm and set a meeting at my house for the next day.

31. Outfit Change

The meeting was at eleven thirty the next morning. Bart showed up first, stone-faced and pale, the bruise on his cheek smaller, but slightly green.

"Good morning," I greeted him neutrally. "How do you feel?"

"Physically fine, but my head don't know which way is up."

Leading him into the dining room, I asked, "You're not carrying or anything, are you?"

"Dope? Shit no, man. But I got to unload what I got back to you, get it out of the house."

"What I meant was, are you carrying a gun? I don't want any at the table."

He looked at me like I was crazy. "What the fuck, Kurt? I've packed maybe *twice* since we've worked together."

"Hey, this is a potentially explosive situation. Just wanted to make sure."

"You think I was gonna do Franks right here in your house?"

"People get crazy."

"Well, that ain't the kind of crazy I get." On the dining room table, I had two shots of tequila waiting for us. Otherwise, there were bottles of water and some sodas in the centerpiece.

Eyeing the tequila, he said, "Are we starting early?"

"Well, this is to loosen me and you up a little. Just us. I don't want everyone drinking during the meeting."

He shrugged. "I guess that makes some sort of sense." We shot the tequila.

He focused on me in an odd way, tilted his head; he was summing me up anew, re-estimating me. It made me feel a little bad, like I'd offended him. There was a knock on the door.

"That'd be Franks. Probably Poins as well. You cool?"

"Just answer the fucking door, Kurt." Bart took a seat at the table.

I steeled myself and answered the door. There was Franks, in his red St. Patrick's FC jersey and a Giants cap, and Poins, in a new black and orange Giants spring training hoodie. Poindexter was his usual expressionless self, but Franks was energized like nothing had happened and couldn't wait to tell us about his vacation.

"Yo, Kurt, my man!"

"Franks," I managed. I nodded Poins's way. "Poins."

"Kurt" was all he said.

"Come on in. We are in the dining room. Bart's already here."

They stepped inside and I closed the door and said awkwardly, "Oh . . . are either of you carrying . . . you know, a gun?"

"What?" Franks asked reflexively. "Um, no man. Why would you even ask that?" But he saw my look and got it. "Oooh. Well, I guess you can't be too careful. But no, man, I ain't carrying."

I turned to Poins, who glanced at Franks. Franks nodded and Poins lifted the bottom of his hoodie to show a small .380 semi-auto in a clip holster jammed inside the front of his baggy jeans. "Yeah, I got my usual."

"Ah. Well, if you could please give it to me for this meeting, I'll just put it on the shelf until you leave."

This was a peculiar side I'd never seen of Poindexter. He had the torn expression of a kid who was told they need to hand over their favorite stuffed animal. He said, "Um, that makes me uncomfortable."

I got serious, but not angry.

"On this rare occasion I'm going to have to ask for it until the meeting is over, or wait outside in your car. Or go home. I asked the same thing of Bart. And my piece is in the gun safe upstairs." (My gun was in the china cabinet drawer behind the chair in which I'd soon be sitting.) I told him, "I won't get offended if you leave."

Poindexter looked at Franks, who gave him a shrug.

"Alright, homes. Your house, your rules," he said magnanimously, handing me the piece. I took it from the holster, ejected the clip and the bullet in the chamber, and put the gun on the coat rack shelf next to the door. The clip went into my pocket.

"Good enough. Let's get down to business. Gentlemen . . . ." I gestured toward the dining room and followed them in.

Upon entering, Franks greeted Bart much the same way he had me. "Bart, my man—"

Bart cut him off without a smile. "I'm not in the mood, Franks."

Franks froze, then dropped his cheerfulness like a mask. "Alright, Bart." Poins and Bart greeted each other by way of an efficient, wordless nod. I sat at one end of the table, near the kitchen; Bart was to my left, Poins to my right, and Franks directly across the far end of the table from me.

Franks eyed the beverages on the table and asked, "Can I grab a beer?"

"Let's not right now. Maybe after we are done talking."

"Shit, all this serious stuff is making me nervous, fellas."

Poindexter popped open a diet cola.

"The fact that you're nervous, Franks, is actually reassuring. This *is* serious."

Franks clearly had a speech prepared. He said, "Bart, man. I'm *sooo* sorry. I'd've never asked you to cover for me if I knew Jericho was a snitch—*obviously*. You 'n' me are friends, man—*mates*. I wouldn't do that to you. And, Kurt," he continued, working his face into a visage of pure contrition. "Man, I would never do anything to threaten you or the outfit. We have a safe little operation here. I didn't know my reputation preceded me." He knew that last bit sounded almost boastful, so he added, "I know it's bad to have a . . . a *public* reputation at all."

Bart was still stone-faced. Contained fury.

He said to Franks deliberately, "You didn't have *any* feeling about Jericho?"

I detected a timing problem with Franks's answer, although I couldn't tell if it was too quick or too slow. "No way! I thought Jericho was cool. He was always solid. A bit of a nerd, if you ask me, college type of hippie, you know. But he's hit me up a few times."

Bart looked at Franks in that appraising way he had at me earlier. "Why didn't you call Kurt back sooner? And don't tell me your phone ran out of juice."

Franks looked at me, at Poindexter, back at Bart, and suppressed a smile. "Well, doncha know, PD and I crashed a party at the Hilton with a shit-ton of ballplayers and all these baseball groupie chicks were there and, well, turns out we managed to do a little business with one of the new outfielders and then it was all tits and blow for the rest of the night."

I asked him, "Did you see that I called—and *texted*? I mean, you had to've."

Poins studied the label on his soda can intently, now and then glancing up at Bart and me.

"Well, I might've heard a buzz and seen a missed call," Franks explained, "but to tell you the truth, my phone was in my pants and my pants weren't on for a while." Franks couldn't help but smile now, broadly. "There was a Jacuzzi involved."

He and Poins high-fived, but their smiles quickly fell from their faces when they saw that we were not amused.

"So, I'm in lockup and you're getting *pussy*, and you think that's fucking funny?" Bart struggled to control the volume of his voice, which made it come out soft and through his teeth, a little like Clint Eastwood.

I could feel Poindexter grow tense, *ready*, prepared for Bart to make a move on Franks; I could see it in the way he'd repositioned his legs.

"No, I don't think it's funny, Bart. I'm just telling you why I didn't call Kurt back right away. I was busy. How could I have known there was trouble back here?"

"Goddamn it, Franks," I interjected. "You should've known something was up because I never call you a zillion times in the middle of the night and leave text messages. There's a time-lapse in your story and a negligence in your behavior that *pisses . . . me . . . off*."

Franks stood, palms up. "How would've calling you back changed anything?" He turned to Bart. "I'm sorry you got busted, man, but it was sort of wrong place, wrong time. It was an accident. I'd take the fall for you if I could."

"Thing is," I said, "you still can."

This shut everybody up, and all eyes turned on me.

"What?" Franks said, unsteady. He sat.

"You *can* still take a fall. So could I. Bart could seriously cut his jail time, or maybe get out of it altogether, if he just rolled over and gave us up."

Bart was quick to speak: "I would never fucking do that, and you know it!"

"Exactly." I stood at my seat. Tension was high. "So let me tell you how things are going to go. No matter what, Franks, you are indirectly responsible for what happened to Bart—"

"Kurt—"

"Shut the fuck up, Franks," I spat. "You are responsible. Now, of course, if Bart hadn't agreed to help you out, or if, say, he had chosen a different profession altogether, he wouldn't be in this mess, granted. But Bart is going to do about three years, looks like, to cover *our* asses. What I'm going to do about it is, I'm going to have a nice little nest egg waiting for him on the other side. Franks, *you* are going to pay his fine."

The Irishman had gained his composure a little. "Uh . . . well, uh . . . sure. How much is it?"

"About ten grand."

Poindexter finally made a sound: "Oh, shit."

"Aw, fuck—I . . ." But Franks saw the look on my face and did some math in his head. "Fuck, well, I can handle that." I watched Franks's expression change as he realized that he was going to get away from this whole debacle for the relatively low cost of about ten thousand dollars. "Happy to, Bart. I'm so sorry this happened." Franks stood and extended his hand. "Will you accept my apology?"

Bart looked at Franks, then Poindexter, then me. He stood slowly and said, "Sure, Franks." It looked like Bart was going to shake, but instead he shot out his left hand and grabbed Franks's right wrist; in one very quick, almost rehearsed-looking move, Bart yanked Franks forward across the table and punched him square in his Irish nose, sitting Franks back in his seat with a howl.

This was not terribly surprising to me. Poins attempted to leap across the table at Bart to defend his master, but I was already standing by. As Poins launched himself at Bart, my hand shot out and grabbed the back of Poins's Giants hoodie, jerking him back toward me hard, clotheslining him and dragging him sideways. As he fell toward me, off balance, I could tell that he wanted to throw the punch he'd had ready for Bart—throw it at *me*—but he thought better of it and he landed against me, his face hitting my chest.

"STOP!" Franks shouted.

He held his nose, blood already dripping from his chin. Sprawled in his seat, he had his right hand extended up and out in a sort of hold-on-one-second gesture. His left hand held the bridge of his nose, expertly, because this was not the first time someone had given in to the urge to punch Franklin Franklin O'Donnell in the face.

"Just stop, guys. Sit down, PD, it's okay."

Bart stood back at his side of the table, arms ready. But you could tell he had cooled—clearly, punching Franks in the nose had been cathartic.

Poins awkwardly pushed away from me, eyes manic, shooting hatred at me and Bart. "Motherfuckers" was all he said as he regained his balance and straightened his hoodie, checking it for damage.

Franks gestured toward Poindexter. "Sit, PD." To Bart he said, "We're done, right?"

"Yeah, I'm done."

My nerves were alive in a beautiful way. I slipped over to the kitchen, got a dish towel, and put some ice in it. Crossing carefully past Poins, I handed the towel to Franks. "Here. You handled that pretty well." I nodded to Bart. "Bart, please sit."

I resumed my spot at the table. "Okay. That happened. Everybody take a breath."

"Goddamn it, Bart. Nice jab," Franks complimented.

And for the first time all day, for the first time since he got busted, Bart broke a smile. "Apology accepted."

Franks started laughing, then me, then Bart. I smiled, but Poins didn't seem to think it was funny.

"Kurt, I'm gonna need some paper towels." The towel was blood-soaked, as was Franks's Irish soccer jersey.

"Gotcha."

"Can we drink now?"

"Yeah."

Bart was back to solemn. "I'm gonna go unless we have anything more to cover."

I looked at him and could tell the episode had sapped his already strained capacity. There was certainly stuff we could all discuss, but I could understand why Bart would want to go if the drinking was going to start. Over the next twenty days, we'd talk frequently.

"Oh, man. I thought we could make up over some whiskey," Franks said. It was easy for Franks to be so easygoing—he was getting out of a prison stretch for ten grand and a poke in the nose.

"It's okay. We're sort of made up."

"Shake my hand?"

Bart's mouth twisted a little but he met Franks's hand. Franks held on: "Look, Bart. I am really truly fucking sorry. And really thankful that you're so stand-up, man."

"I'm sorry, too." He got his hand back. "For me, I mean. Sucks." He did not say goodbye to Poindexter. I followed him to the door.

"Well done, Bart."

"I believe him, mostly," he said, nodding toward the other room. "He's just a fucking idiot. No surprise."

"Yeah. How's your hand?"

He looked at it, knuckles a little red. "No biggie. Just a little attention getter."

"Alright. Drive safe."

In the kitchen, I turned on some old rock and roll and brought Jameson and glasses to the table. Poins rubbed his neck where the zipper of his hoodie had left a welt from my violent yank.

I said, "Sorry about that, Poins. I didn't want it to turn into a brawl. Franks handled it perfectly. Now Bart will feel a little justice has been done. He'll keep his mouth shut. Less grudge this way." I poured us shots and lifted my glass. "Sláinte."

We drank.

"So, what are we going to do now, Kurt?" Franks asked. Two narrow paper towel twists were shoved up his nostrils to stem the flow of blood.

"Well, *you*, for one, are going dark for a while. You'll have to stop any face-to-face business for a couple months."

"Dude! How will I survive? After I pay Bart's fine—"

"*Your* fine."

"Whatever. I'll be broke, man."

"That's all you got?"

He sighed. "I have a lot of irons in the fire."

"Of course you do. I'll cover you. But look—I'm taking you out of circulation for a sec."

"Fuck, man."

"I want you to hire another guy. Or rather, I'd like it if Poins here hired another guy."

I suddenly had Poins's attention.

I asked Poins, "Can you find a guy that you can trust, who can talk the talk—someone who *doesn't* look like a gangbanger?"

He thought about it for a second. "I know a guy."

"Good." I poured another round. "So, Franks: I hereby am promoting *you* to be my number one, my first lieutenant. You are going to get the keys to the kingdom. If you can keep your shit together."

Holding his nose with one hand, he nasally proclaimed, "I *can* keep my shit together!"

"Great. Okay!" I said.

We drank to that. And thus, my great undoing began.

32. So Rookie

Imagine my surprise when I had my first overdose!

Remember that guy, Hob? One of the clients I inherited from him was named Winston. He threw an annual party up at his exquisitely restored Eichler home in Diamond Heights. I went to Winston's party and I brought Franks with me, as I felt he could at least pretend to fit in with hippie lawmakers, retired artists, and techie billionaires who had learned to swap their hoodies for blazers. This was not your normal posh crowd, mind you, as everyone was openly taking drugs, but everybody also knew how to keep their shit together and not embarrass themselves.

Everybody except for me.

So, we arrived around eleven in the evening to a party that was clearly under way with no sign of slowing down. A well-known San Francisco DJ spun old-fashioned acid house to a fully catered event featuring two tended bars on opposite sides of this seven-room split-level architectural masterpiece. Winston, who was white haired, wiry, and handsome in shimmery slacks and a black turtleneck, ushered us inside immediately, took our coats, and showed us to one of the bars. I knew a good portion of the guests, and I introduced Franks around. He acted like a normal human being, thank God, and people were pleasantly delighted by his Irish accent. Lord knows the boy could chat, and chat he did, and I soon lost track of him.

Time passed and I needed a fix.

Heroin is not a popular drug among these types, but Winston was amenable to my needs and in fact paired me off with the only other person there with whom I could fix. Luanne was her name, Japanese lady. Winston provided us an upstairs guest room with a supply of booze, and he told us to be careful and to not be strangers.

A floor-to-ceiling mural of Andy Warhol's *Banana* was painted on one of the walls. The bedspread was a matching yellow. There was a small side table and two chairs near the window, and we sat down with our drinks and could hear the muffled thump of the music and walla-walla chatter of the guests downstairs. It was comfy in the room, but this was supposed to be a quick in and out sort of thing . . . well, as quick as these things go at any rate. There was a moment of chit chat before both of us politely and simultaneously offered our supply to the other. We laughed and the ice was broken.

"Let's do mine," she said, winking. She had big almond eyes and a silver bridge piercing on her nose.

"You sure? Mine's pretty awesome," I said.

"Maybe, let's save it for later."

This sounded kind of flirty to me and a bit promising. She was around my age, I guessed, but presented a little younger. As she cooked up, she asked how much was my normal and I said a couple tens, and she asked if I was sure, and I was pretty sure. There's something intimate about the act of shooting up, and she said I should go first so she could make sure I'd be okay cuz this stuff was damn good, even if I was a pro. She helped me tie off, her pretty smooth face close to mine, and we caught each other's eyes and she smiled. Then she did me up and she was right—it was damn good.

I woke up, startled, with Luanne and Franks standing over me, faces filled with worry. Luanne was pulling something from my nose. I was on the floor of Winston's upstairs guest room. I got up on my elbows and looked down to see vomit on my shirt.

"What the fuck happened?" I croaked. Luanne sighed.

"He's okay," she said, then repeated that I was okay over her shoulder. She said to Franks, "I told you it was pretty fast."

Franks's face filled with relief and he held the side of my head with one hand. "Kurt . . . you fucking overdosed, man. We almost called an ambulance."

"Oh, shit," I said.

Luanne made a tense grin. "You're gonna be fine, Kurt. The Goddess was too strong."

"The Goddess." I repeated.

"The heroin, honey."

I looked at the naloxone inhaler in her hand and touched my nose, runny with the drug.

"You're lucky she had that shit with her, Kurt," Franks said. "She came and got us, but she knew what to do. Thank God, man. You scared us."

Winston cleared his throat and Luanne and Franks parted so Winston and I could see each other. Winston looked none too pleased, but wasn't furious. "Oh, Kurt. I'm glad you're okay. This is so unlike you."

"I'm sorry, Winston," I said. My voice was thick. I felt woozy, and a little dope sick like I needed to re-up. "I didn't fuck up your party, did I?"

He smiled and waved his hand as if to ward off an invisible fly. "Oh, lord no. Everybody here is high themselves. Just not on anything that's going to kill them." He touched Luanne's shoulder and asked, "He's not going to have to go to the hospital or anything, will he?" He caught my eye. "Will you?"

"No," Luanne said. "I mean, *I've* never gone," she admitted.

Everyone was relieved. Winston said, turning toward the door, "Still, please clean up and stop this nonsense. If you can't, you should probably leave. There are shirts in the closet."

"I'm sorry, Winston. I'll get my wits together and call myself a ride."

"Do what you need to do. I love you and am glad that you're okay. That would've made for a sucky Christmas if you'd, you know, *died*." Clucking his tongue, Winston left, closing the door behind him.

I struggled to my feet and stumbled to the adjoining bathroom. I removed my stained, half-buttoned shirt and looked in the mirror. Death not-so-warmed-over stared back at me. I stooped and drank water from the tap with cupped hands.

"Goddamn, I feel like shit."

From the other room, Luanne called, "You're going to need to do a little bump pretty soon. All the dope in your system has kinda gone away from the naloxone." This sounded impossible.

I heard Franks say, "You gotta be kidding. He just almost died, fer chrissake."

"Well, that may be, but I know what I'm talking about." Luanne entered the bathroom with a burgundy button-down shirt in one hand and fresh beer in the other. She looked me over; I was half naked with gray body hair, my former brawn melted under junkie skin and bones, track marks up and down my arms. She let her eyes wander, though, which was slightly unsettling, considering. She read the tattoo on my arms. "What is *amor fati*? Love something?"

"What it is right now is horribly ironic."

"You should drink this and put this on."

I took the beer and put on the shirt.

"You okay?" she asked.

"I don't know."

"What are you going to do?"

Franks had been listening, of course. He said loudly, "We are going to go downstairs and join the fucking party. What you need, Mr. Kurt, is a big fat rail."

This did *not* sound like what I needed. For the first time in a long while, I could finally see the horrible darkness of my life.

I announced to them, "I'm going to have a drink, take a bump of H to settle my nerves, have *another* drink, and call a ride home."

Luanne looked a little disappointed. How she could still be flirty was beyond me. I couldn't even look at the creature in the mirror. She said, "Well, I'm going to fix. Can you help me a sec?"

Franks was in the doorway. "I'll be down at the party," he said and disappeared.

I looked at Luanne. In all this commotion she hadn't fixed and she was feeling the itch. One good turn. I said, "Sure, Luanne. Is there some whiskey up here?"

33. *Welcome Back to Sober January*

I knew what I had to do the moment I woke up the next day. It was a little past noon and I sat up in my own bed, already putting my plan together. The bed was empty, the house was empty. I had made it home from the party in one piece, somehow. And I had a plan.

I was going to kick.

I was going to detox, and I'd do it right at home with a little help from my friends.

I made a plan to return to Sober January.

For over twenty-five years (way before the Month of Darkness), every January, I would go cold turkey, no drugs, booze, or cigarettes. I'd start on January 2 and take January 26 (birthday) off for good behavior, then resume until the 31st. Sober January was a way to hit reset and let my body and liver recover from the year's worth of damage. I had quit the Sober January tradition when I quit everything else positive in my life. Now I would dust off SoJan, as we called it, and I would get off the smack.

While this sounded like the talk of a desperate addict, I committed my mind to it.

I took a chance and called Dolly.

“I have the feeling I’m going to regret answering this call,” she said.

“I’m kicking and I need your help.”

There was a pause. “You can’t just call me and say this shit.” I could hear odd background noises.

“Where are you?”

“Bi-Rite.” There was the metal clang of cans in a shopping cart. “Kurt, call someone else.”

“Please, Dolly. You’re a nurse. And I’m totally serious. I’m kicking and I don’t want to go to a hospital to do it.” There was a longer pause. “Hello?”

“I’m here. Look, I’m sure you’re serious. And I actually don’t doubt you can go through with it because when you set your mind to something, you’ll do it. But you’re probably going to relapse again in a couple months.”

“Wow. That’s fucking encouraging. Look, I’ll never know unless I try. I’m going to do it and I’ll be a lot more successful if you help me. You helped your cousin—and that guy in Western Addition with the pink topknot.”

“Kurt, I’m not coming back to you.”

“I’m not asking you to come back to me. I’m asking for your assistance. Please.”

“Goddammit.” Then I heard her say to someone, “Can I leave this here for a second?” Then she was out on the sidewalk, Seventeenth Street. I could hear it. I drank the large glass of water I’d smartly left next to the bed. “When are you planning to do this?” she asked. She lit a cigarette.

“January second.”

“That’s smart. Oh, hold it—is this like that Sober January thing you used to talk about but never did anymore?”

“Exactly. Except I’m doing it.”

“Fuck, Kurt. Okay. So, that’s eight days from now.”

“Oh, my God. Thank you, Dolly.” There was a long, sighing pause.

"I'm going to send you a list of supplies to get."

"You are the fucking best."

"Whatever. There're a couple great websites. Also, you'll need a full-time babysitter. I can't do that—I won't do that."

"Of course. I'll get Bryan."

"It's going to take you most of January."

"Perfect."

She made a frustrated groan. "Goddammit, Kurt. I shouldn't help you. I'm not coming back to you. Get that straight."

"I don't want that. I mean, I don't *expect* that. I just need someone who knows what they're doing. I'll be eternally thankful."

"Again, *whatever*, Kurt. Look, right now for the next eight days, you're going to want to go hard until January, you know, like a last hurrah—but *don't do it.* Don't die before you do this. That happens. Please keep it together until January; I don't want to see you in a box."

"I'll take it easy. I'll get supplies. I'll set it up with Bryan."

"Give me Bryan's phone number. I'll need to talk to him."

"I'll text it to you."

"Goddammit, Kurt. Don't fuck this up. You'll get no second chance with me to do this."

"I know—I won't fuck it up."

"Call me at the end of the month if you're really still interested and this isn't just you being high."

"I will, and I'm pretty sure this isn't just me being high. I just woke up."

"That doesn't mean anything. Just call me on the thirtieth."

"Okay."

"I reserve the fucking right to back out, Kurt."

"Okay."

"Goddammit. Bye."

"Bye, Dolly. Thanks—"

The call ended, cutting me off. All bullshit aside, Dolly was a good one. Very smart for leaving me. I did her wrong, her and so many others. What an asshole.

Anyhow, I called my buddy Bryan and set things in motion. I gave him the lowdown and offered him a generous payout. He didn't want to have anything to do with it, even with the money, but also, he would do anything to get me off the junk, so he agreed.

I had no idea what I was getting into. I had only Hollywood notions of what getting off heroin was like. *Trainspotting*, *Man with the Golden Arm*, *Basketball Diaries*. There was no story about it, fiction or nonfiction, that made it sound pretty.

A couple days after Christmas, I called a meeting to tell the crew. Franks, Poindexter, and the new guy, August, sat around the big dining table. All were skeptical.

"No offense, man, but I'll believe it when I see it," Franks said.

"Ye of little faith."

August glanced at Poins, almost as though he was making sure it was okay if he spoke. Poins nodded affirmatively. August, who had still not grown very comfortable with me, said, "So . . . you're different when you're clean? I never can tell when you're even high." The tonal quality of his voice was that of a teenager, sounding out of place at the big kids' table. Again, there was the glance at Poins to see if what he said was within bounds. Poins nodded. This kid might've been a drug dealer, but he looked like a techie intern.

Franks said, "Straight or high—he's always kind of a dick."

"With different levels of sleepy," Poins added.

"Yeah," August said. "I've never tried the heroin. As far as I can tell, it just sort of makes you tired and a little sweaty."

"Want to try?" I teased.

"No thank you."

Franks went back on topic. "So, you're going to do it *here*. Do we need to babysit you?"

"No, Dolly is going to help me. And Bryan."

"Dolly?" Franks asked. "Wow."

"Bryan?" August inquired.

"Bryan's an old friend of mine."

Franks and Poins exchanged a look.

"Look, you guys. Bryan's going to be here full time for a few weeks. You are bound to bump into each other. If any of you fuck with him, I will cut you loose. He's closer than family." I looked at Poins directly when I said this, then at Franks. "Clear?"

Franks put his hands up in a surrender gesture. "No problem."

"Good. Poins?"

"Sure, homes."

"It's settled, then. I'm starting January second. Franks—I'm handing all the H over to you. It's gotta be out of the house."

"What about the blow?"

"The bulk of that can stay. Not as much a problem."

Poins grinned. "You gonna wear a diaper?"

"What?" I asked.

"A diaper, man. My cousin wore a diaper when he kicked cuz he shit himself."

Franks and August both groaned.

"I don't know about that," I replied. "But I'll do what I have to do."

This was comedy gold to Franks. "That's fucking rich, man. Brilliant. *Diapers.* This Bryan must be quite the friend."

"Shut it, Franks."

"Should I get you a walker and a bedpan?"

Poins piped in, "*Depends.*"

"Wow. A rare instance of funny from Poins." I stood and a grin crept across my face. "Fuck you both." I added, "After I get through with you, you'll both need a walker and a bedpan."

August said, "Yeah, I'm pretty sure I'll never try heroin now."

!!!

I had my last drink and last fix on New Year's Day. It was tradition that I'd start Sober January on the second of the month because New Year's Eve parties generally went into the next day. With all that in mind, the wheels had been set in motion, and Bryan and Dolly had been in communication to coordinate their efforts.

Bryan recruited another mutual friend, Rick, with whom to tag-team my care and oversight. These guys were good old friends of mine who, despite our disconnection of the last few years, were as close to me as brothers, and they could literally be trusted with my life. They arrived in the afternoon on the first of January; Bryan's minivan was filled with a load of supplies from Costco that that Dolly told him to get. I met them in the driveway. I hadn't seen Bryan in probably six months, but I hadn't seen Rick in a couple years. Rick stopped dead when I greeted them in the driveway.

"Holy shit, Houston," he said, looking me up and down. I was in sweats and a long sleeve T-shirt with a couple days of beard growth. "What happened to you? Where'd you go? I thought there was a homeless guy in the driveway."

"Yeah, I know. Thanks." I was embarrassed and couldn't muster a witty retort. Still, he embraced me and looked at my face.

"Looks like we are just in time. You'll be okay, buddy."

Rick's a funny guy, straightforward and easygoing, hard to rattle. Worked as a union glazier for most of his adult life. He was built solid, with hands made of sandpaper and iron. Bryan was also solid. We'd spent the '90s tearing up San Francisco nightlife, then the Playa at Burning Man. He'd been a ranger and was quick on his feet in emergency situations.

Bryan tugged on my ill-fitting T-shirt. "After you get clean, we'll need to fatten you up. The world isn't right when I outweigh you."

I examined a package of adult diapers, slightly horrified. "Is this really necessary?"

Bryan grinned. "Dolly's orders. She said sometimes you might not be able to make it to the toilet in time."

"What have I gotten myself into?"

"Exactly, Kurt." He leveled a gaze at me and said slowly, "What *have* you gotten yourself into?"

After we stowed the supplies, we got ourselves some drinks and waited for Dolly. We caught up with each other. While I'd gone criminal and become addicted, Bryan and Rick had domesticated. Bryan had a daughter; Rick had a wife and a pet rabbit.

At five o'clock, the doorbell rang, and there was Dolly.

She looked good, sleek brown hair drawn back, sunglasses, blue jeans, and a green sweater. In her arms was a large bag of still more supplies.

"Well, look at you," she said. "You look like a poster boy for the needle exchange."

"Thanks for coming, I think. Come on in. The boys are in the dining room."

"Good. Let's not drag this out." She handed me the bag and took off her sunglasses. "Did you do a sweep?"

"Of course."

"Where's the stuff?"

"Franks took away the smack inventory. I have one more shot of my personal supply and I was going to do it and give the works to you."

"That sounds okay . . . but I'm going to do a sweep, too."

"Be my guest."

"I know all your hiding places."

"Look, I'm not fucking around, Dolly. If I didn't want to kick, I wouldn't pretend. I know you know all the hiding places and I knew you'd do your own sweep."

"I'm glad you're taking this seriously, Kurt." Her expression softened slightly. She was as beautiful as ever and the afternoon sunlight through the foyer window made her more so. "Let's get started with the boys and I'll give you guys the detox 101." I went in to hug her and she said "Don't" and walked past me.

Bryan and Dolly had hung out on a number of occasions but Rick had maybe met her once. Dolly drank water while we had beers. We sat around the dining table, and Dolly set out a few products as though she was presenting at a recovery seminar. We sat on one side of the table, Dolly on the other. It felt very official.

"Guys, welcome to Kurt's detox. It will be a shitty three weeks, sometimes literally."

"I'm not wiping up anything, Kurt," Rick said.

Dolly responded, "You may change your mind on that, Rick. Now listen: I'm going to tell you what to expect in the order of what's going to happen. Some of the stuff varies from person to person, but a lot of it is the same. Kurt is essentially going to go through the worst flu of his life, especially the sweats, fevers, shakes, chills, nausea, puking, muscle aches—" Dolly was counting on her fingers. "— headaches, dry mouth, sleeplessness, nightmares, hallucinations, and possibly violent emotional swings."

Bryan and Rick looked at each other. "Sounds like any Sunday morning with Kurt," Bryan quipped.

"Funny," I said.

"Also, the person going through detox is going to beg you to get him a fix, or get him some drug substitute, will bargain with you, offer you money, threaten you, cry, scream, throw a tantrum, et cetera."

Rick gazed at me, shaking his head. I said, "Hey, I haven't done any of those things yet. Gimme a break."

"You'll owe me."

"For sure."

Dolly held a large prescription bottle. "This is Suboxone. This stuff makes this process way better for all involved. It cuts down the craving, a little like methadone, doesn't get you high. But this isn't the usual Suboxone cure, because the usual cure just replaces junk with different junk. On my method, you'll be giving Kurt microdoses of Suboxone on a limited basis for a couple weeks. You'll still get sick, Kurt, but it'll probably keep you from going completely haywire. I've written down instructions here in the bag with the rest of the pills." She put the bottle back in a small white bag.

"How'd you get that stuff?" Rick asked.

"I'm a nurse. I know people." She paused and took a sip of water. "Any other questions?"

Bryan said, "Please, go on."

"When Kurt wakes up tomorrow, he's going to want to fix. By the end of the day, he'll be sweating, nauseated, and irritable. He'll want to gnaw his arm off." She looked at me. "You're going to barely sleep and probably be up for a couple days. The flu symptoms will start the following day." She pushed forward the Pedialyte, Imodium, cold medicine, aspirin, and Dramamine. "Keep him hydrated, make him comfortable. Watch a bunch of TV. You can smoke cigarettes, if it doesn't make you puke. Have a big puke bowl handy. Shit, have two of them in case you need to empty one while he's still puking. Kurt, you're going to get the runs, and if you don't make it to the john, you'll probably want to wear the diapers because no one wants to wipe up even their own shit—or have your friends do it. A few days in is where the crazy really starts, with the pleading, the fever dreams, the cramps, the sweating. Bryan, Rick: change the sheets because it's going to reek in his bedroom. Also, sometimes, Kurt, you might feel like you're having a heart attack. It's not. Just a panic attack that lasts for a couple days."

I remember thinking that I'd perhaps made a mistake at that point, and the look showed on my face. Bryan rubbed my shoulder. "Kurt, it's okay. You got this—*we* got this."

Dolly was relentless: "Now, after about a week or so, it's going to seem like you're out of the woods, but you're *so* not. Even with the drugs, the craving will be there. Your head will start to clear and you'll be overconfident. Also, your tracks will be healing up and itchy. Your whole body will be itchy. Bad headaches the whole time. Cold medicine is your friend."

This horror story went on for another twenty minutes, after which I followed Dolly around as she checked places she thought I might've hidden extra stashes. In my bedroom upstairs, she looked through my nightstand and said, "A-ha!"

"What?" There was no way.

She brought out my Glock case. "Having this around is not advised."

"What am I gonna do?"

"I'm serious. The cure makes you go loony toons."

"Give it to Rick. He's a gun guy."

With the gun case in one hand, she disappeared into the walk-in closet for about five minutes, making all sorts of noise. Finally, she came out, stood in the middle of the room and said, "Well, I have to admit it: you really cleaned your place up. And the big stash of coke is locked up in the study?"

"Yeah."

"You sure that's safe?"

"I know this is going to sound wrong, but . . . well, it's not my real problem. I'm not going to do any. It's across the house and I have babysitters and I really don't need it like I do the H."

"Hmmm," she muttered skeptically. "What is the plan with Franks and them?"

"They may stop in but they should have what they need."

"You really think you can trust Franks to take care of things without fucking it up?"

"I wasn't sure at first, but it's been months since I made him lieutenant and he's been the most reliable I've ever seen him."

"Interesting." She looked me in the eye. "Hey, have a seat a second." She gestured to the chair. I held her gaze and sat down.

"Why are you suddenly kicking?"

"I OD'd and almost died."

"Yeah, I heard. But . . . you sure that's going to keep you from relapsing? Usually, a person needs more than that to stay off the junk."

"Well," I started. Really, almost dying was the main reason. But there were others. "I feel like things are slipping away. My self-respect really took a hit that night I OD'd. Total loser. I feel like if I don't make a move now, I may never make a move."

Dolly sat on the edge of the bed. "So, that's all?"

"Well, I lost you. My friends stay away. My sister hates me." I was starting to depress myself. "I need to start getting shit back that's falling away from me. Kicking has to be the first step."

"Hmmm. Okay." She stood up. "For what it's worth, I don't think it was your junkie ways that killed it for me. It was the drug dealing itself. Being a criminal was fun for a little while, but there's no future in it for me." I saw a glint of tear reflecting off her eye. "There's no future there for you either." She looked at me, and her look said, *Goddamn it, maybe we could've gone the distance . . .* She shrugged off that look and said, "Now, where's your works? Let's do your last dose and I can get out of here."

!!!

Things were pretty chill the first day, and all we did was talk and smoke cigarettes. I drank water, while they had beers. We hung out in the family room, put on a movie, and sometime in the early afternoon I started to get a little antsy, but it wasn't so bad, so I muscled through it. I distracted myself by playing with Joplin. My nerves started to come undone, and the cat scattered. After a while, I asked them if I should have some Suboxone, and Bryan said, "Dolly said not yet."

By around eight at night, I was sweating and nauseated, but still, they wouldn't give me anything. I smoked a cigarette and had a horrible bout of flatulence and finally vomited. That's when they led me up to my bedroom and gave me a small dose of the Suboxone and an over-the-counter sleeping pill. They told me that I was to stay up in my room for a couple days if possible, and they would run food to me and keep me company. I felt horrible, but I drank some water and slept for a couple hours, waking up sweaty and sick and filled with craving. Then it got worse.

I won't bore you with the details because it's pretty repetitive. But there were all the things: cramps, vomiting, endless dry heaving, shitting (the diapers were unnecessary, fortunately), very bad shaking, headaches like an exploding tumor, a painful unscratchable itching, crawling skin. Sunlight hurt my skin. I didn't count on all the sleeplessness and boredom. No one told me there'd be night terrors and evil fever dreams. It really did feel like the worst flu. I spent an hour calling for Joplin in the middle of the night, screaming for the cat, and Bryan had to come in and calm me down. I don't remember that part.

There was a recurring night terror about being stuffed into a hole too small for me and all my bones being broken and skin torn off as I suffocated.

I tried to read, and had some success, but identifying with Richard III of England was not exactly the right headspace for a junkie on detox. It was a mad Elizabethan kaleidoscope of rhyming couplets, thees, thous, and thys.

Several days later, the vomiting and shitting stopped, though the mood swings, sleeplessness, and headaches resumed for at least a week. I drank lots of water and Diet Cokes, smoked a carton of cigarettes. I tried to eat, but nothing tasted good, stayed down, or satisfied. I binge-watched *Battlestar Galactica*, the remake *and* the original. The track marks on my arms were well on their way to healing, which seemed like a miracle because I had thought they might be permanent. Hunger returned; my depression turned into dull self-recrimination. It was at the end of the third week that I had a very odd feeling, and that was the feeling of not being sick at all, no pain or headache, no sniffles or sweats, and no physical craving for smack. The idea of heroin itself filled me with loathing, associated directly with the huge shithole of pain I'd just emerged from.

One day, Joplin was curled up next to me for the first time in a couple weeks. I got out of bed, took a shower, and went downstairs to find Bryan fixing breakfast for the three of us. Rick had taken apart his Mossberg 12-gauge and was dutifully cleaning it on the kitchen table. They looked over at me, both of them visibly satisfied.

"Well, look at Kurt, all up on two legs," Rick said.

"I do believe you've gained about ten pounds. You look great," Bryan added.

"Thanks guys. I feel pretty good. A little weary though."

"That was some horrible shit, Kurt," Rick commented.

Bryan looked at me, then Rick, saying, "I thought we'd have our little postmortem over breakfast."

"What?" Rick asked.

"Kurt's term," Bryan replied.

"Postmortem is just a meeting about all the shit that just happened and what we learned—that kind of thing. Wrapping things up so we can move on."

"Well, we learned how many times a grown man can shit, piss, and puke in a ten-minute period," Bryan said.

"That's a valuable lesson," Rick added.

We sat down at the breakfast counter with eggs and coffee.

"Before I forget," Bryan said, scrolling through his smartphone, "Dolly says 'congratulations but don't fuck it up,' and she's 'not helping you anymore.' She also says the following: 'Tell Kurt he should probably go to Narcotics Anonymous so he doesn't relapse. He won't do it but tell him.'"

"Yeah," I said, "that's not going to happen."

"She continues: 'Tell him he should get out and walk around, go shopping, maybe go to the beach. Stay outside for four or five hours.' She doesn't have an explanation for this."

"Sounds pretty nice," I said.

"'Tell him to not drink for as long as he can stand it. Tell him to get some exercise and go kick his punching bag.' She keeps going, there's a list."

"Alright. I'm all ears."

"She says, 'Tell him to let Franks handle the smack from now on or get out of that line of business entirely. Tell him to not dive into the blow. Take vitamins.' Then she added this: 'Tell him that he should stop kicking himself and move on.' Last thing is, 'Tell him not to call me and good luck.'"

I finished my breakfast and coffee. "Well, all that sounds like Dolly."

"You owe her, man," Rick told me.

"This is true. I owe you guys, too. What did I miss while I was gone? My cat was here when I woke up."

Rick pondered, saying, "I have to say, I think those dudes that work for you are a little sketchy."

"Well, they *are* criminals," I said, smiling.

"I've known plenty of guys *in the life*, Kurt," Rick admitted. "And these guys . . . well, there's something about them. I don't think they respect you."

"Huh" was all I could say.

Bryan added to this. "They seemed pretty sloppy, too. They came in a couple times, and they opened up your office and hung out and partied. They invited me in." He shrugged guiltily. "But they were at your supply pretty liberally and restocked themselves without weighing out, and spilled some and would've forgot to shut the safe if I hadn't said something."

"All this happened while I was upstairs?"

"Yeah, you were crashed out. I checked on you a couple times. This was about a week and a half ago."

"Well, shit."

"My advice to you, Kurt," Bryan said, "is that now that you have your faculties again, I'd take control of your business. These guys are going to fuck it up. I'd check your books and rein it all back in."

"You keep books?" Rick asked incredulously.

"Of course—it's a business."

"Huh."

We were silent for a moment. Finally, I said, "Well, I'll work it out. I gotta think about things." I stood up. "Fuck Dolly. I'm going to reward myself with a beer. We made it through! Why don't we all pile into Bryan's minivan and go out to Beach Chalet, have a drink, maybe walk around?"

"That's a great idea," Bryan agreed.

Rick exclaimed, "Drinks on Kurt!"

34. Last Rite

Imagine my surprise when, one day, I found myself clean of heroin!

I couldn't and didn't say I wasn't an addict anymore. But on Chris Feist's birthday, January 22, I had no heroin in my veins and hadn't for twenty-one days. I felt alert, alive, healthy, and clear—which was always how Sober January went no matter what level of debauchery I was cleaning up from. And like previous countless Sober Januarys, I would soon grow bored. I didn't hit the booze too hard, either, and until that day, January 22, I had stayed off the cocaine.

Bryan's suggestion that the crew had gotten sloppy during my absence had made up my mind that I was going to retake the helm of this criminal ship. A look at the books and Franks's sloppy attempt at keeping them straight strengthened this decision.

So there we were again—the gang—at the dining room table, the command center, Franks, Poins, August and me sitting around, everyone with drinks, music playing in the background—and no drugs. This was the first time Franks and Poindexter had seen me for a couple weeks and I'd put on over ten pounds of healthy weight. The color in my cheeks had returned.

Uncharacteristically, it was Poins, sitting shoulder-to-shoulder with his protégé, August, who was first to comment: "Hey, Kurt, you look like your old self, man."

"You look better than ever, literally," August commented.

Franks had suspicions about the meeting, and I could tell he had rehearsed a number of reactions that were at the ready. He said, "You *do* look great, Kurt. Better than a long time. Let's try keeping you healthy." I interpreted this as *Please don't take my power away.*

But I was definitely there to take his power away.

"Let's have a cheers to my full recovery." I clinked my beer against theirs; they seemed not quite as enthusiastic as I.

"Excuse me," Franks said, cocking his head. "What the fuck are we listening to?"

"Pretty chill, huh?" I replied.

"Iron and Wine," August said. "My parents listen to this stuff."

"It's shite," Franks said.

"Whatever. I find it relaxing."

"Okay, gramps," he jeered.

"What the fuck?"

I looked at Poins. He shrugged. August was about to say something when Poins stopped him with a smack to the shoulder.

"I'm kidding, man," Franks relented. "It's fine. Just not like you. You're usually more of a Rage Against the Machine–Alice in Chains kinda guy."

"I still am. I just thought this would be more soothing. Can we please stay on fucking topic?"

"Easy, man. By the way, what *is* the topic?"

"The topic is, I'm coming back and taking full reins of the business again."

Silence. Poins and August looked at Franks, who tried on a look of sober acceptance.

"Cool," he responded carefully. "Are you sure you're ready for that?"

"Well, ready or not, I think it's necessary. Now—Franks—I am very appreciative of you taking the wheel when we needed you, and for the most part I think you held it together. Sales are good." My voice sounded level and annoyingly corporate. "To that point, I think that's where your strengths lie—in *sales*."

August laughed. "Classic. You totally sound like HR right now." His grin vanished when he saw Poins didn't find it amusing.

"Well, in a way, August is onto something," I continued. "I think the bookkeeping portion got away from you, Franks."

"All the money is there, Kurt. And more. I don't see the problem."

"The expected ROI is indeed reflected in the bank account, but how we got there is poorly documented."

Franks scoffed. "I don't know what all that shit means. Can I get some whiskey?"

"Be my guest. Pour us all some." I paused, then continued unemotionally, "And yes, it's evident that you literally don't know what I mean."

"Look, I told you I have a hard time with all this bookkeeping stuff. What's important is that all the money is back in the bank with a little bit extra." He lifted his shot glass. "Here's to the return of Kurt, the micromanager." I was the last to lift my glass.

"Funny." We clinked glasses and all drank. "You can still run the sales crew, Franks."

"Goddamn it, Kurt—you know I can't show my face around town. They're still looking for *The Irishman*!"

"I understand that you are a criminal superstar, *Irish Guy*. You should continue to keep your head low for another couple months. That's really not that long. You still make money. And I think we can grow the crew by one more person. But I have to interview. August here was a perfect addition. Let's stay in that vein."

"Thanks for saying so, Kurt," August said brightly. Poins glared.

Franks said, "Well, I still don't think it's a good idea for you to have a shitload of heroin in the house." He was stalling about the heroin, which made me nervous. But he also had a point: was I ready?

"Give me a few days to make sure my head is on straight. Say, Saturday. I won't give you hell if the supply is in shambles. You did your best and . . . well, the money is all there."

Poins was a hard one to read, but watching him, I could definitely see turbulence under his stony façade. August didn't give a shit; he seemed genuinely happy to have this new Kurt in charge. Franks was doing his best to roll with it. He sighed and poured us another round.

"Alright, well, what's most important is that Kurt is off the horse and back in business. Sláinte!"

The ease with which this transition occurred was unsettling. I had the feeling my sobriety was getting in the way of their scheming. Their acquiescence was forced, reluctant. But I let it all roll—eyes wide open.

!!!

On January 25, the day before my birthday, Franks came to the door with a backpack loosely slung over his shoulder. He was alone.

He took off his yellow sunglasses. "Here I am, as promised."

I ushered him inside, glancing around the stoop outside for Poins before closing the door. Joplin, seeing Franks, followed us back to my study. Franks set a large gray metal lockbox on my desk and sank into one of the teal accent chairs across from me. A digital scale waited there, next to my laptop with the spreadsheet ready. I think somewhere in my subconscious, the fact that I treated my criminal activity like a business made it somehow less sinful. I opened the gray lockbox, taking account.

I put the heroin on the scale and eyed it. And eyed it. I sat down. It was a shimmering, sexy white pile. It was a thing of beauty. The heroin was as pretty and inviting as a young cunt spread and waiting. Glancing up, I saw Franks watching my face, my wanton face.

He tried not to smile as he said, "Everything okay?"

"Yeah . . . well." I licked my lips. "You did some good business. We'll have to re-up. Can you at least give me the shorthand of how it was distributed?" I sat at my desk, ready to input his account. The heroin lay there like a porn star with her legs spread asking me to fuck it, fuck it hard it was so horny oh please just give it to me stick it in I need your cock so bad please fuck me hard.

Franks said, "So . . . I divided it up between Poins and August, two ounces a week each to start. I think that was near the beginning of January . . ." It was hard to concentrate on Franks's words because the heroin was talking dirty to me.

C'mon, Kurt, how can you just let me lie here like this with my pussy so wet? You'll just slide right in, no one has to know. I'm in fucking heat and need to feel you inside me. You can do me any way you want . . . I swear if you even fucking touch me I'm going to cum, I'm going to squirt all over the place you're so fucking hot, please.

". . . And that was all in one lump, see, because August was going to Reno for a convention and he knew some people up there . . . Kurt?"

I snapped back. "Well, shit. Look, we can't do business like that, Franks. That's why I'm taking it back." I stood up and scooped the heroin back into its plastic bag, careful to scrape every grain of dust back in, then I sealed it, put it in the gray box, locked it, opened the safe, put it in, shut and locked the heavy iron door . . . but I could still hear the heroin's muffled, agonized need for sexual release groaning from inside the safe.

I composed myself. Or so I thought.

"Hey, man, you look a little . . . I dunno . . . you okay?"

"Yeah . . . hey, look, I got some stuff to take care of . . . you need to re-up or anything?"

"No, I think we're good."

I walked him hurriedly to the door. He said, "So . . . isn't your birthday tomorrow?"

I had totally forgotten. For exactly the length of time since the heroin had arrived.

"Yeah, that's right."

"Whatcha gonna do?"

"Hadn't really thought about it."

"Maybe I'll drop by with a bottle or something."

This in itself was an odd thing for him to offer, but I said, "Um, sure, okay."

When Franks left, I went straight for the whiskey. I was strong enough—*just*—to not go for that slutty heroin. What I did was smoke through a pack of cigarettes and finish the whiskey. When I woke up, it was my birthday.

!!!

In the morning, Joplin, her bad fluffy self, was curled up on the wedge of the pillow next to me, purring low in her sleep. I sank my nose into her fur; she had this delicious smell. I can smell it now in my memory as I record this. Etched indelibly in my brain, along with my mom's smell, and Dolly's. Limbic memories followed me across planes of the living.

That last morning, I was alone in the house. Or so I thought. Actually, I could hear someone else—some*thing* else—downstairs, coming from my study, moaning for release. It was that whore, heroin. I turned on the stereo and pumped heavy metal at high volume all through the house. It was almost noon, so I made a massive egg scramble and popped open a beer.

My phone buzzed with birthday texts that I didn't answer. I walked listlessly from room to room, the music volume obliterating everything. Joplin followed me around, like she knew I needed company. *Oh, Joplin.*

After a while, I switched from the beer to making fancy cocktails, a stalling technique to avoid going into straight whiskey drinking. I made a margarita on the rocks. I kept a burning cigarette nearby, whether I smoked it or not. It was clearly time to bust out the cocaine. Fortunately, I didn't have to go to the drug safe to do that as I had returned to the habit of having the house stash in the wooden box in the middle of the dining table. As I cut myself a line, it was only then that I finally realized that the music was too fucking loud and had been blasting for hours. I turned it off.

The silence was alarming.

I remember I made this rant, this dialectic fugue with myself, and I understand now that I'd kind of flipped my lid under the influence of coke, alcohol, and the still-firm grip of heroin's slutty ghost; also, that landmark fiftieth birthday, also how stuck I was; also, the subconscious knowledge of my epic failure as a human—all haunting me into the rambling speech I made to no one as I lurched from room to room.

I got my biggest suitcase from the garage and brought it upstairs. Joplin followed me around, and I responded to questions and accusations she was hurling at me. I spoke loudly, to drown out the orgasmic wails coming from my drug safe.

I'll try to recreate the rant, which is oddly clear in my head.

It started as though I was already in conversation:

"I'm not guilty of shit. What I am is *awake* . . . for the first time in a while. It's all bullshit. Bloody bullshit." I threw socks and boxers into the open suitcase on my bed. I trudged downstairs to hit the blow and the bourbon again. I was taking the bourbon straight now. "*Your* despair?! You *die*, you fucking bitch!" The cat stood her ground and rubbed against my leg. Why was I packing? Where was I going?

"Yeah, maybe I'm running from myself, so what? I'm out of here. If I don't, I will take revenge upon myself." Then I was in the bathroom loading up my old leather shaving kit. Excedrin PMs, Q-tips, and expired contact lens packs. I ranted at the mirror.

"God, I love myself. This is my problem. I love myself too much. But I've created a life that is loathsome. How can I love myself in a world I hate? I did this all to myself."

In the bedroom, Joplin lay on the pillow, accusing me with one eye. Somebody was downstairs. Somebody was having loud sex in my study? Dolly?

I continued, "It's not love. It's not love—it's hate. Because I've always said this: you can't truly hate something you haven't loved. Hate is a power of emotional investment that inhabits the same space as love. How can I love my hateful deeds? How can I do such hateful things if I truly love myself?"

I packed my green retro sharkskin suit, the one with the crotch ripped out and repaired. The one I wore in Amsterdam, a twenty-four-hour layover fiasco, replete with Arab grifters and the British whore and her daughter; I almost dumped their pimp off the bridge. Was I going to Amsterdam?

"I'm the bad guy. I'm the villain. Hero? But that's a lie. Villain or hero, both are flattery.

"My conscience hath a thousand several tongues,

"And every tongue brings in a several tale,

"And every tale condemns me for a villain."

A-ha! During my detox, I read Shakespeare's *Richard III.* I *was* Richard the Third, King of England, and Joplin was all the ghosts haunting me.

I looked at her and said, "I shall despair."

That's when the doorbell rang. And rang.

I looked over and Joplin was gone. All was quiet in the house except the echo of the doorbell in my head. There was a glass of water on the nightstand. Somewhere in that psychotic episode I had switched to water in a moment of harm-reduction clarity. The doorbell rang again. I went to the window and looked down at the front stoop, and there was

Franks, looking up and waving at me with flowers in one hand and a bottle in the other.

Goddamn. What had I been doing? On the way downstairs, I looked in the mirror and saw that I'd changed into something semiformal: dark gray Armani slacks and a rich, buff-satin blue Brunello Cucinelli button-down. When had I changed? When had I shaved my week's beard growth into a fucking goatee? Why would I even do that?

Everything looked in order as I crossed through the house on the way to the door. I had tidied up.

"Happy birthday, motherfucker!" Franks said when I answered the door.

"Uh, hey . . . did you phone?" I was a little glad to see him actually, but it was weird. He and I hadn't hung out one-on-one for years.

"I called and texted you like five times. But I said I was gonna come over yesterday. Is it okay? Look!" He brandished a very expensive bottle of bourbon. "And I brought you these!" He pushed forward a bouquet of wilting drugstore flowers. This was actually funny.

"Okay. Get in here, you fucking mick."

Franks came inside and took note of the place appreciatively, and also the broken pile of coke on the dining table. "I see you started without me." He put the bourbon on the table and turned to me. "Let me see you." He grabbed my elbow and confronted me, giving me the up-and-down. "Are you going somewhere? You look all . . . you look cleaned up."

"It's my birthday" was all that came out.

He continued to study me. "Well, you're half loaded but I see you haven't got into the smack. Good man! I won my bet with PD. You have a vase?"

We sat at the table pouring this extraordinary bourbon for each other. The cheap daisies graced the centerpiece. I felt the clearest I had all day. We talked.

Franks began, "My Da used to fancy himself a hardcore republican, member of Sinn Fein, knew fellas in the 'RA. All that. Of course we were like two hours from the border and we didn't even *have* family in the North, so it always seemed like a bit of fantasy that he was so patriotic about Ireland. But on that fiftieth birthday of his, he and the boys got very drunk and decided that they were going to start some shit up at the border near Monaghan-town. They got themselves so worked up. They piled into the car and sang football hymns—soccer songs—all the way to Monaghan. And they ran out of gas."

"Sounds like good luck to me."

"Well, you see, back then, all the roads in Ireland, even the biggest ones, were just wide two-lane roads. It's different than out here. You overtake, er . . . *pass*, people on the shoulder. So these boys ran out of gas about two kilometers short of the border, dead in the street, and Dad jumped out from the passenger side and was immediately hit by a bakery truck and killed. I was ten years old."

I was so used to Franks joking around—he was never serious—that I waited for the punchline. But that was it. I said, "Well, that's a fucking sad story."

"It's the only turning-fifty story I know." He smiled and lit two cigarettes, one for me. "So, I'm going to let you go to wherever you were off to, but I have this last present that you can do whatever you want with."

Franks dug into his coat on the back of the chair and came out with a small zippered works kit, much like I used to have. A kit for shooting dope.

"I got this back in December before you decided to kick, but the gear in here is so good that I didn't *not* want to give it to you. You seem like you can at least safely keep it and get rid of it." He unzipped the bag and broke it open showing two sealed syringes, spoon, cotton, rubber, water bottle, lighter, alcohol swab, and vial of white powder. "You can probably sell it. It's only a gram but it cost me $300. Afghani Khost

Blond. They call it *Ghost Blond*. You know I'm not on the shit, but I gave it a little blast and it was pretty unbelievable. If you want me to take it with me, it's cool. Just thought I'd give you the choice."

I looked at it and immediately said, "Nah."

He started to zip it up again when Ghost Blond screamed at me, "NO PLEASE FUCK ME FUCK ME FUCK ME!!!"

As casually as possible, I said, "Well, hold on. I know a guy who'd love this. I'll give it to him as a present."

Franks looked at me. "You sure?"

"Yeah."

"You're going to be okay?"

"Yeah, man. I'm good. I just made it all night with ounces of shit in my safe. Never touched it."

"Fair enough."

He slid it to me and put on his coat. "Well, I must be off, sir. I'll leave the bottle for you to finish. Happy Birthday."

I walked Franks to the door and he turned to me that one last time, started to say something then said, "Never mind. See you, big man. Happy birthday."

I closed the door and locked it.

I got the bourbon and the leather kit bag and went into the living room with its big bay window overlooking downtown San Francisco. The sun was just going down and was shooting molten rays off the skyscraper windows like a broken disco ball, scattering sharp diamonds as the sun fell below the horizon. The building lights blinked awake one by one at the coming darkness.

Joplin was on the arm of the sofa, kneading it. That spot was hers and the black leather was long ruined by her claws. Punctured away, like a thousand needles stabbing into skin for a decade.

She meowed her scratchy meow at me. I gazed at the heroin kit on the coffee table, reached over and unzipped it.

Fuck me, it begged.

I looked over at Joplin and said, "One more time around the block. Whaddya say, Jops?"

PART 7 - KEENAN

TIMESTAMP=2032-07-30T:22:16:09-23:55:51Z

35. The Luxury Suite Melee

So there Stoli and I were, jumping off the N Judah train at King and Third, in front of the ballpark. He wore his St. Pat's FC jersey and camo Giants cap under a light North Face jacket. I wore my 2010 World Series replica jersey, a standard Giants cap, and a jacket far too thick for the current weather conditions. He wore steel-toed army boots for stomping, and I wore trainers for running away. Because, you see, we were expecting a violent reaction to my presentation—or at least *I* was. Stoli didn't see what the big deal was; he didn't see what cause there would be for a physical reaction after being faced down by your reincarnated murder victim whose embodiment was the unimpeachable proof of an afterlife.

On the corner near the Willie Mays statue, we had a short pregame meeting. I took a key chain out of my pocket and examined it. On one end of the chain was my house key, and on the other end was a purple tube of glittery fluid inside of which was a three-inch tactical ice pick defense key chain with which I supposed I could stab an attacker in the thigh before they punted me across the room. It would give them a gouge that would really smart, before they easily throttled the life out of my skinny midget body. But hey, it was something.

Stoli, on the other hand, had a black tactical attack pen made of military aircraft aluminum capable of puncturing through a human skull. It looked like a beefy executive ballpoint pen, and it could actually write, but it was designed to disable an enemy, either with the blunt back end or the pointed tip. We felt inclined to come armed, but the ballpark had pretty stiff security with a pat down and a body scanner. Guns and knives would be impossible, but nondescript defense tools designed to evade security were perfect. Then there was Stoli himself, who was a highly trained man killer who had indeed killed men in Afghanistan, though perhaps only through the scope of an M24 sniper rifle.

"So have you ever actually taken someone out in hand-to-hand combat?" I asked him on the way to the park.

"Look, I've cleared a lot of structures and had to break a few bones to do it, but I never killed someone with my bare hands, no—do we really have to talk about this here?"

I poked Stoli in the pudgy gut roll that fell over his belt.

"You sure you can take Poins?"

"Stop that. Yes. He's just a punk. I could put him face down in under two seconds."

"He's pretty tough. He's survived prison a couple of times. I've seen him in action."

"Don't be nervous. I could sincerely put the hurt on both those guys before they knew what hit 'em."

Outside the ballpark, next to the Mays statue, it was reassuring to keep talking because in this new life as Keenan Solomon Harris, I had never felt as terrified as I was at that moment. And while I was now in possession of the knowledge that there was life after death, I had built Franks and Poins up into the kind of boogieman proportions that only a five-year-old could conjure. I asked Stoli, "Do you have your pen?"

Stoli looked down at me and made a very parental face. *So annoying!* He knelt on his haunches and talked at face level to me. "Everything is going to be okay, Keenan. We got this. I've never seen you so worked up."

I sighed. "I'm sorry. I feel very vulnerable as a child who is not quite four feet tall and barely forty pounds."

"Look, we are going to stick to our plan, top of the sixth, and when we start, you'll stand behind me on the counter or something so nothing can happen to you. You'll have your say, hopefully get your answers, and we'll leave. And we'll be done with this whole thing."

"Really?"

He hesitated. "Well, actually I doubt it'll go that smooth, and I also doubt we'll be done with the whole thing."

"What is there after this showdown anyway?"

Stoli stood up and zipped his jacket. "You live your life, Keenan. Go to ball games with your Uncle John."

"You hate baseball!"

"It's grown on me."

"I'm pretty sure after today, they'll never let us back in."

"It's not going to end up that messy. Stop worrying. Were you like this when you were the other guy?"

"No."

"Well, be a little more like him right now. Let's go and beat the crush."

"I hope they don't take our tactical gear."

"Please be quiet."

And we were off. We sailed through security.

As we stepped off the escalator and made our way to the suite, Poins was waiting for us. It immediately dawned on me how different our expectations of the day were: we were here to deliver cosmic justice; Franks and Poins were here to deliver customer service.

Somehow, Franks had got Poins to wear a tie and jacket, and he stood there in front of the suite like a gangland valet, neck tattoos extending up past the starched white collar of his shirt, Giants-orange blazer and black tie, disgust barely hidden by his forced, blank face. All I could think was *Oh, my God, how humiliating!* Franks must've really thought he hit the jackpot with Stoli. If I was nervous before, I was close to a panic attack now. Stoli was right, I needed to channel the ol' Kurt Houston on this one, chill the fuck out. Unfortunately, the former me had drugs and alcohol and two hundred pounds to make him brave.

I took Stoli's hand. Never had I felt so five years old.

When Poins saw us winding toward him through the growing crush of patrons, his posture shifted, and his inked-up fingers straightened the black tie. He did a subtle head-crane, as if to look for others in our party. When we reached him, he actually said, "Welcome to GameDaze," then opened the door for us.

We were about fifteen minutes shy of the first pitch. Franks had put on his Britpop playlist, which meant he was also nervous. This particular suite was narrow but deep, with a lower lounge at the field end, stepping up to a homey reception area. The private bathroom was on the right as you came in; the front window had a sweeping view of the field, overlooking third base, with stadium seating directly outside, below the window. In front of the viewing window was the long counter with barstools, and behind that were three cocktail tables. The split-level step-up to the reception area was notable because it was a natural choke point with a couch on one side and a short black cast-iron rail and yucca tree on the other. The upper level had a small wet bar, a mini-fridge, a baseball-bat-legged side table, and a massive flat screen so you could be at the game without having to personally witness it.

As we entered, the Happy Mondays issued from the speakers as Franks set champagne on ice. There were finger foods on the left and a tub of beer and sodas on the right, with uncorked wine on the side table. Franks had gone all out to host what he thought was going to be a roomful of Giants fans ready to party down. On one hand, you could see it as great hosting and perfect marketing for future suite reservations; on the other, I saw it as Franks thinking he had a shot at something bigger. Franks himself was dressed in his schmoozy finest—no FC jersey, no Giants gear, just business casual in khakis and a button-down. It all made me very queasy.

In any case, we entered and Franks gave us a "Welcome to GameDaze!" with a hand-sweeping flourish. He too looked past us as the door closed. "Where're the others?"

Stoli was ready. "On their way. Well, actually, one group dropped out. They were supposed to fly down from Seattle but the planes were grounded because of the storm up there."

"Oh, shit! Well, I hope the others come because we have a shitload of food and drink. Anyhow—what can I get you, John?" Then he knelt to me and said, "There's the little man. How're you, Keenan? Fist bump!"

"Good!" He held out his fist and I hit it as hard as I could with my little five-year-old fist, knuckles forward.

"Ow!" He smiled, shaking his hand. "You got a real bruiser here," he said, laughing.

"Yeah, I'm thinking kickboxer," Stoli agreed. "I'll have a Jameson rocks and a light beer, please."

"You got it. Can I get you a soda and some fries, little man?"

I wanted to say, *If you call me* little man *again, I'm going to fucking stab you in the junk with my tactical key chain.* But instead, I said, "Yeah, that would be great." I ran past him and climbed up on a stool at the big window. I glanced back around the room, sizing it up, memorizing everything.

Stoli removed his coat, hanging it on a hook near the door. "You've gone the extra mile, Frank. Impressive."

Franks handed him his whiskey and beer. "That's how we do it here."

"What's Poindexter doing out there? He should be in here drinking with us."

"He's working."

"My people are stuck in traffic on a party bus coming up the Peninsula. They're already going to miss the first pitch. There's no need for him to be out there. Have him join us."

"Well . . ."

"I'm requesting—as your *paying* guest."

Franks smiled. "Say no more." He went outside and had a word with Poins. When Poins joined them in the suite, he wore something close to a smile.

"Thanks, homes," he said to Stoli as he grabbed a beer. He wedged a finger inside his shirt collar as if it were choking him. Indeed, his dusky flesh bulged out over the top. "Your pub is cool, man."

"Thanks," Stoli said. The three of them took seats in the lounge area as I ate fries and drank a cola, pretending to study the crowd.

"How has it been after the opening?" Franks asked.

"Gangbusters. Exhausting."

Polite small talk continued as the game started as everyone joined me at the window with food and drinks. Earlier, I warned Stoli to watch his liquor after the opening round because he was going to need all his faculties come the sixth inning. When the bottom of the first ended (0–0), Franks turned to Stoli.

"So, what's up with your people, John? They're going to miss a great game." Franks's voice was edged with something like a whine, as though he was missing his chance somehow, like he went to the lame party and was regretting it.

Stoli frowned, looking at his phone. He stood up and said, "Let me call them. This is ridiculous." He crossed up into the lounge and started an extended monologue. I don't know if his phone was off, if he really dialed somebody, or if he was talking into a voicemail. It was a terrific bit of theater.

"Hey, Roy! What's up, man? You're missing the game!" Stoli paused as if he were listening into the phone. He looked over at Franks and Poins, both of whom hung on his every word. The top of the second inning started and Arizona hit a single on the third pitch. The crowd made a surly roar. "Yeah, whatever, Roy. You hear that?" Stoli held the phone toward us, toward the game, then back. "That's the fucking Diamondbacks scoring because you're not here! Hey . . . put Jenny on—you're not making sense." He moved the phone away from his mouth and said, "Their bus broke down in Millbrae and they had to pull off the freeway. They're at some bar, waiting for a ride into the city." He returned to his phone. "Jenny! I can barely hear you. What the hell happened? . . . Oh . . . oh . . . oh, shit . . . I know. Roy sounds pretty lit. When did he start? Oh. On the bus? Damn. Well, of course he kept going. So, what's the plan now? Food? Look, there's food *here*. Just call an Uber limo and have them deliver you here directly. We are waiting for you. Look, I'm starting to get pissed. My host knocked himself out to make this special. My man Frank here can take care of all of you, if you know what I mean." Stoli winked at Franks, who suddenly perked up. "Look, just handle your people and get the hell over here. Text me when you're at will-call. Bye."

Stoli ended the call and looked at the expectant Franks and Poins.

"Well, that sounds *iffy*, as you Americans say," commented Franks. Poins undid the top button of his shirt and loosened his tie. I pretended to be absorbed by the game and the fried cheese sticks in front of me.

Stoli shrugged it off. "Oh, don't count them out. These guys are crazy billionaire techies who do whatever they want, whenever they want. It wouldn't be unusual for them to show up during the eighth inning and keep partying after the game and rent out the presidential suite at the St. Regis. It has happened."

Glancing at Franks and Poins, this embellishment seemed to quell their doubts for the time being and indeed renewed some enthusiasm. I had to hand it to Stoli—he had natural improv skills. He'd make a top-notch con man. Years on the street will do that for you, I guess.

The second, third, and fourth innings flashed by. I grew less nervous. Part of my plan was a prepared speech, a litany of accusations, arguments, aggrievements, and what I referred to as proof-of-life facts to throw in their faces. I was as ready as I ever would be. Stoli kept his drinking pretty low-key, but he was building a small buzz, I could tell, and just before the top of the fifth, he took a suspicious bathroom break that I'm pretty sure was sponsored by Franks's cocaine. This was a curse and blessing, as it might sober him up, but also might over-rev him since he was such a drug lightweight.

The score was Diamondbacks 4, Giants 2.

As the fifth inning started, Poins left the suite on an errand. Franks got all of us another drink (root beer for me) and announced, "So, I hope it's okay, but Poins went to grab an old friend of ours who is at the game. She has shite bleacher seats so I told her to come over. You'll like her—she's very pretty." He winked at us.

Uh-oh. I glanced at Stoli, who was also cogitating. He said, "Well, I guess it's cool until Roy and Jenny get here with their crew."

Franks nodded. "For sure. She has her own seat. She's just coming to say hi."

This seemed suspicious to me. It would be absolutely in character for Franks to hire a pro, (i.e., prostitute), to shake Stoli down, soften the target, as it were (an ironic choice of words, yes). This could prove problematic if we couldn't get rid of her before The Show.

If there were a Camera 2 in this narrative, I would say *go to Camera 2* for my editorial aside:

When I died and was reborn on my own birthday and given a name that shared the initials of my former self, I knew there was a cosmic puppet master directing events on this planet, third from the sun, a small system on an outside arm of the Milky Way, a galaxy of two hundred billion stars, give or take.

But through the years, I forgot about the puppet master, as events rolled at me with a fair amount of randomness, and the decision-consequence matrix of this reality seemed to operate with no thumb on the scale. I got comfortable. Of course, when Franks's cousin Sean showed up at my house that one time, and when Stoli returned to fulfill his destiny, I should've recognized the puppet master's handiwork. I had let my guard down.

So when the door of that Giants suite opened and *she* walked in, I felt the puppet strings like a noose around my neck.

There she was, Dolly Velasquez in the flesh, a still very good-looking flesh, to be sure. I froze, mouth agape, as Franks introduced her to us: "Fellas, this is Dolly, a good old friend of mine . . . and apparently she's a closet Giants fan—I did not know."

She said, "Hi, guys. I know nothing about baseball except the beer is expensive." She flashed that Dolly smile. The years had been good to her: she was slim and healthy looking. My guess was she was around forty now, and her thick dark hair had no hint of gray.

Franks continued, "This is John and his nephew, Keenan . . . you alright, little man?"

I nodded and managed, "Uh-huh." Franks chortled, but John saw something was up with me, and he turned to her.

"Hi—sorry, your name is *Dolly*?" Stoli asked this pointedly and looked at me. I nodded slowly.

"Yep," she said. "For *Dolores*. Like the street."

"Nice," Stoli said, "Can we get you a drink? What's your flavor?"

"Bourbon," she said.

And so we invited my ex-girlfriend into our midst. I mean, why the fuck not?

I forced my eyes back to the baseball game. The bottom of the fifth was just starting; the Giants had just pitched three and out.

Think, think, think. We have to abandon the plan and flee. I am not prepared to go on with this new audience member. No fucking way. We could do this another time. It was just a cosmic justice jack-off session anyway.

Someone touched my shoulder and tousled my wispy ginger-brown hair. I turned and . . . there was Dolly, face level, looking so beautiful and genuine, engaging me.

"Hi, Keenan. I'm Dolly. Are you having a good time?"

My breath hitched. I managed a "Hi." I was so close to hugging her and saying *I'm so sorry I'm so sorry I miss you so much I wish I had never been that guy please forgive me I really did love you I'm sorry.*

But instead, I started to cry. Like a five-year-old. Perplexed, Dolly stood up, glancing over at Stoli. Stoli was also perplexed, but for different reasons.

"It's alright. I got this. He always gets tired around this time of the game. Gimme a sec." He came over to me as Dolly skulked away to refill her drink. "Whatcha need?" Stoli asked me in a low voice.

"Bathroom," I managed.

He picked me up and said, "We are going to have a little time-out. Back in a jiffy."

"It's all good, John," Franks said. "Take your time."

I glimpsed all of their embarrassed faces as we ducked inside the bathroom. Stoli locked the door and set me down.

"Oh, my God, Keenan. What's happening? Is this an act? Or is it for real? I'm lost."

I pulled myself together and wiped my nose with some bathroom tissue. I wasn't quite hyperventilating.

"We have to abort. I can't do this."

He was gobsmacked. "What?" he hissed back at me. It was then that I realized that he'd been drinking harder than I suspected. He wasn't *drunk*, per se, but he was on the way. With a side order of cocaine. This was a disaster. "Look," he continued, taking a knee. "We *have* to go through with it! Don't you see? It is *ordained*. The fact that Dolly is here is a *message from God*. This is all *supposed* to happen, Keenan. Kurt. *Kurt*. This is your time to get it all out—for you to reveal the nature of reality to these fucking career criminals. They *can't* get away with murdering you! I'm not letting you blow this chance and I'm not going to go through this again. This is it, motherfucker."

"But Dolly!"

"I know! I can't believe you used to date her. What a number!"

"That's not what I meant. I don't want to fuck with *her* head. If all goes well, these guys are going to be seriously psychologically damaged for the rest of their lives!"

"Oh, Keenan. You vastly overestimate the human ability to absorb a message such as yours. Besides—face it—she's here for a reason. God is a *fuck-with*! K-S-H! Kurt Sebastian Houston. Keenan Solomon Harris. I've thought about this a lot. This isn't your grandfather's reincarnation—it has a purpose, and this is it. Come on!"

The stadium shook with a massive cheer, and a gleeful shout came from the suite on the other side of the bathroom door. There was a knock on the door and Franks's voice: "We just ran in two, you guys! We're tied up! Everything okay?"

"Everything's great! Out in a sec!" Stoli looked at me and said quietly, "Take a breath, take a piss, and let's do this. Everything has led to this moment."

He was right. The situation was ridiculous, but apparently this was a ridiculous puppet master we were dealing with.

I said to Stoli, "Okay, but give me till the bottom of the sixth for my speech, okay?"

"Alright."

So we rejoined the party, and Dolly gave us a little sympathy wave as we emerged. Poins had returned to his suspicious mode, staring me down with his shark-cold eyes. The three of them had taken the window seats as the Giants started to surge. I, meanwhile, sat on the couch in the upper lounge area, girding my loins and gathering my wits. When the inning ended, Franks got up and refreshed everyone's drink. It also seemed everyone refreshed their noses in the bathroom, and I could only shake my head at Stoli. I pretended to watch the big flat screen on the wall as the others retook their seats. I called Stoli over.

"Dude," I hissed, "Stop with the powder or I'm out of here. This is the most serious event in your adult life."

He gave me a look. "I used to be a sniper in a war with the Taliban."

"Still." I hesitated. "Stop that shit."

"Okay."

The minutes inched along. Stoli pretended to mess with his jacket near the front door, looking for something, then he messed with the door itself. The other three were distracted. When Stoli turned around, I knew it was time. There was a sudden ringing in my ear. Maybe it was stress, I don't know, but the top of the sixth ended and Stoli stepped forward. I got up and stood in the center of the upper lounge between Stoli and the door.

"Hey, you guys, can I have your attention? Keenan has a little performance thing he wants to do for you," Stoli said, my emcee.

The three turned and smiled in a courteous, curious way.

Franks was pleased to be past my tired tears. "Great! Whatcha got for us, little man?"

They arranged themselves in a row, audience-style.

"First of all," Stoli began. "Can I get a stool from over there?" Poins grabbed a stool and handed it to Stoli, who set it down, center. I climbed atop it and sat. "Next," Stoli continued, "and this is part of the magic trick—I'll need your cell phones."

They chuckled.

"Mine's in my coat near the door," Dolly said.

Franks brought his phone out without hesitation, but not Poins. "C'mon, PD," Franks nudged. "It's a magic trick, for chrissake. It'll be fine." Poins reluctantly extracted his phone from inside his coat and handed it to Stoli, who took them and disappeared into the bathroom, then reappeared.

"Is that part of the trick?" Franks asked humorously.

"Sure is," Stoli replied. He stood between them and me, but a little to the side so they could see me on my stool. "With that, I give you the Great *Houston*!"

This word, *Houston*, definitely gave them pause. Did they hear that right? Their faces showed confusion, smiles faltered, as though trying to reconcile the meaning of this stage name: *How-stun?* Like their former boss? They looked at each other uncomfortably.

My fear was gone. In its place was a joyful anger. And relief. This was it, and whatever happened, happened. And I was on fire.

"Greetings! Franks! Poins! Dolly!"

Poins's smile, what there was left of it, fell. Franks and Dolly didn't catch my familiar tone. I mean, I was a five-year-old on a stool, who, they supposed, was about to perform a magic trick with their phones.

I continued, "I want to apologize for the elaborate charade we've been orchestrating. This has been a long time coming. I mean, ever since I died. You see, I may look like a kid named Keenan, but I'm actually the reincarnation of Kurt Houston, your former boss. Who you killed."

The stadium suddenly shook as the first batter was up to start the bottom of the sixth. With the game tied up, spirits were high.

Dolly's face was frozen; Franks's mouth moved but nothing came out, and he searched the faces next to him, then Stoli's.

"W-what did he just say, John?" Franks quavered.

But Poins was furious, and took a slow step forward.

"I knew it, Franks. I told you something was up with these motherfuckers." Poins looked about to explode, sizing up Stoli as he waited for Franks to say the word.

"John, what's going on?" Franks asked, putting down his drink and taking his feet.

"It's Keenan's show now, Frank. I just work here."

I couldn't help myself. "Look, you all heard correctly. You may see a five-year-old boy, but it's me—*Kurt*. It's taken me all this time to grow up enough so I could find you and face you down. Because I need to know: why did you kill me, Franks?"

The batter, on a full count, hit the ball into left field, well within view of our windows. The crowd ignited at full volume, masking Dolly's quick, gasping shriek. She staggered back on her seat, and Franks helped her sit.

I remember thinking, *Sorry, Dolly . . . I didn't really count on you being here.*

Poins was a pit bull on a leash as Franks held him back by his coat collar. Franks said, "Hold on, PD—this has to be a joke. A bad fucking joke. But, I mean, who would . . ." And Franks did a funny thing, head swiveling to Dolly, taking a step back. "Is this your idea of being funny, Dolly?" Poins glanced at her too, then at me, then Stoli. Poins was lost with no place to put the violence he so wanted to unleash.

"What are you talking about?" she asked plaintively, blood drained from her face. I'd never seen Dolly in such a state. "Who are these people? What's going on?" Her shoulders shook and she looked like she might vomit.

The roar of the crowd was so continuous now that I had to almost shout. "Dolly, don't worry. This wasn't for you. You just had the bad luck of showing up at the wrong time. You see, it was Franks here who slipped me the fentanyl shot ten years ago that killed me. And I died but was reincarnated into a little baby in Campbell."

"This is insane," Franks protested.

Stoli's countenance was grim but alive, almost as though he was having a good time. He set himself firmly in place at the top of the single step that separated the fore from the aft of the suite. He reassured them, "Look, everyone, this doesn't have to get messy. Keenan's just going to say his piece and then we are going to go. He just wants you to know that your actions have consequences."

"Fuck this," Poins spat, as he jerked away from Franks.

"Please, stand back, Poindexter," Stoli warned, hands forward.

"Whatever," he grunted, as he attempted to barrel through Stoli. With stunning grace, Stoli sidestepped Poins, aikido-style, and dropped him on his back, right there on the step, and finished with a quick jab to Poins's nose, a relatively mild jab, a warning that said, "I'm not the guy you think I am, so back off."

This happened so surprisingly fast that it managed to stop Dolly's hysterics. Poins groaned and half-sat up, hands on his face; Stoli used his boot to topple him back down the stair in front of Franks. Poins, stunned, but still clearly not done, got on one knee. Blood ran down his chin, and he shot fury at us through watery eyes.

"Holy shit! Poins! John! Stop!" Franks shouted over the white noise of the stadium outside. He put himself between the two men. "Okay. Everybody, take a breath." He glared at Poins. "PD, stand the fuck down." Then he looked at Stoli and me. There was something close to a grin on his face. "I think I know what's going on now. It's the only thing that makes sense. It has to be Bart!" He glanced at Dolly, then Poins, then back at us. "Bart is the only one who could put this together. I get it—he's pissed because he did time. This is payback for getting rolled. Okay, ha ha. He's got a sick fucking sense of humor. Where is he? Outside the door?"

Stoli stood relaxed but ready. I felt the same way, so I jumped down from the stool and approached them, staying a safe distance behind Stoli.

"Bart didn't put us up to this, Franks. It's me, Kurt."

"Stop it!" Dolly croaked.

Franks was losing patience. "Look, you little fucker. I don't know why or how they trained you to do this little act of yours, but it stops right now. It sucks, because I actually liked you. And you, too, John. This breaks my heart that it was all some sort of joke. I thought we coulda done some business." He paused. "You guys should just get the fuck out now." He patted his pants for his missing phone. "Give me back my phone."

I was not to be deterred. "Fucking Franks. It all comes down to business for you. Remember the time you came over to my house when Dolly and I were screwing in the living room and you had this quote-unquote great idea about starting a coke-dealing taxi service? Remember that one, Einstein?"

Dolly looked sick. Poins was again upright, a pile of blood-soaked napkins at his feet, a napkin-twist up each nostril. To add insult to injury (literally), he was still wearing his bright Giants-orange blazer, blood on the lapel, one of the pockets ripped.

"Hey, that was a good idea," Franks protested, then paused. "I see what you're doing. Kurt could've easily told Bart that story. This is bullshit. You're not going to get us to believe that Kurt is risen from the dead. Stop this horseshit and get the fuck out of my suite." Franks started toward Stoli.

"I'm sorry, Frank," Stoli apologized. "You're going to have to wait until he's done."

"You can't take us both on." Franks edged forward.

"Try me," Stoli said through his teeth. Franks edged back again.

I continued. "Poins—I mean, *Steven Hightower*—remember when we were on our way to shake down that dealer guy near Parnassus and I asked you why they called you Poindexter, and you said because you were smart? I always thought that was funny." He stared at me malevolently. "Remember, why I called you Poins?"

There was a pause and Franks looked back at Poins, who seemed to be unraveling a little. Terror and fury are a volatile combination. Among them, I saw the first little crack of doubt. Poins replied, "Because Shakespeare." He took a step forward.

"What's my birthday, then?" Dolly suddenly challenged.

"We are not humoring these assholes, Dolly," Franks cut in.

"July eighteenth. You're a Cancer. And I always made the joke that you had to be a Cancer because you were more addictive than cigarettes."

Dolly gasped. Franks would have none of it. "Dolly, pull yourself together. There's a thousand ways Bart could know that."

"How?!"

"Bart isn't here, you stupid Irish fucker," I barked at him in my small voice.

"Swear words coming from your little mouth sounds really fucked up," Franks replied.

"So I've heard."

Poins panted, and he growled, "That sounds a lot like Kurt, Franks."

"Stop it, you two! He's *five*! Calm the *fuck* down!" And with that, Franks tried to shoot past Stoli, who clotheslined him by the neck and threw him back, staggering him into Poins's arms. Franks gained his feet quickly, filled with new anger. "What the fuck do you *ass*holes want from us?"

I ignored him. "While we're on the subject—*did* you set up Bart?"

Franks blew out a sigh. "See, I *knew* it," he said to Poins and Dolly. At this point, it was only Franks who hadn't started to believe I was Kurt, and he was disgusted with them. He turned back to me. "I didn't set up Bart. You can tell that to him, since I'm sure he's outside having a good fucking laugh." He gestured to Stoli. "So, where'd you learn those moves, John? Did Bart find you in prison? Do you guys have a pact or something?"

"I was in the Army Rangers, Frank. In Afghanistan."

This bit of news deflated Franks a little, but Poins didn't react.

I said, "Franks—Bart disappeared back east after he got out on parole. I checked."

"Whatever."

"This isn't happening," Dolly whimpered.

"You knew Jericho was hot, didn't you?" I accused Frank.

"Jericho?" He paused, mentally scrolling back. "Look, I didn't know nothing. I mean, he was acting weird, but that guy was *always* weird."

"So, he was quote-unquote acting weird and you sent Bart in anyway? Goddamn you."

Dolly and Poins looked skeptically at Franks.

"Look, it's a risky business. I didn't know anything for sure."

In a trance-like voice, Poins suddenly locked eyes on me and declared: "There . . . is . . . no . . . death."

I said, "Poins—I *did* die. It wasn't pleasant." I continued with Franks, "The question is: would you have gone to meet Jericho if you were in town?"

Franks hesitated too long.

"That's what I thought," I said. "Now, lastly, Franks, why did you give me the hot shot?"

"Now!" Poins shouted.

Poins made his move. With a gurgling war cry, he charged at us again, Franks on his heels. I scrambled back up toward the door. Stoli was expecting something like this. As Poins shot to the right, Stoli moved to meet him; but Poins was only feinting and instantly sprang left, bringing with him a right hook. Had Poins not been so short, this might've done some serious damage, but being down a step, it merely struck Stoli's chest. Franks was the other problem. He collided with Poins, who had dodged left. Tall and skinny Franks, with what only could be called spindly limbs, tangled up with the shorter, tank-like Poins. Stoli was right there to capitalize on this accident—this slapstick maneuver—and he used his body to guide both of them into the iron railing, which made a terrific yawning squeal as it bent backward, partially coming free of the wall, crushing the yucca tree behind it, and completely stopping their forward momentum.

This all happened in the space of three seconds. Our two foes became wedged between the wall, the rail, and the upper lounge step, which they had still hadn't managed to cross. It felt like everyone was playing their rehearsed part, everything happening on cue. That said, a lot of noise had been made just now, and I wondered if it would finally alert security. Outside the suite, the stadium was still making plenty of noise.

The flat screen said DIAMONDBACKS 4, GIANTS 6.

"This isn't happening," Dolly repeated.

Stoli, who had managed to keep his feet, stood above them rubbing his clavicle. "Goddammit, you guys. Let Keenan finish and we'll go. It doesn't have to be like this."

Franks pulled himself off of Poins, who was slow to get up. Stoli watched him closely. Poins got on all fours and sat back, still wearing his orange blazer, now thoroughly ruined. The corner of his left eye looked like it had caught one of the iron rungs and was bleeding.

Stoli told Poins, "That was a nice move, but Frank here fucked it all up."

Somehow, we maintained the standoff.

Franks clenched and unclenched his right hand, grimacing. "I think I fucked up my hand." He looked at us wearily. "Look, I don't know why you are doing this shit, but just get it over and get the fuck out. How am I gonna explain this mess to management?"

I approached again. "Shit, you guys are exactly like I left you: total fuck-ups."

"Yeah, yeah, yeah. Well, say you *are* the reincarnation of Kurt 'Biggest Junkie in the World' Houston: you were a fucking pathetic old waste-oid who started out pretty cool, but in the end was a real prick. And a junkie."

"Granted. But that was no reason to kill me."

Franks exploded, "I DIDN'T FUCKING KILL YOU, YOU FUCKER!" Lips twitching, eyes bulging, shouting at a five-year-old.

"Well, August didn't kill me!" I said. "Setting up that poor kid was lower than low."

"We didn't set him up! He got popped and kept his mouth shut. He did the loyal thing."

"You let him take a fall for *your* murder, you asshole! And, Poins—"

Poins shifted his terrible gaze from Stoli to me, dripping hate.

"Poins, how could you do that to that kid? He looked up to you."

He shrugged and said, "Them's the breaks, homes."

"Having him shivved was *the breaks*, too, motherfucker?"

Staring straight at me, he repeated, "Them's the breaks."

Franks sucked in air. "Are you fucking kidding me, Poins? You said—"

"THEM'S THE BREAKS, FRANKS!" he shouted turning, taking a threatening step toward his boss.

"Goddamn it," Franks said.

Dolly squatted on her haunches in the corner, leaning against the wall, under the long window counter. She whispered *This isn't happening this isn't happening* over and over.

I continued: "Yeah, poor white-bread August, taking a fall for Franks's fentanyl. Yeah, I read my autopsy report. But I knew it was bad from the moment I shot it. There I was, just out of detox, and you leave me with a birthday present of shooting works and a bag of Afghani super-junk. Yeah, I shouldn't have shot it—*I was weak*. But I didn't shoot a lot, and you don't *need* a lot when it's cut with fucking fentanyl. It was a classic hotshot, and you know it."

"*Really*, you little fucker? You came back from the dead to tell me *this*?" Franks started laughing. And laughing. Poins dragged himself to one of the cocktail tables and used water from a bottle to wash the blood off his face. He finally tossed aside the ruined coat and took off the shirt and tie. He was now in just stained slacks and a wifebeater tank top. Poins's squat torso, a combination of muscle and fat, was decorated with an impressive display of tattoos: a kaleidoscopic mishmash of gangland runes scrawled without reason.

Dolly suddenly spoke up, clearly turning something over in her mind. "So, Franks . . . where'd you get this supposed super-junk anyway? You didn't really use the stuff."

Poins splashed the rest of the Jameson down his throat.

Franks said, "That's the funny part—the dope was actually a birthday present from Poindexter; he told me to give it to Kurt. I just, well . . . I just *said* it was from me." Franks shrugged. Dolly's jaw dropped, and a boil of rage brought her out of her crouch.

She turned to Poins: "You *ass*hole!" She looked at me, her face in a new sort of anguish. She seethed at Poins, "*That's* why you wanted the fentanyl . . ." Dolly's words trailed off, then she ran at Poins, arms swinging, screaming, "YOU PIECE OF SHIT!"

But her attack was nothing to Poins, and he stopped her cold with a straight punch to the face, dropping her like a sack. "Them's the breaks," he said to her crumpled body.

"Poindexter!" Franks shouted. "What have you done?" He fell to Dolly's side.

Stoli braced himself, saying to Poins, "There's something wrong with you, man."

Poins smashed the Jameson bottle on the table and slowly approached us with its jagged menace, locking his gaze on me.

"Fuckin' right there's something wrong with me . . . and it's that little motherfucker right there." He gestured at me with the broken bottle. "You're the same pompous fucking know-it-all jack-off you always were." Poins spat blood on the ground as he stepped forward. "Getting clean is really what killed you, Kurt. Me and Franks had everything covered. So, I did what I had to do. But you just couldn't stay the fuck dead."

He took another step.

"Hold it right there, PD," Stoli said. "Look, I think we are actually done now, and we can go. No need to make this worse."

That's when I put it all together. I said, "Oh, shit! It was *Poins—of course!*" I was both elated and mortally embarrassed. "Oh, my God! I've spent five years obsessing over the wrong killer." I laughed. "Shit, Franks doesn't have the stones to murder someone. What was I thinking?! Of course, it was Poins!"

"STOP CALLING ME POINS, YOU ARROGANT FUCKHOLE!" he bellowed.

But then this high drama scene was instantly silenced by a loud pounding at the front entrance. We all froze. A voice shouted through the door: "Hello! Sorry to bother you—it's security. We've had some complaints. Can we come in, please?"

There was this weird moment when we all looked around the room and realized what a disaster the place was. We were fucked. Blood was everywhere in the forward lounge. "Coming!" I blurted, edging backward, moving away from the standoff. When I reached the door, I shouted, "Okay, I'm unlocking it!"

But the thing wouldn't unlock. The lock was frozen in place. I looked at the doorjamb and it was covered in dried glue—epoxy. "Stoli, what the fuck?" He looked back at me and saw the problem.

"Oh—shit—I'm sorry—it was supposed to be a precaution."

That's when Poins made his move.

"Watch out!" I shouted.

Poins lunged the broken bottle at Stoli, who reflexively held up his left hand. The jagged glass gored Stoli's palm open like a crushed steak. Poins swung a left hook up into Stoli's groin. Stoli groaned as he fell to his knees, pulling his damaged hand to his body like a broken wing.

Poins sidestepped Stoli and leveled his eyes at me.

"Poindexter!" Franks jumped up from where Dolly lay slumped. The Irishman put a hand on his partner's back. "Stop this shit! We can still fix this."

I didn't have a clear view of what happened next because Poins was between me and Franks. But I heard Poins shout "SHUT THE FUCK

UP!" and his right arm made a flourishing backhand spin, a somewhat graceful pirouette. Behind him, Franks dropped from view. Poins again locked his gaze on me and cursed, "Fucking Kurt."

He came for me.

I hammered my little fists on the door, screaming, "Help! Help!"

But Stoli wasn't done. From the ground, he grabbed the back of Poins's belt with his good hand. Poins grunted with rage and spun, swiping at Stoli's arm with the bottle, slashing it through the St. Patrick's FC jersey. Stoli let go with a gasp, and Poins proceeded to stomp and kick the downed man.

Seeing Stoli getting stomped triggered the crazy in me and I found myself running toward Poins, the short ice-pick-like tactical key chain in my hand. The front door shattered behind me as I dove through the air. My target was Poins's left kidney, and I knew full well the three-inch weapon would be only a slightly painful distraction. *Fuck it*, I thought and I jammed it in Poins's side, jabbing as hard as a five-year-old could jab. Poins gagged out a scream, turned quickly, saw me, raised his fist and—BAM!

That's all I remember.

!!!

The rest of the account comes from Stoli, paraphrased.

"It wasn't the ripped hand that did me—it was the punch to the balls. That totally took me down. And when he saw I was down, he just kind of dismissed me as a threat and immediately moved on to you. Like the Terminator. That's when I finally realized how scary this guy was. I've seen this psycho behavior before—on the battlefield.

"In any case, somehow, I got him by the belt and slowed him down, but this *really* pissed him off. While I can appreciate that this was the moment that may have saved you, it was also the moment that got me stomped. But, you know, I've been stomped before. You learn how to be stomped. So, as I was stomped, I remembered the tactical pen in my pocket, which I could feel stabbing me in the thigh every time I hunched up for a kick. But I couldn't reach it. I'd almost lost hope.

"But the kicking stopped suddenly and Poins made this weird animal growl, so I looked up and saw you had stabbed him with *your* silly tactical key chain. Oh, man, that was a *very* stupid thing for you to do. You must really like me."

"Just tell me what happened," I said.

"Everything was in slow motion—you know, the adrenaline. I'm on the floor and I see him wind up like a boxer, a brawler—a prison fighter—and he throws a hard straight punch to the top of your head. Not some back-of-the-hand slap-down—he clocked you with purpose."

"That's why I dropped so fast."

"He wasn't punching Keenan. He was punching *Kurt*."

Stoli continued, "To add to this chaos, ballpark security busted through the door and wood and glass flew everywhere. Poins stood over you like some weird monster, about to deliver the death blow; but I finally had my own stupid tactical pen in my hand and I jammed it as hard as I could up into Poins's junk. Right into his ball sack. My leverage was shit but I gave it all I could. It stopped him long enough for security to take him down. They piled on him."

"Tell me about Franks and Dolly—oh . . . and thank you for saving my life."

"Sure thing. Well, it was the cops busting in that woke Dolly up. She said the big crash of the front door made her sit straight up after Poins knocked her out. She was down maybe sixty seconds? It all happened so fast. So, Dolly sat up and saw Franks lying on his side, a couple of feet away, in a big pool of his own blood. He was twitching and still holding his neck as blood pumped through his fingers, she said. She saw his fingers go limp. That's when she thinks he bled all the way out. Poins had got him across the throat with that bottle."

"I think I saw him do that. Franks was trying to help Dolly, and Poins just slashed him."

"So, the cops came in and grabbed Poins. I passed out for a second, and when I came to again, a paramedic was kneeling over me. Dolly was yelling for someone to help Franks, but it was too late. Dolly's face was a gory mess from Poins's punch. And to top it all off, as the cops dragged Poins out, he shouted, 'There is no death! There is no death!'"

Poins wasn't exactly right, wasn't exactly wrong.

"What a mess," I said, "I kind of feel sorry for Franks."

"Me too, Keenan. And Dolly. She looked bad, but she seemed lucid. I saw her talking to the cops before they put us in the ambulance. And . . . well, the rest of it was in the news."

"That's right. What was it? Something like 'Notorious Gangster *The Irishman* Killed in Ballpark Brawl'? Something like that."

"Something like that."

36. Epilogue

Let me tell you what happened after the melee.

After Poins smashed me, I blacked out and woke up in the ambulance on the way to the hospital. There was an EMT lady with a round face that looked like my sister. She smiled.

"You're going to be okay. We're just going to the hospital to make sure," she said calmly.

"What? . . . is Stoli okay?" That's when I realized there was a bandage on my head and I was strapped onto a gurney in a moving ambulance, sirens blaring.

"Stoli?" she asked. She looked up, then back down at me. She grinned. "You mean *John*? He's okay. He's right here."

I lifted my head and saw Stoli sitting in a jump seat not three feet from me. He had a massive wad of bandaging on his left hand and another bit wrapped around his right forearm. He also had a black eye.

He smiled. "Hey, Keenan. We did it."

I glanced at the lady, then at Stoli. "Finally. We did it."

"Your parents are meeting us at Zuckerberg General."

I put my head back and replied, "Zuckerberg General. I'll never get used to calling it that."

"I don't think your parents are going to let us hang out anymore."

"Sure, they will. Just maybe no more baseball games."

"Hallelujah."

!!!

By the way, that big fight was two years ago. Since then, we moved to Los Gatos, just down the street from Campbell. That's how we have this cool attic where I recorded all this. It's been a few weeks since my last entry and the summer is almost over. Hard to focus these days. Seems like forever ago that all that stuff at the Giants game went down. There's a scar just above my hairline where Poindexter went at me.

Franks's murder and everything got Poins life in prison. No parole. Too many strikes against him already. Then Poins killed himself in lockup, maybe testing his theory about there being no death. I bet he woke up as a dung beetle.

Hard to admit, but I'm real sorry about Franks. While I can't say I was *all* wrong about him—he was a real lowlife—he wasn't the cold-blooded killer I thought he was. In fact, he might've saved Dolly's life, stepping in like he did. It's hard to think of Franks as heroic. I dunno.

At the ballpark, after they whisked Stoli and me away in the ambulance, the cops grilled Dolly about what happened. She kept her mouth shut about reincarnation and dead drug dealers. I mean, what could she do? She was quick on her feet, and made up a pretty believable story about how Franks and Poins were crazy on drugs and alcohol and got into a fight over the game. And when Stoli intervened, things got out of control. Good ol' Dolly. The last we heard from her was a get-well card sent to the brewery. I feel bad about her part in this. She didn't deserve it. But I'm thankful for her showing up—she helped solve the mystery of Who Killed Kurt Houston.

Bart is still disappeared.

Just so you know, the Eleventh Street Brewery is a success and the Harrises are financially secure for the first time ever. As you can imagine, Lou and Drew were plenty upset about the Luxury Suite Melee, as we now call it. The whole fiasco almost broke up their partnership with Stoli and the brewery. But in the end, they really didn't blame Stoli, and they knew that if it weren't for him, things could've been much worse. These days, we all go out of our way to *not* talk about it, and you'll never see a Giants game on the TV.

Also, I've checked up on my sister, Rae, a few times. She still lives in my old house and seems happy. I think she has a boyfriend. Also, she changed her name back to Houston, from her old married name of Walker. I think about her every day . . . when I can remember, anyways.

As you can maybe tell, I'm not quite myself anymore, whatever that means. It all keeps slipping into a sort of, um, an, uh, into the present, where all I can think of is lunch and video games and playing outside and my kickboxing team and my new little sister, Sabine.

Recently, I sat Stoli down and explained to him what I thought was happening to me and told him to not be upset. I also told him not to be sad and, in fact, to be happy that I was turning into the kid I should be.

But he *was* sad. He said, "I feel like I'm losing a best friend."

"I'm sorry. What you are really gaining is a full-time nephew. Please look after me and steer me straight." Then I said, "Not too straight . . . that'd be boring."

"I'll try to keep you out of trouble."

"Make sure I don't grow up to be an asshole again."

"I'll do my best."

Anyhow, I think I was brought back from the dead because Kurt Houston died at the wrong time. I don't know why, but somehow his death wasn't part of the Big Plan, so things had to be set right. I trip on how my story feels guided by an invisible hand, about how there is like a cosmic order to things. Not like religion, just like . . . *how things are?*

I have a theory on why it took five years for Kurt to be placed inside a fresh body. It wasn't some sort of religious formula, it was timing. The grand plan of Keenan's story had to wait for all the elements of necessary coincidence to align the paths of the Harrises and Stoli and Franks and Poins and even Dolly. So now, with the mission completed, and maybe because I saw too much extra-dimensional connectedness or something, the old me is being phased out of—or maybe phased *into?*—the life of an honest-to-goodness seven-year-old named Keenan Solomon Harris. This is how I think of it now.

All this heavy shit hurts my brain, so I think I'm going to call it a day and hide the recorder. Sorry I don't have more right now. I'm hungry and feel like catching up with Ralphy and Tina and the gang.

See ya!

UNTITLED

TIMESTAMP=2032-09-25T:12:20:31-12:20:59Z

Final record

Sorry I forgot about you! I caught a snake yesterday! Gopher snake, like so big. Me 'n' Ralphy and the guys were playing patrol. So cool. Also, did I tell you I have a little sister now?! I'll try to remember to talk to you. You know.

Hey, someone is coming upstairs. I gotta go. Talk soon.

Afterword

A Short History of the Keenan Harris Tapes

In February 2065, Professor F. C. Roberts of Stanford University contacted our publishing company with a curious discovery of fifty-three hours of digital audio recordings found in the attic of a home in Los Gatos, California. Dr. Roberts described the contents of the recordings as a reincarnation fantasy posing as a novel. He thought it was probably more valuable as an anthropological oddity than as literature.

Dr. Roberts was given the recordings by a couple (identities withheld by request) who had just purchased the Los Gatos property in which the recordings were found. Those new owners somehow accessed this archaic Sony technology and, stunned by their contents, contacted Dr. Roberts for advice on how to handle the "Tapes," as they termed the digital recordings. They have since been known as the "Keenan Harris Tapes" in academic circles.

The metadata on the audio files (in the now defunct m4a format) is from the summer of 2032. The data has been confirmed as authentic, as was the recording device. The Sony DCM-A30 Portable Audio Recorder (no longer in production) on which the recordings had been found was wrapped and rewrapped in plastic and duct tape with a note that said,

"Please listen to my story." This package was sealed in a plastic box, also wrapped in duct tape. It sat in a far recess of the attic under loose insulation for over thirty years before it was discovered.

When our team started investigating, it did not take long to find a man by the name of Keenan Solomon Harris. Dr. Harris is a psychologist practicing cognitive behavioral therapy in San Francisco. He remembers nothing of the recording and firmly believes the whole matter is a prank left behind by his late father, who was prone to such jokes. Even so, Harris has confirmed many of the names and relationships, including the late John Galvin (died 2040), his mother and father, Drew (died 2052) and Louise Harris (resides in Montara, CA), as well as Dr. Claveria (retired), and his childhood best friend, Ralph Malkmus. Dr. Harris also claims that he remembers little before age seven, at which time he received a head trauma that all but erased his memory before the incident, obliterating much of his childhood.

As for the identities surrounding the late author, Kurt Houston, all of these were confirmed as well, supporting the veracity of the story on the tapes. His sister, Rae Houston, passed in 2043. Christopher Feist was indeed murdered in a liquor store. The gang identities—Franklin O'Donnell, Steven Hightower, Bart Montgomery, Dolores Velasquez, and August Williams—have all been verified via city records. All are deceased.

Additionally, all the geographical locations are confirmed, from the addresses in Houston's story, to the 7-Eleven of Harris's story. The Eleventh Street Brewery has become something of a San Francisco destination.

In conclusion, the field of Transmigration Science has embraced the likelihood that the story as told by the Keenan Harris Tapes is factual. Not since the work of Dr. Ian Stevenson has the existence of transmigration been more confirmed. The search continues.

—R. Adams, PhD
Editor

THANKS

Many thanks to Dennis Adams, Dr. Wes Brown, Chris Faiss, Claudia Figallo, Brian Garvey, Deirdre McCarthy, Michael A. Miller, Shane O'Neill, Jeffery Weissman, Chris Zegri, Ricardo Zegri, and Lang Zerner. Thanks to Creative Arts Charter School. Thanks to Bernard Schweizer for all his guidance and support.

!!!

Also by K.S. Haddock

The Patricidal Bedside Companion